✦ Dedication ✦

For the ones who know summer isn't all sunshine.
Who crave what blooms in the dark—the twisted, the tender, the untamed.
May you always find someone willing to bury ~~*bodies*~~ the past with you.

✦ Note to Readers ✦

The world of Cypress Vale doesn't offer gentle love stories, and the woods of Silver Hollow least of all. Camps are meant to be places of laughter and safety, but these trees remember every secret, every scream, every vow spoken in the dark. When I began writing Camp Silver Hollow, I wanted to capture that place where devotion tangles with danger—where love can feel like salvation one moment and destruction the next.

Inside these pages, you'll find obsession, violence, blurred morality, and bonds that burn hotter for the shadows wrapped around them. This isn't a story of safe choices or tidy endings. The people you will meet here are messy, hungry, and relentless—haunted by loss, driven by loyalty, and willing to bleed for what they refuse to let go.

If you're here, it means you're drawn to the shadows too. You crave the unsettling pull of the forbidden: the quickening of your pulse when danger is near, the ache of wanting what should be off-limits, the shiver of intimacy that feels as much like trespass as it does like belonging. This book was written for readers who know that sometimes survival looks like ruin, and that love in the dark often demands a price.

Some chapters may leave you breathless with longing. Others may press against your comfort, sharp with fear, guilt, or violence. Many will linger in that uneasy space between horror and desire, where every touch carries risk and every choice cuts deep. If you find yourself torn between recoiling and leaning closer, aching even as you flinch, then this story has done what it was meant to do.

Above all, I hope *Camp Silver Hollow* stays with you—the way campfire smoke clings stubbornly to your clothes, the way shadows stretch long after the flames have died, the way the woods whisper even when the night is silent. Stories like this are not written to comfort. They're written to haunt, to thrill, and to remind you that in Silver Hollow, love isn't gentle; it's survival.

Mori Belle

So, settle close to the fire. Let the dark press in. And remember, in Silver Hollow, nothing stays buried forever

✦ Content Warnings ✦

Camp Silver Hollow is a dark romance rooted in trauma, obsession, and the kind of love that takes hold amid ruin. It contains mature and potentially disturbing themes that may not be suitable for all readers, so please continue with care.

Content includes:

- Emotional neglect and psychological trauma (past and present)
- Toxic parental relationships and gaslighting
- Verbal abuse and parental cruelty
- Bullying and peer cruelty
- Psychological manipulation by authority figures
- Gaslighting and cover-ups by adults in power
- Grief and survivors' guilt
- Substance use (marijuana and alcohol)
- Sexual harassment by an adult male toward a minor (non-graphic, early scene
- Voyeurism / non-consensual sexual observation
- Sudden death and unexplained disappearance of counselors
- Profanity and explicit language throughout
- References to past trauma, sexual and emotional repression
- Graphic violence and murder
- Descriptions of dead bodies and blood
- Blood in water imagery
- Knife use (non-sexual and symbolic emotional contexts)
- Torture (restrained, implied physical and psychological suffering)
- Vigilante justice and morally gray protagonists

- Obsessive relationships
- Dubious morality in main characters
- Body disposal and cover-up of murder
- Graphic body disposal
- Explicit sexual content with intense emotional context (MF)
- Public and semi-public sex scenes
- Depictions of emotional vulnerability through sex and touch
- Sacred violence and emotional fusion post-murder
- Religious and spiritual symbolism around death and intimacy

This isn't a summer camp story about healing. It's about choosing each other through pain, rage, and ruin—and setting the world on fire just to feel safe in each other's arms. The love is feral, the loyalty is unforgiving, and survival doesn't come without blood on your hands.

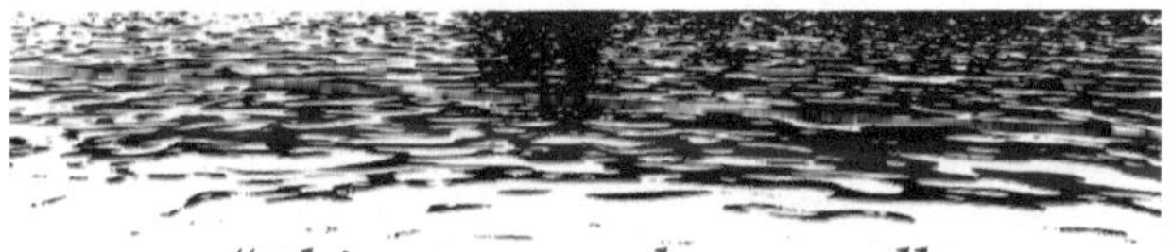

"This summer, love smells like pine needles, lake water ...and blood."

✦ At a Glance ✦

Camp Silver Hollow

The Summer Darkness Bloomed

Mori Belle

Here at Silver Hollow, we believe in three things: teamwork, self-discovery, and smiles that never fade. Whether you're exploring the scenic trails, roasting marshmallows by the lake, or discovering your true potential through the power of community, we promise this summer will be one to remember.

PLEASE NOTE:

- All campers must abide by lights-out protocol.
- Emergency drills will be held weekly.
- Campers should not enter the woods unsupervised.

AND REMEMBER HERE AT CAMPSILVER HOLLOW,

WE DON'T BELIEVE IN BAD ENDINGS.

ONLY CHARACTER DEVELOPMENT.

✦ Prologue ✦

✧Ms. Dee✧

Every summer, they come like clockwork—bright-eyed, half-feral, dragging ghosts behind their duffels.

Some think the woods are healing. That if you just breathe enough pine and sleep under the stars, the hurt don't stick as deep.

But I've been here long enough to know Camp Silver Hollow don't fix what's broken.

It just shows you where the cracks start.

You wanna know the truth?

This place eats secrets and spits out stories. And every year, at least one kid walks into the trees thinking they'll come back the same.

They never do.

And maybe that's not a curse.

Maybe it's the only honest thing we got left.

✦ 1 ✦

Popcorn and Heartstrings

Ashgrove, Oregon

☽ June 24th ☾

✧Emilia✧

The Ashgrove Commons Mall aged like a childhood friend you never realized was falling apart until they smiled. The two-level structure still clinging to life, its tile floors dulled by time, the corners of the space buzz with tired fluorescence, and the faint smell of rain-soaked concrete floats throughout. The theater, which was once its heart, is now in desperate need of renovation after decades of neglect. The once vibrant neon colors of the black galaxy carpet now faded and moldy, fingerprint smudges staining every surface of the glass, and an old claw machine that's been broken longer than most of the staff has worked here.

The lights above the concession stand hum faintly, flickering with that erratic, stammering blink that might've driven someone else crazy—like they're winking in Morse code, trying to signal out of this place. But I barely notice them anymore. The longer you work here, the more your brain learns to tune it out, folding the stutter of fluorescents into the background hum of the mall's artificial heartbeat.

It isn't just the lights. It's also the constant echo of too-loud movie trailers, the soft pop of soda machines that never quite dispense right, the faint chemical sweetness of stale butter. There is a tangible rhythm to it, the kind that doesn't care if you're breaking inside, as long as you clock in on time.

My eyes are fixed on the glass display in front of me, where the popcorn shimmers under a tired heat lamp like something fossilized in amber—shiny, stale, and too still. The candy racks beside it lean unevenly, half-empty and untouched. Dust gathers in the corners of the shelves in soft gray smudges, and the whole setup has the look of a forgotten offering.

It's late morning on a Tuesday, and Ashgrove Commons Mall is dragging on at its usual pace, the same as it has for the last four years since I graduated high school—sluggish and strange, like time itself is walking through molasses. The food court smells faintly of old grease and synthetic citrus from the janitor's mop bucket. Stores echo with hollow pop songs no one is really listening to. A lone toddler screaming two corridors away, the sound bouncing off the linoleum like a trapped bird.

This is the kind of place where ghosts might linger just to pass the time. Not the violent kind—just the bored ones, the ones who haven't realized yet that nothing here ever really changes.

Shifting my weight from one foot to the other and look toward the ticket booth where Wes is leaning out in all his glory, radiating sunshine. My happier half, effortlessly charming a group of girls who are clearly flirting with him. He laughs at something one of them says, all warmth in his threadbare theater polo, one arm slung over the window ledge as if he belongs in some cheesy movie about mall romance.

I pretended to rearrange the candy rack, anything to avoid feeling that tight pinch behind my ribs. Not jealousy. Not really. Just that quiet, familiar voice reminding me I don't fit in the easy spaces he fills so well. He belongs with people who smile like that. People who sparkle. I keep my gaze fixed on the counter, the way you do when you're used to being background noise. I don't sparkle. I'm not even worth a second look, but I know he would never stand to hear me say that.

Then he looks up and catches me staring, his face lighting up like it always does when he sees me—not in a way that makes me feel exposed, but in a way that makes me feel like maybe I'm not entirely invisible. The light hits his eyes really bringing out the broken glass look they have; the way it refracts through them is mesmerizing.

He mouths a goofy little, "Hi."

My lips twitch despite myself.

Jason, our shift lead, sticks his head into the concession stand, looking half-asleep as usual.

"Break time," he mutters. "You good here for a few?"

I nod, and he wanders off.

A few minutes later, Wes strolls behind the counter like he's never belonged anywhere else. His hip brushes mine as he reaches for a soda cup.

"Hey," he says, eyes crinkling.

Though my insecurities are whispering for me to, I don't move away. "You're supposed to be out front."

"It's dead." He fills the cup with ice, the sound sharp in the quiet. "Besides, I missed you."

My lips curve before I can stop them, and I duck my head to hide it. The air between us feels warm, like standing too close to something that might burn if I leaned in.

"You're going to get written up again," I murmur.

He shrugs, unbothered. "They'd have to care enough to read the reports."

I curl my lips inward, biting back a smile. "You think you're charming."

"I know I'm charming." He leans his hip against the counter, close enough that I can smell the faint detergent scent of his shirt. His voice drops, teasing. “It’s one of my better qualities.”

I cut my eyes at him. “You’re lucky I like you.”

“Correction,” he says, nudging my shoulder with his. The touch lingers longer than it needed to. “You love me.”

I do. That is the problem.

I'm worried loving me would be like water on soft wood—creating a slow erosion he wouldn’t notice until it’s too late. But Wes—he doesn't flinch. He moves through the world like someone who knows exactly where the damaged spots are and loves them anyway.

He makes me feel soft in a world that has only ever required me to be angular. Around everyone else? My walls remain high, but around Wes... they tremble.

And every time he looks at me like this—like I am the only thing that makes sense—the voice in my head whispers that it won’t last. That eventually, someone like him will figure out that wanting someone like me is a mistake.

But, for now, I let myself enjoy the way his smile lingers.

✧

It's just before one when our break starts, and we walk down to the food court side by side. The mall is quiet but still alive, elevators humming, distant chatter drifting through the corridors. A pretzel place is still open, buttery garlic knots half-heartedly baking beneath a heat lamp, while a couple of teenagers slouch against a boba counter, scrolling their phones.

Sophie's already waiting at one of the round food court tables when we arrive, her arms crossed over a folded-up brochure, her mouth twisted into a scowl. Her hair is pulled back in a frizzy ponytail. The moment she spots us; she uncrosses her arms and holds the brochure aloft like it was evidence in a court case.

"Okay," she says without preamble, "I need a favor, and Mom is being the actual worst."

I blink several times. "You're opening with that?"

"Because I'm panicking. I've only been on summer break for a month, and I'm already losing it in that house."

She drops the brochure in front of us. It's glossy and colorful, featuring an old-timey pine tree logo and faded summer photos of canoes, misty lake mornings, and towering evergreens splashed across the front. Wes leans in closer to read it while I just stare at my sister, waiting.

"Camp Silver Hollow," she announces, the name landing like a spark between us. "It's the place I told you about, the one out near the Cascade Mountains. They still have spots for the second summer session, but Mom says she's not paying for something that sounds like an artsy cult."

I arch a brow, the corner of my mouth twitching.

"She literally said that," Sophie confirmed, rolling her eyes with an edge that doesn't quite mask the hope flickering underneath. "but... There's a scholarship thing. If I get someone to volunteer as a counselor, I can go for free."

Across the table, Wes looks up from his lo mein, fork pausing mid-spin... "Volunteer? Like... the whole summer?"

Sophie nods, the motion quick and full of nervous energy. "Just six weeks. You get food and housing, and there's even a stipend. Kind of. I think the counselors are all your age, probably mostly college kids."

She turns to me fully then, and I see the moment her confidence falters. Her eyes go wide—hopeful and scared at once. "I know you're going to say no. But I had to ask."

My hand pauses halfway to my mouth, suspended like the moment is too fragile to break. Even the food-court hum seems too quiet, like the whole place was holding its breath with her.

"I'll do it," I say, biting into the french fry.

Sophie blinks slowly, thrown. Then her eyes spring open. "Wait. What?"

"I'll volunteer," I repeat, softer this time, as if it were the most natural thing in the world. "You want to go, and I've got no plans. Easy decision."

For a heartbeat, she just stares—mouth open, eyes shimmering in disbelief.

"Are you serious? Are you actually serious right now?"

I shrug, trying to play it cool, but my throat feels tight. "Yeah. You're worth it."

Sophie looks like she's been hit in the chest with sunlight—eyes wide, face wobbling between disbelief and joy. She swallows once, hard, and nods like she can't quite trust her voice.

Wes nudges my knee under the table, a quiet, grounding touch, and I glance at him.

"Then I'm going too," he declares, voice steady, like there was never another option.

Sophie gasps, then laughs—a small, incredulous sound that cracks around the edges.

"You guys. You guys. You're both insane. But you're also perfect. And I love you."

Something warm presses up beneath my ribs, tightening my throat before I can swallow it down. I blink hard, staring at my hands so neither of them would see the way my breathing hitched. She deserves this—somewhere bright, somewhere soft. A summer that belongs to her.

Wes leans back and stretches, arms behind his head, looking pleased with himself.

"Summer camp," he says with a lazy grin. "I can rock with that."

And across the table, Sophie beams as bright and warm as sunlight after a long storm.

By four o'clock, our shift is officially over. The theater is now still with the dinner lull, but the mall around us is alive—stores still buzzing, customers drifting in and out.

Wes, Sophie, and I walk out together through the west exit, the sky outside streaked with early summer gold. The parking lot stretched long and warm under the sun, the asphalt still slick from the earlier rain, the neon sign above the arcade still glowing faintly in the light.

As we pass a grimy corner near the exit, I slow. A man stands half in shadow, smoking a cigarette. He reeks of sweat and cheap beer, clothes stained and skin sallow. Sophie is a few steps ahead when his voice cuts through the air, acerbic and sour.

"Bet you taste as sweet as you look, sweetheart."

She freezes.

I stop mid-step, stomach turning.

Before either of us can react, Wes's voice slices through the space—low and final.

"Don't."

He was already moving, stepping in front of us like a wall. Not yelling. Not bristling. Just still. Too still.

"You've got five seconds to walk away and forget you ever opened your mouth."

The man scoffs, half-laughing, but the sound dies in his throat when Wes looks at him.

That look. Quiet and blazing. Not angry. Focused. Dangerous.

The man blinks. Reconsiders. He mumbles something I couldn't catch and shuffles off toward the parking lot.

Silence stretches. Sophie exhales shakily beside me, but I can't take my eyes off Wes.

His jaw is set, hands flexing once, then again. So still. Not breathless. Not shaking. Just controlled. Like he's holding something barely leashed beneath the surface.

But it doesn't scare me. It draws me in.

Is this what it means to be protected? To be loved so fiercely, it scorches the edges? My pulse kicks, fast and unfamiliar, as if my body knows something I don't. It isn't really fear, but not quite desire — something deeper, messier. The kind of heat that makes me wonder if I'd burn or bloom.

The sun begins to dip low, casting long shadows across the pavement, and for a moment, everything feels quiet. Safe.

As we reach the car, Wes pauses and pats his pockets.

“Shit. Forgot my keys in my locker. Be right back?”

He jogs off without waiting for a reply, calling over his shoulder with a flash of a grin.

Sophie and I climb up to sit on the edge of the trunk, legs swinging. The metal is warm beneath us; the kind of warmth that soaks through and makes the world feel like maybe it isn't all jagged edges.

She watches Wes jog back toward the mall, her shoulders rising and falling with a small breath. "Bet Mom's halfway into a bottle by now and calling it self-care."

I hate that she said it so casually. Hate that she'd learned to. She never should've had to grow up that way—and yet she had.

My mouth twitches, going dry. "Only self-care she knows is Vince's approval."

"Or his wallet."

We laugh, but it's a brittle sound, the kind that lets us pretend, just for now, that things aren't falling apart behind closed doors.

Sophie picks at the peeling edge of the camp brochure, quieter now. Her voice dropping, "do you think it'll be good? Camp, I mean?"

I look over. Her expression is open, a little nervous, a little hopeful. She's still so young in some ways, still waiting for something to feel like it belongs to her.

"I think it might be the best thing we've done," I said softly. "Especially for you."

She smiles. Not big, but real. The kind of smile that doesn't try too hard or hide behind sarcasm. It creeps in slowly, tugging at the corners of her mouth like it was learning how to be there. Her eyes crinkle just slightly, soft and a little shiny, and for once—just once—she doesn't seem guarded or bracing for it to disappear. It's the kind of smile that screams, *maybe this time, it'll be different.*

And I hope with everything I have that it will be.

She looks down, then nudges my knee with hers. "Hey. Thank you again. For saying yes."

I leaned, nudging her back. "You don't have to thank me. You're my sister."

She hesitates, then blows out a breath and whispers, "I actually sent the application in weeks ago. I was just worried if I asked too early, it'd give you too much time to get in your own head."

I blink, then laugh softly, the sound gentle and knowing. Of course she did—always thinking ahead, always careful of me. Because she knows I'd do anything for her. Always.

We sit in silence after that, watching people trickle in and out of the mall. A mother dragging a whiny toddler. A couple arguing over a receipt. Somewhere in the distance, someone's car alarm chirps. Five minutes pass. Then six. The kind of minutes that feel slower than they should, the kind that stretch wide in your chest where silence starts to feel like weight instead of peace.

Sophie rests her chin on her knees, fingers absently pulling at a thread on her hoodie. I lean back on my palms, eyes squinting into the late-afternoon haze. The heat shimmers off the pavement, blurring the edges of things. Talking isn′t necessary for us. This is the kind of silence that doesn′t press on my ribs—easy, familiar, lived-in.

Somewhere beyond the row of parked cars, a shopping cart rattles in the breeze, its wheels twitching on their own—still no sign of Wes. The moment holds long enough for unease to settle in the back of my throat—but not enough to call it fear. Just that familiar hum of wondering.

Then he appears, returning a little breathless. His hair looks slightly mussed, windblown maybe, and his shirt isn't sitting quite right around the collar. There′s a faint mark on the side of his arm that could've been from leaning on something. He doesn't explain, but I don't push—just watch as he smiles brightly, jangling his keys in one hand as he unlocks the car.

"We should grab a couple things for camp," he announces easily. "That drive through the forest's gonna be a long one. If you want, we can stop at Bargain Cove so you can create the perfect camp experience. And of course, we definitely need gas station snacks for the drive. Road trip rule."

Sophie lights up again. "Yes! Slim Jims, gummy worms, those weird marshmallow peanuts."

Wes grins and opens the back door for her with a mock bow. "Your chariot awaits."

I slide into the passenger seat, the leather warm from the sun, and watch him as he starts the engine. His profile is soft in the fading light, framed by the gold of dusk—the kind of light that clings to everything, like the day doesn't want to end. His mouth moves as he banters with Sophie, casual and warm, but my attention has drifted somewhere quieter. Somewhere beneath the surface, beneath the ease and practiced charm.

There's a shift in the way his knuckles flex on the steering wheel. The way he doesn't meet my eyes right away, just glances sideways, like something in him is still catching up to the moment. Trivial things, easy to overlook. But I felt them anyway—not as doubt, not as distance, but as something weightier. Something he carries with purpose. And still, he doesn't flinch under the weight. He wears it like armor, like choice.

When he finally glances over, it isn't the grin or the banter that catches me. It's the warmth behind his gaze—steady, fierce. The way it lands on me like a promise.

My heart stutters. Not from fear of him, but of myself, of how much I want to love him freely, fiercely. Of how badly I want to believe this could be real, that I could lean into it without breaking myself in the process. Because that look—God, that look—makes it so easy to forget everything that has ever told me I wasn't allowed this.

I lean my head against the window, throat tight, chest aching. The world outside blurs in amber streaks, trees stretching long in the late sun, and still, all I can see is him.

✧Wes✧

The second the sliding doors open, cold air blasts over us as if we'd stepped into the Arctic. Bright lights, sugar-colored chaos, and rows of cheap treasure greet us—everything a broke logging town teen could dream of before disappearing into the woods. The whole place smells like plastic and potential.

"Alright," I say, pushing a bright blue shopping basket into Emilia's hands. "We're stocking up for summer survival. All on me."

Emilia raises a brow. "You're not serious."

"Oh, I'm very serious." I grab a pair of oversized flamingo sunglasses and jam them onto my face. "Camp Silver Hollow doesn't know what's coming."

Sophie squeals and darts toward the bins near the front. "This is the best day of my life!" She's already piling stuff into a basket of her own—a pineapple-print water bottle, neon gel pens, a squishy stress avocado. I follow with Emilia beside me, her fingers brushing mine as we walk.

"Just grab what you like," I tell her quietly. "No arguing."

She shakes her head, but the corner of her mouth twitches. "You're ridiculous."

"Ridiculously generous." I nudge her. "Let me spoil you a little."

"Our version of spoiling is camp flip-flops and bubblegum chapstick."

"Hey," I chirp, plucking a twin-pack of said chapstick from the rack. "This stuff smells like nostalgia and poor decisions."

She takes it, just long enough to roll her eyes and tuck it into the basket. "One thing. That's it."

I don't push. Not yet. Because I know what it means for her to even take that much. She isn't used to taking—not gifts, not help, not softness. She'd spent so long convincing herself she didn't need anything that even the smallest indulgence feels like too much, like she has to earn every scrap of comfort. So I let her set the pace, because spoiling her isn't about the stuff; it's about showing her she doesn't have to brace for disappointment every time something feels good. Not with me. Not anymore.

Sophie comes bounding back, arms overflowing with ridiculousness. "They have waterproof mascara and glitter face paint! I'm going to be an actual forest fairy. This is... Wes, I don't know how to thank you."

"You're doing it right now," I tell her with a grin. "Just keep that sparkly energy all summer. We'll need it."

She beams like I handed her the moon.

We move aisle to aisle, picking through bins like pirates in a plastic sea. I hold up a pair of frog-themed shower sandals and give Emilia my best salesman pitch. She snorts, trying to walk away, but I see the way her hand lingers on a lilac bath towel—soft, plush, slightly out of place among the chaos.

"You like it." I state.

"I don't need it."

"That wasn't a question."

She stares for a moment before running her fingers across the edge. Her expression goes unreadable—too still, like she is trying not to want it. I know that look. That hold-your-breath-until-you-don't-feel-anything look. I'd worn it too. I pluck the towel off the shelf and add it to our pile without waiting. She doesn't argue this time.

In the next aisle, Sophie finds a journal with moon phases on the cover—soft black with silver foil embossing, the kind of thing that looks like it belongs in a spellbook collection. She turns it over in her hands, then glances at me with a grin. "It looks like something Em would pick," she whispers.

She's right. It is exactly Emilia—quiet, intentional, full of magic no one noticed at first. When Sophie holds it out, Emilia pauses. Really pauses. Her eyes scan the cover like it might be a trick, like wanting something isn't allowed. Her fingers hover just short of taking it, and for a second, I wasn't sure she would.

But then she takes it. And the way she does—it isn't casual. She folds her arms around it like it's delicate, like someone might try to take it from her. Like it had been meant for her, and she didn't quite believe she was allowed to keep it.

Something in my chest pulls tight. Not the painful kind of tight. Not fear. Not even love—it is deeper. A kind of ache that lives somewhere in the marrow. Because I knew what it meant to grow up convincing yourself you didn't need soft things. To flinch at wanting. To treat joy like a visitor, not a right. Watching her hold that little journal like it was a piece of herself she'd been missing—yeah. That broke me a little. In the best way.

We load up on camp basics: cheap flip-flops, bug spray, toothbrush holders shaped like bears, and little mesh laundry bags. Somewhere between the glow sticks and citronella candles, Sophie starts comparing them like we were prepping for the Hunger Games. "They'll never see me coming," she declares, wielding a pool noodle like a sword.

Emilia is laughing. Really laughing. That low, surprised kind that feels like a win every time.

I drift closer, looping an arm around her shoulders as Sophie pretends to fence with an inflatable flamingo. "She's literally vibrating with excitement," I whisper.

"She's never had anything like this before," Emilia admits, voice soft. "None of it. You're... making it feel real."

I kiss her temple before I can stop myself. Not big. Not dramatic. Just enough to say *I see you.* She leaned into it—just a second, just enough.

"She didn't get handed much," she mutters. "I just want her to have something that feels good. That's all I've ever wanted."

Something inside me clenches—low, steady—as if her words snag on something raw inside me. The way she said it—quiet, offhand—like it wasn't the most heartbreakingly beautiful thing I'd ever heard. Like it wasn't everything.

"I know," I concede. "That's one of the first things I ever loved about you."

She looks up at me then, something open in her eyes. Something raw. I didn't look away.

By the time we made it to the register, our cart looked like a clearance aisle had exploded, but I didn't care. Sophie chattered nonstop while Emilia kept insisting I didn't need to do all this. I let her insist. I let her roll her eyes and mutter about overkill. And then I paid for it all without blinking. Because this—this was easy. This was nothing compared to what she deserved.

The checkout beeped like it was announcing something sacred. The cashier didn't look twice. No one ever did. But I saw them, Emilia tucking a bottle of glitter sunscreen into Sophie's bag like it was armor, Sophie holding onto that ridiculous inflatable frog like it was treasure. This wasn't just a shopping trip. It was hope, packed in plastic.

We stepped back into the fading light, bags in hand, the sky shifting toward evening in soft lavender strokes.

"Alright," I said, swinging the keys in one hand. "Now: snacks. Then I'll take you lovely ladies′ home."

Sophie cheered like we'd just won a championship. Emilia slid her hand into mine without a word.

And just like that, I was gone again. Hopeless. Completely hers.

✦ 2 ✦

Home Shitty Home

☽ Evening ~ June 24th ☾

✧Emilia✧

Ashgrove isn't the kind of town that lets you forget anything. The streets here feel stuck, caught between peeling porch paint, rain-stained siding, and hand-lettered gas station signs still advertising smokes for $3.99. Even the air feels soggy with memory—mildew and cedar bark, pavement always damp from the last rain.

Our neighborhood is quieter than most—not the good kind of quiet, but the kind that comes from too many closed doors and too few safe places. Fog hangs low in the streetlights, soaking into cracked sidewalks and moss-choked gutters, homes sagging under the weight of the years and newer regrets.

The door creaks open, and the smell hits me first: boxed wine, burnt toaster crumbs, and cheap microwave dinners. It's always the same. The scent of surrender soaked into the walls. No matter how long I'm gone, it never stops clinging.

It seeps into your skin, that smell. Gets under your fingernails, in your clothes, between the folds of memory where even good moments go to die. I used to think I could scrub it out—change the curtains, light candles, open windows. But nothing can lift the weight of a place that has given up.

The TV flickers low in the living room, casting a weak glow over a mess of limbs on the couch. I don't even have to look to know.

Mom is slouched on one end, her signature tank top clinging to her like a memory that doesn't know when to quit. Faded lettering across her chest read Famous—which would be ironic if it didn't already feel like a punchline. Her jeans are tight, belt studded, cigarette dangling from her lips like it had grown there. Red, chipped polish on her nails, smoke curling around her mascara-smeared eyes. Her coppery hair, wild and teased from too many nights of not bothering, catches the glow from the floor lamp in a way that almost makes her look alive.

Almost.

She used to be beautiful. Still is, in a faded rock star sort of way. Like if you squint hard enough, you could see the girl she once thought she'd grow up to be. But these days, all that's left is brittle edges and slurred laughs. Her mouth is twisted in a lazy grin as she sips from a red Solo cup, lounging like she doesn't have two daughters still residing under her roof.

Vince takes up the other end, stretched out like he owns the place. He always did that—acted like the furniture was his, like we should be grateful for his presence. His biker vest hangs open over a tight, faded shirt stamped with a grinning skull. The kind of thing you'd buy to look hard, except on him, it doesn't feel like an act. Thick silver chains hang around his neck, one holding a cheap cross that clinks when he moves.

His jeans are worn in the way that comes from years of hard living, not style. A beer bottle dangles from his tattooed hand, and his arms, lean and sinewy, are covered in ink that looks more like bad decisions than art. The kind of man who probably used to ride logging backroads drunk and swore he'd outrun the sheriff on a gravel turn.

There's always something in the way he watches the room—like he's waiting for an excuse to break something that isn't his. Trouble isn't something he causes; it is something he wears, easy as breathing. And worst of all, he is always just bored enough to be cruel.

The news anchor's voice murmurs from the TV in a dull, practiced cadence.

"Breaking News: A body was found earlier this evening behind Ashgrove Commons. The victim was a middle-aged male who sustained significant trauma. Police are currently investigating."

Sophie freezes beside me. Just stops moving, as if her brain short-circuits. Her eyes lock on the screen, wide and too quiet. When she finally speaks, it is barely a whisper.

"Was that the...?"

She doesn't finish. She doesn't have to. I feel the rest of the sentence unspool in her head like a thread unraveling too fast.

The man from earlier. The mall. That feeling that had followed us home like something oily under our skin.

I can't let her think about it. Not here. Not now.

"Don't," I warn, my voice low and clipped, a warning honed by years of keeping us safe. I grab her wrist and pull her toward the hallway. "Just go."

My hand trembles around her wrist, but I don't let go. Can't. I need her out of there, need her past the hallway and into a room where cruelty can't reach. My voice comes out definitive and steadier than I feel. The fear sits under it, thick as smoke, burning the back of my throat.

She doesn't fight me. Just goes, quiet and rattled, casting one last glance at the TV as we disappear down the hall.

Behind us, Mom lets out a slurred laugh at something Vince mumbled. The anchor keeps talking. But I'm not listening anymore. I've heard enough. And seen more than enough to last me a lifetime.

✧Sophie✧

We're almost past the living room. I can see the corner of the hallway, maybe ten more steps, and we'll be free. I've been holding my breath without meaning to, just trying to get through it like always, when Vince opens his mouth—because of course he does.

"Kinda funny," he drawls, tilting the neck of his beer bottle in a lazy circle like the motion could make him smarter. "You spend enough time loitering around that mall, someone's bound to put you down like a stray."

I stop. Freezing so hard it's like my body forgot how to move. I turn slowly, my whole spine locking into place as I face him.

"What did you just say?"

He finally looks at me—slow, smug, and deliberate. Like he is savoring it. One corner of his mouth pulled into a smile that doesn't come anywhere near his eyes.

"You heard me, sweetheart. Maybe if whoever killed him had a better eye, he'd have picked prettier targets. Clean up the gene pool a little."

A beat of silence passes. It feels like something inside me cracks, like the pressure from everything—*everything*—was finally starting to split open. I see my mom shift on the couch, not even lifting her head.

"Vince, shut up," she groans, as if *we* were the inconvenience.

But he isn't finished. Vince never knows when to shut the hell up. His eyes stay glued to me like a dare.

"Not like I'd miss either of you. This place might actually be quiet for once."

Before I could take a step forward, Emilia is there, sliding in front of me like a wall I hadn't asked for but always seem to get.

"Don't," she warns, her jaw clenched so tight I think she might crack a molar. "Just don't."

But it's too late. My pulse is hammering, heat building behind my eyes. I am not done.

"You wouldn't care if we ended up on that news, would you?" I say, the words scraping out of my throat like they had claws.

He laughs—that ugly, bitter kind of laugh that isn't even human. Just sound and cruelty mixed in one low, empty note.

"Long as it didn't interrupt the game. Not really."

Something flickers behind Mom's mascara-smudged eyes, but all she manages is a sluggish, "Ugh. Not tonight, babe..."

Like it was just another night. Like it was all background noise to her wine buzz and whatever Vince fed her that made him feel necessary.

"Don't start acting like you give a shit now, Marla," Vince mutters, already turning back toward the TV like we don't exist.

I want to scream. Throw something. Shake her until the numbness cracks. How could she keep choosing him?

"Let's go, Soph," Emilia says, her voice low, clipped, final—the way it always gets when she is seconds away from snapping herself.

I hate that tone. Not because it's cold—but because I know it too well. It means she is holding herself together with tattered resolve, fingers curling tight around the last shreds of control. It means she is bleeding somewhere I can't see.

I let her pull me down the hallway, my feet moving before I could decide whether or not I wanted them to. The moment we are out of view, it all comes spilling out in a hiss between my teeth.

"Why do you just let him run his mouth like that?"

Emilia doesn't even flinch. Her eyes are fixed forward like she's already shoved it all into a box and slammed the lid shut.

"Because it's not new," she answers. Flat. Numb. "And because we're leaving tomorrow and I won't let him ruin this for you."

I kick the baseboard on impulse, just to hear something break. Just to feel the jolt of it through my foot. "Still sucks."

"Yeah." Her voice doesn't change. "But it's better to just not give him the satisfaction. Ya know, just let the rain take care of him."

We keep walking. The hallway light buzzing above us, one bulb flickering with that sick yellow glow that makes everything feel tired. I didn't want to say it out loud, but the words came anyway, quieter this time, like I was afraid of how true they were.

"You always act like you don't feel it."

She doesn't answer. Not really. Just keeps walking, her silhouette rigid in the half-light. But the silence behind her says plenty.

And I hate how well I understand it.

✧Emilia✧

Our room is small—a full-size mattress pressed against the far wall, a shared dresser near the door, and posters curling at the edges from too many humid summers and forgotten thumbtacks. The PNWC's damp air never really leaves anything untouched. But it's ours. The one place Vince has never set foot into, like even he knows it's off-limits. That makes it sacred.

I drop my keys on the nightstand with a soft clink and pull the plastic Bargain Cove bag onto the bed, careful not to wake the dust that seems to cling to everything in this house. I open it slowly, almost like a ceremony.

One by one, our treasures spill out. Cheap, colorful, unapologetically bright—like magic on clearance, disguised as survival. A hot pink flashlight, the kind with a rubber grip that Sophie had claimed within seconds. A lavender neck pillow that matched her hoodie so perfectly it felt fated. Two mini fans shaped like popsicles, a watermelon lip balm that smells like summer, face wipes with smiling cartoon fruit on the package, and a glittery journal she swore she'd actually write in this time. Matching water bottles with Chaos Crew printed in silver sparkles. Her idea, obviously.

I rolled my eyes and called them dumb in the store. Then we bought two.

She flops backwards onto the bed behind me; arms folded behind her head like she doesn't have a care in the world. Like, the whole interaction with Vince never happened.

"You always make things feel like more than they are," she says, smiling up at the ceiling.

"You deserve more," I reply without looking up. I was already lining up the travel-size shampoos and soaps like soldiers along the edge of the bed. Lining things up in neat rows has always steadied something in me. Order in a place that doesn't have any. "I won't always be able to protect you. So for now... I do what I can."

The words come out softer than I meant them to. But true. If I could make her world lighter by even an ounce, I'd carry the rest without complaint. Packing isn't just a chore; it is a declaration. A signal to the universe that we are leaving, even if only for six weeks. Even if only for now.

Sophie's striped swimsuit sits folded beside a few soft shirts and her new sandals, tags already cut. I'd watched her grin like a kid opening a birthday present when she tried them on earlier. That grin was worth everything.

My side of the suitcase was thinner. A few pairs of shorts, and a handful of old tank tops I could wear a few times each before washing. I tuck my birth control pills between my deodorant and toothbrush. Mundane things. Necessary things. The kind of control I can cling to, even if nothing else in my life feels steady. I'd handed over most of our budget without hesitation. She hadn't even realized I'd done it.

"You need it more," I'd told her in the checkout line when she questioned it. "I'll share yours."

I didn't mind. I never did. Let her have the glitter and the colors and the soft new things. Let her feel like something is hers for once.

I'd keep the weight. That is mine.

Later that night, the lights are off. Sophie sleeps soundly, her breath slow and even, the kind of peaceful rhythm I always listen for without realizing. I stay still, careful not to shift the mattress or disturb her. She needs rest. Real rest. The kind that doesn't come easy in this house.

I lay beside her in the dark, scrolling numbly through my phone. Headlines blur past—disasters, scandals, lives unraveling in real time—and none of it feels real. It was just noise. Background static to the quiet panic that never fully left my chest.

Then, my screen lights up with a message from Wes.

"Almost time to trade chaos for cabins. I'll take any excuse to be lost in the woods with you."

A soft smile tugs at my lips. Fleeting. Fragile.

I read the message again, slower this time, like maybe the second read-through would make it safer to hold. Wes always had a way of cutting through the mess, finding a thread of something sweet and steady in the middle of the storm. Of course, he'd say something like that. Of course, it would make me feel like the floor wasn't caving in for a second.

Hope is dangerous. But tonight, I let myself have a little. Just a taste. Just enough to keep going.

From the other room, the TV murmurs, too quiet to make out the words, but I don't need to. It's still looping the news story. Same dramatic voiceover, same faces frozen on the screen, same nightmare they keep replaying like it matters what order you watched it in.

I lock my phone and set it face down on the nightstand, letting the darkness take over again. Then I turn on my side, curling around Sophie without really thinking. My arm drapes gently over her waist, fingers brushing the soft cotton of her shirt. She mumbles something incoherent in her sleep but doesn't wake. I rest my forehead against her shoulder and close my eyes.

"We're getting out," I whisper into the dark, like maybe the universe needs to hear it just as much as I do. "Even if it's only for a little while."

And I mean it. Even if it is six weeks. Even if the woods are only a pause button. It would be something. A breath. A break.

For her. For me.

For us.

✧

The dream comes severe and sudden, as if it had just been waiting for me to close my eyes.

I was thirteen again.

The house is too quiet. That kind of quiet that isn't peaceful, just waiting. The TV in the living room crackles low in the background, a laugh track rising like it didn't know any better.

Sophie is asleep in our bedroom, curled beneath the covers, still clutching the ragged stuffed bunny she hasn't let go of in three years. I kiss her forehead and tell her I'll be right back. Just getting a glass of water. Just two minutes.

I should've known better.

The kitchen floor is cold under my feet. The air reeking of beer and cheap aftershave, sour and sharp. I keep my steps light, holding my breath like that could make me invisible.

It doesn't.

He is already there.

My father stands hunched over the sink, a bottle dangling from one hand, his mouth curling around slurred curses as he mutters to himself. Something about my mom. Something about being disrespected. Something about me.

I freeze mid-step, heart rattling against my ribs like it wanted out. I should turn around, should leave the light off, should let the thirst burn in my throat all night if it meant not seeing him like this.

He turns.

"The hell are you sneakin' around for?"

His voice is jagged and mean. I don't answer. Don't move. I've learned by now that silence is safer. That sometimes if you are small enough, quiet enough, he'll just lose interest.

Not tonight.

He steps towards me, slow and swaying, and I can already see it coming. The shift in his eyes. That snap of fury that has no trigger. The belt isn't in his hand this time. Just the bottle.

"Look at me when I'm talkin' to you," he barks.

I flinch. And that's all it takes.

The glass shatters first. Then comes the back of his hand, fast and mean, sending me sprawling backward into the counter. My head slams against the edge, and pain blooming white-hot just above my eye. I don't even register the scream until I feel blood spill down into it.

The room blurs. My knees are giving out. The world tilts.

All I can think about is Sophie still sleeping, safe behind that closed door. She can't hear this. She can't wake up. I won't let him touch her. I won't.

The world narrows to a pinpoint of dark, soft, and heavy, the closest thing to mercy I've felt all night.

I jolt awake, chest tight, breath ragged and shallow like I'd been drowning in sleep.

The room is dark. Hot. The sheets stuck to my skin.

Sophie remains sleeping beside me, undisturbed, her little body curled toward the wall. Her breathing is steady. Peaceful.

I let my head drop back onto the pillow and reach up, fingers brushing the scar above my left eyebrow. The glass cut down along my brow bone and nicked the top of my eyelid. It had healed clean, considering, but it still felt jagged under my fingertips, like the skin remembered.

I'd lied to doctors. Said I slipped down the stairs. Said I didn't remember. And maybe, eventually, I didn't. Not all of it. Just enough to stay standing. Just enough to keep breathing.

For a second, I just breathe. In, then out. One, then two. But it isn't enough.

My lungs feel tight and my body restless, a kind of too-much that won't let go. I don't want to sit in it, but I don't want to go back to sleep and see him again either.

I grab my phone from the nightstand and type with trembling fingers.

"You up?"

I don't wait for a reply. I already know he'll meet me at our spot.

I press a kiss to Sophie's forehead, careful not to wake her, and slide silently from the bed.

The window opens with a familiar creak. The humid night air rolling in, thick with pine, damp earth, and the faint sweetness of blooming red huckleberry shrubs.

My bedroom sits at the front of the second floor, just above the sagging porch roof. Years ago, I'd claimed the sloped shingles beneath my window as mine—a perch where I could breathe, where the weight of the house didn't press in quite so hard. Directly across the narrow stretch of side yard, Wes's room faces mine. His splintered balcony, half-sheltered by overgrown ivy and shadow, has become our shared middle ground. On nights like this, when sleep is too far and the world feels too close, it is the bridge we meet on.

I climb out barefoot; the shingles cool beneath my feet. The sky above stretched out like a held breath, smeared with stars and slow-moving clouds. The air is heavy. But it feels better out here, away from walls. From memories.

Across the narrow gap, Wes waits on the small balcony outside his room, hoodie unzipped, pajama pants slung low on his hips like he doesn't know how dangerous he looks. The moonlight makes everything about him glow, his collarbones, the hard line of his stomach, the soft curve of his mouth.

I let myself look for a bit too long.

Get a grip.

But around him, I never quite can.

He catches me looking. Of course he does.

His mouth tilts into a half-smile, lazy and warm.

"That look better be for me, or I'm gonna be heartbroken."

I roll my eyes, but it doesn't land. Not with the way my chest aches.

"What if it is?"

He shrugs, all casual mischief.

"Then I guess I should keep standing here like this..." he subtly flexes a few poses, "give you something worth climbing over for."

The smirk is still there, but softer now. Gentle under the teasing, like he knows exactly why I'm out here. Like he's offering me something steadier than a joke.

I step across the gap without answering, and into the only place that ever felt like solid ground.

He doesn't just hold me; he catches me, as if I'm something he'd never let fall. More than just a weight he is willing to carry; it feels like he genuinely wants to.

The way he steadies me sends a tremor through my chest, sweet and frightening all at once. How badly I want to stay right here.

"You just like seeing me half-dressed in moonlight," he murmurs, brushing his nose against my temple.

I want to laugh. I almost did. But it catches in my throat—because somehow, even wrapped in humor, he always left space for my hurt. Like the jokes were just scaffolding, holding up something more careful underneath.

I feel him take a deep, slow breath, anchoring me. His hands move, settling on the small of my back, and he presses my body closer. In the shadows, his eyes—stormy and intense—study me, and I feel the unspoken weight of his attention. It is his way of saying: I know what you are, and I won't let go.

I flush.

"Would that be such a bad thing?"

His hand comes up to my cheek, thumb grazing along my skin in that way he did; never pushy, never asking for more than I give.

"You ever wonder," he cuts through the silence, voice barely a breath, "what it would feel like if we didn't have to keep stealing these moments?"

I nod. This time, when I lift my face to his, I don't hesitate.

The kiss isn't soft. It is full of everything we haven't said. Breathless and deep, pulled from something that's more than just us. His hands are steady at my waist, holding me like I'm something precious. And for once, I let myself believe I am.

When we finally pull apart, my breath catches in my chest. His eyes remain on me, dark, unreadable, too full. "I should go," I whisper.

He captures my wrist gently before I can move. His voice follows me as I step away. "Don't forget... you're not alone in this world."

I turn, just enough to meet his gaze over my shoulder. "Promise."

And then I slip through the window, back into the dark. But I don't feel quite so alone anymore.

✧Wes✧

I don't move.

I just stand there, watching her disappear back across the roof like something sacred I'm not sure I deserve to touch. Her frame shifts in and out of the shadows, the moonlight catching in the loose strands of her hair, gilding her like something already halfway to a dream. She doesn't look back.

She doesn't need to.

I can still feel the heat of her in my hands. The press of her lips. The way she'd looked at me like I was something solid when the entire world kept cracking underneath her.

When she's far enough away, far enough that I know she won't hear me, I let the words slip out on a breath I hadn't realized I was holding.

"If only you understood... I'd burn this whole world if it would bring some peace to you."

Not in the dramatic way people say things they don't intend to follow through on. Nor in a teenage fantasy or some lovesick metaphor. I meant every word. If it ever came down to it, I'd light a match and walk away smiling, as long as it meant she could finally rest.

I stand there a while longer, just listening. The soft creak of her window breaks the silence, the familiar groan of old wood sliding closed behind her. It settles into place like a heartbeat, and I know she is back inside. Safe.

My chest eases, just a little.

The moon slips behind a cloud. The stars go quiet. And the night, for a breath, feels like it's holding something between its teeth.

I run a thumb across my lower lip, tasting the last ghost of her Burt's Bees chapstick. I can still feel the press of her body, the faint, sweet scent of her hair lotion clinging to my hoodie, a smell that belongs only to her and nowhere else. She is all contrasts, that girl: pale as paper, yet she dressed like a shadow. Her black-painted nails that dig into my back sometimes, her skin flushing with heat right before she breaks. A hurricane beneath the surface, and I am the lighthouse, built only to stand for her. I take a deep, shaky breath, the humid air thick with the memory of her, and the sudden, wrenching realization that I'd have to wait until morning to touch her again.

Tomorrow, we leave for Silver Hollow.

A few hours from now, the sun will rise, and we'll pack bags into my car, like we're just two normal kids headed to some stupid camp job. We'll smile like we don't have ghosts crawling up our spines, and she'll keep that fire in her eyes like nothing can touch her. Like she hadn't just woken up from a memory that nearly split her in half.

And me, I'll keep pretending I don't watch the world for cracks she might fall through. That I'm not quietly taking inventory of every hurt written on her skin. I will continue to always be something warm, something constant for her.

Maybe up there, tucked away in the old-growth forest and the fog that never fully burns off, in the loamy scent of pine and moss and lake mist, we can pretend the world is something else.

Something quieter. Kinder. Maybe we can even believe it.

Even if only for a little while.

✦ 3 ✦

Silver Hollow's Smile is Paper-Thin

☽ Wednesday, June 25th ☾

✧Emilia✧

It's a little after 7 a.m. too early to be thinking about anything but coffee, let alone hope. But something about this morning makes it hard not to wonder: Could this really be the start of a good summer?

I don't trust hope. Not really. It has teeth, and it bites the second you let it get too close. But in this moment, it flickers anyway—thin and gold and begging to be held.

I know I shouldn't let my thoughts wander there. Not yet. But there's a flicker I can't quite shake. Quiet. Unreasonable. They're all the same.

The house was still asleep when we left—shadows tucked into corners, the hallway light casting that jaundiced, flickering glow we both knew too well. I hadn't slept. Not really. I'd lain there beside Sophie, listening to the creak of Vince's floorboards and counting the seconds between.

My bag was already packed. I'd triple-checked it at 5 a.m., careful not to wake her as I folded her new hoodie tighter than it needed to be, like it would hold something together.

Leaving didn't feel triumphant. It felt like slipping out of a house fire barefoot.

But the second I closed the car door, and he looked at me like I was already free, I almost believed it.

The sun is barely up when we leave Ashgrove. I ride in the front seat of Wes's dusty sedan, a coffee cup warming my hands, the windows cracked just enough to let in the early summer air. The radio plays low, shuffling between indie tracks and old songs I half-recognize from our childhoods—songs Wes deemed worthy of our road trip playlist.

We aren't driving more than ten minutes when Sophie starts talking. She's leaned between the seats, curls pulled into two French braids, phone in one hand, the Silver Hollow brochure in the other.

"Okay, but how big do you think the lake is? Like... canoes and rope swings big, or just, like, a sad puddle with a dock?"

Wes gives a half-laugh. "I don't think 'sad puddle' counts as a summer camp lake."

"I just want there to be lots of fun stuff to do," she says. "Like bonfires and color wars and maybe archery. Unless we're not allowed near weapons."

"That might depend on how annoying you are after week three," I tell her, keeping my gaze fixed on the window.

Sophie makes a mock-offended sound and slumps back with a dramatic sigh. "I'm just saying, six weeks in the woods sounds way less intense if there's at least some fun."

Towns shrink around us—shuttered diners, crooked mailboxes, peeling Americana like ghosts in daylight. Gas stations giving way to long stretches of forest, the kind that swallows sound. Sophie's chatter fills the silence, jumping from speculations about activities to wondering if the cabins have bunk beds or if we'll be stuck sharing with someone who snores.

After about forty-five minutes of carrying on, her excitement finally starts to wane, and we don't talk much for the next hour. We don't need to. Sophie is sprawled across the back seat, dozing with her earbuds in and a rolled hoodie under her head.

The towns blur by—names like Coquille and Sutherlin, places that feel more like memories than maps. Rusting gas pumps stand like grave markers beside boarded-up diners, and the signs for scenic overlooks are all sun-faded and tilting. By the time, the forest presses in, the radio fades to static, and

Wes hums under his breath, filling the silence like he is trying to hold it all together.

The road narrows as we climb farther north, winding past shuttered farm stands and forgotten backroads, until even the suggestion of a town disappears. I keep my elbow braced against the door, watching the trees blur past, taller now—like the landscape is unraveling. Civilization thins to patches. One town has a single blinking stoplight. Another, just a diner and a church.

The air changes too—cooler, crisper. Like a breath taken after too long underwater. Like the trees have been holding it in for years.

Sunlight filters through the branches in golden, syrupy streaks. Pines give way to hardwoods that loom high and wild. Lakes shimmer through the trees like secrets that almost don't want to be found.

The scent of moss and bark creeps in through the window, thick, wet, and old. It smells like memory—like something forgotten waiting in the woods.

I pretend my heart isn't galloping. Pretending my hands aren't clenched in my lap.

Wes glances over at me, a soft smile tugging at the corners of his mouth.

"You, okay?"

I nod, even though inside, I am fraying.

His hand lands gently on my thigh, steady and warm.

"We're gonna be fine. Whatever this summer brings, we'll handle it."

The weight of his touch is grounding. He's always been my anchor. Solid. Unshakeable. The one good thing that never flinches when everything else collapses.

But even anchors can slip. Even steady things rust. I don't want to think that way, not with him—but some part of me always does.

Somewhere in the second hour, Sophie stirs and sits up, her voice groggy.

"Are we almost there?"

"Not even close," Wes announces, glancing at the clock. "Still a little over an hour. We've gotta go deep into the Umpqua National forest to get there, remember?"

"I feel like we've crossed into a different century."

I smirk. "We're entering no-cell-service territory. Brace yourself."

Sophie makes a face and pulls out her phone. "Only two bars. Ugh, I hate that."

We stop once, at a rural gas station that looks like it hasn't changed since the seventies. The bathroom has a flickering light and smells like wet pine needles.

When I come out, Wes is leaning against the hood, sunglasses on, sipping a convenience-store soda like it is the most natural thing in the world to look that attractive surrounded by peeling wood paneling and bug-zapper hum.

"You want to turn around?" he asks as I join him.

I shake my head, even though my stomach twists with something close to dread.

"Nope. I already committed. For Sophie. Can't back out now."

He offers me a sip and bumps my shoulder gently." Just remember, we can survive anything. Together."

Back in the car, the road grows bumpier, snaking through mountain curves and overgrown shoulders. The trees crowd in closer, taller, the canopy casting long shadows even as the sun rises higher.

Wes drives one-handed, his knuckles brushing my thigh now and then, the other resting lazily on the wheel while his playlist hums softly over the speakers. He'd made it last night—called it Silver Hollow Summer like a joke—but every track is one I know by heart.

It's just after noon when Sophie lets out a frustrated sigh.

"Ugh... nothing's loading. My phone's already losing signal."

"Told you," I say, not bothering to look back.

"We're off the grid now," Wes adds, eyes flicking to the rearview mirror.

Sophie groans and slumps in her seat. "Ugh, great. No phone for the rest of the drive. This is going to be the longest hour ever."

"We're not that far," Wes offers. "And once we get to camp, you won't even notice. You'll love it."

I glance out the window as we pass a rest stop. It looks... too quiet. A vending machine stands crooked beside a faded picnic table, and the posted map had clearly been water-damaged long ago. Something about it felt *off*. Like the kind of place people disappeared from in horror movies.

I half-expect the vending machine to flicker to life on its own. The map on the board looks like it hasn't been updated since the world stopped caring. Even the trees leaned in like they were trying to listen.

A few more turns later, the trees thinned, and the road curved to reveal a hand-painted wooden sign:

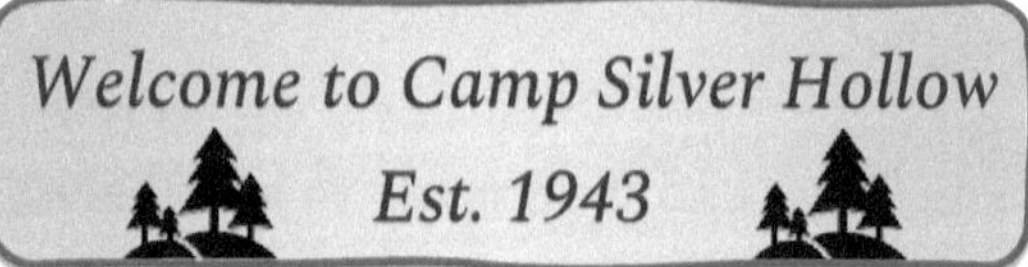

✦ 4 ✦

Welcome to Camp Silver Hollow

✧Emilia✧

The old camp gates creak open as Wes's car bumps along the gravel path that curves wide into a clearing, wooden buildings scattered like storybook props. A faint whiff of smoke hangs in the air. The whole place is dipped in filtered sunlight that feels too golden to be real.

Wes parks beside a few other cars, the engine ticking quietly in the stillness. It's just before 11a.m. when I climb out and stretch, my boots crunching into gravel as I take it all in—breathing in pine, damp earth, and something else. Older. Quieter. Not the emptiness of Ashgrove, but this doesn't feel like a fresh start either, it feels like a held breath.

Camp Silver Hollow looks like something pulled from a dream I don't remember having—familiar and eerie all at once. The mess hall stands at the center, all worn wood and wide porch steps, as if it had been waiting for us. To the left, cabins spill out between the trees, scattered like secrets, barely visible through the pine. Painted signs point toward a nature pavilion and an art building to the right, beyond that, more tucked-away structures, that I assume are for staff. The lake stretches out behind it all, still and silver, the surface too calm to be real. Just beyond its edges the woods grow denser, and *something* leans into the shadows and my stomach unsettles.

It isn't pristine. Nothing here sparkles. The wood sags in places, paint chipped on the signs, but the bones are strong. Like it had survived too much to fall apart now.

Before I can fully settle into the silence, the moment fractures.

A pack of sun-tanned, well-dressed counselors strut toward us like they own the gravel they're walking on. Silver Hollow T-shirts cling to toned frames, sunglasses perched with practiced ease. Their laughter is bright but hollow.

"Oooh, new blood. Finally," a barely dressed girl exclaims, twirling a strand of hair as her gaze drags over Wes.

A guy with sculpted arms and a smug smile whistle "you here to lead nature hikes and break hearts?"

Wes chuckles, breezy and unreadable. "Just a volunteer counselor."

Another girl—tall, sleek, with olive skin and ice in her eyes—flicks a glance at me.

"Cute. You two a package deal?"

Wes slides his arm around my waist. "Yeah. This is my girlfriend, Emilia."

A ripple of disbelief moves through them. Thin smiles. A low, "Seriously?"

I stiffen. I know this feeling. The scrutiny. The silent verdict: 'You don't belong.'

Wes exhales, his fingers brushing mine in quiet reassurance.

Then a piercing, falsely cheerful voice cuts through the tension like a knife.

"Okay, okay! That's enough," calls the camp director, stepping into view like a set piece from a retro brochure. Vintage blouse. Too-bright smile. Not a hair out of place. Her eyes scan the group like a casting director sizing up extras.

"You all have things to prep for tomorrow," she chirps. "Chop chop!"

With performative groans and mock salutes, the group scatters.

"Well, if it isn't our scholarship stars," she announces as she closes the distance between us, her smile switching on like it was on a timer. "Emilia. Wes. Welcome to Camp Silver Hollow. I'm Crystal Vaughn."

She gives Wes a long once-over, then looks past us.

"And this must be the charming Sophie."

Crystal's eyes softened slightly, the smile losing just a fraction of its performative shine. "The rest of the campers won't arrive until tomorrow. You'll have today to get settled, and you can spend it with my daughter, Lila. She'll show you around."

I follow her gaze to a girl leaning against the side of the mess hall, arms crossed, clearly unimpressed by her mother's display. She has wild brown curls, sun-drenched and untamed in the best way. She doesn't wave, but she does smile and gives a small nod.

"Cabin Three," Crystal says to Sophie. "You'll be bunking with Lila."

Then she turns back to us, her tone brightening again.

"And you two will be in Counselor Cabins A and B. Work assignments are posted daily inside the mess hall. We all have jobs to do. Let's make this a smooth, sunny season, yes?"

She walks off before waiting for a response, leaving a waft of high-end perfume in her wake.

Inside the kitchen, the air is warm and heavy with the scent of melted butter and something vaguely cinnamon left over from staff breakfast. It feels warmer here, both in temperature and in presence.

Behind the counter stands a tall, wiry Black woman in her sixties, her long salt-and-pepper hair half pulled back in an elegant vintage twist, secured with a carved wooden pin. Her floral apron is stained in ways that feels earned, embroidered with a name tag that reads 'Miss Dee.' She doesn't look up when I walk in.

"You, Emilia?" she asks.

"Yes, ma'am."

"Hm." She eyes me once, then nods. "You're one of the ones with sense. Not one of those kids runnin' around trying to charm their way into nothin. Good." She turns toward the counter. "Wash your hands, grab an apron. You're on prep. Grab those cucumbers and start slicing. We've got lunch to throw together."

The thunk of knives against cutting boards soon becomes our rhythm.

After some time, her voice cuts through the hum of the kitchen.

"Caught the show out front when you arrived."

I hesitate. "Yeah. That was something."

"They've run the place for years now. I call them 'The Inner Circle.' Same shiny teeth, same rot under the surface. Crystal sees what looks good in a brochure. Doesn't mean it's what's right."

I don't say anything, but my grip tightens on the knife.

"I'm not here for them, though," she continues. "I'm here for the kids who show up looking for magic. For some of em this is it."

Finally, she looks up, her sharp eyes pinning me in place.

"But you. You've got that haunted look. Like you came here hoping to disappear."

"I guess I did."

She wipes her hands.

"Well, you didn't come alone—you brought a shadow. The kind who'd follow you anywhere, no questions asked. You can see it in his eyes, the way he looks at you. That boy wears devotion like it's stitched into his skin."

I blush, heart fluttering.

"Hold on to that," she says. "It's rare. Someone who'll stand between you and the fire without flinching."

✧ Wes ✧

The mess hall hums with the clatter of trays, the screech of worn benches, and the low buzz of overlapping conversations. It smells like instant coffee, powdered eggs, and the kind of wood that has soaked up decades of weather and sweat. Long tables stretch across the room beneath antler chandeliers that look more haunted than rustic, their bulbs flickering like they can't quite commit to staying on. The whole place has the charm of a cabin that hasn't realized it should've retired years ago.

Some of the paid counselors were already lounging in groups, plates half-eaten in front of them, voices high and artificially bright. I pick a spot near the middle—not close enough to the counselors from earlier to seem interested in hanging out, but not tucked in the corners either. Neutral ground feels like the best option for everyone.

When I spot Emilia walking in, something settles in my chest. She always does that—just existing, just showing up—is enough to make the world feel a little less tilted. I catch her eye and give a slight nod, motioning for her to join me. She hesitates only a second, then walks over and slides onto the bench beside me.

As we start to eat, I stay close as always, letting the world blur around us. My hand rests on her thigh beneath the table, fingers grazing over the fabric of her jeans. Every time we reach for the same drink, our fingers brush, lingering just a beat longer than necessary. Even in this loud, crowded space, we move like we're synced up to a private frequency no one else can hear.

"I hate how they looked at us earlier," I say under my breath, keeping my voice low enough that only she could hear it. "Like they know me better than I do."

She keeps her eyes on her plate. "They think you belong with them," she says, quiet and resigned, like she's already made peace with the idea.

I lean in closer, not letting go of her gaze. "I belong with you."

Something flickers in her eyes—fear, maybe. Or maybe it's want. The kind that trembles just before it decides to stay.

And maybe it isn't the first time I've said it, but it was the first time it felt like she almost believed me. There is a flicker in her eyes, a fragile kind of trust pushing back against the doubt. Even if I could still see the voice in her head whispering that nothing good ever lasts, at least she hasn't turned away.

The moment breaks with the crash of a tray slamming down beside us.

Sophie plops onto the bench like she'd been launched there, beaming, and breathless, a new friend running up behind her. "This is Lila," she says with a dramatic flourish. "Her mom's the director, but don't hold it against her."

Lila gives us a crooked grin and tugs her curls into two loose buns with a practiced. "My mom thinks camp should be like a reality TV show crossed with a country club," she says, wrinkling her nose. "It's gross."

Sophie is practically vibrating with excitement. "She's cool. She already told me where to sneak snacks and how to get out of the brutal hikes."

I lean toward Emilia with a grin. "I like her already."

Lila glances across the room and tips her water bottle toward a table near the far wall. Where the group of counselors from earlier sits like they are the cast of some exclusive Netflix reboot—hair too perfect, voices too loud, clothes too clean for this late in the day.

"You're gonna want to know who's who," Lila announces. "That—" she points subtly with her bottle— "is the 'Inner Circle,' as Ms. Dee calls 'em. Brianna's the ringleader."

My eyes follow hers to the girl in the center of it all. Brianna. Golden-skin, hair honey-blonde, and airbrushed-looking even under this tragic lighting. She sits with one leg crossed over the other like she's claimed the entire table as her personal throne. Her arms are folded with calculated casualness, her face glowing like a photoshoot, but her eyes... her eyes are icy, cold, like glass just waiting to shatter someone.

"She's basically camp royalty," Lila goes on. "Looks like a goddess, acts like a queen bee. Manipulative, cruel, and too smart to get caught. You'll learn quick—don't trust her smiles."

I watch as Brianna leans toward the guy beside her, laughing like whatever he just said was the funniest thing in the world. Her hair shimmering as she flips it over one shoulder. Nothing about her feels accidental.

"That's Mason," Lila continues. "Her boyfriend. Classic golden boy. Shirt always half-buttoned, baseball cap never off, and just enough charm to make you forget he's dangerous."

Mason is sprawled across the bench like he owns it, legs wide, posture dripping with fake ease. His eyes slide to Emilia, and I catch the second-too-long pause before he looks away. My jaw clenches before I can stop it.

"The loud one with the Bluetooth speaker?" Lila nods toward a guy bouncing in his seat. "That's Zach. Thinks pranks are a personality. Not the brightest bulb."

As if on cue, Zach stands up, waving his arms like he's hosting a rave in his head. His backpack is lit up in rainbow pulses, some god-awful remix blasting from the speaker strapped to it. Someone yells for him to shut it off, but he turns it up instead.

Lila doesn't even blink. "The one with the thousand-yard stare? That's Chloe—tall, brunette, intense eyes. Coffee cup's basically a limb. She's here for the vibes and the gossip. Pretends she's above it all, but she's Brianna's little spy."

The way Chloe pokes at her food you'd think it had offended her, then laughs quietly at something Brianna whispers. Her mouth says, 'I'm bored,' but her eyes are always watching.

"And Aubree," Lila adds, tilting her chin toward a platinum blonde with highlighter-perfect cheekbones and lashes that could probably swat flies. "She'll act like your best friend while low-key destroying you. Flirts with everyone and lives for drama."

Aubree is practically glowing, her glossed-up lips smiling sweetly at someone across the table. Her laugh is high-pitched and fake, like the soundtrack to a breakup montage.

I give a low whistle. "So basically, if we're not rich, fake, or cutthroat, we're not invited."

"You're catching on," Lila chimes with a smirk. "They mostly ignore new counselors unless you catch Brianna's eye. If she sees you as competition... Game on."

Emilia gives a quiet, crooked smile. "I'm safe then, 'cause trust me, I'm not giving off threat to the throne energy."

Lila takes another sip of her water, her gaze still on Brianna. "Doesn't matter. If hurting you makes her feel prettier, funnier, or more important, she'll do it. That's how she operates."

From across the room, Brianna's gaze slides towards our table like a predator spotting movement in the brush. Her smile widens, slow and deliberate, stretching across her face like a threat wrapped in gold foil.

And just like that, I know Emilia has been noticed.

✦ 5 ✦

As the Day Fades

✧ Emilia ✧

Outside, the late afternoon sun slants warm through the trees, dappling the gravel path in soft gold. The light feels almost too gentle, too forgiving for a place that bristles with unspoken rules and sharp-edged smiles. Crickets chirp lazily somewhere off in the brush, and the scent of pine and charcoal from the distant fire pits mingles with the lingering tang of dish soap still clinging to my sleeves.

Wes and I head out through the back door of the mess hall, the hinges creaking in protest as it swings open. Sophie and Lila follow a beat later, still chattering quietly about some bizarre craft project one of the campers attempted during free time. I don't realize we've stepped right into the shadow of the picnic tables until the door groans closed with a metallic thud too loud in the hush of late afternoon. It startles me, slicing through the warm quiet like a warning bell.

Their laughter reaches us before their words do—low and lazy, the kind that curls under your skin. Shadows stretch long across the gravel, pooling at their feet like they're anchored in something darker. Somehow, we've walked straight into their territory.

They're already there, like they'd been waiting—lounging across the benches as if the whole world were their private set. The Inner Circle. All glossy hair and curated indifference, venom tucked behind their smiles like lipstick knives.

They look at me and Wes like we don't belong, but Aubree's eyes lock onto Wes first, keen and calculating.

"Well, well," she purrs, tilting her head and batting her lashes with a slow, mocking smile. "Look who's still slumming it."

Her gaze lingers on Wes in a way that makes my stomach knot. It's the kind of look that says he could do better, or he belongs with me, or worse—he will leave you soon enough. The words hang between us like a blade.

A flicker of something—hurt, doubt—ripples through me, but I swallow it down hard, trying to keep my face neutral. I can feel Sophie glance sideways, and even Lila's eyes darken just a little.

Zach raises his drink, a sly grin pulling at the corner of his mouth. "She's got potential," he says with a slow smirk, eyes sliding over me. "If you squint. Or maybe if you're desperate."

Chloe snickers, crossing one long leg over the other and tossing her braid over her shoulder with practiced disdain. "God, Zach, you're such a jerk. But honestly, I'm surprised she showed up at all. Most strays know to keep to the trees."

Sophie stiffens beside me, voice razor-edged and defensive. "Seriously?"

Chloe gasps, hand to her chest in exaggerated surprise. "She speaks! I thought she was just the mascot. Do you bark on command or just growl?"

Their laughter swells—bright and hollow. It's a sound designed to wound, and it works.

Sophie's face flushes with humiliation, but she doesn't back down. "You're disgusting."

Chloe's gaze cuts from Wes to Sophie, then lands on me with a razor-thin smile. "Isn't it cute how the rescue pets try to act tough?" Her voice is syrupy sweet, but her words sting like nettles. "Better make sure you don't get too comfortable, Em. Around here, soft things get eaten alive."

The jab isn't casual. It's pointed, her eyes daring me to react. My spine goes rigid. My hands twitch at my sides, nearly stepping forward—not for me, but for Sophie. To shut her up. To cut that cruel smirk from Aubree's face and make her bleed regret.

But before I can, Wes steps forward, calm, and deliberate. He slides between them and us like a wall I didn't realize I needed. His presence fills the space, sudden and absolute.

"That's enough."

He doesn't shout or raise his voice. It's quiet, controlled—like a promise and a warning all at once.

The air changes. Tightens. Even the trees seem to hold their breath.

Laughter stutters, then breaks off, brittle and uneven. Aubree's eyes flash, a flicker of annoyance or maybe surprise. Chloe shifts on her bench. Zach's mouth twitches, uncertain. For the first time, they don't know how this scene ends.

Brianna finally cuts through the silence with a cutting laugh. "Okay, I'm bored with this. Let's go swimming one last time before the campers show up tomorrow and ruin all our fun."

The others immediately start nodding and gathering themselves like a pack obeying the alpha's call.

Her words roll out cool and casual, but everyone knows what's really happening. They're backing off because Wes put them on notice. Brianna's just putting on the queen's mask, making sure it looks like the choice was hers all along.

I'll take it.

The Inner Circle peels away, still smirking, but their confidence is thinner now, forced. Their shoulders stiffen; their footsteps quicken.

Beside me, Sophie exhales slowly, the tension in her spine loosening just a little. Lila crosses her arms, jaw set in quiet rebellion. When her eyes meet Sophie's, something passes silently between them—a bond forged in shared defiance, their irritation boiling into solidarity.

"Come on," Lila says, turning toward the trail that leads to the art center. "Let's enjoy having the whole place to ourselves before the other campers show up."

She doesn't wait for a reply, striding off like she knows how to outrun the sting of other people's cruelty by making something beautiful with her hands.

Sophie follows—slower this time, but not small. Not crushed. She gives one last look over her shoulder at me, at Wes—and there's a flicker of gratitude in her eyes.

I'm left with Wes's steady presence beside me and the slow thrum of adrenaline fading from my pulse.

The sun keeps shining, golden and soft.

But something under my skin has shifted.

✧Wes✧

While the rest of the counselors enjoy their swim, we choose to hide out near the cabins. Emilia and I linger in the quiet, tucked into the shade where the building blocks the last slants of sun. The breeze carries the faint scent of pine sap and campfire smoke, soft as a memory. Tree branches whisper overhead, rustling gently in the hush between dinner and dusk.

She leans back against the wooden siding, arms folded loosely over her chest. I can tell her shoulders ache from the long day, from smiling when she didn't feel like it. From being seen but not really seen.

I watch her in that quiet way I know helps, hands tucked in my pockets, body angled slightly toward hers. There's a stillness I try to offer her, the kind that calms instead of crowds. I'm not just waiting for her to speak. I'm waiting to understand.

"Tell me what you're thinking," I ask, stepping closer. My voice is low, edged with concern. I reach out and brush a strand of hair from her face, tucking it behind her ear with a touch so gentle I can see the ache ripple through her.

She hesitates, eyes flicking toward the woods, the gravel—anywhere but me. "It's hard to feel like we belong here."

The words hang between us, fragile and bare—a quiet confession.

I don't flinch. I never do.

"We don't have to belong to anyone but each other," I say, and there's something in my voice I hope she hears—something fierce and tender all at once.

Then I kiss her.

Soft at first, like I'm asking. Like I'm offering her an escape, or a home, or both. The world around us fades—branches swaying, birds calling somewhere deeper in the forest, the distant clatter of trays from inside the mess hall. None of it matters.

Her fingers twist in my shirt, pulling me closer. My hands slide to her waist, anchoring her to me, and the kiss deepens, heat rising between us. My mouth moves against hers with growing urgency—

still careful, still reverent, but hungry now, like I've been waiting all day to breathe her in.

She parts her lips, matching me, letting me in.

The contact sends a ripple through her—a pulse of something hot, passion-fueled, and real. Her back presses into the wall, and I follow her there, the rough wood at her spine grounding her as much as the weight of my body. My hand slips beneath the hem of her shirt, resting at the curve of her waist, fingers splayed against bare skin. The touch sends sparks through my bloodstream, all thought unraveling into sensation.

She exhales into me, a sound soft and breathless.

And then—

"Ahem."

The sound cuts through the quiet like a rock through glass.

We break apart, startled, breath still tangled, and turn to find a sunburned lifeguard standing awkwardly ten feet away. His shirt is untucked and slightly damp, like he's just climbed out of the lake—or had fallen in by accident. He squints at us, blinking like he wandered in from a dream he doesn't quite understand.

"You seen everyone?" he asks. "Trying to… you know, keep track."

There's a long beat of silence before I lift a hand and gesture vaguely behind us. "They're at the lake."

The guy nods like that obviously makes perfect sense and shuffles off, back towards the old boathouse he came from, muttering unintelligibly as he goes.

Emilia exhales a breath she had been holding, then laughs—quiet at first, then more freely—as she presses her face into my chest. My arms come around her instinctively, solid, and warm, and she lets herself linger there.

"Only day one," she murmurs against my shirt, voice muffled but smiling.

I laugh too, pressing a kiss to the top of her head. "We're gonna survive this place."

She nods, even if she's not entirely sure it's true. But with her, maybe survival isn't the only thing worth hoping for.

✧Emilia✧

After dinner that night, the sun sinks behind the trees, casting long shadows that stretch across the forest floor like they're trying to hold on to something. The air has that dusky, almost sweet smell—pine, dirt, something distant burning. A breeze carries the faintest whisper of wood smoke and lake water. Fireflies flicker in and out of focus, like the night is blinking slowly awake.

Wes and I walk along the edge of the lake, and for once, I don't feel like I need to say anything. The gravel shifts beneath my feet, the shoreline curving ahead, the water catching the last light like it's memorizing it. It glows—just barely—but enough that I can still see the way the ripples move, almost as if the whole lake is breathing.

He reaches for my hand, and I let him take it. His fingers lace with mine without hesitation, he's always known how to hold me, he knew before I did.

I don't pull away.

There's a quiet in the trees that doesn't feel empty, it feels sacred. Making this moment feel sealed off from everything else. The noise, the past, the weight I always carry with me. It's still there, of course, but somehow it feels lighter. Easier to bear with him walking beside me.

His thumb brushes the back of my hand. I glance at him. The light is too low to see the exact look in his eyes, but I feel it. Steady. Warm. A little dangerous, even. Not in the way that scares me, but in the way that makes me want to run toward it instead of away.

And maybe that's what scares me most.

Because there's a part of me that still doesn't trust this. That's waiting for the moment he realizes I'm too much—or not enough. That I come with shadows I never invited, fears I've buried so deep I can barely name them. I've always known how to take care of people. But being taken care of... that's harder.

Still, his hand is in mine, and we keep walking. And I think... maybe it's okay to be wanted. Not just needed. Not used. Not tolerated.

Wanted.

Maybe it's okay to stop bracing for the moment when it all falls apart.

Maybe I don't have to belong to this place, or these people, or the version of myself I had to become to survive them.

Maybe it's enough to belong to this. To this quiet. To *him.*

Tomorrow, the campers show up. Everything will change—noise, expectations, masks slipping on like uniforms. But right now, in this soft, flickering moment, the world feels quiet enough that I can actually hear my own heartbeat. And it's not racing. It's not screaming.

It's steady.

I squeeze his hand a little tighter. Just to be sure he's still there. Just to be sure I am.

And for the first time in a long time, I let myself fall a little more—not with panic, not with fear, but with something close to peace.

Something dangerously close to hope.

☽ Camp Day 1 ~ Thursday, June 26th ☾

✧Emilia✧

The morning hums with motion, new campers dragging duffels across gravel paths, counselors shouting names over the buzz of chatter. The scent of pine hangs thick in the air, laced with sunscreen and something faintly metallic drifting off the flagpole. The sun's already rising, casting everything in this golden, storybook kind of light. I stand just outside it, arms crossed, a bit shielded behind my sister and her friend, watching it all unfold like a play I forgot I was in.

Crystal balances on the crooked wooden platform near the flagpole like she was born to perform, megaphone in one hand, camp schedule in the other. She claps for attention, far too eager, ponytail bobbing as she beams at the crowd.

"All right, campers! Once you're unpacked and fed, we'll be breaking into rotating activity groups. You'll get to try everything, from crafts to canoeing, all led by our incredible staff."

She gestures like she's unveiling prizes on a game show. One by one, the counselors step forward to a polite little round of applause.

"Noah Ellis, Nature Specialist—he knows every tree, bug, and bird in the Cascade Range. If you like mud and moss, follow him."

Noah gives a stiff nod, hands stuffed deep into his pockets.

"Harper Kim, Arts & Crafts—if glitter and glue are your thing, you'll love Harper."

Harper throws up both hands, her purple hair catching the light like amethyst.

"Tanner Blake, Waterfront Lifeguard—he's in charge of keeping you all from drowning. Seriously."

Tanner salutes from behind his aviators, lazy smirk right on cue.

"Valentina Santoro, Drama & Talent Show—she's got flair and fire. Get ready to perform!"

Valentina blows a kiss that earns her a few whistles from the older campers.

"Jesse Browne, Music & Campfire Songs—if you can hum it, she can play it."

Jesse lifts her hand, guitar strap snug across her shoulder as if it belongs there.

"Mattie Greene, Maintenance—don't bother him unless something's broken. And even then, maybe don't."

Mattie doesn't wave. Doesn't smile. Just stands there, arms crossed, his eyes hidden under the brim of his cap.

"And last but not least, Nurse Trudy—currently enjoying the shade on the mess hall porch, but you can usually find her in the infirmary. If you're bleeding, dizzy, or just fishing for attention, she's your girl."

Trudy gives a nervous little smile from her perch on the mess hall's screened porch, colorful scrubs and teal Crocs catching the light as she adjusts her glasses.

Crystal's voice tightens just a little. "But let's keep this session emergency-free, shall we? No surprises, alright? Everything is going to be perfect."

That word sticks in the air like a splinter. *Perfect.* My skin prickles.

She closes with a dazzling grin. "See? Something for everyone." Her eyes flick down to the clipboard, already losing interest. "You'll meet your junior counselor when you check in at your assigned cabins. They'll handle the day-to-day stuff—lights-out, bathroom rotations, cabin rules. Try not to break them. Some of them are new this year."

Scattered laughter breaks out, mostly from the kids who've done this before.

Lila leans toward Sophie and mutters, "Let's hope my mom assigned your sister or Wes to our cabin."

They slip away fast, heading straight for Harper's station to stake their claim. I stay where I am.

The kids are buzzing—nervous, excited, a little wide-eyed. Half the counselors are genuinely trying; half of them are just coasting on charm. And Mattie? He doesn't move at all. Doesn't even glance at the campers. His eyes are glued to the counselors.

Not all of them.

Just the inner circle.

✦ 6 ✦

Meet & Greet

☽ Camp Day 1 ~ Thursday, June 26th ☾

✧Emilia✧

The morning hums with motion, new campers dragging duffels across gravel paths, counselors shouting names over the buzz of chatter. The scent of pine hangs thick in the air, laced with sunscreen and something faintly metallic drifting off the flagpole. The sun's already rising, casting everything in this golden, storybook kind of light. I stand just outside it, arms crossed, a bit shielded behind my sister and her friend, watching it all unfold like a play I forgot I was in.

Crystal balances on the crooked wooden platform near the flagpole like she was born to perform, megaphone in one hand, camp schedule in the other. She claps for attention, far too eager, ponytail bobbing as she beams at the crowd.

"All right, campers! Once you're unpacked and fed, we'll be breaking into rotating activity groups. You'll get to try everything, from crafts to canoeing, all led by our incredible staff."

She gestures like she's unveiling prizes on a game show. One by one, the counselors step forward to a polite little round of applause.

"Noah Ellis, Nature Specialist—he knows every tree, bug, and bird in the Cascades. If you like mud and moss, follow him."

Noah gives a stiff nod, hands stuffed deep into his pockets.

"Harper Kim, Arts & Crafts—if glitter and glue are your thing, you'll love Harper."

Harper throws up both hands, her purple hair catching the light like amethyst.

"Tanner Blake, Waterfront Lifeguard—he's in charge of keeping you all from drowning. Seriously."

Tanner salutes from behind his aviators, lazy smirk right on cue.

"Valentina Santoro, Drama & Talent Show—she's got flair and fire. Get ready to perform!"

Valentina blows a kiss that earns her a few whistles from the older campers.

"Jesse Browne, Music & Campfire Songs—if you can hum it, she can play it."

Jesse lifts her hand, guitar strap snug across her shoulder as if it belongs there.

"Mattie Greene, Maintenance—don't bother him unless something's broken. And even then, maybe don't."

Mattie doesn't wave. Doesn't smile. Just stands there, arms crossed, his eyes hidden under the brim of his cap.

"And last but not least, Nurse Trudy—currently enjoying the shade on the mess hall porch, but you can usually find her in the infirmary. If you're bleeding, dizzy, or just fishing for attention, she's your girl."

Trudy gives a nervous little smile from her perch on the mess hall's screened porch, colorful scrubs and teal Crocs catching the light as she adjusts her glasses.

Crystal's voice tightens just a little. "But let's keep this session emergency-free, shall we? No surprises, alright? Everything is going to be perfect."

That word sticks in the air like a splinter. *Perfect.* My skin prickles.

She closes with a dazzling grin. "See? Something for everyone." Her eyes flick down to the clipboard, already losing interest. "You'll meet your junior counselor when you check in at your assigned cabins. They'll handle the day-to-day stuff—lights-out, bathroom rotations, cabin rules. Try not to break them. Some of them are new this year."

Scattered laughter breaks out, mostly from the kids who've done this before.

Lila leans toward Sophie and mutters, "Let's hope my mom assigned your sister or Wes to our cabin."

They slip away fast, heading straight for Harper's station to stake their claim. I stay where I am.

The kids are buzzing—nervous, excited, a little wide-eyed. Half the counselors are genuinely trying; half of them are just coasting on charm. And Mattie? He doesn't move at all. Doesn't even glance at the campers. His eyes are glued to the counselors.

Not all of them...

Just the inner circle.

✦ 7 ✦

The Things We Don't Say

☽ Camp Day 4 ~ June 30th ~ 39 Days to Go ☾

✧Emilia✧

The counselors are gathered on the cracked concrete pad outside the timber-framed lodge, the smell of damp pine and sun-warmed wood rising with the morning, squinting into the sunlight as the campers fidget in front of us. Crystal stands front and center, clipboard in hand, and a smile that is all teeth.

"Happy Monday, campers! Excited to be kicking off our first full week. Okay, I want everyone in their specialty groups right after breakfast," she called out, her voice syrupy sweet with a sharp edge beneath it. "We'll rotate later this week, but today's for everyone to shine where they're strongest."

I stand slightly off to the side, arms crossed. Sophie leans toward me with a mock whisper. "Think if I pretend to love plants, she'll let me go with Harper?"

Crystal's ears are sharp. "Actually, you and Lila will be joining Noah this morning. He's got a butterfly release and identification project he's very excited about." Her smile thins into something tight and decisive—the kind that isn't up for debate.

Noah gives an awkward wave from the edge of the group, his hair already ruffled and his clipboard hugged tight to his chest.

Lila groans under her breath beside us. "That boy's enthusiasm is exhausting."

Sophie elbows her. "Don't knock butterflies until they land on your soul or whatever."

Crystal keeps moving like she hadn't heard them. "Emilia, you'll be assisting Aubree with prep for the relay race this afternoon. We'll need stations set up and camper pairings coordinated; think of it as a chance to... collaborate."

My jaw tenses, but I nod once. "Sure."

Zach arrives last, sauntering up with his hair still wet from a rushed shower. Crystal flicks her eyes at him.

"You'll be helping Noah too, with Wes. Try not to set anything on fire this time, hmm?"

Zach gives a lazy salute. "No promises."

Crystal looks around one last time, then snaps her clipboard closed with a sharp clack.

"I expect energy, enthusiasm, and excellence from all of you today," she said with that same brittle brightness. "And let's keep visits to Nurse Trudy to a minimum, yes? We want to project health and confidence."

Then her eyes land squarely on Lila, lingering just long enough to draw blood.

"Try not to slouch, sweetheart. Presentation matters."

Lila straightens half an inch, her smile tight. "Right. Wouldn't want to disappoint the butterflies."

I watch the way Lila's jaw tightens, the flicker of something unspoken behind her eyes. It isn't just defiance—it is restraint. The kind you learn when you've been bitten before for speaking too loud. My chest tightens, a quiet sympathy blooming. I know that look. Know what it feels like to stand next to someone who uses love like a mirror—only reflecting you when it suits them.

Crystal doesn't respond, but her smile turns icy before she pivots and walks off, leaving the rest of us to scatter.

✧

The sun is high, and the field behind the lodge is already drying out, the grass still heavy with dew and the earthy scent of fir needles. Aubree stands in the middle of it with a laminated map of the racecourse, twirling a marker like it was a magic wand.

“Okay, so we'll need three water buckets, two tire flips, and a trust-fall station,” she said, tossing the map at me without really looking. “Think you can handle the setup? You look… strong.”

I catch the map. “You've got the plan. I'm just the muscle, right?”

She grins, flipping her hair over her shoulder. “Exactly. But we'll call it teamwork, so it sounds fair.”

The sun is beating down on the field like it has something to prove, and sweat collects at the nape of my neck despite the breeze off the lake, clinging to the strands of hair that has fallen since tying it up. Aubree's perfume hangs in the air—overwhelmingly citrusy—like it is trying to cover something rotten. Her shadow keeps drifting too close, and every time I shift to adjust a cone, she adjusts too, mirroring my movement with the practiced ease of someone who'd studied how to get under skin without leaving fingerprints.

She kneels to start laying out cones, then says, too casually, "Wes is on nature duty today, right? That's kind of a bummer. I was hoping he'd be on field rotation with me."

I don't answer. I remain focused on lining up the cones, careful and silent.

"He's such a flirt when he's relaxed," she went on. "I swear, the way he smiles at me? It's like... sparks. It's probably just his natural charm, but I'd be lying if I said I didn't love it."

She glances sideways at me, trying to catch a flicker. "You're lucky, I guess. I mean... he has been circling you for years, hasn't he?" Her voice dipped into that syrupy, fake-sweet tone. "That kind of history—it makes guys feel obligated sometimes. Like they owe you something for sticking around."

"Maybe I envy that," she adds, almost too low to catch. "Having someone who sees you that way, even when you're not trying."

I don't respond. My jaw clenches, and I keep adjusting the cones.

"But I don't think that's really who Wes is," she continues, lazily twirling a piece of her hair. "He's a free spirit. Wild. He needs someone who doesn't cage him in. Someone who knows how to play with that kind of energy instead of smothering it."

I crouch down, face tilted toward the grass, so she doesn't see anything slip through.

She kneels beside me like we are co-conspirators. Her voice drops to a near-whisper. "There's this... pull between us. You've seen it, right? I catch him watching me sometimes. It's like he forgets you're even there. And the way he talks to me? Teasing, all low and warm. Like he's interested. Like he's wondering."

My hands still on the cone, but I don't look up.

"I bet he wonders what it'd be like. Someone different. Someone who doesn't come with all that heavy, brooding baggage. You act like you're this tragic little mystery, but honestly?" She smiles at me like I am something pathetic. "You just look tired."

My ears ring. Not loud—just enough to make her voice feel distant, like I'm listening underwater. I dig my nails into my palm to stay present, to keep from floating too far above myself.

I am.

Not the kind of tired you could sleep off. The kind that sits in your bones. Tired of keeping everything together. Of playing nice. Of letting people like her talk like this and pretending I didn't care.

I stand up slowly, brushing the dirt from my palms with deliberate care. "You done?"

She rises too, standing too close. Her voice softens in that awful way that makes it sound intimate.

"Not even close."

She tilts her head, eyes sliding over me like she is assessing damage. "You think he's yours because you've been around the longest. That's not love, Emilia. That's familiarity. And that fades. Guys like Wes? They don't settle for girls who suck the air out of the room. They go looking for fire."

I don't flinch, but my fingers curl slightly at my sides.

She leans in, her breath warm and smug. "He wants more. He just doesn't know it yet. But when he figures it out? You'll feel it the second he pulls away. And I'll be right there when he does."

My voice comes out quiet, but sharp. "He's not a prize you win, Aubree."

"Oh, I know," she says, her smile turning saccharine. "But it'll still feel so good when I take him from you anyway."

✧Wes✧

The chalk squeaks across the old blackboard, Noah's voice rising with enthusiasm as he sketches the life cycle of a Painted Lady butterfly. He stands beside his diagram like it is sacred—wings, antennae, transformation—it means something to him in a way I'll never fully understand, but I like watching him in his element. Makes me want to protect it. Protect *him*.

Across the pavilion, Sophie and Lila sit on the bench closest to the open air, sketchbooks in their laps. Lila's is tilted at an angle, her pencil gliding across the page while Sophie leans over, whispering something with a crooked smile. Probably about the butterflies. Or Noah. Or both. Art makes everything more tolerable for them; it grounds things.

Zach, naturally, is the opposite of grounded. He keeps pretending the netting poles are javelins, tossing them from hand to hand while Noah ignores him with the patience of a saint.

I lean against one of the beams, arms crossed, eyes drifting until I catch sight of her.

Emilia.

Out near the edge of the field, setting up cones like the world depended on their spacing. Her shoulders are tense with concentration, legs braced in the grass, fingers brushing dirt from her palms. Her hair has started to come loose, dark strands whipping across her cheek. She keeps trying to tuck them back behind her ears, but the wind doesn't care. It never did. And she never looked more beautiful.

The scar above her eyebrow catches the sun for a second, like it is daring the world to look away. She doesn't hide it anymore, not from me. And every time I see it, I remember what she survived. How strong she is. How lucky I am.

I still remember the night I touched that scar for the first time—how she flinched without meaning to, then let my hand linger anyway. Like she was trying to believe that being seen didn't mean being hurt.

She didn't know what she did to me. The way she moved, completely unaware of her own gravity, pulled at something primal in my chest. I'd never wanted to keep anything before her. Not like this. Not with this kind of ache.

My gaze trails lower, over the worn camp T-shirt clinging to her in all the right places, down to the curve of her hips in those cutoffs she probably didn't think twice about wearing. But I think about them—a lot.

I think about the way she tastes when she lets go. The soft, desperate sounds she makes when I kiss her so deeply she forgets how to breathe on her own. About pulling her into my lap, fingers tangled in her hair, making her forget anything that ever hurt before me.

About taking my time—making her feel safe enough to fall apart in my hands.

I want her so bad it hurts sometimes. Not just her body—though, God, yes—but all the buried parts she tries to keep hidden from the world. The rough edges. The wreckage. The wildfire of her temper. I want to burn in it. To mark her so deep she'll never feel clean of me.

There are days when I swear I can still feel her even when she isn't near me. Like she's soaked into my skin. Like she belongs there.

God help anyone who tries to take her from me.

Noah claps his hands together, jarring me out of it. "Alright! Grab your water bottles, everyone. Time to meet some butterflies in the wild!"

Zach groans but helps wrangle the younger campers. Sophie and Lila stand, Sophie rolling her eyes toward me with a smirk. "You're holding up the adventure with your brooding. Let's go, Nature Boy."

I grin, but my feet are already moving. I jog across the grass toward Emilia, slowing when I reach her side. She looks up, startled for a second, then relaxed. That tiny shift in her shoulders. The flicker of relief in her eyes. She's been holding something in.

I cup her face, thumb brushing her cheekbone. "I love you," I whisper, only for her. "I know I say it a lot, but it never feels like enough."

Then I kiss her—really kiss her. One hand still on her face, the other curling around her waist and pulling her in like I need her closer than skin. She tastes like summer air and tension, like something breaking open and being rebuilt in the same breath. I kiss her until she melts into me, until I feel her exhale like I'd just unknotted something inside her.

Something had been sitting heavy on her all morning. I don't know what, but I feel it leave with her breath.

When I pull back, she looks steadier. Like I'd put her back where she belonged.

Behind her, Aubree stood with a clipboard, eyebrows raised. Watching us.

I meet her gaze with a practiced smile—nice, bland, civil. The kind of smile people use when they're saying something they don't mean.

"Appreciate you keeping her entertained," I say, voice polite. "But she never stays bored for long."

I don't wait for a reply.

When I rejoin the group, Sophie raises her brows. "Everything okay?"

"Better now," I tell her.

Lila laughs. "Alright, Romeo. Lead the way before Noah starts naming butterflies after us."

We head toward the tree line, and I don't look back.

I don't need to. She is mine.

And if anyone ever tries to change that...

They'll learn real fast what I'm willing to do for her.

✧Emilia✧

The days settle into a rhythm as two weeks slip by, each one stitched to the next with sunlight, sweat, and the echo of mosquito bites being slapped away. It's too easy, how the repetition numbs everything. Like the camp is trying to wear us down—not with malice, but with mundanity.

Even the air has a rhythm—mosquitoes whining near the lake, the scent of sunscreen and bug spray clinging to everything like a second skin. It isn't chaos. It is erosion.

Mornings start with whistles and soggy cereal. I rise early to help Dee prep breakfast, the kitchen already sweltering with heat from the ovens and Dee's fluctuating mood. Pancake batter sizzles on the griddle, occasionally spattering across my apron as Dee barks orders and curses about campers who don't understand portion sizes.

After breakfast, the camp fragments, groups scattering like dropped marbles.

At the craft hall, kids crowd Harper's long wooden tables, elbows knocking paint pots, glitter floating in shafts of light. Their voices rise and fall in waves, laughter blending with groans as glue dries crooked and resin molds trap air bubbles. Harper weaves between them like a storm contained in a person—sharp eyes, faster hands, her own half-finished projects strewn like casualties.

Down at the lake, sunlight turns the surface silver and mist curls in the corners where the trees overhang the water. Tanner lounges at the edge of the dock, shirt abandoned somewhere, sunglasses tilted just so. He rarely speaks. Just watches as campers shriek and splash in the shallows. Occasionally, he tosses out a lazy warning, but mostly he looks like he's waiting for something more interesting than water safety.

In the clearing, where ferns creep near the edges, Valentina dances across the half-finished amphitheater stage, her portable speaker clipped to her belt like a sidearm. Campers trail behind her in a kind of choreographed chaos, limbs flailing, some mimicking her precisely, others too shy to try. Her voice is everywhere—cheering, correcting, casting roles no one asked for. She's magnetic. Exhausting.

And Jesse, always with her guitar, sits on a rough wooden bench by the firepit, gently strumming as kids gather like moths. Her melodies drift across the camp, threading through the trees. Soft, haunting things that make even the squirrels pause. When she sings, the air itself seems to hold its breath.

Sometimes, I walk the trail to the nature pavilion just to watch the hush fall over the group there. Noah kneels in the dirt, hands hovering over strange plants or bugs—fuzzy lichen, black beetles, the kind of mushrooms that look like they belong in fairy tales, whispering facts the kids strain to hear. He gives them names; Latin ones, old ones—and tells stories that don't sound like stories at all. They feel like secrets.

But not everyone lets the summer soften them.

Zach's pranks evolve quickly. What starts with silly string and whoopee cushions morphs into sabotage. One morning, Sophie's favorite boots are stuffed with pine needles and fish guts. Another day, someone pours glitter glue across my laundry, turning my favorite black shirt into a sticky mess of stars. Zach just laughs when I confront him, shrugging like mischief is his love language.

Chloe trails behind him, always ready with a whispered insult she delivers like a compliment. She eyes Sophie's clothes with theatrical pity and makes remarks about my hair like it's a science experiment gone wrong.

Brianna, sugar-slick and smiling, pretends concern. "You okay, Em? You look... tired." Her voice always carries just enough volume to draw attention. "Have you tried ice on those undereye circles?"

I say nothing. But I memorize the way Brianna walks. How she bites her nails when she thinks no one's looking. The way her eyes always flick to Wes when she thinks I'm not paying attention.

And then there's Aubree.

She attaches herself to Wes like a shadow with better lipstick. She touches his arm when she talks. Leans into his space. Her laugh is just a little too loud, too rehearsed. She's pretty impossible not to notice, but it's the way she looks at me, over Wes's shoulder, that makes it sting. Like she knows exactly what she's doing.

Wes, for his part, doesn't acknowledge her. Not really. When Aubree touches his arm or leans in too close, he doesn't flinch, but he doesn't respond either. His eyes always find mine, like he's tethered to me no matter how crowded the camp is. And when they do, there's a softness there—something wordless and fierce, like he's reminding me I'm the only one who matters. It's not a performance. It's a promise.

Mason. He isn't as loud as the others. But his silence is worse. He watches the cruelty unfold, eyes bright with amusement. He plays along, echoes Zach's jokes, smirks when Brianna purrs something acidic. He never starts it, but he never stops it either. His hands are clean, but his shadow always lingers at the edge of trouble.

Sophie takes it quietly. Tries to rise above. But I see the way she flinches when Chloe brushes past her. The way her smile cracks sometimes, just for a second, before she patches it back on.

And through it all, the forest waits.

The wind never moves quite right here. The trees lean in like they're listening. Shadows shift too fast or not at all. And at night, when I lie awake in my narrow bunk, I swear I hear the trees whispering to each other. Not threatening. Not friendly.

Just... watching.

Wes

The camp feels different lately. Tense. Like the air itself is charged with something waiting to snap. I watch from the edges, knowing there's more going on beneath the surface than most want to admit. The way those kids circle Emilia and Sophie is not just typical camp drama anymore. There is something colder beneath the surface, like they are sharpening their claws just to get a reaction. Brianna's eyes hold a quiet cruelty, all sweetness barely masking the poison underneath. They don't realize they are chipping away at something fragile, stirring a fire that will not burn out easily.

I don't like it. Not one bit.

Because Emilia is not just some girl to me. She is everything. The storm I never saw coming and the calm I did not know I needed. I would cross any line, break any rule, do whatever it takes to keep her safe. Even if she does not know how much she means to me yet. Even if the world wants to test her limits every damn day.

She doesn't deserve this. No one does. But there's just something about her pain that cuts deeper. Like it echoes in a way I can't ignore. She doesn't have to say it out loud for me to feel it; I'll always be there when everything falls apart, even if she tries to carry it all alone.

Let them try. They are messing with something they do not understand. And when it comes to her, there's nothing I wouldn't do.

✧Emilia✧

The hiss of the shower finally goes quiet. A few stray droplets tap the tile, echoing faintly through

the thin cabin walls. I lay curled in my bunk with the curtain half-drawn, facing the wall, pretending to be asleep.

I can still hear them—Brianna, Aubree, Chloe—chattering in hushed tones by the vanity, voices edged with amusement like they were telling secrets meant to hurt someone. Probably me.

They never whisper when they want me to hear. Just lower their voices enough to make the laughter sting worse.

"I'm just saying," Aubree says in that syrupy voice, "I wouldn't have survived junior year looking like that. Imagine showing up here and thinking you're competition."

Chloe lets out a low, conspiratorial laugh. "Wes must be into rescue projects."

A pause, then Brianna's voice, smooth as a polished blade. "Everyone wants to feel chosen. Even strays."

Something clatters—probably a lip gloss rolling off the counter. They giggle like it was part of the punchline.

I exhale through my nose, fingers curling into the thin blanket beneath me. My body goes tight with stillness, every muscle clenching like it can shield me from being seen.

Eventually, the lights click off, plunging the room into a soft darkness broken only by moonlight slipping through warped shutters. Footsteps pad across the wooden floor, bunks creak one by one, and the sounds settle into late-night silence.

I wait another ten minutes before shifting. Just enough to slide my arm beneath my head and let the tension bleed out slowly.

The breeze outside pushes gently at the shutters, making them creak and sigh like the woods are breathing just outside.

I let my eyes drift closed. For a moment, I think I might actually sleep.

Then I hear it.

Tap. Tap.

Not loud. Not frantic. Just... deliberate.

I freeze. The sound come again—closer this time. Right outside the window, no more than three feet from where I lay.

Tap.

I hold my breath, my mind running through every logical possibility: a tree branch, a raccoon, maybe one of the girls sneaking out to meet someone by the dock.

But it doesn't stop. It shifts.

The tapping gives way to something softer. Stranger.

A voice—maybe. Not a full word, not anything clear. Just the shape of one. Formed around breath, like someone trying to speak underwater.

I sit up slowly, the curtain rustling as I move. My pulse thunders in my ears, and still, I try to tell myself it is nothing. It has to be nothing.

The room is quiet otherwise. No movement from the other bunks. No footsteps toward the bathroom. Just the whispering. Soft. Slurred. Right outside my window.

I slide from my bed and creep to the shutter, bare feet silent on the worn wood floor. The air smells faintly of lavender body spray, old shampoo, and the sharp mineral tang that clings to the bathroom from too many damp towels being left too long.

Every instinct screams not to look.

But I look anyway.

The slats of the shutter are parted just enough for me to glimpse the clearing beyond.

At first—nothing. Just shadows tangled with moonlight. The grass shimmering with dew, and mist curling low across the ground.

That's when I see it.

A shape—tall, indistinct—standing at the edge of the woods. Not moving. Not breathing. Just... watching.

But as quickly as it emerged it's gone.

Not walked away. Not faded.

Gone. Like it had never been there at all.

The mist swirls low through the underbrush like it had been stirred by something not meant to be seen. My skin prickles. Not from cold—but like something invisible had reached through the glass and brushed a finger down my spine.

The whispering stopped. The air inside the cabin felt heavier now, like it had been disturbed and hadn't settled yet.

I stand there for a long time, watching the mist.

When I finally climb back into my bunk, I don't close the curtain.

I just lay there, blanket pulled up to my chin, staring at the ceiling beams, waiting for the sound of someone breathing who wasn't supposed to be there.

I don't sleep the rest of the night.

✦ 8 ✦

More Than Survival

☽ Camp Day 17 ~ July 12th ~ 27 Days to Go ☾

✧Emilia✧

The morning light spills through the warped screen of my cabin window, painting pale gold bars across the foot of my bed. I blink against it, dry-eyed and heavy-limbed, dragging myself upright with a groan. My body aches in that bone-deep way it always does after a night of fitful sleep: half dreams, half dread. I don't even remember what woke me. Just that I'd rolled over sometime in the night and found Wes's hoodie beside me on the bunk, the scent of pine and salt and him pulling me back from the edge of something unnamed.

Now for day seventeen.

Seventeen...

Somehow both endless and not enough.

I rub my eyes and throw off the thin sheet, stretching until my joints crack in protest. The sun has already begun baking the gravel paths. I dress on autopilot, tugging on my frayed cutoff shorts that are older than most of the campers, the hem curled and torn from years of wear. Familiar. Lived-in. Mine.

I reach for the black tank top that used to be plain until Zach got his hands on it. Thanks to him and his glitter bomb prank, it now shimmers faintly in the light, permanently dusted with silver like a cursed disco ball.

I scowl at my reflection in the tiny square mirror propped on my bunk shelf. My scar catches the morning sun, a pale slice above my left brow, jagged where it cuts through to my eyelid. I touch it, just for a second. Not to hide it. Just to remember.

With a sigh, I grab my flannel—the soft, faded one I wear when I need armor. It smells like smoke and coffee and Wes; the sleeves rolled to my elbows. Too hot for flannel. Too necessary to care.

My boots thunk softly on the worn wooden steps as I make my way toward the kitchen. The camp is already waking around me: screen doors slamming, sneakers pounding gravel, the distant screech of a whistle, a faint call of a Steller's jay in the trees, and a kid already crying about sunscreen in his eyes. The world is too loud too early.

Dee is already elbow-deep in biscuit dough when I push through the swinging back door of the mess hall. She doesn't look up as she continues kneading.

"You're late," she said gruffly.

"I'm early," I counter, tossing my flannel over the back of a chair and reaching for an apron. "You just wake up at war-crimes o'clock."

That gets the corner of her mouth to twitch.

She hands me a mixing bowl. "Stir." Eyebrows raised and a warm smile cracking as she adds, "Not like you're good for much else."

I smirk. "You're a poet, Dee."

"Don't I know it." She wipes her hands on her apron, then finally glances up, eyes scanning me from head to toe. "That *the* glitter tank?"

"Forever and always," I state grimly.

"You gonna let 'em keep getting under your skin, or you planning to grow some teeth?"

I don't answer right away. My hands stir in rhythm with the quiet hum of the kitchen, metal scraping ceramic, the soft whirr of the fridge kicking on. It's calm here. Honest. A little too hot and always vaguely smelling of onions and woodsmoke, but honest all the same.

"They don't get under my skin," I say eventually, but it sounds weak, even to me.

Dee raises a silver brow. "You sure about that?"

I don't answer.

She moves closer, wiping her hands clean before leaning one hip against the counter beside me. Her voice drops, lower and softer. "They think they're untouchable, those ones. All smiles and poison. But it never lasts. Sooner or later, the world's gonna catch up to them."

I keep stirring.

She leans in just enough for her words to land between us like a secret. "And maybe, just maybe we'll be lucky enough to see it happen."

My hands still.

Her voice isn't bitter. Not quite. But there is something behind it. Something earned.

I look at her. Really look. At the deep creases carved by time and truth, the salt-and-pepper hair pulled back in a careful twist, the faded floral apron stained by years of breakfast battles, and the quiet, knowing weight behind her eyes.

"They'll fall," I mutter quietly.

She nods. "They always do. The trick is to stay standing long enough to watch."

Dee doesn't say anything for a moment after that. She just watches the tree line through the smudged window as if it might answer for her.

I follow her gaze. The trees don't move, but I swear they're listening. Like the forest itself is holding its breath—waiting for something to fall apart or fall into place. Maybe both.
I don't want to fall apart anymore. But I'm not sure I know how to be whole, either.

"Every summer," she murmurs, "they come through here dragging ghosts behind their suitcases. Doesn't matter how hard they smile or big a show they put on."

I don't respond, but my shoulders go tight.

She goes on, voice low and sure.

"People think the woods are gonna fix 'em. Like sleeping under the stars is some kind of miracle cure."

Then she turns to me, gaze steady.

"But Camp Silver Hollow don't fix what's broken. It just shows you where the cracks start."

She shrugs then, with her smile returning like a veil. "Anyway. Breakfast ain't gonna fix itself."

The back door bangs open then, and a counselor breezes in, shouting about needing juice refills and pancakes for a picky camper who only eats smiley faces. Dee turned with a roll of her eyes, barking orders like she hadn't just handed me a piece of the armor I didn't know I was missing.

But I stand there a beat longer.

Because maybe she's right.

Maybe surviving means not just withstanding the storm, but outlasting it.

And maybe... maybe that is what I'd been doing all along.

✧

It's just after the afternoon heat breaks, and most of the campers are off at swim time or prepping for the evening campfire. I wander into the nature pavilion, expecting it to be empty; except for maybe just Noah, quietly tending to his plants or checking on the terrariums he keeps in the back corner.

Instead, I pause in the shadows near the doorway when I hear laughter, cruel and mocking.

The Inner Circle is here.

Brianna Cross stands by one of the screened butterfly enclosures, the lid tilted open, her finger trailing along the rim. Butterflies flit around in chaotic spirals, no longer contained. Chloe leans against the table nearby, smirking as she watches the delicate creatures flutter aimlessly, some already making their way toward the open screens leading outside.

Noah stands a few feet away, his face pale and tense, his hand half-raised as though he wants to stop them but doesn't dare.

"God, this is so pathetic," Zach says with a snort, poking at an overturned container of caterpillar host leaves. "You spend all summer with bugs, man? No wonder you're still single."

"Yeah," Aubree adds, voice sickly sweet, "maybe if you could actually talk to people, you wouldn't have to whisper to butterflies to get attention."

Brianna plucks a small paper label off the tank and rolls it between her fingers. "Papilio glaucus," she reads in a fake breathy tone, mocking him. "Look at you, naming your little winged girlfriends like it's gonna make you less weird."

Chloe bursts into laughter, tossing a dried leaf at Noah. "Bet he writes love poems to them. Poor guy probably thinks one of these bugs is gonna flutter into a wedding dress someday."

The lid clatters to the floor. A few of the more delicate butterflies escape into the rafters, some frantically bumping against the screens.

One smacks against the screen, dazed, like it can't understand why the sky has turned solid. Another falls to the table, its wings trembling like a heartbeat.

My stomach twists. This isn't teasing. It is precision. Intent. Destruction disguised as amusement.

Noah moves forward instinctively, hand outstretched to shoo them gently back, but Brianna steps in front of him, smirking.

"Careful," she taunts, eyes glittering, "don't get too attached. Nothing this pretty will ever want to stick around you for long."

Something about the way he stands there, frozen and trying not to flinch, reminds me of my sister. Of how small you learn to make yourself when the world doesn't offer safe places.

I step in just then, my voice low but cutting. “Funny. You talk like someone who knows exactly what it's like to be left behind.”

“Wow, protective and pathetic. Must be exhausting pretending anyone wants you around.”

That one hits harder than I wanted it to. It lodges in the softest part of me, the part that still can't believe Wes has really chosen me. The part that is always waiting for the other shoe to drop. For him to realize he can do better. For everyone to realize it.

I cross the room and kneel by the fallen terrarium, carefully setting it upright and checking on a few trembling butterflies clinging to the mesh. The air smells like damp soil and broken stems, the sweetness of the butterflies' nectar jars turned sour in my nose. I work silently, my presence like a slow-burning rebuke.

“You really gonna play butterfly babysitter now?” Zach mutters, but his voice lacks confidence.

“You've got five seconds to leave before I tell Crystal what happened,” I say, my voice calm but unyielding.

They laugh; shrewd, knowing. Of course they do. Crystal would never do anything. Not to them. Not when their perfect smiles and polished reputations reflect everything she wants the camp to be.

Chloe rolls her eyes. "Whatever. He should be thanking us. He needed to let them go anyway."

They file out reluctantly, tossing a few final taunts over their shoulders, but the damage is done.

When they're gone, the quiet doesn't feel peaceful. It feels like a held breath. Like the air itself isn't sure what will happen next.

I gently coax a trembling black-and-blue swallowtail back into a mesh enclosure and turn to Noah, who stands frozen, his face taut with emotion.

"They've always been like that?" I ask softly.

Noah lets out a breath he'd been holding. "Yeah. Every year. Same games. They wreck things because they know they'll never get in trouble. They're Crystal's golden shining stars. Good-looking, popular, fake." He looks over at the screen where the butterflies are still swirling frantically. "I guess I thought if I stayed small and quiet, I'd be left alone."

"They were just peacefully existing. That shouldn't be a reason to hurt them. Some people just like breaking things that remind them what they're not."

That makes him smile; small, but real. "Thanks... for stepping in. Most people don't."

"They're not people I care to impress," I reply, standing and dusting off my hands. "And anyone who spends time helping something fragile survive instead of crushing it? That's the kind of person I do want to know."

He blinks, clearly surprised by the sentiment. "I'm... not really used to people seeing it that way."

"Well, maybe the right people are finally starting to." I give him a knowing look. "Besides... I think you're more connected than you think—to things that matter. You just haven't been given the space to prove it."

Part of me wonders what Wes would've done if he'd been here. If he would've stepped in like I had, or if the sunshine in him would've cracked into something darker. But he isn't here, and maybe that's why I needed to be.

I stare at Noah for a long second, and for the first time, something unspoken passes between us; recognition, maybe. Understanding. A spark of human connection.

Noah glances over at the door where the Inner Circle disappeared. His jaw tightens, but his voice is even.

"They always get away with it," he says. "Year after year, no matter what they do. But..."

He gently closes the lid on the terrarium I had helped him fix, eyes watching the butterflies settle.

"...eventually, the world balances the scales. One way or another."

I pause, unsure whether to say anything. His tone isn't threatening exactly, but there is a weight behind the words—a quiet certainty.

I give a slow nod, not pressing him, but as I turn to go, a flicker of something settles in my chest.

Something I can't quite name.

After lunch, I slip away. I can't stay in the mess hall another second; not with Aubree's laughter still echoing in my skull, or with Sophie's tight smile over a tray of gray spaghetti.

I don't know where I'm going. I just know I need to move. To breathe. To be somewhere that doesn't hurt.

I find myself wandering toward the trailhead, gravel crunching under my boots. Wes falls into step beside me without a word.

We walk with nothing but the sounds of the forest between us.

The air is different here—cooler, stiller. Pines press in overhead, casting dappled light that dances across his face. We don't speak. We don't need to.

Eventually, we reach a place where the ground softens into moss, a clearing where the trees lean in like they're listening.

We settle against a wide, flat boulder. Our backs brush against the cool stone. His knee bumps mine. I tip my head back, eyes half-closed.

"I think I hate it here," I say quietly.

He doesn't answer right away. I feel his breath slow and steady.

"You don't have to like it," he says at last. "You just have to survive it. But not alone."

He shifts slightly beside me, close enough that I can feel the heat of him—steady and solid. Like an anchor in a place where everything else feels like it's slipping sideways.

"Plus, you don't hate everything here," he says gently.

I don't answer. I don't need to. The way my body leans toward his says it for me.

I hate the camp. The noise. The masks. The pretending.

But him? I love him like breathing.

His hand finds my side. Fingers resting lightly above the waistband of my shorts. A question, not a command.

"I don't want to *just* survive."

He turns. His eyes, so pale they're nearly clear, hold something else now. Something deep. Something clawing.

"Then take what you want."

The words crash through me unexpectedly, like he sees all the parts of me I try to hide and still doesn't flinch.

I don't think. I just move.

Turning, I lean in my lips brush his—soft at first, a test, a flicker. Then it deepens. Molten. Immediate.

My fingers slide into his hair, tugging gently, needing more.

I don't feel small here. I don't feel forgotten. Just wanted; completely, irrevocably.

He tastes like heat and danger and something sweet beneath it.

And just like that, the world fades.

It's just trees. Breath. Heartbeats.

A voice cuts through the stillness. Distant. Calling his name.

The forest collapses around us. Shatters.

We break apart, breathless.

The chill rushes in all at once, like the air remembered what it was supposed to feel like.

His forehead presses to mine. "Later."

"Promise?"

"Always."

We stand. The hush returns, but it's different now. Charged. Heavy with what almost was.

✧

Campfire smoke curls into the dusky sky, drifting in lazy spirals above the clearing. The lake is just out of sight, but I can hear the water, steady and slow, lapping against the dock. Around the firepit, kids crowd close, marshmallows glowing golden at the tips of their sticks, laughter rising and falling like waves. It's easy, almost dreamlike—like nothing bad has ever happened here.

I linger at the edge of it all, half in shadow, just beyond the reach of the firelight. Sophie waves me over from a log across the circle, her smile open and warm. I pretend not to see her.

Behind me, the woods press in—silent and watchful. The air at my back is colder here. Sharper. The hair on my arms lifts before I even register why. Something's out there. Not just an animal. Not just wind. Something older. Slower. Watching.

My body responds instinctively, the way it always has when something isn't right. A quiet tightening, a stillness I learned too young. I feel ten years old again, waiting for a slammed door. For footsteps too heavy. For the world to shift on a breath. I know what it is to go still. To go small. But I don't move.

Because deep down, something stirs in answer. It isn't fear. Not exactly. It's quieter. Heavier. Like recognition.

I think of the butterflies in Noah's pavilion; so delicate, trembling against mesh, still shining even as everything around them broke.

It should terrify me, but it doesn't.

Instead, it feels like truth. Like something darker. Something already mine.

Sophie calls my name again, and this time I go, settling beside her on a worn log. The fire crackles in front of us, casting long shadows and painting flickering warmth across the faces nearby. The scent of pine smoke clings to the air, warm and thick, wrapping around me like a memory.

Sophie curls up beside me, tucks her knees up, her voice hushed as she recounts a camper's dramatic retelling of a ghost story that clearly started as a Scooby-Doo episode. I smile, listening without really hearing. My attention keeps slipping, always, inevitably, toward him.

Wes is crouched at the fire's edge, the firelight catching on the angular cut of his jaw and the tousled mess of his dark hair. He moves with quiet purpose, tugging a stubborn branch from the pile beside him. Then, without a word, he reaches behind him and draws his knife.

Not a pocketknife. Not some flimsy camping tool. His knife. The one he always carries, sheathed at the small of his back like it belongs there. As if it is an extension of him.

The firelight trembles across his features, shadows leaping like startled animals as he moves. Even the air seems to hold its breath around him.

The blade gleams for half a second before slicing clean through the branch. No effort. No flourish. Just a swift, practiced motion, controlled and sure. He does not explain. He does not show off. It just is.

Across the fire, Mason's laugh cracks too loudly, trying too hard.

"Seriously, man?" he calls, waving a half-eaten s'more in the air. "You really gotta bring that thing everywhere? Who do you think you are, Bear Grylls or something?"

A few others chuckle with him, ready to pile on, expecting Wes to snap or toss back something cutting.

But Wes does not look at him.

Not at first.

His eyes lift to mine instead, just for a second, and it is like the universe narrows to that one glance. Heat fans through me, low and consuming, curling into places I try not to name. It is not the knife that does it. It is the calm in his gaze. The quiet restraint. The storm he holds back like it's nothing.

Then, without breaking stride, he slips the blade back into its sheath at the small of his back, rising to his feet as smoothly as if the moment had not happened at all.

"Comes in handy," he says, finally looking at Mason. His voice is quiet but steady, a flat kind of calm that sounds almost bored. "You would be surprised how many problems a good blade solves."

The fire pops, sending a spray of embers into the dark.

No one laughs after that.

Mason shifts, suddenly all shoulders and uncertainty, and a few of the others glance at each other like they are not quite sure whether to keep poking or back off. Wes does not look at any of them again. He just moves to tend the fire, like nothing happened, like the knife was never there at all.

But I saw it. The precision. The ease. The way his hand moved, like he could do it blindfolded in the dark.

And maybe it should unsettle me.

But it doesn't.

It settles into my chest like a spark sinking into dry leaves. Slow at first. Then steady. Then sure.

There is something about the way Wes moves through the world—silent and chiseled and fiercely loyal. Something that calls to the parts of me I never let anyone see. Not even Sophie. Something ancient and electric.

Something mine.

The laughter resumes, quieter this time. Softer around the edges. But I am no longer really listening.

Because across the flames, Wes catches my eye again.

And I know, without a word, without a single touch, that this night is not over yet.

Not even close.

The fire crackles between them, sending sparks into the dark tree line. I watch Jesse lean forward, elbows on her knees, her eyes catching the flames.

"Listen," she says, her voice dropping low. "You might think Camp Silver Hollow is just...a place to roast marshmallows and paddle canoes. But there's a story you should know. A story the counselors tell each other when the lights go out. Only, most of them don't believe it. Until they see...things."

Valentina chimes in, her grin Cheshire-like in the firelight. "They say that every thirty years, something bad happens here. Not just a camper getting scared, not just a storm knocking down a tree. Something...darker. Something that touches the camp and the lake, even before the cabins were built. And it never stays buried for long."

A hush falls over the circle—a log shifts. Somewhere in the trees, a branch snaps, perfectly timed, and a few kids jump. I squeeze Sophie's hand, feeling her startle against me.

"Some people say it started long before the camp," Jesse continues, rocking back on her heels. "That the land itself is...angry. Scarred. There are stories of disappearances, of fights, of people who never came back from the lake or the woods. People who shouldn't even have been here in the first place. Some say it's revenge. Some say it's...witchcraft."

Valentina leans closer to a small group at the edge. "Every thirty years, things happen. Fires, drownings, fights, strange visitors. Some of them you've probably heard in whispers. Others were never reported. And those who survive...well, they never talk about it the same way again."

Jesse tilts her head, letting the words hang in the air. "They say every cycle has its own...events. Things happen that leave a mark on the camp. Some of it gets whispered about, some of it never fully explained. But everyone agrees—something stirs, and it always comes back. Watching."

Sophie shivers, pressing closer to me, whispering, "Do you think it's true?" I swallow hard, my marshmallow forgotten on its stick. I glance at her, trying to hide the chill that runs through me, but part of me thrills—drawn to the dark, dangerous edge of it. It's wrong, I know, but it feels inevitable.

Valentina's voice drops to a whisper now. "Some say the lake remembers everything. That the land remembers. That whatever curse touched it one long time ago never left. And it waits. Waiting for the next cycle. The next thirty years. For someone—or something—to come back."

A gust of wind skitters through the clearing, tossing ash into our hair. I feel Sophie shiver against me. Another camper tightens their sweater. I lean back, scanning the darkness, aware of the weight of unspoken things pressing in.

Jesse grins faintly, leaning back. "So if you hear things at night...if you see shadows where there shouldn't be any...don't be surprised. And whatever you do, don't go wandering alone near the lake after dark. You never know what's already watching."

The wind switches directions with it carrying the scent of pine smoke and something colder from the trees beyond. My pulse quickens, the warmth of Sophie at my side doing nothing to calm the stirring inside me.

Valentina sits back, letting her voice soften, almost playful, but still carrying the chill of the tale. "And remember—every thirty years, Silver Hollow reminds you. That it's not just a camp. It's a story that doesn't end. And it has a way of finding the next person to live it."

The fire pops again, loud, and some of the kids flinch. Sophie buries her face in my arm, quiet except for a low hum of tension. I tighten my hold on her, heart hammering as my eyes drift to the fire again, to him, to the shadows between the trees, and I feel that familiar pull. Even as some of the others try to laugh it off, I can feel the story rooting itself deep.

Jesse and Valentina exchange a glance, the kind only conspirators share, and I watch the silence stretch, long and tense, before anyone dares to speak again.

The woods groan with a sudden gust of wind, branches creaking as though in answer. Somewhere.

A few of the younger campers huddle closer to their friends, fingers gripping sleeves or sticks. One lets out a nervous laugh, too brittle, and another stares into the dark as if it might reach out and grab them. The flames jump and crackle, throwing long, twitching shadows across the circle, and for a heartbeat, I feel like the darkness itself is leaning closer, listening.

I keep my arm around Sophie, but my eyes can't leave him. Every flicker of the fire makes me think of him with his knife, the quiet strength and control in his movements, the way he always protects without a word. And yet—there's something darker there tonight, just beneath the golden warmth I know so well. It's dangerous, electric, and it pulls at me in a way I didn't know I needed, stirring something deep I've been holding back. It's wrong, irresistible in a way that makes my chest tighten, and I can't tear my eyes away, can't ignore the tug at a darkness that wants to grow.

✧

The campers are all tucked in now, their voices long since faded behind screen doors and cabin walls. The warmth of the day lingers on my skin, clinging to the dry twilight breeze like summer doesn't want to let go. It's late, dark enough that the Douglas Firs blur into shadows, but the moon hangs low and full, casting everything in a pale, silvery glow. The fire behind us still crackles softly in the pit back by the mess hall, the scent of woodsmoke faint on the wind, distant now, more memory than presence.

Laughter drifts faintly behind us as the last of the counselors either turn in or trail off in twos down the other winding camp trails. Wes and I wander further, side by side, past the old boathouse where the decrepit dock stretches over the lake's dark mirror, still and edged with shadowed reeds. The air smells like woodsmoke, pine, and a little like the ghost of sun-warmed earth. His hand brushes mine, and instinctively, I turn my palm toward him.

He takes it.

His fingers are rough, warm, calloused in places that tell stories I haven't heard yet, and I feel that ache again—the one that's been following me all summer like a second heartbeat. It thrums low and steady, quiet but impossible to ignore. Every part of me knows when he's close. It's like my body has rewritten its geography around him.

We don't say much. We don't have to.

The path curves again, right where the woods thicken and the old trail to the boathouse veers off to the left. Here, between the hush of pines and the gentle lap of water against the lake's edge, there's a tree I've never really noticed before. It's tall, weathered, half-wrapped in moss and lichen—unremarkable at first glance, but under the moonlight, it feels like something else entirely. Ancient. Watching. The kind of thing you'd pass a hundred times before realizing it's always been waiting.

Wes stops near it. It's a massive Douglas Fir, weathered—the bark cracked and furrowed with time. It looks like it's been standing there forever, rooted deep and unmoving, long before any of us ever set foot in these woods.

"This one's been here forever," he says softly, brushing his fingers across the bark.

I watch him—the way he touches it like he's reading something only he can see. He pauses, and I catch the faint shift of his shoulders as his hand drifts behind him; familiar, fluid. There's a flash of metal as he pulls the blade free with ease, like an extension of himself. Like it always has been.

For a split second, I tense. Old reflexes. But then I see his face—softer now, half-lit in moonlight—and all that tension slips right back out of me.

"What are you doing?" I ask, teasing, trying to steady the flutter in my chest.

He doesn't answer right away. Just grins that lazy, sun-drenched grin of his—the one that gets under my skin and makes everything feel too bright.

"Leaving something behind."

He leans in close to the bark, pressing the tip of his knife into it. The blade moves with quiet precision, no hesitation, no wasted motion. I watch as he carves not just letters but a symbol—our initials, W and E, looped into each other in an elegant, interwoven design. It's not just a mark. It's intentional, intimate. A secret emblem, the kind you'd walk past a hundred times and never notice unless you knew what it meant. The "W" curls into the "E" in a fluid sweep, stylized and ornate like something sacred. Something only we understand.

"Now it's official," he murmurs as he finishes, his voice low and rough around the edges. "We're forever."

The words hit somewhere deep. Not flashy. Not dramatic. But honest. Like he's not just saying it—he means it. Claims it.

He lifts one hand to brush over the still-fresh carving, fingers dragging gently across the wood like he's sealing something in place. With the other hand, he slides his knife smoothly back into its sheath at the small of his back. My eyes follow the motion, catching on the shape of his body, the easy strength in it. And just like that, the air shifts.

There's a heat between us now that wasn't there a moment ago. Or maybe it was, and now it's just risen to the surface. It's not fear. It's not nerves. It's something else entirely, like gravity pulling every part of me closer to him.

I reach out, letting my fingertips find the fresh carving. His hand is still there, and our fingers tangle, slow and deliberate. The bark is rough beneath our skin, but his touch is warm and steady.

"You always carry that thing?" I ask, my voice quieter now, rougher.

His lips twitch, eyes flicking up to mine with something like a spark. "It's been a useful tool more than once," he says. "Some things are just... multipurpose."

The glint in his gaze is playful, but there's something else beneath it too. Something darker. Something truer.

He steps in closer. My breath catches.

One hand lifts to tuck a strand of hair behind my ear, and it's the gentlest thing in the world. His knuckles graze my cheek, and I forget how to think. "Do you know what you do to me?" he asks, barely above a whisper.

I don't answer. I can't. But the part of me that always second-guessed—always braced for rejection—went quiet. Just for a second.

Just long enough for my body to answer for me and give him what I'd been holding back. Catching his mouth with mine before the question even finishes hanging in the air.

It starts gently but deliberate. His lips taste like heat and memory and something I can't name. It's not a kiss meant to be rushed. It's a promise. A question wrapped in fire.

His mouth is on mine like it's been waiting, like he's been holding back until now, and I feel the restraint bleed out of him as his hands slide to my waist and pull me in. It starts slow, an ache stretched across seconds, but quickly sharpens, deepens. I clutch the fabric at his back as he presses me against the tree, mouth hot, hands sure.

He lifts me with ease, and I wrap my legs around him without a thought, without hesitation. The rough bark at my back, the strength of him under my fingers—it's all sensation, all heat and breath and the press of something that's wanted this just as badly and just as long.

His hand slides beneath the hem of my shirt, fingers splaying across my waist like he needs to memorize me. My hips tilt toward him, chasing friction, and he groans low into my mouth. The sound wrecks me.

I gasp against his lips as he grinds into me just enough to make my head fall back, and he takes full advantage, mouth trailing down my throat, teeth scraping just enough to make me tremble.

His mouth finds that spot just beneath my jaw and lingers there, breathing heat into my skin like he's trying to brand me without leaving a mark. My fingers tighten at his shoulders, nails catching the fabric of his shirt.

"You feel that?" he mutters, voice thick, rough with restraint. "You do that to me. No one else."

My breath stutters, caught between a moan and a whimper as my body arches into his. The weight of his words sinks into my chest like gravity, like truth. I want to tell him I feel it too—how it's always been like this, how being close to him makes everything else fall away.

But I can't speak.

So I show him instead, rocking my hips against his, pulling him impossibly closer, letting my hands roam like I'm trying to memorize the shape of him by touch alone.

His fingers dip lower, teasing the waistband of my shorts, and every nerve in my body is a live wire, sparking with want. I grip his shoulders, eyes locking with his. There's nothing playful in his expression now—just raw hunger and something deeper. Possession. Worship.

"Here?" I manage to whisper, but my voice is already gone to heat and want.

His forehead presses to mine. "I don't care. I just need you."

I don't want him to stop. I don't want to think. I want to burn.

His mouth finds mine, deeper this time, hands moving with purpose now as my legs tighten around him and his hips meet mine in a rhythm that leaves me aching.

His breath hitches against my mouth, and then he's kissing me again, slower this time, deeper, like he's trying to memorize the shape of my hunger.

I feel the shift in him, the way his hands roam with more certainty now, sliding beneath the hem of my shirt to press against bare skin. He touches me like I'm something sacred, like he knows exactly how to unravel me. I gasp as his mouth trails down the column of my throat, my back arching instinctively to bring us closer.

"You're mine," he whispers, breath hot against my skin, "and I don't care if the whole damn forest hears it."

The way he says it, quiet, almost reverent, undoes me completely. My hands find the hem of his shirt and push it up, hungry for skin, for contact, for something real. Something only he can give me.

Clothes shift. Breath tangles. Bark scrapes against my spine, grounding me as everything else starts to float.

His hand finds the hem of my cutoffs, tugging them to the side with a practiced sort of urgency, just enough. The denim bites at my hip as he lines us up, rough and sweet all at once.

He's warm and solid between my thighs, all strength and intention, and when he sinks into me, it's not with a rush. It's with a groan so low and broken it steals every thought from my head.

We move in sync, slow at first, like a dance we've done a thousand times but are still trying to perfect. He watches me like I'm the only thing he's ever wanted, his name a whisper on my lips between gasps, repeatedly, like a prayer.

I clutch at him, nails biting into skin, needing more, needing all of him. The rhythm builds—friction and breath and the quiet snap of something I can't take back. We're too close, too far gone.

His mouth finds mine again, messy, and urgent, and I lose myself in it, in him, in this.

And when it finally breaks over me, it isn't just pleasure. It's devastation. It's surrender.

He follows me over the edge, stifling his groan against my shoulder, and for a moment, everything is silent but our breathing.

The world falls away.

This isn′t just lust. This isn′t just some stolen moment.

This is a claiming.

And above us, etched into the heartwood of a tree that′s weathered a hundred Oregon winters, our symbol remains, unmoving. Eternal.

Ours.

✧Wes✧

We walk in silence, her shoulder brushing mine every few steps as we follow the gravel trail back toward the cabins. The moon is high, barely veiled by wisps of cloud, painting her in soft silver light. She looks untouchable like this. Fierce and fragile. Like something the world shouldn′t be allowed to hold—but somehow, I get to.

And I don't know how I got so damn lucky.

She glances over, catching me staring, and rolls her eyes with the faintest smile. "What?" she murmurs.

I shake my head, barely holding back the truth. Everything. Everything about her. Her meek tongue. Her stupid glitter tank top. The scar above her eye that I hate and love in equal measure. The way she kisses me, like I am the only thing keeping her tethered to the earth.

"You ever stop and think about how insane this is?" I ask softly as we reach her steps. "That out of everyone... I get to be the one walking you home?"

She blinks, caught off guard.

"I just... I don't take it for granted, Em," I add, voice low. "You choosing me. I don't think I'll ever stop feeling like I've stolen something not meant for me."

She opens her mouth like she wants to argue, but I don't let her.

I kiss her instead, slow, and fierce, like I meant it to echo in her chest the way she echoes in mine. When I finally pull back, she is breathless, eyes wide in the dark.

Her voice is quiet but steady. "You make it really hard to walk away from you."

I touch her cheek, brushing my thumb over the scar. "Then don't."

She leans into me, just for a second. "I'm scared of how much I feel when I'm with you."

I don't hesitate. "Then be scared with me."

She stares at me like she wants to memorize my face in this moment, like she already knows she'll replay it later.

I reach up and tuck a loose strand of hair behind her ear.

Her skin is soft and warm as she leans into my hand, looking up at me like she doesn't know whether to kiss me again or cry. "I love you, Wes."

"I love you too, Em—in more ways than you know."

She slips inside without another word, quiet as a whisper, and I stand there for a beat longer. Just breathing.

Then I turn and head for my own cabin, gravel crunching beneath my boots.

The night has grown still. Too still.

A flicker of movement catches my eye near the tree line—Mattie. Sitting on the camp swing just beyond the fire circle, rocking back and forth like he'd been here the whole time. Watching.

His eyes meet mine. He doesn't speak. Just stares.

Doesn't smile. Doesn't blink. Just rocks.

Something cold skitters down my spine. Not fear. Just that crawling, bone-deep sense that the world has tilted by half a degree and no one else has noticed.

I nod once in his direction, more out of instinct than anything, and walk on.

Let him stare. Let the firs whisper whatever secrets they want.

I have what I need. And I'll rip the light from the sky before I let it slip through my fingers.

9

He Was Laughing

☽ Camp Day 22 ~ July 17th ~ 22 Days to Go ☾

✧Emilia✧

The early light filters through the gaps in the wooden cabin walls, casting long, thin stripes across the rough pine floorboards. The faint scent of damp earth and cedar drifts in through the cracked window, mingling with the faint smokiness from last night's campfire. Outside, the distant call of a crow echoes, sharp and solitary.

I woke up feeling different.

There was none of the familiar weight pressing down on my chest, none of the stiffness in my limbs that usually followed a night of twisting through nightmares. The ache in my back was still there, but not from restlessness.

I push the tangled sheets aside and swing my legs over the edge of the bed, letting my feet rest on the cold floor. Wes isn't here, but I can still feel the shape of him in the places we fit together. A faint echo of his touch clings to my skin—the scrape of rough tree bark, raw along my back where we'd pressed too close, tangled up in the dark like branches woven tight in an ancient forest. It hurts just enough to remind me we are real. That maybe what we have is real too.

There is a new warmth curled inside me. Not just body heat, but something deeper. A sleepy, humming buzz that lingers in my blood and bones, soft and heady. It's like the forest itself had breathed into me overnight—the quiet pulse of moss beneath roots, the slow drip of dew from needles, the hush between the rustling leaves.

For a moment, I let myself believe this is what it feels like to be safe. To be seen. To be truly wanted—not just for the way I move through the world, but for the pieces I usually keep hidden.

We can make it.

Maybe this strange, passionate thing between us is strong enough to last beyond this place. Beyond the trees and the secrets.

But even in the quiet, something else lingers. A whisper, cold and uncertain, weaving through the edges of my mind like smoke.

I push it away.

The cabin around me stirs with movement. The thin fabric curtains rattle softly in the morning breeze, and the wooden floor creaks under their shifting weight as the other girls begin their morning routines. The smell of sunscreen mixed with cheap perfume and the faint tang of pine sap cling to the air.

Aubree stands at the sink already, lining her eyes with precise, practiced strokes, while Chloe brushes through her thick brown hair with bored, distracted swipes. From behind her curtain, Brianna mutters something clipped and impatient, directed at one of them: "How many times do I have to say not to touch my hair products? I will not run out before we leave this hellscape." Their voices fill the air in small, purposeful bursts, thick with that same low-grade hostility they wear like perfume.

Normally, I would have felt the pressure of their presence like thorns pressing into my skin. But today, they can't touch me. I am floating somewhere above it, wrapped in the haze Wes left behind. I let their noise roll past me like wind through trees.

I move quietly to the corner near my bed and begin getting ready—not to disappear, not to dull myself down, but to show up. My hand hovers over the makeup bag I have been ignoring for weeks, then dips inside. A sweep of mascara. A touch of color to my cheeks. It feels strange, like slipping into an old version of myself I thought I had outgrown. But when I look in the mirror above the sink, I don't hate the girl looking back. She looks sharper, steadier—like she might know who she is.

I leave my hair down, letting the loose waves fall around my shoulders, and step outside into the warm, pine-scented morning.

The mess hall buzzes with the usual chatter, the clink of trays, and the dull scrape of plastic chairs dragging against the floor. The windows stand open, letting in a breeze that carries the scent of damp pine needles and fresh coffee. Somewhere beyond the treetops, a jay calls out—a sharp, raucous note that cuts through the low hum of voices.

Wes is already seated at one of the long tables near the windows, his easy smile catching mine as I walk in. He has that relaxed posture he always wears around other people—one hand curled around a cup of coffee, the other resting on the back of the chair beside him.

I sit down next to him, letting my shoulder brush his, and let myself exist in that small, quiet space we created. Around us, a handful of the specialist counselors carry on sleepy conversations, the kind that comes from routine more than interest.

Near the serving line, Noah stands with his tray, talking to Crystal. His voice is quiet but edged with something sharp—something that makes me look up.

“This time they took it too far,” he says. His face is tense, his jaw tight, his fingers curled white around the tray in his hands like he's holding back more than words. “I’m not kidding. If you’re not gonna do anything, somebody eventually will. And it won’t be pretty.”

Crystal’s smile, though practiced, doesn't quite reach her eyes—they flicker with exhaustion, like someone carrying too many secrets. She lets out a slow sigh, brushing a strand of hair behind her ear. Her tone is patient, almost maternal, but there is a flatness to it. “Noah, you know how they are. It’ll blow over. Just keep your head down.” The air between them crackles with a quiet, unsaid warning.

He shakes his head, barely containing the frustration vibrating off him in waves. “It’s not just harmless pranks anymore. They’re pushing people. Someone’s going to break.”

Her smile falters for a beat, but she doesn't answer. She turns away and busies herself stacking coffee cups near the drinks station, ending the conversation with her silence.

The tension lingers like static in the air long after Noah walks away.

A few minutes later, Crystal circles back to where Wes and I are finishing up our breakfast. She tucks her clipboard against her chest and gives us both a nod. "You two are heading to the lake this morning. Tanner's already there, but I need you to help him keep an eye on the kids."

She pauses, then adds under her breath, "He's a good guy, but you know how he gets. Sometimes I think he forgets he's not a camper."

Wes stands, stretching lazily, and shoots me a crooked grin. "Looks like we get the fun job this morning."

I smile back and rise to my feet. My hand brushes his briefly as we move toward the door—a silent promise tucked between our fingers.

The lake waits beyond the trees, wide and still, a mirror to the sky. The surface is glassy, broken only by the occasional ripple from a drifting pine needle or a fish breaking the surface in a lazy arc. The cool scent of water mingles with resin and earth, grounding me in the moment even as unease curls low in my gut.

I walk alone from the cabin, towel and water bottle in hand, the morning sun already warm against my skin. My new flip-flops—the ones Wes had bought me during our Bargain Cove run—slap softly against the gravel path. Until now, they'd only been used as shower shoes, never quite escaping the mildew-slick floors of the communal stalls. But today, they feel like something more. I can feel the texture of the gravel under the soles, not in a painful way, just more present than in my boots. Like the earth beneath me isn't letting me float through it unnoticed.

I wear my bathing suit under an oversized camp shirt that clings to the backs of my thighs in the heat, fabric soft from too many washes. The edge of my towel brushes my knees, and the ombré jewel-tone water bottle Sophie had picked out for each of us bounces lightly against my hip. Chaos Crew shimmers across it in silver sparkles, just obnoxious enough to make her proud.

I pass the mess hall, where Chloe stood tucked between the dumpsters, one hand wrapped around her usual to-go coffee cup, the other raising a cigarette to her lips. She doesn't look at me as I walk past, but I catch the flick of her lighter and the quick exhale of smoke curling upward in the sunlight. Her eyes are half-lidded, heavy with whatever mix of exhaustion and disdain she wakes up with most mornings. The sharp tang of cigarette smoke tangles with the earthy smell of damp leaves and rotting pine cones nearby, a bitter contrast to the fresh morning air.

Farther down, I spot Noah crouched beside the picnic table near the nature pavilion, a half-folded trail map spread out in front of him and a clipboard propped against one knee. He is muttering to himself, scribbling something down with quick, precise motions—probably a hiking plan. The way his brows knit together makes it clear he isn't in the mood for interruptions, so I don't stop.

The path opens wider as I near the lake. Laughter echoes through the trees, and the sunlight breaks across the water in long, shimmering stripes. A few campers splash in the designated swim zone, their shrieks carrying up in uneven bursts. Wes is already in the lake, wading thigh-deep with that easy grace he always carries—like his body just knows how to exist in space without effort. He hadn't waited, hadn't hesitated. Of course, he hadn't.

I follow the worn boards of the dock until I reach the edge and set my towel down, along with the water bottle. From here, I can see Tanner at the top of the lifeguard stand, perched like a king on a weathered throne. His sunglasses are low on his nose, the lit joint pinched carelessly between his fingers and only partially hidden in the curl of his palm. He looks half-zoned out already, his gaze drifting over the water, unfocused but alert, as he mutters something about sunscreen and water safety before returning to his personal cloud.

I hesitate for a second longer before peeling off the oversized shirt and folding it on top of my towel. The sun hits my bare shoulders, and the breeze ghosts over the rest. The warmth feels almost too sharp against my skin, exposed beneath the endless sky. So much skin, so many eyes. I sit on the edge of the dock, feet dangling in the water. Wes is only a few feet away, standing at hip depth now, the lake lapping gently at his sides. He turns at the sound of my movement and looks up.

His eyebrows raise, slow and deliberate. "Well damn, Em," he says, a lazy grin tugging at the corners of his mouth. "Didn't know you owned anything like that. You trying to kill me or just boost morale?"

I kick my foot hard, sending a splash right at him. It lands clean across his chest.

He laughs, startled but unbothered, and wades a little closer, water swirling around him. "Noted," he says. "She's armed and dangerous."

I smirk and let my feet sway in the water, feeling the warmth of the sun on my back and the cold of the lake on my toes. I hadn't even noticed Sophie climbing onto the dock until her voice rings out behind me.

"Clear the runway!"

Before I can react, she launches herself off the dock just a few feet down from where I'm sitting, hitting the water with a cannonball that sends a shockwave of spray right over me and Wes. Droplets hang in the air, sparkling like scattered diamonds in the sunlight before falling in shimmering curtains around us. The splash stirs the lake's surface, sending ripples that lap gently against the wooden dock.

She surfaces with a triumphant gasp, her grin wicked and wide. "That's for giving me and Lila latrine duty. You're welcome."

I wipe water from my face, laughing as Wes gives her a half-hearted dunk in retaliation. The sound of their laughter echoes across the lake, light and unguarded in a way that makes something inside me unclench. The water looks so inviting—sunlight glinting across it in fractured mirrors—and for a moment, I don't want to be the girl sitting on the dock, half in, half out. I want to be weightless with them.

So I slide forward, toes first, then calves, the cold closing around me with a sharp, breath-stealing gasp. It shocks the heat from my skin, steals my breath, and replaces it with something clean and alive. Wes's hand brushes my arm beneath the surface, steadying me before he lets go, his grin softening into something quieter. Sophie splashes again, triumphant that she's gotten me in. I sputter, then laugh, shaking water from my hair.

We drift together, shoulders occasionally bumping as the lake rocks us in small, steady waves. The three of us float in the shallows as time drifts by lazily, wrapped in a rare, suspended moment when nothing feels wrong yet—just the warmth of the sun, the sharp scent of lake water, and the weightless joy of letting ourselves be kids again.

A little farther up the shoreline, Mattie crouches beside the kayak rack, tightening bolts with a rusted socket wrench. His work shirt is already damp with sweat, the collar darkened and clinging to the back of his neck. Every movement is focused, deliberate, like whatever he's fixing is the only thing keeping the lake from swallowing the rest of us whole.

Zach crouches nearby, too low, and too quiet to be up to anything good. I spot him just in time to watch him sneak towards Mattie's pile of tools, swipe a couple of socket heads, and tiptoe backwards like a cartoon villain. He ducks behind the changing stall, snickering to himself.

Mattie doesn't even lift his head.

He freezes mid-turn of the wrench, eyes narrowing like he can smell the mischief. Then he stands slowly, jaw clenched tight, glancing down at his tools while taking silent inventory.

Zach doesn't stick around to see the fallout. He bolts towards the trail with a laugh, the stolen pieces still clutched in one hand.

Mattie's voice follows him, low but sharp enough to carry. "You keep carryin' on like that, Zach," he calls, "and one day it's gonna come back to bite you hard. Hope you're fast when it does."

He doesn't yell. He doesn't need to. The quiet fury in his voice hits harder than any shout could. Around them, the forest is alive with subtle sounds—the rustle of leaves, the distant call of a raven, the soft crack of twigs beneath cautious steps. It feels like the woods themselves are waiting for something to break the fragile calm.

Mattie crouches again, retrieving the remaining tools and checking them over with quick, precise movements. His jaw is set in stone now, the veins in his forearms pulled taut as he picks up the next bolt and keeps going—like this is the only thing keeping his hands from balling into fists.

Wes glances at me, his expression unreadable, then back towards Mattie, who is moving a little slower now, but not because he's tired. No, something is simmering beneath his skin. Not just annoyance. Containment.

Wes brushes his hand over mine under the water, anchoring me in the moment again.

"Come on," he tells me softly. "Bet I can still beat you to the diving platform."

"You wish."

"Winner gets a kiss," he adds with that familiar crooked grin.

"Guess that means we both win," I quip, and slide into the water, the lake folding around me as we take off side by side.

For a little while, it feels like we could outrun everything else.

Later at lunch, I sit with Wes, Noah, and Jesse at one of the counselor tables near the back of the mess hall. The clatter of trays and chatter of voices surround us in waves, a constant hum that makes the air feel heavy and close. The fans in the corners do little more than stir the heat. I can feel the sweat prickling beneath the collar of my camp shirt, my hair still damp at the roots from the lake. The long, tangled waves sticking to the tops of my shoulders and clinging to my collarbone whenever I shift, the weight of it like wet rope down my back.

Jesse sits across from me, guitar case leaning against the bench beside her like it is an extension of her body. She always has it nearby, carrying it like some people do a purse or a utility knife. Her jeans are frayed at the knees, one thread hanging loose where it had caught on something, and the black flannel tied around her waist looks like it has been through its own series of wars. Her mascara is smudged slightly under one eye, but in a way that looks intentional, like a soft shadow rather than a mistake.

She taps her fork against the rim of her tray, eyes flicking up to meet mine as a smile tugs at her mouth.

"I think you might be the reason lunch's my favorite part of the day," she says lightly, like it's just another observation. "Even the mystery meat doesn't feel so tragic when you're sitting across from me."

The comment lands like a surprise flick to the ribs. Not harsh, not painful, just unexpected enough to leave me blinking. My heart stutters, a sudden heat blooming within me. I feel the familiar tightness in my throat, like I swallowed a secret too big to hold. It is both thrilling and terrifying—this small moment of being truly seen. I freeze, toast halfway to my mouth, heat crawling up my neck before I can think better of it. A flush creeps up from my collarbone like a tide I couldn't hold back. I'm not used to being flirted with. Not like this. Not in a way that feels teasing and real at the same time. Not in a way that makes me feel seen.

I don't say anything in response. Not because I am uncomfortable, just... thrown. I'm not sure what expression I'm wearing, but whatever it is makes Jesse's smile widen a little. I must look bewildered, because she gives me a small shrug and turns back to her food, like it's no big deal. Like she'd just mentioned the weather.

Across the table, Wes rests his chin in his hand, elbow propped up as he watches the exchange with quiet amusement. His pale blue eyes look like broken glass in the midday light, sharp and unflinching, but not cold. There is a spark in them, the kind that says he found the moment funny in a way he'd never admit out loud. Not jealous. Not annoyed. Just amused. Like watching a cat paw at a mirror. Like he already knew how it would end.

I catch his gaze and hold it for a beat longer than I mean to. The noise of the mess hall seems to blur at the edges again, softening to a low, forgettable murmur.

Lila and Sophie slide onto the bench beside me with trays in hand, their conversation already in full swing. Lila's earrings jingle as she leans in, her voice laced with exasperation.

"You will not believe what we just heard," she pants.

"Zach," Sophie says, drawing out his name like a warning, "has apparently been bragging about some big prank he's planning for the trail hike."

Lila rolls her eyes, spearing a carrot stick with her fork. "Apparently, he wants it to be 'one for the books.' His words."

"He says it's going to be a 'legendary' moment," Sophie adds, using air quotes. "Like he wants it to be the kind of thing campers talk about for years."

Jesse groans. "Seriously? What else is there for him to do at this point? How much worse can he actually get?"

"I don't want to find out," Wes chides without missing a beat.
His voice is quiet, almost amused, but something underneath it is sharper. Like a wire pulled tight.
Sophie gives a nervous little laugh and pushes some peas around her tray. "I mean... it's probably not that bad, right?"

"Or it's a total disaster waiting to happen," Lila counters, biting her lip. "But I kind of want to see it?"

Jesse looks over at her. "Yeah, until we're all cleaning up shaving cream and glitter until August."

"I don't even think it's about the prank anymore," Wes says. "He just wants to be remembered."

Noah, who'd been silent up until now, sets his fork down too hard. The clink echoes louder than it should have. "He always wants to be remembered. He doesn't care who he hurts to get it."

We all turn toward him. His expression is flat, but his jaw is tight.

Around us, the chatter dulls, replaced by a tense hush. The weight of the moment pressing in, thick as the humidity that clings to the pines.

Noah stands, collecting his tray in one hand, his voice a low mutter as he steps away from the table. "Those kids need to get what they deserve." The words barely reach us before he disappears through the mess hall doors.

Sophie hesitates. "You okay?"

My fork hovers over my tray, appetite thinning by the second. That familiar, tight feeling curling low in my stomach. Zach pulling a prank isn't exactly news, but whenever he talks like this, loud, confident, grinning like he knows something no one else does, it never ends well.

Especially not for whoever ends up in the crosshairs. And the worst part is, you never know until it's too late.
I force a breath through my nose and try to let it go.

Wes reaches across the table and nudges my water bottle with his finger, his eyes still soft on mine. I know that look. A silent reassurance. *I'm here. You're okay.*

But the unease is already crawling back in.

When the bell rings to signal cleanup and activity transitions, the mess hall stirs into motion. Trays scrape against tabletops, benches screech across the floor, and counselors start rounding up their campers for the afternoon trail hike. I dump my tray, wipe my hands on the hem of my shirt, and linger by the door, letting the others pass me in a slow current of laughter and footsteps.

My fingers brush the worn wood of the doorway. It is warm from the sun, splintered in places from years of contact. I stand still for a moment, not quite ready to move.
The air has shifted. Not colder, not louder. Just... off. Like a moment held too long. Like something had stopped that wasn't supposed to.

The laughter fades behind me, muffled like it was happening underwater. I can still hear the clink of utensils and the occasional shout from a camper outside, but it all feels distant, like I'm not part of it. The air presses tighter around me. The fine hairs at the back of my neck stand up, prickling like static.

I turn my head slowly, scanning the clearing and the trees beyond. Nothing. Just the dappled light

through the leaves and the usual hum of summer. But the feeling doesn't go away.

Not *someone* watching.
Something.

I shake my head, blink hard, and make myself take a breath. Probably just leftover nerves from hearing Zach's name. Or maybe it's the quiet tension that's been building up in me all day, coiled just beneath the surface with nowhere to go. It is probably nothing.

I tell myself that twice, maybe three times, before I step forward and join the others on the trail. My feet crunch over the gravel path, and the sound of voices slowly swell again as I catch up.
I never look back.

✦ 10 ✦

Somebody's Eyes are Watching

✧The Hunter✧

I watch because no one else will. Not the ones who laugh too loud or turn their eyes away when cruelty crawls just beneath the surface. Not the ones who write off hurt as weakness or let bruises bloom without question. But I see. I always have.

I am not here for vengeance, not exactly. I am here for balance—for those who suffer quietly, swallow shame, endure the wrongs that others just walk past. I move like silence itself, not to punish all, but to answer the ones who take too much and feel too little.

Today, the weight tips toward a boy named Zach McKinley.

I hear him before I see him. Crude laughter. The snap of a branch beneath careless boots. The sticky thump of a water balloon slapping against an open palm. Zach's voice is sharp with excitement, slicing through the trees like a blade.

"I swear to God, it's gonna be legendary," he says. "Fake blood. All over her. Right in front of everyone."

Mason snorts in response, his voice thinner, uncertain. "Dude, what did she even do?"

Zach scoffs, and there's a sneer in the sound. "She exists. She strutted around all morning like she was queen of the lake, all cozy with her golden retriever. Somebody has to knock her back down."

There's a pause. Then both of them laugh, loud and harsh, like gravel in a blender. It echoes through the woods with no regard for who might hear.

"I'm heading to the ropes course," Zach says. "Gonna wait 'til everyone's in sight. She won't know what hit her."

Mason steps trail off in the opposite direction, his voice fading. Zach is alone now, humming tunelessly under his breath, the water balloon cradled under one arm like a prize he earned. He doesn't notice how the woods behind him go quiet. How even the breeze that stirred the leaves moments ago seems to still. The birds have stopped. The trees no longer rustle. There's a hush in the underbrush, like the forest itself is waiting.

He doesn't hear me. They never do.

He paces a slow arc through the trees, nearing the ropes course, until he finds a clearing just shy of the main trail. There, beside a stump capped with damp moss, he crouches down and pulls the water balloon free. He examines it like it's precious, fingers turning it slowly in the light. The deep red liquid sloshes beneath the thin membrane, viscous and rich like real blood. He chuckles low in his throat.

His tone is gleeful, self-satisfied—the kind of voice used by people who have never been made to reckon with their own cruelty. He glances toward the path, calculating his timing, then scans the tree line. There, just off the trail, a cluster of low brush offers cover. He shifts toward it, boots crunching softly on dried pine needles, and sinks into place.

"She looked way too happy this morning with lover boy, like she forgot who she actually is," he murmurs. "Let's see what he thinks when she's soaked in blood."

His smirk is a tight twist of malice as he crouches deeper, eyes locked on the approaching trail. He is still. Waiting. Focused.

I step forward.

There is no warning. No sound. The moment folds in on itself like a held breath.

He senses me too late.

His head jerks toward me, but his eyes never get the chance to register fear. The rock in my hand is smooth on one side, jagged on the other. I bring it down with all the force of judgment behind it.

It lands against the side of his skull with a sickening crunch, splitting skin, shattering the delicate bone above his temple. The balloon slips from his hands and bursts against the ground with a soft pop, red liquid spreading like a mimicry of death, but not enough to cover what comes next.

Zach jerks, gasping, blood already pouring down the side of his face in thick ropes. His eyes roll wildly, mouth opening in a startled scream that never fully forms. I hit him again. The second blow caves in part of his forehead. A piece of bone pushes inward, and this time the sound is wetter. More final. His legs buckle beneath him.

He drops to his knees, swaying, trying to catch himself on trembling hands slick with pine needles and soil. Blood patters to the forest floor in irregular drops. He looks up at me, dazed. Not defiant. Not pleading. Just confused.

I grab him by the front of his shirt before he can fall. My fingers twist in the fabric, and I haul him upright, his body limp weight. His breath stutters in his chest. I can smell the iron of the blood, sharp and metallic, clinging to the air. His face is ruined. Part of his brow is gone, and one eye is already swelling shut.

I lean in close. My hand clamps around the base of his jaw, thumb beneath his chin. I look him in the eye when I do it. He should know who ended it.

With a sharp, practiced motion, I wrench his neck. It breaks like a dry stick. The sound is clean and final, louder than it should be in the hush of the clearing. His head lolls to the side, and he exhales one last, involuntary breath as his body goes slack.

I let him drop. He lands on his side, mouth slightly open, blood trickling from his nose, pooling in the dirt beneath him. His arms are bent awkwardly. One leg twitches—a leftover nerve spasm—but he is already gone.

I breathe in slowly through my nose, tasting the metallic sharpness in the air. The blood is darker now, thickening in the cool shade. It spreads from the open gash in his head, soaking into the leaves, the moss, the soil. The forest accepts it.

I crouch and take hold of his ankles, dragging him through the brush, away from the stump, away from the path. I don't care if twigs catch in his hair or his limbs scrape against the roots. He doesn't feel it. He won't.

I leave him nestled in a pocket of shadows beneath a low canopy of pine. Blood dots the trail where I pulled him, but the forest is forgiving. With time, even the stains will disappear.

I don't pose him. I don't linger. I am not here for art.

Zach was loud. He was reckless and cruel. He wanted to humiliate someone already carrying too much. He laughed at her pain before it even happened. He took pleasure in the thought of breaking something fragile just because he could.

That was enough. Now he is gone.

I slip back into the trees long before the first group rounds the bend. My heartbeat is steady. My hands are clean. The breeze stirs again behind me. The birds begin to sing.

The trail remains quiet and the balance holds.

✧Emilia✧

The sun has already begun to dip behind the trees, flickering through the canopy like it's trying to hold on, when the shouting starts.

At first, I think it's just campers goofing off near the dining hall—someone chasing someone else, laughing too loud, breaking a rule they'll pretend not to know. But then a whistle cuts through the air, sharp and urgent, slicing clean through the humid stillness. It isn't the usual kind of whistle. It doesn't call attention. It warns.

My head lifts automatically, eyes searching the tree line. There's movement near the trailhead, where the path leads off toward the ropes course and deeper into the woods. Counselors are running, one after another, their strides too wide and uneven for anything casual. I take a step forward before I realize I've moved. My heart kicks harder in my chest.

Something's wrong.

I follow the motion like a leaf dragged downriver—weightless, aimless, already too late. My legs carry me faster than my thoughts can catch up. Somewhere behind me, laughter still spills from the dining hall porch, sharp and oblivious. The sound doesn't match the air anymore. I round the side of the mess hall just in time to see Wes and Noah emerge from the trail, faces pale and locked in focus, a stretcher suspended between them.

Zach's body is on it.

The white sheet thrown over him flutters slightly as they move—too light, too thin to mask the truth beneath it. One of his arms slips off the side, limp and swinging with every step. The sight roots me to the ground. My breath stutters in my throat.

He looks so small.

I don't remember him ever seeming small before. He was loud. Always in motion. Smirking. Leaning too close when he talked. But now he looks like a child curled in sleep—except for the way his fingers dangle and the slack shape of his jaw beneath the sheet.

Campers have begun to gather despite being told to stay back. Their voices rise all around me, buzzing like hornets caught in a jar.

"Is he dead?"

"What happened?"

"Oh my God, that's Zach—he was with our group."

I can't stop staring at the shape beneath the fabric. My eyes trace every inch, trying to make sense of what I'm seeing. Something doesn't add up. There, on the side where his arm hangs limp, leaves are tangled in his hair, dark and matted. A smudge of dirt cuts across the pale skin of his wrist. Near his temple, just beneath the edge of the sheet, something glistens. It's darker than the rest. Thicker.

There's too much damage for a fall.

Crystal arrives like she was waiting for this moment. Her expression is set—just enough grief around the eyes, tension in the mouth. Poised. Practiced. She steps in front of the stretcher and waves the growing crowd back with both hands.

"Zach... Zach took a horrible fall while scouting a new route for the ropes course," she says. "We think he slipped, hit his head. It was a freak accident."

They fall limp, like soaked paper that tears the moment you try to lift it.

"He was brave," Crystal continues, eyes shimmering as they sweep across the faces of the crowd. "He wanted to help set up tomorrow's course. This isn't anyone's fault. But please stay with your groups. No more wandering off."

Her voice catches just enough to sound believable, but the way she glances toward the stretcher doesn't sit right. There's no flicker of real grief. Just a calculation in her eyes, like she's already picturing how to phrase the parent email.

Just behind me, I catch Mason's voice, hoarse and cracking, like he hasn't caught a full breath since finding the body. He's flanked by Brianna, Aubree, and Chloe. They're clustered together in stunned silence, Aubree's hand pressed tightly over her mouth.

"I thought it was a prank," Mason says finally. "He was supposed to jump out and make a scene. I waited. It didn't happen. I figured he chickened out… so I went looking." His voice breaks. "I didn't know he'd be…"

Chloe doesn't speak. Her face has gone stark and unreadable, color drained. Even she looks shaken.

Some of the counselors nod, absorbing the story like they're willing it to make sense. Like, if they accept the narrative quickly enough, it won't touch them.

The body is carried toward the service road, where a long white van waits behind the maintenance shed like a silent predator. Its side bears no markings, but everyone knows what it is. The coroner's office, summoned without fanfare. No sirens. No flashing lights. Just the inevitable waiting out of sight.

I don't follow as they pass me.

I just watch.

Nearby, I catch Dee standing near the kitchen doorway, arms crossed, eyes shadowed beneath the brim of her ball cap. She mutters something under her breath, too quiet for anyone else to hear. But I catch it.

"It's always the cocky ones."

The sheet ripples once more before disappearing behind the trees. The air swells with something unspoken. Thick. Heavy. A silence that doesn't just follow death—it announces it.

My hands are clenched in the fabric of my shorts. I didn't realize I was gripping them until my nails bit into my skin, hard enough to leave marks. I let go slowly, one finger at a time.

I tell myself it was just an accident. Just a fall.

That's what they said.

That's what I'm supposed to believe.

But the words don't sound like mine. They don't settle in my chest the way truth usually does. They feel distant. Like someone else's lines handed to me in a play I didn't audition for.

Around me, the camp begins to exhale.

Crystal's voice drifts away as she walks with the crowd, offering reassurances that sound more hollow than comforting. Counselors usher campers toward the mess hall now, redirecting them with quiet voices and forced smiles. Dinner is next. As if nothing happened. As if grief can be postponed until lights out.

I don't move.

The world around me keeps moving—like a slow, relentless tide—while inside I feel the jagged shards of silence fracture every part of me. The rehearsed words, the hollow reassurances—they all feel like lies shaped to keep the darkness at bay.

I stand at the edge of the clearing long after the van has gone, after the last murmurs fade. My eyes are still locked on the path where Zach's body had been carried. The ground there looks the same as always—worn dirt, half-lit by the fading sun—but it doesn't feel the same.

There is something wrong. Not just today. Not just Zach.

This place.

This camp.

This summer.

Something dark coils beneath it all, quiet and unseen. I can feel it. A tension in the air like a storm forming beneath the soil.

And yet, as I stand here, unmoving, a darker truth threads through me—one that chills me deeper than death itself.

I'm not entirely afraid.

Something in me understands this silence. Something in me... accepts it.

And I don't know what that means.

I should be scared. I should feel sick, furious, and shattered. But instead, all I feel is stillness. A terrible, echoing calm.

That night, camp doesn't breathe right.

The mess hall goes quiet too quickly. Laughter stutters like it is being rationed. Even the fire pit feels wrong—wood burning too fast, flames too low.

Crystal held a counselor "check-in" where she never once said Zach's name.

"Let's just... focus on stability," she'd said, smile too tight. "We don't want the kids scared. We are their anchors."

But we aren't anchors. We are barely holding ourselves steady.

The air outside feels off—too still, like the woods are waiting for someone to admit what we all already know. I watch Brianna stir sugar into her tea without looking up, eyes red-rimmed but dry. Chloe hasn't said a word since dinner. Even Lila is quiet. Not cold. Just distant, like her thoughts are somewhere else entirely.

I can't take it anymore. The walls of the mess hall press in, and every flicker of the lanterns feels like a scream that hasn't found its voice.

I find Wes on the dock after lights-out. He doesn't say a word. Just reaches for my hand. His thumb brushes over mine again and again, like he is checking to make sure I am still real.

I let him.

And for a little while, we just breathe in the dark—side by side, the trees whispering in the night breeze, secrets fold into the rustle of needles and the sigh of the earth. The fire pit's embers flicker weakly, casting long, trembling shadows that dance like ghosts across the water. We sit with the weight of all that was lost, and all that is yet to come, pressing down between us like a silent promise.

Something we can't quite name yet.

But it's already settling in our bones.

Whatever innocence this place had pretended to offer is gone.

✦ 11 ✦

Truth or Coverup

✧Emilia✧

The sun has already begun to dip behind the trees, flickering through the canopy like it's trying to hold on, when the shouting starts.

At first, I think it's just campers goofing off near the dining hall—someone chasing someone else, laughing too loud, breaking a rule they'll pretend not to know. But then a whistle cuts through the air, sharp and urgent, slicing clean through the humid stillness. It isn't the usual kind of whistle. It doesn't call attention. It warns.

My head lifts automatically, eyes searching the tree line. There's movement near the trailhead, where the path leads off toward the ropes course and deeper into the woods. Counselors are running, one after another, their strides too wide and uneven for anything casual. I take a step forward before I realize I've moved. My heart kicks harder in my chest.

Something's wrong.

I follow the motion like a leaf dragged downriver—weightless, aimless, already too late. My legs carry me faster than my thoughts can catch up. Somewhere behind me, laughter still spills from the dining hall porch, sharp and oblivious. The sound doesn't match the air anymore. I round the side of the mess hall just in time to see Wes and Noah emerge from the trail, faces pale and locked in focus, a stretcher suspended between them.

Zach's body is on it.

The white sheet thrown over him flutters slightly as they move—too light, too thin to mask the truth beneath it. One of his arms slips off the side, limp and swinging with every step. The sight roots me to the ground. My breath stutters in my throat.

He looks so small.

I don't remember him ever seeming small before. He was loud. Always in motion. Smirking. Leaning too close when he talked. But now he looks like a child curled in sleep—except for the way his fingers dangle and the slack shape of his jaw beneath the sheet.

Campers have begun to gather despite being told to stay back. Their voices rise all around me, buzzing like hornets caught in a jar.

"Is he dead?"

"What happened?"

"Oh my God, that's Zach—he was with our group."

I can't stop staring at the shape beneath the fabric. My eyes trace every inch, trying to make sense of what I'm seeing. Something doesn't add up. There, on the side where his arm hangs limp, leaves are tangled in his hair, dark and matted. A smudge of dirt cuts across the pale skin of his wrist. Near his temple, just beneath the edge of the sheet, something glistens. It's darker than the rest. Thicker.

There's too much damage for a fall.

Crystal arrives like she was waiting for this moment. Her expression is set—just enough grief around the eyes, tension in the mouth. Poised. Practiced. She steps in front of the stretcher and waves the growing crowd back with both hands.

"Zach... Zach took a horrible fall while scouting a new route for the ropes course," she says. "We think he slipped, hit his head. It was a freak accident."

They fall limp, like soaked paper that tears the moment you try to lift it.

"He was brave," Crystal continues, eyes shimmering as they sweep across the faces of the crowd. "He wanted to help set up tomorrow's course. This isn't anyone's fault. But please stay with your groups. No more wandering off."

Her voice catches just enough to sound believable, but the way she glances toward the stretcher doesn't sit right. There's no flicker of real grief. Just a calculation in her eyes, like she's already picturing how to phrase the parent email.

Just behind me, I catch Mason's voice, hoarse and cracking, like he hasn't caught a full breath since finding the body. He's flanked by Brianna, Aubree, and Chloe. They're clustered together in stunned silence, Aubree's hand pressed tightly over her mouth.

"I thought it was a prank," Mason says finally. "He was supposed to jump out and make a scene. I waited. It didn't happen. I figured he chickened out... so I went looking." His voice breaks. "I didn't know he'd be..."

Chloe doesn't speak. Her face has gone stark and unreadable, color drained. Even she looks shaken.

Some of the counselors nod, absorbing the story like they're willing it to make sense. Like, if they accept the narrative quickly enough, it won't touch them.

The body is carried toward the service road, where a long white van waits behind the maintenance shed like a silent predator. Its side bears no markings, but everyone knows what it is. The coroner's office, summoned without fanfare. No sirens. No flashing lights. Just the inevitable waiting out of sight.

I don't follow as they pass me.

I just watch.

Nearby, I catch Dee standing near the kitchen doorway, arms crossed, eyes shadowed beneath the brim of her ball cap. She mutters something under her breath, too quiet for anyone else to hear. But I catch it.

"It's always the cocky ones."

The sheet ripples once more before disappearing behind the trees. The air swells with something unspoken. Thick. Heavy. A silence that doesn't just follow death—it announces it.

My hands are clenched in the fabric of my shorts. I didn't realize I was gripping them until my nails bit into my skin, hard enough to leave marks. I let go slowly, one finger at a time.

I tell myself it was just an accident. Just a fall.

That's what they said.

That's what I'm supposed to believe.

But the words don't sound like mine. They don't settle in my chest the way truth usually does. They feel distant. Like someone else's lines handed to me in a play I didn't audition for.

Around me, the camp begins to exhale.

Crystal's voice drifts away as she walks with the crowd, offering reassurances that sound more hollow than comforting. Counselors usher campers toward the mess hall now, redirecting them with quiet voices and forced smiles. Dinner is next. As if nothing happened. As if grief can be postponed until lights out.

I don't move.

The world around me keeps moving—like a slow, relentless tide—while inside I feel the jagged shards of silence fracture every part of me. The rehearsed words, the hollow reassurances—they all feel like lies shaped to keep the darkness at bay.

I stand at the edge of the clearing long after the van has gone, after the last murmurs fade. My eyes are still locked on the path where Zach's body had been carried. The ground there looks the same as always—worn dirt, half-lit by the fading sun—but it doesn't feel the same.

There is something wrong. Not just today. Not just Zach.

This place.

This camp.

This summer.

Something dark coils beneath it all, quiet and unseen. I can feel it. A tension in the air like a storm forming beneath the soil.

And yet, as I stand here, unmoving, a darker truth threads through me—one that chills me deeper than death itself.

I'm not entirely afraid.

Something in me understands this silence. Something in me... accepts it.

And I don't know what that means.

I should be scared. I should feel sick, furious, and shattered. But instead, all I feel is stillness. A terrible, echoing calm.

That night, camp doesn't breathe right.

The mess hall goes quiet too quickly. Laughter stutters like it is being rationed. Even the fire pit feels wrong—wood burning too fast, flames too low.

Crystal held a counselor "check-in" where she never once said Zach's name.

"Let's just... focus on stability," she'd said, smile too tight. "We don't want the kids scared. We are their anchors."

But we aren't anchors. We are barely holding ourselves steady.

The air outside feels off—too still, like the woods are waiting for someone to admit what we all already know. I watch Brianna stir sugar into her tea without looking up, eyes red-rimmed but dry. Chloe hasn't said a word since dinner. Even Lila is quiet. Not cold. Just distant, like her thoughts are somewhere else entirely.

I can't take it anymore. The walls of the mess hall press in, and every flicker of the lanterns feels like a scream that hasn't found its voice.

I find Wes on the dock after lights-out. He doesn't say a word. Just reaches for my hand. His thumb

brushes over mine again and again, like he is checking to make sure I am still real.

I let him.

And for a little while, we just breathe in the dark—side by side, the trees whispering in the night breeze, secrets fold into the rustle of needles and the sigh of the earth. The fire pit's embers flicker weakly, casting long, trembling shadows that dance like ghosts across the water. We sit with the weight of all that was lost, and all that is yet to come, pressing down between us like a silent promise.

Something we can't quite name yet.

But it's already settling in our bones.

Whatever innocence this place had pretended to offer is gone.

✦ 12 ✦

The World Kept Spinning

☽ Camp Day 23 ~ July 18th ~ 21 Days to Go ☾

✧ Emilia ✧

I thought there'd be silence. Not peace, nothing so gentle, but the kind of hush that follows a tragedy. Stillness. Reverence. Shock.

But the mess hall is alive. Too alive.

Laughter echoes off the walls, sharp and careless. The wide windows stand open to the morning air, letting in the damp scent of moss and wet earth. The breeze carries the sharp cry of a jay somewhere out by the tree line, a jarring reminder that life outside the cabin walls hasn't stopped either. Forks scrape against chipped plates with a shrill clatter that sets my teeth on edge. A pitcher of orange juice crashes to the floor and spills in a slow-spreading puddle, sticky and bright. No one even flinches. A kid at the end of the table snorts milk through his nose while someone retells a story I wish I hadn't heard.

Mason leans back in his chair, easy and loose, his grin too wide as he tells Chloe and Aubree about a prank from last summer — something about a glitter bomb in the staff bathroom. The punchline lands with a bang of laughter, like the whole table has been holding their breath for the release.

Zach's name is barely even said. Just implied. Tossed around like set dressing for Mason's joke. A prop in someone else's memory.

It feels wrong. Like he never even existed, like the old growth forest didn't take him. I didn't know Zach well. But I saw his body. I saw what was left.

And now Mason is laughing about glitter. Aubree's wheezing like it's the funniest thing she's ever heard, drumming her heels against the floor, and Chloe just sips her coffee with that perfect, practiced ease like they're on break from a photoshoot, not a crime scene.

Brianna, though. She doesn't laugh.

She watches Mason with the sharp kind of quiet that says she hasn't forgotten anything. That maybe she's counting every breath he takes, weighing them against what's been lost.

I slip into the seat beside Sophie, my skin too tight, the room too loud, every sound scraping raw across my nerves. The wood bench is rough beneath my legs, the varnish long worn away. I can feel every scrape and groove digging in, grounding me in a place I wish I wasn't. The air smells of burnt toast and too-strong coffee—normal things that suddenly feel unbearable.

"They're acting like..." I stop, the words sticking like grit in my throat.

Sophie stares into her bowl, her spoon unmoving in the soggy cereal. "Like nothing happened?" she murmurs. Her voice is soft, almost apologetic. "I don't think they know how else to cope."

I want to say, cope with what?

But I bite my tongue.

✧

The days that follow dissolve like sugar in rain. The weather shifts almost daily—misty mornings, afternoons heavy with sun that bakes the dirt paths dry, and nights that fall cool and damp enough to smell the rain waiting in the clouds. But none of it matters. Each day feels the same, as thin and brittle as paper ready to tear.

No memorial. No moment of silence. No email to the parents.

Crystal just carries on like death is an inconvenience we all agreed not to mention.

On Day 25, she's back to shouting across the clearing about "leadership potential" and "building trust" while campers wobble blindfolded across balance beams, their arms flailing, laughter shrill and unsure.

The scent of pine sap and sunscreen hangs heavy in the air. Beyond the clearing, the forest looms dark and watchful, the shadows between the trunks cool and deep even in the midday sun. The contrast feels like mockery—playacting safety on ground that's already taken a life.

I stand under the sun, my shirt sticking to my back, watching Aubree giggle as she lets a ten-year-old nearly fall and think: Zach is gone, and this is what we're doing?

✧

Day 27, the fire circle is packed again.

Chloe tells a ghost story about a girl in the woods who whispers your secrets in your sleep. Her voice is slow and syrupy, pulling the kids closer with every word.

The firelight catches her cheekbones, making her look almost ethereal—like she belongs in the kind of story she's telling. The kids lean in, wide-eyed, oblivious to the real ghost that haunts this place.

They love it. Their shrieks of delight curl into the air like smoke.

Someone passes around popcorn in a paper bowl, and when it hits the flames — one stray handful tossed too close — the smell turns sharp. Burnt sugar and ash.

It clings to my hair, my clothes, my skin. It sticks in my throat, sweet and bitter, like grief disguised as something harmless.

✧

By Day 28, I overhear Dee muttering in the kitchen while scrubbing a pot that looks older than I am. The air is warm and heavy with the scent of dish soap and boiled vegetables, steam fogging the windows above the sink.

"Kids bounce back quick," she says, her voice gruff.

Then quieter, almost to herself, with a heaviness that clings to me like steam:

"Sometimes too quick."

I don't think she knows I heard her.

But what she said sticks with me, curling into the cracks I've been trying to patch shut.

⟡

The only place I can breathe is the woods.

And the only thing that can ground me anymore is Wes.

We've spent hours beneath that tree.

Curled in the moss, wrapped around each other, stealing time like it's the only thing we have.

Our initials are carved there, deep in the bark, his W looping into my E — a secret promise no one else knows exists. Moss creeps thick along the trunk, damp and cool beneath our hands when we trace the grooves of the letters. The air smells of cedar and wet earth, the lake glinting through gaps in the trees like a secret no one else can find. The grooves are still fresh. The wood hasn't grayed yet.

Some afternoons, we lie in silence, the world hushed around us except for the lake lapping at the shore, the wind threading through the trees like it's humming a lullaby just for us.

Other times, I'm in his lap, our mouths pressed hard together, fingers tangled in each other's clothes like we're trying to crawl inside one another.

There's no pretending out here. No lies.

Just the truth of his hands on my skin and the way he looks at me like I'm something he doesn't think he deserves.

✧

On Day 30, as we watch the sunset together at our spot, he gives me a stone.

Smooth and pale, veined with iridescence like lightning frozen in quartz.

"It reminded me of you," he says.

I tuck it into my jacket pocket and know I'll never let it go. I press my hand there sometimes, just to feel its shape. Just to know he chose it.

Later that night, we're walking back through the trees when Wes stops, brows lifting.

"There," he says, tilting his chin to the right.

Two figures moving fast down the trail to the lake.

It takes a beat, but I recognize Chloe's laugh — syrupy and bright, the sound of someone who's used to getting what she wants.

She's wrapped around Tanner, her legs swinging behind her as he lifts her off the ground, their mouths already locked.

Wes grins. "Wanna see where this goes?"

I hesitate. "Kind of feel like we shouldn't..."

But he's already moving, pulling me along until we're crouched near the warped siding of the old boathouse.

Inside, Chloe's back is pressed to the wall, one arm thrown over Tanner's shoulder, the other holding a lit joint. The glow of it flares like a firefly in the dark.

He kisses her neck while working at the button of her shorts. She giggles against his skin, a puff of smoke drifting between them like fog.

She moans when he sinks to his knees.

I freeze, wide-eyed, caught between the horror of watching and the shame of not looking away.

Tanner tugs her bikini bottoms down, slow, and cocky, and presses his mouth between her thighs like it's the most natural thing in the world.

Chloe arches with a soft, needy sound that makes my stomach twist.

She threads her fingers through his curls, takes another hit, and exhales, gasping his name.

I should look away, I know I should.

"We should go," I whisper, even as heat floods my face, my breath shallow.

Wes's hand is already on me, sliding up the back of my leg, fingers teasing beneath the hem of my shorts.

"You sure?" he murmurs, voice low against my ear. "You're breathing kinda heavy, my love."

I swallow hard. My heart's beating too fast.

He smirks, eyes dark and knowing, but when I nudge him again, he lets out a soft sigh and leads us away.

We slip back into the trees, the echo of Chloe's moans fading behind us.

Wes's fingers lace with mine, his thumb tracing slow circles over my knuckles, steadying me.

We don't head back to the cabins as planned.

Not yet. Not anymore.

My pulse is racing, burning through the calm he's trying to hold.

Before I can think twice, I lean in and press my mouth to his—hard and hungry.

His breath hitches, surprised, but doesn't pull away.

I push him gently but insistently backward, toward the slope just off the trail—soft moss cushioning the earth beneath, damp, and cool against my knees as we fall together into shadow. The scent of cedar and wet earth clings to the air, grounding and dizzying all at once.

His back hits the ground with a muffled thud, and I straddle him instantly, heat flooding my cheeks.

I grind down, threading my fingers through the curls at his neck to pull him closer.

His jeans sit just low enough, and I tug at the waistband, sliding my hand under to brush the warmth of his skin.

I pull my shorts to the side without hesitation, needing him—needing this—right here, right now.

His voice is low, steady, and rough as gravel:

"Watching those two lit a fire under you, huh?"

I catch my breath, heat swirling faster.

"They knew exactly what they wanted," I murmur, "and so do I."

The stretch steals my breath for a heartbeat, heat blooming sharp and sweet. It feels reckless and perfect, like we're crossing a line we can't come back from.

Wes smirks against my neck, biting lightly,

"And that's me. You're mine."

His claim sends a jolt straight through me, making me grind harder, needing to hear it again.

Wes's hands settle firmly on my hips, thumbs pressing into my skin, steadying me even as I lose control.

He guides my movements, slow and deliberate, making me feel seen and claimed in every stroke.

"Yes," I breathe, voice trembling but fierce, "yours."

He pulls me closer, hips lifting to match mine, making my body shudder with the perfect rhythm—his rhythm.

Every touch, every movement is electric, wild, and intimate all at once.

My nails dig into his chest, my voice rising in a breathless mix of need and surrender.

He groans deep in his throat, his hands possessive on my hips,

"Such a good girl, taking what's yours."

His words unravel me, everything building sharp and fast, until it's too much—until I can't hold back the sounds spilling out of me, raw and needy.

I lose myself in the fire between us—rough moss beneath, his skin against mine, the fading light filtering through trees.

His lips find mine again, claiming, sealing the moment.

"Say it," he murmurs.

I meet his eyes, breath catching,

"I'm yours. All of me."

He smiles against my mouth,

"And I'm never letting go."

A few nights later, just before the storm breaks, I find Sophie.

She's curled in a rocking chair alone on the mess hall screen porch, barefoot, knees tucked up, her journal open across her thighs. Her pen moves like it's dancing, no hesitation, just flow.

The air is thick, buzzing with that charged, metallic stillness that comes before a storm. The clouds above us are heavy and low, tinged with that eerie green-blue cast like something bruised.

The scent of rain is already in the air—wet earth and cedar, sharp and electric. The forest around camp has gone unnervingly still, like every branch and needle is bracing for the downpour.

The wind lifts the edge of her page.

She doesn't look up when I sit beside her.

I watch her for a while — how her face softens when she writes, how her forehead creases in that way it does when she's letting something true out.

Finally, she closes the journal with a quiet breath and says, almost like she's talking to herself, "Sometimes I pretend nothing ever happened. Just so I can enjoy it."

It takes me a second to realize she's not talking about Zach. Or camp.

She's talking about everything.

Our whole life.

The way it was before Dad started drinking, and Mom started leaving for days at a time. Before the screaming and slamming doors. Before I became the one who held her when she cried.

I take her hand. "You don't have to pretend with me."

Her eyes glisten, but she just nods, squeezing my fingers. A tear slips down her cheek, and she brushes it away with a smile that almost convinces me it was never there.

Outside, the first drop of rain hits the porch railing.

Then another. And another.

The sky finally opens, and for a moment, we just sit there and listen. The rain hits the forest in waves, a low, steady roar on the leaves and roof above, until it feels like Mother Nature is holding her breath with us.

✦ 13 ✦

Shallow Waters, Deep Cuts

☽ Camp Day 36 ~ August 1st ~ 7 Days to Go ☾

✧ Emilia ✧

The morning tastes like aftermath—wet air heavy with the metallic tang of last night's storm. Mist clings to the lake like gauze, winding through the cedars at the shore as if the storm lost something it's still searching for. The sky is a watercolor bruise—gray bleeding into blue—and the forest feels blurred, like it's still holding its breath. Damp moss scents the air, mingling with the sharp freshness of rain-soaked pine. There's a hush that isn't just quiet, but fractured, like something had broken in the night and nature doesn't know how to fix it.

I pull on my flannel. Not armor today. Just for warmth. Comfort in cotton form. The fabric is soft and faded, worn thin at the elbows. It smells faintly of pine smoke and that clean, subtle scent that always clings to Wes, like something unshakably safe. I wrap it tighter around me like a memory I'm scared I'll lose.

We gather around one of the back corner tables in the mess hall. Wes, with his arm slung over the back of my chair, Sophie tucked into her usual rocking rhythm with a spoonful of untouched oatmeal, Lila scowling into her mug like she wants to set it on fire. Noah sits rigidly, picking apart his toast in silence, while Jesse's already halfway through a melody, head tilted and fingers dancing across her guitar.

The music drifts lazily through the air, filling in the gaps where conversation fails.

"I swear," Lila mutters, clinking her spoon against ceramic with venomous flair, "the only reason my mom put you on lake duty today is because she hates you."

"She doesn't hate me," I say, though the words taste like a lie.

Sophie snorts gently. "She definitely hates you."

"I don't think it's personal," Lila adds, twirling a lock of hair around one finger. "She just hates anyone that doesn't fit into her fake-ass Pleasantville fantasy."

I let out a quiet, crooked laugh. It's too accurate not to, but the sad part is, it's true. I've never been a clean enough line in her picture-perfect coloring book.

Noah glances up briefly, sympathy flickering in his eyes, but he stays quiet. Jesse breaks the tension with a light strum and sings under her breath, "Aubree and Chloe, devil's debutantes…"

Wes squeezes my knee beneath the table, a silent anchor.

It helps. But it doesn't stop the dread from sinking in.

Lake duty. With them. More campers swarming in for sunshine that hasn't even shown up. With Chloe and Aubree prowling the dock like apex predators in slinky bikinis.

Fantastic.

The chill still clings to the morning when I trudge toward the lake, heels sinking into the damp ground. I skip the swimsuit, pulling a dark navy camp shirt I swiped from Wes over a pair of cotton shorts and lacing up my boots like I'm going into battle. I won't be getting in that water; not with the weather, and sure as hell not with them.

The lake stretches out in front of me, wide and cold, the surface glassy except for the lazy drift of fog that snakes along the edges like it doesn't want to let go. I plant myself halfway out on the dock, far enough that the water's deep beneath me so the kids won't be splashing around right at my feet, but I can still keep an eye on my group.

Laughter echoes over the water.

Chloe's giggle is sugar-dipped poison, sharpened for effect.

Tanner's low drawl blends with hers, careless and amused.

My eyes drift to the end of the dock where they're tangled together on the lifeguard stand. Chloe's perched on Tanner's lap in a way that might look innocent from a distance, but up close, every shift of her hips is calculated. Intentional. I can see the thrill she gets from teasing him, from knowing there's nothing he can do about it with all these eyes around.

Last night's memory stirs uninvited. Hiding in the trees. Watching them slip off together, shadows sliding into the boathouse. The flicker of a joint between her fingers. The low, breathy heat of her moans. I remember the way Wes's breath hitched beside me and how mine did too. I knew it was wrong, voyeuristic, but there was something intimate and electric in being pulled into someone else's secret. Like it lit a fuse under my skin.

Watching them now, that same flicker stirs again, heat blooming low in my stomach. My cheeks flush. Shame tangled with lust.

But not for them. Never for them.

It was Wes then. It's Wes now. Always Wes. Every look. Every accidental brush of skin. His hands. His mouth.

Heat coils through me until...

"Aww," Aubree croons behind me, voice sticky-sweet. "Reminiscing about one of your little late-night rendezvous with lover boy?"

I stiffen. Her words land with all the subtlety of a blade slipping between ribs.

She peels off her cover-up like it's a stage reveal, every movement languid, deliberate. Her bikini is hot pink, blindingly bright even under weak sunlight, an announcement, not an outfit. Skin golden, toned, glistening like a photoshopped ad for sin.

"Better enjoy those moments while you can," she purrs, stepping closer, close enough that I can smell her sunscreen and sugar-sweet body spray. "Because soon, all you'll have are those memories."

She winks. And dives.

The splash is clean. Perfect. Of course it is.

I stare at the ripples she leaves behind, stomach twisting. The water churns in soft rings around her as she floats effortlessly on her back, her smirk gleaming like it's carved from cruelty.

"I mean..." she adds, drifting closer, voice all honeyed venom. "Why would he want something like you..."

Her eyes rake down my frame, slow and surgical, carving out pieces I didn't know I was still protecting.

"...when he could have aaallll this?"

Her hands glide down her flawless body like a taunt in slow motion.

She kicks off with a splash and glides away, hair slicked, smile triumphant.

I can't breathe. My chest feels hollow, ribs locked tight as if my lungs forgot how to work. My heart thunders hard enough that I can hear it in my ears, a sickening pulse that drowns out everything else.

My vision narrows to her smirk, cutting through the water like a blade, bright and cruel.

The voice in my head, my mother's voice, slithers out of its cage: "No one's ever gonna want to stick around you. He's too good for you anyway."

I clench my fists. My breath snags in my throat.

I sense it a second too late.

The shift in the air, the way the dock trembles with weight not mine—

Then they hit.

They come at me all at once, barreling across the dock. A coordinated assault. Campers—boys charged up with the energy of Aubree's attention, and her cheers of approval.

A shove.

Hands grab at me.

And then—

The lake swallows me.

Cold. Violent. Loud.

The water is a fist around my throat, yanking me under.

I kick, fight, gasp as I break the surface. My hair sticks to my cheeks. My boots pull me down like weights.

Laughter erupts behind me.

Bright and cruel and fucking endless.

I claw up the ladder, dragging myself free, soaked and shaking, rage and panic tangled in my chest. My hands are shaking so hard I fumble the towel near the bench, snatch it up like a lifeline. The moment I find footing, I run. I don't think. I don't stop. I leave the sound behind, the shock, the ache.

Mattie is a statue by the fire circle. Still. Silent. His eyes locked on mine.

I don't stop to read the look. I run.

✧

The bathhouse is mercifully empty. Steam curls through the air, thick and fragrant.

I strip fast, boots slamming to the floor, soaked shirt peeling from my skin like a second betrayal. I yank on the shower knob too hard and stagger under the blast, scalding water mixing with the salt of my tears.

"Fuck," I gasp.

I lean against the wall, shaking, forehead pressed to the tile. Without warning, the sobs come fast and raw, ripping through me.

I slam a fist weakly against the tile, the sound swallowed by steam. Anger burns hot and useless beneath the grief, coiling in my stomach like something venomous with nowhere to go. I want to scream, to shatter something, to make them feel even a fraction of what they carved out of me. But all I can do is choke on it.

The door slams.

I go still.

That's not the wind.

I spin, heartbeat lurching.

My towel is gone.

"Shit..." I whisper.

I check the benches, the hooks, the corners.

Empty.

No clothes. No cover.

"Are you fucking kidding me?"

Panic claws at my throat. How could I have been so dumb?

I spot my boots near the door. Oh good. But everything else has been ripped away from me.

There's no time. No option. No way out.

I force my feet back into the soaking wet boots—squelching, cold, disgusting—tightening the laces with shaking hands.

"The boots just dragged me down. Now they're all I have."

The wind hisses outside.

They're probably still down at the water. Far enough that maybe, just maybe, I can make it with no one really seeing me like this.

I push the door open and sprint into the field, wearing nothing but wet boots. One arm flies to cover my chest, the other twists behind me to shield what I can.

And I run straight into them.

Chloe and Aubree. Standing center stage.

Chloe twirls my shorts around one finger like a trophy.

"Thought we heard thunder," she sing-songs. "Had to get everyone out of the lake!"

I stumble, gasping, twisting sideways to shield myself as best I can with shaking arms.

Campers stare.

Some laugh.

Some point.

Heat crashes into me like a breaking fever.

My vision sways. The world tilts.

Every laugh slices deeper. Every stare strips me bare.

I don't cry. I won't. I can't.

I bite down hard on my tongue and shove forward.

"Better run back to your little boyfriend, freak," Aubree calls sweetly.

I bite down harder on my tongue and shove forward.

Through the laughter.

Through the fucking humiliation.

Past Mattie, still unmoving by the fire pit, his gaze locked on mine like he sees something I don't understand.

My feet slap the ground, towelless, boots squelching, hands clutched around my body with a death grip.

I stumble. Recover. Keep going.

The cabin looms ahead like a finish line.

I reach the door and throw myself inside.

Collapse onto my bunk.

Blanket up.

No towel.

No clothes.

No dignity.

Just the suffocating silence of humiliation.

✧ Wes ✧

The sun filters through the clouds in patches, sharp and silvery, like light trying to break through something too thick to yield. I'm halfway to the mess hall when I see Sophie running across the gravel path, her curls bouncing wildly, eyes too wide.

"Wes." She grabs my arm, breath catching like she's been holding it the whole way here. "You need to find Emilia."

My stomach drops. "What happened?"

Her voice cracks. "Something bad. At the lake. The girls… the other counselors." She swallows hard, glancing behind her like she's afraid the memory's following. "I was headed to her cabin, but I saw you first."

I don't ask anything else. I just run.

The cabins blur past. Gravel stings under my boots. The air's thick with leftover rain and something bitter I can't name.

I take the steps two at a time and wrench open the door to our cabin.

She's there. Curled in bed like she's trying to disappear. Knees to her chest, face pale and blotchy. Her hair is wet—lake-wet. Dirty. Wrong.

Her eyes meet mine and then flick away fast, like even that hurts.

I cross to her slowly, afraid that if I move too fast, she might shatter.

She doesn't speak right away. Just pulls the blanket tighter. When she does, her voice is a whisper unraveling thread by thread.

She tells me everything.

The dock. The shove. The chilly water swallowing her.

The fucking laughter.

The stolen clothes.

Aubree's voice like venom laced in sugar.

Her boots the only thing left.

And all I can do is sit there, jaw locked, heart howling.

I pull her against me. No words. No plans. Just her tucked under my chin, my arms a wall around her shaking frame.

I don't try to fix it.

I just hold her.

And for once, it feels like it might be enough.

When I finally ask if she wants to get some food, she shakes her head.

"I can't go to the mess hall," she says, voice so small it almost doesn't exist.

I nod, brushing a strand of damp hair from her cheek. "Nature pavilion?" I say gently. "It's quiet. Out of the way."

She hesitates, then gives the smallest nod.

I move slowly, going to her duffel. I pick clothes I know she loves. Not just comfortable, but safe; things she's wrapped herself in on bad days. A soft, oversized t-shirt. Worn-in cutoff jean shorts. Her favorite socks.

I kneel in front of her like it's a ritual, helping her into each piece with careful hands. Like dressing something breakable. Like dressing someone you love.

Her boots are still soaked, so I grab her Converse instead. She doesn't stop me when I lean down to lace them up, just watches, quiet, like maybe letting me help makes it hurt a little less.

She doesn't say much. But when I brush out her hair, her eyes flutter closed. Her body finally starts to breathe again.

And when she ties her braid to the side, I can see it—her fingers still shake, but her spine is a little straighter.

Before we leave, she pulls on the flannel I know better than my own skin.

I watch her settle into it, the way her shoulders square just a little.

She doesn't say why she chooses it. But I know.

She's putting it on like armor.

And I could fucking weep for her.

We walk in silence, the trees tall and drowsy above us, the sky low like it's ashamed of what happened this morning. The grass clings to our shoes. The air smells like wet wood and distant smoke.

Noah's already at the pavilion, laying out maps and sorting gear for the afternoon hike. He hears us coming and looks up. One glance at Emilia, and his

whole posture shifts—jaw set, eyes hard. He doesn't say anything right away. But something passes between us. Something unspoken and old.

"Hey," I say. "Mind if we eat here instead of the mess?"

He just nods. "Of course."

Emilia sinks onto the bench beneath the screened roof like her bones don't quite belong to her. Trees sway around the edges of the clearing, their shadows pooling like protection. The place feels held, wrapped in something quiet.

I kneel beside her, cupping her cheek. "I'll be right back." I place a gentle kiss on her forehead before walking away.

She nods, barely looking up.

I glance at Noah and tilt my head slightly.

Watch her.

He nods. No hesitation.

I cut across the field, boots damp with dew, the mess hall looming ahead like a necessary evil. The clang of dishes filters through the open kitchen window. Inside, Ms. Dee stands at the sink, hands moving in a rhythm older than the camp itself.

She doesn't look up. Doesn't have to.

"Heard 'em all talking about it," she mutters, rinsing a plate and setting it gently on the rack. "Jackals. Circle the weak. Always have."

I swallow the knot rising in my throat.

She jerks her chin toward the counter. "Saved a couple trays. Figured you'd come."

I step forward. There are two trays—sandwiches, sliced fruit. Two peanut butter cookies on one. A large brownie on the other. Not much. But more than enough.

"Added a few treats too..." she says, quieter now. "She's a good kid."

My chest aches. "Thank you."

She just nods once and turns back to the sink.

Outside, I spot Sophie across the field. She sees me and waves Lila over, and they fall into step beside me. They don't ask questions. They don't say anything at all.

Back at the pavilion, Emilia's hunched over her moon phase journal, pen scratching across the page. I can see the shape of her pain—how it coils and clings to her, like something she believes she deserves. How she's been taught to wear shame like a second skin.

And I hate that for her.

I ache for her.

I sit beside her and wrap an arm around her waist. She leans in without hesitation, like gravity knows where she belongs. Her breath isn't quite steady, but it's closer.

Sophie breaks the silence first, her voice thick with fury. "I cannot believe them. What the hell is wrong with people?"

"They're not even funny anymore," Lila snaps, folding her arms tight across her chest. "They're just assholes. Vicious little assholes."

Noah, still by the gear bin, finally speaks. His voice is low. Grounded. Final.

"I saw part of it."

He doesn't look over. Just keeps working. "Told Crystal things are escalating."

He pauses, turns a map over slowly, then looks up. Eyes steady. Calm. Cold.

“They’re gonna push the wrong person too far,” he says. “And someone’s gonna get hurt.”

The words settle like fog in the clearing.

No one moves, no one argues. Because we all feel it. We all know it’s true.

Conversation softens after that. Lila and Sophie gently steer the topic toward the talent show, chatting about ideas, costumes—things they know will lift Emilia at least an inch out of this place.

I shift closer, stealing a glance at the time. I have to get back to Nurse Trudy soon, but I don’t want to move. Not yet.

Emilia stays beside me, tucked into my side like something precious and I hold her a little tighter.

Just in case the world decides to tip again.

✧ Emilia ✧

The sun has burned through the clouds at last, casting long ribbons of gold across the wet grass, but the warmth barely touches me. I walk with Wes toward the open field, his hand wrapped around mine—rough, steady, and warm despite the morning chill. I grip it like a tether to solid ground, afraid that if I let go, the fragile gravity holding me upright might vanish entirely.

I don't want to let go.

But the hike looms ahead—mandatory, inescapable—and I can already see the cluster of campers and counselors beginning to gather in the clearing, their voices floating over the field like birdsong. Normal. Safe. Unaware. My stomach twists.

Sophie and Lila flank my sides before I can take another step. Silent at first, no fanfare, just presence. Like they know words might crumble me. They each give Wes a small nod, subtle but fierce, a mutual understanding passed between them.

"We'll stay close," Sophie says, her voice light but her eyes sharp.

"Real close," Lila adds, tipping her chin—and there's a quiet fire in her that steadies something in me.

Then Jesse appears, ever the jester in denim and charm. She falls into step with a grin that doesn't quite meet her eyes.

"Of course, you know I've always got my eyes on you too," she teases, flashing a wink in a weak

attempt to lift the mood. Her voice is teasing, but it lands softer than usual—like she's trying to summon levity rather than swimming in it.

Sophie groans. "God, Jesse, reel it in."

"Oh, please," Lila scoffs, sliding her sunglasses down her nose to give Jesse a once-over. "You think she's impressed by recycled flirtation?"

Jesse gasps in mock offense. "Excuse me, this is premium-grade flirtation. Refined over years of trial and error."

"That explains a lot," Sophie mutters with a grin.

The banter is easy, familiar. Their rhythm wraps around me like a blanket—frayed, but warm. And for a moment, a breath, a flicker.

I almost smile.

Wes grins at the three of them, all bright teeth and sunshine warmth, but his hand squeezes mine a little tighter before he lets go. "You better bring her back to me," he says, mock stern.

Sophie throws him a salute. Lila flashes a thumbs-up. Jesse tosses a backward peace sign as they start toward Noah, who stands like a general in the middle of the field, clipboard in hand, campers orbiting around him.

But I don't follow yet. I linger.

Wes steps back to me, his eyes searching mine. Not demanding. Just seeing. He lifts his hand to my cheek, his callused thumb tracing a slow, reverent line across my skin.

"I'll be waiting with open arms the second you get back," he murmurs.

When he kisses me, it's soft and warm, a fragile ember glowing in the dark—brief, flickering, like something borrowed from a world I'm not sure we belong to. But beneath that warmth, something deeper simmers, a low hum vibrating through my bones. A promise.

I close my eyes for the briefest second, let myself lean into the feel of him. The steady rhythm of his breath. The way his presence always finds the cracks in my armor and fills them—not to fix me, but to hold me together.

When I open my eyes again, something shifts.

Beyond Wes's shoulder, near the dumpsters at the edge of the mess hall, Mattie stands half-shadowed by slanting light and the thin veil of mist still curling off the wet ground. A rusted engine part lies open at his feet, grease staining his hands and sleeves. A hammer dangles loosely from one fist.

But he isn't focused on the work.

He's watching.

Not the scene. Not the campers. Just them.

The Inner Circle.

His eyes are dark, unreadable, like storm clouds gathering heavy over still water. Not curious. Not kind. Simply watching.

My stomach twists tight, a cold knot tightening with each silent heartbeat.

He doesn't smile, doesn't wave, and for some reason, that's worse.

I turn my face away before he can see the way it unsettles me. The way it clings. But the chill stays lodged beneath my skin, crawling like something cold and wet behind my ribs.

Wes doesn't notice. Or maybe he does and just doesn't ask. Either way, he squeezes my hand once more before stepping back, his eyes holding mine until the last possible second. I nod, barely, then force my legs to carry me forward.

Across the field, Sophie, Lila, and Jesse are waiting. Like lifelines stretched across a tide I'm afraid to cross.

This is the part where I keep going. Where I pretend not to notice what's unraveling beneath my feet.

My steps start slow. Each footfall is heavy, like I'm dragging pieces of the morning with me. But the air smells cleaner now—sunlight warming damp grass, woodsmoke curling faintly on the breeze—the kind of scent that belongs to quiet mornings and things that feel far away.

I focus on that. I let the rhythm of my breath anchor me. Each inhale a thread, each exhale a knot. In, out. In, out. Like stitching myself back together, one quiet breath at a time.

But some seams feel too thin.

And I don't know how long they'll hold.

The tightness in my chest loosens. Just a little.

Wes's kiss still lingers on my lips—warm and grounding, like a touch I tucked into my pocket.

But the weight of Mattie's stare clings to me like fog.

I rub the back of my neck, trying to chase the sensation away, fingers brushing the skin where his gaze settled.

It doesn't help.

Still, I keep walking.

I don't look back—not at the shadows pooling behind me, not at the storm biding its time, not at the eyes I still feel pressed into my skin like fingerprints in wet cement.

Something lingers.

Thick and invisible.

Watching. Waiting.

And I don't know if it's reaching for me... or wanting to see if I'll break.

Collateral

✧ The Hunter ✧

The fog is lifting, wisps of it still tangled in the upper boughs of cedar and Douglas fir like ghosts reluctant to leave. The ground is still damp from last night's storm, moss dark and spongy underfoot, and the air carries the faint, resinous scent of pine and wet earth. The camp is emptying one footstep at a time toward the trailhead; their laughter thins as they disappear into the woods, a parade of oblivious souls playing summer.

I watch from the trees just beyond the mess hall. I don't hide. I never have to. People rarely look past their own stories long enough to notice what's watching them. Especially here. Especially now.

Chloe leans against the mess hall doorway like it owes her something. One hip popped, her expression the usual bored disdain. Crystal stands in front of her, arms crossed, jaw tight. Chloe mutters something about nausea, about not feeling well. I can't hear every word, but the tone says enough.

For a moment, Crystal hesitates. It's faint, but it's there, that flicker of feigned concern, like a thread about to be pulled. Then her face hardens. She waves Chloe off with an irritated flick of her fingers, saying, "Whatever. Do what you want."

And just like that, when no one's around, Crystal's mask unravels.

Across the clearing, Jesse lingers behind the others, her voice lifting in some flirtatious joke meant for Emilia. I watch Emilia walking beside Sophie and Lila, three girls moving as one. Protective. Guarded. The dynamic bends around Emilia like a campfire everyone wants near but fears getting too close to. They orbit her in quiet protection, pretending they aren't afraid of what might happen if they look away.

And Lila... Lila Vaughn is nothing like her mother. I've watched them both. The mother is all polished image with rot beneath. But the daughter? There's something real in her. Some wildness still intact. The world should count itself lucky.

The last of the group disappears into the trees. The camp quiets. Even the birds seem to hush.

Inside the kitchen, Chloe brushes past Miss Dee. She mutters something about being relieved Crystal bought the act.

"Thank God she believed me. No way I was going on that stupid hike."

No intention of hiking, no interest in heat or bugs or bonding. As if any of this is surprising.

Dee doesn't even look up from her prep, just grumbles something low and sharp.

"Yeah, yeah. Nobody's surprised, sweetheart."

A woman who sees more than she says. I like her.

Chloe slips out the back door, cigarette already perched between her fingers. Coffee, in the other hand. Her little ritual. She heads for the patch of gravel near the recycling bins, her usual spot.

I don't follow, not yet. I wait, all around me, the camp is still. Doors shut, windows sleep behind drawn curtains. The trees draw long shadows across the dirt, and it feels like the forest itself is holding its breath.

There's a quiet before violence. A lull. Reverent. Sacred. And it's almost time.

Standing alone, arms crossed, chin high, trying to look unbothered. Her cigarette burns like a fuse.

Even the birds seem to still, as if the forest knows what's about to happen. The world holds its breath, waiting for the violence.

I watch from the shadows. Still. Invisible.

She lied, of course. Not about the nausea. Not about the heat. Just about caring. She never cared to come, never cared to show up for anyone but herself. Today wasn't different in that way, but her cruelty was.

Sharper.

Directed.

Something in her had shifted. I'd felt it at breakfast, seen it in the way she looked at Emilia, like a girl she wanted to peel the skin from just to see what was underneath.

Chloe always carried venom, but today, she'd spit it with purpose.

I step forward. Quiet as breath, as shadow. The pine needles don't crunch beneath my feet. She doesn't hear me.

She's smirking to herself, lips curled like she's remembering something awful and enjoying it all over again.

Typical.

She's always been a plague in a pretty package.

I don't give her the satisfaction of seeing me coming.

My hand wraps around her throat in one clean motion. She startles like prey, a sharp inhale that never finishes. Her eyes widen, but her body's too slow, too spoiled by years of never needing to run.

My grip finds the hollow beneath her jaw—that fragile bridge between breath and terror.

I drive her into the siding. It cracks in protest, a brittle gasp that feels almost human.

She gags on instinct, nails raking down my forearm, skin breaking beneath her frantic scrabbling. Her legs kick out, catching air. Her coffee spills, splashing hot against her thigh before the cup clatters to the gravel with a wet thud.

The cigarette drops and rolls beneath a bin, forgotten.

The cigarette's bitter stink fuses with scorched coffee and the sharp tang of sweat. It coats my tongue. Burrows into my lungs. A scent that smells too much like memory.

I don't speak. There's nothing to say.

Her breath hitches and stutters. Then stops.

Her face blossoms with color, rosy pink to violent red to something near purple as the pressure builds. Her eyes bulge slightly, mouth opening on a broken, voiceless rasp.

Her lips twitch, forming the ghost of some last, clever cruelty. But the words die in her mouth, silenced like the rest of her.

There's no audience now. No mirror to admire her venom. Just dirt and air and me.

She tries to buck forward, but her weight is nothing. A girl wrapped in brittle bones and ego.

Her body weakens, limbs twitching in dying resistance.

Then, a shift.

That final tremor.

The way her hands stop clawing and instead slide uselessly down my arms.

And the moment her eyes—those bright, mean eyes—flicker. Dim.

Gone.

Stillness overtakes her like a decision. One I made for her.

I hold her one second longer. Two. Just to be sure.

I can no longer feel her pulse beneath my fingers.

It disappears. Not fades—disappears.

I let go.

She drops like wet laundry, limp and graceless in the dirt. Her cheek hits stone. No breath follows.

She's quiet now. Finally. The air feels cleaner now, without her in it.

There's no need for flair. No performance. She wasn't worth the poetry.

But just as I turn to vanish, a flicker of movement stops me.

Tanner.

He ambles across the clearing, headed toward the lake, humming some lazy tune. His shoulders slouch in that perpetual stoner sprawl, like the world doesn't exist unless he feels like looking at it.

He doesn't glance my way. Doesn't pause. But I can't shake the feeling.

Did he see?

I can't be sure.

And I can't afford to be wrong.

So I follow.

The dock groans beneath Tanner's weight as he settles at the edge, feet dangling over the lake like he's ten years old again and the world is safe. He flicks his lighter open and closed—rhythmic, bored. Then lights a joint and breathes it in like a blessing.

He hums again, off-key, lazy. Content.

Inside the boathouse, I watch through a narrow seam in the slats. The cool wood walls close around me, still damp with lake air. The scent of pine and mold, old oil, and rusted hooks.

I'm still shaking from Chloe. Not fear. Not guilt. Just adrenaline. Stillness pretending to be calm.

This wasn't the plan. Tanner wasn't meant to die today.

But he'd wandered into the path of it. Too close. Too soon.

He isn't art. He isn't even a challenge. Just a risk I can't afford to leave breathing.

I step out into the light.

He hears me just before the first blow. His head turns, mouth already parting in lazy curiosity.

Then the oar connects with a hollow, meaty crack, like wet wood splitting.

The sound lands heavy in the air, then bounces back from the water's edge. The lake flinches. So do I.

His head snaps sideways, blood blooming across his temple in a jagged fan, dripping instantly down his neck and soaking the collar of his tank top.

He slumps, dazed, barely catching himself on an elbow. His eyes go wide with incomprehension, like he's still catching up.

"Wha—?"

Another strike, lower this time, across the jaw. Bone gives. Teeth splinter. His head whips sideways, and a spray of red speckles the wood behind him. He tries to crawl away, but doesn't make it more than a foot before I bring the oar down again.

And again.

Skull meeting wood. Over and over.

Each strike fractures the world a little more.

Bone cracks. Blood gurgles. Breath turns into a bubbling whimper.

It's not normally rage that drives me, not quite. It's the weight of inevitability. The ugly, graceless kind.

Rage drives me now. Cold, focused rage—not because I hate him. Because I can't leave loose ends.

The top of his head splits open like fruit under pressure. Blood soaks the boards. His fingers twitch.

Then, nothing.

Just my breath, ragged and real, and the slow groan of the dock settling beneath me.

The soft lap of the lake.

And the creak of the dock beneath us.

Tanner lies splayed on his back, limbs bent wrong, one eye open and glazed.

Blood seeps between the damp boards, dripping into the dark water below. The smell of iron mingles with the lake's algae-sweet rot.

I don't stage this one. No reason. This isn't art. It's removal.

I grab his wrists and drag him to the edge. His head bumps once against the wood with a dull knock.

Then I let go.

He vanishes beneath the surface without a sound, the water swallowing him whole.

I crouch there, breathing hard, watching the water settle. The silence feels too loud.

I wait for guilt. It doesn't come. Just the ache in my forearms. Just the quiet.

My fingers close around the rusted handle of the old bucket that hangs from the dock.

Scoop. Splash. I rinse the blood from the planks. From my skin. From my face.

The water is cold. Bracing. Honest.

Another scoop. Another rinse.

When it's done, the dock is just damp.

The lake looks the same.

But I know it's not.

Something has changed.

Something has deepened.

The lake remembers.

And so do I.

I vanish into the trees once more.

Quiet. Unhurried.

Like I was never there at all.

15

Echoes and Embers

✧ Wes ✧

The sunlight slants low through the trees, gold and amber pooling across a forest floor still damp from morning fog. It's the kind of late afternoon light that makes everything feel softer, slower—like even time itself is exhaling. The group fans out into the main clearing as they return from the hike, voices overlapping with the kind of tired contentment that only comes after hours in the sun. But the second I spot her, it all fades.

My stomach dips, sharp and sudden, like missing a step in the dark. It's ridiculous—hours, not days—but her absence hit harder than I'd admit to anyone else.

She's standing near the edge of the campfire circle, backlit like something out of a fever dream, dirt smudged on her leg, a few loose strands of hair curling around her face. I barely remember moving—just that suddenly, she's in my arms.

It's breathless. Exaggerated. A reunion that has no right to feel this intense after just a few hours, but we cling to each other like we've been pulled from wreckage. I wrap both arms around her and press my face into her neck. She's warm. Real. Home.

Sophie groans, dramatic and fond. "Okay, Romeo, we were gone for like... three hours."

Behind her, Lila sips from her water bottle and giggles, eyes twinkling. "Let them have their moment. It's kinda cute."

Emilia tilts her face up to mine, and I rest my forehead against hers. The air between us crackles, familiar and electric. I breathe her in, grounding myself in the scent of sun-warmed skin and that smell that's distinctly her—that always makes me want to bury my face in her shoulder and stay there.

Something in my chest unknots. Like I've been underwater without realizing it, and she's the first breath I've taken in hours.

Her fingers are warm, but her grip's a little too tight, like she's bracing against something only she can feel. It's small, almost nothing—but it feels like the tremor before a quake, a tension that doesn't belong in a moment like this. I skim a knuckle under her chin and tilt her face toward mine. "Hey." Her eyes flick up—not startled, guarded. Something about it makes my chest go tight.

"You good?" I murmur, low, just for her.

Her fingers tighten at my waist. "I am now."

Lila and Sophie have launched into trail stories, animated and breathless as they describe umbrella-shaped mushrooms, a camper who nearly passed out when a garter snake slithered past his ankle, and a tree that looked like it was bleeding sap.

I smile, half-listening, nodding along. But my eyes keep drifting back to Emilia. The way her lashes fan against her cheek when she blinks. The quiet way she leans into me like she doesn't even realize she's doing it.

And then...

"Returned her safe and sound!" Jesse sings out, slinging an arm around Emilia like she's showing off a victory. "And still totally in love with you, despite my very best efforts to steal her heart."

Emilia hides her face in my shoulder with a soft, embarrassed giggle.

I laugh, the sound catching in my chest. "Guess I'll keep her then."

My thumb brushes over her hip, tracing slow, idle circles. I don't know what's coming next, but I know I'll hold on as long as she lets me.

✧ Emilia ✧

We don't make even five steps before the air shifts. Something's wrong.

Near the mess hall, voices drop into hushed confusion. A cluster of people stands frozen, backs to us, whispering and staring in the same direction.

The way everyone's standing—rigid, necks craned like something unspoken is holding them there—tells me it's not just rumor. And just like that, the gravity snaps and I float, unmoored.

Chloe.

She's sprawled near the back wall of the mess hall, limbs bent wrong, as if someone had dropped a marionette mid-performance. Her skin looks waxy in the patchy shade, too still, too pale for summer heat. A clump of hair clings to her cheek, damp, and limp. Her mouth is parted, like she was about to say something.

I stop walking.

All the breath in my lungs turns to stone.

Crystal's voice cuts through the silence like a scalpel. "Heat exhaustion," she says, loud and overly clear. "Poor girl didn't say anything until it was too late."

Her tone is strained, fake concern painted over something brittle and cold.

I move closer, trying to see past the blur of limbs and faces. There's something off. The bruising on Chloe's neck is subtle, but unmistakable. A shadow, a bloom of pressure, just under the surface.

And the wall behind her—

The mess hall's siding is dented, the wood splintered inward, like the building itself remembers what happened even if no one will say it out loud.

My skin goes cold.

I blink, willing the image to shift, to prove me wrong. But it stays the same. The bruises. The dent. The stillness that doesn't belong to sleep.

A rumble breaks the moment, a low mechanical groan that pulls everyone's attention. A van appears at the edge of the trees, familiar in a way that makes my stomach twist.

It's the same one that took Zach—and my stomach drops.

Only, it's not a coroner stepping out.

It's Mattie.

He climbs out of the driver's side like he's done it a hundred times before, casual and practiced.

I feel myself start to float, like the world has lifted an inch off its axis. Like nothing is anchored the way it should be.

Why is Mattie driving?

And if he's driving now... was he the one driving that day, too?

Crystal claps her hands with forced cheer. "Alright, campers, time to head to dinner!"

Then, too loud, too bright: "You three—Mason, Noah, Wes—can you help Mattie with the... uh..."

She pauses.

"Body? We need to get her... into town."

Her choice of words makes my skin crawl.

Mason shrugs with a dark laugh. "Always knew she'd go out dramatically. Honestly kinda fitting."

Noah's reaction is instant. His face tightens, jaw clenched. "Not funny," he snaps. "Shut up."

But Wes—

Wes doesn't speak.

He just looks at me.

Our eyes meet and in the quiet stretch between us, I feel it: the weight of everything neither of us is saying.

I don't move. I just wait.

A tether of silence pulling taut.

And beneath it, the slow rot of something I can't name.

✧

The mess hall is quieter than usual.

There's still the usual din of trays being slid along the buffet line and the occasional burst of laughter from somewhere too far away to feel real, but everything sounds a little muffled. Like the walls are listening. Like the air remembers.

I follow Wes inside, and for a moment, I don't breathe. The overhead lights feel brighter. The smell of grease and ketchup turns my stomach,

cloying and heavy in the already close, humid air. A dozen conversations swirl together in forced, brittle tones, but no one says her name.

Wes and I drift to our table in silence. I don't remember sitting down—just the feel of the bench under me and the way his knee nudges mine beneath the table. He hasn't let go of my hand since we left the counselor cabin, and I'm not ready to ask him to.

Around us, counselors and campers eat like they've convinced themselves this is just another Thursday. Brianna is picking at a salad, her gold bracelets clinking softly every time she stabs at a crouton. Valentina chews gum with exaggerated slowness, blowing a pink bubble that bursts too loud for the room's uneasy hush. Jesse hasn't touched her food.

No one talks about the fact that Chloe's bed is empty.

No one talks about the gurney that rolled behind the kitchen just hours ago.

They're all waiting to see who breaks first.

Across the mess hall, someone drops a cup. It clatters to the floor and rolls under a table. No one moves to pick it up. The sound echoes longer than it should.

Then I hear them.

Brianna. Aubree. Mason. Whispering too loudly to really be whispers—the kind of whispering meant to be overheard.

"I swear he's just... gone," Brianna says, her voice pitched just enough to carry. "No one's seen him since the hike."

"Tanner?" Mason asks, feigning innocence. "Didn't he and Chloe used to fuck?"

Aubree snorts, flipping her hair. "Used to? Please. Hooking up with him is probably why she faked sick to skip the hike."

There's a pause. Long enough for the air to thicken.

The whole mess hall seems to lean in without meaning to—forks pause halfway to mouths, chairs stop creaking mid-shift. Everyone is listening, pretending not to.

Then Brianna again, voice curling sharp at the edges. "And now she's dead. And he's just what? Missing?"

A plastic fork snaps between someone's fingers. Across the room, heads turn.

"I'm just saying," Mason adds, shrugging. "It's weird. And people are talking."

"Maybe it wasn't heat exhaustion after all," Aubree murmurs. She says it like she's not sure if she believes it. Like she wants someone else to confirm it first.

My stomach twists.

I lean in close to Wes, my voice low enough that only he can hear it. "There were bruises," I whisper. "On her neck. You saw them too, didn't you?"

His jaw tightens, but he doesn't answer right away. I watch the muscle twitch near his temple, the flicker of something cold in his eyes. His fingers press slightly harder around mine, anchoring me.

"I saw them," he says finally, just above a breath.

I nod, heart racing. "Then why would Crystal say heat exhaustion? Why lie unless... unless there's something worse?" My voice breaks on the last word. "Unless she's covering for someone."

He turns toward me, resting his forearm along the table so we're shielded, tucked into our own small world.

"I don't know," he says. "But you're not wrong."

The words steady me—more than they should. It shouldn't matter this much—just hearing someone else confirm what I saw—but it does. It feels like the only thing tethering me to reality, like proof I'm not losing my grip.

"But what can we do?" he adds softly. "We go to Crystal, she shuts it down. We say it out loud, and suddenly we're the ones spreading rumors. Maybe they want this to blow over. Maybe that's the point."

I stare down at my tray, appetite long gone. A smear of ketchup looks like blood.

"She made my life hell," I whisper. "But this? Pretending she just... collapsed and that's the end of it?" I shake my head, throat burning. "That's not right. And Crystal knows it."

Wes doesn't say anything at first. Just watches me like he's trying to take some of the weight from my shoulders without asking for it.

Outside, the last rays of sunlight filter through the windows, casting long shadows over the mess hall.

The murmurs around us fade into a dull hum, like the world is holding its breath.

I squeeze Wes's hand once, then pull it back slowly, my fingers brushing against his palm like I'm afraid to let go but know I have to.

"We'll figure it out," he says quietly, as if promising both of us.

I nod, even though the knot in my chest tightens.

The tray in front of me is forgotten. Somewhere behind us, a screen flickers with the camp's old home videos—laughing faces, bonfires, summer days that feel impossibly far away.

I watch the shadows crawl up the walls, distorted by the flickering screen at the front of the room. For the first time since everything started, I let the silence settle heavy between us, like ash after a fire.

Maybe that's all the truth can be for now—unspoken, waiting, ready to burn when the spark finally hits.

✦ 16 ✦

What the Silence Hides

☽ Camp Day 37 ~ August 2nd ~ 6 Days to Go ☾

✧Emilia✧

The sun filters through the screened windows of the craft cabin in slow, syrupy rays, casting gold flecks across the warped floorboards. It's too bright, too still. The scent of pressed flowers and school glue lingers in the air like it belongs to another time. Maybe a safer time.

Outside, the trees sway in lazy arcs, their branches etched dark against a sky that feels too big for the room I'm in. I can almost smell the wet pine seeping in through the screens, a green, resin-thick breath that doesn't belong to the careful neatness of pressed flowers. It's the wrong kind of calm — the kind that makes every creak feel like an accusation.

Sophie hums as she sketches, her pencil strokes delicate and sure. Lila's laugh bubbles up nearby, soft and fleeting, like wind catching the edge of a curtain. Around us, campers whisper and giggle, scissors snipping through dried petals and sun-faded paper, as if the world didn't tilt sideways yesterday.

I stare at the materials—paintbrush poised above a scrap of sun print—but I don't move. I can't remember what I'd meant to paint, or if I even cared.

Chloe's face won't leave me alone. Not the smirk she used to wear like armor; the one from yesterday—slack, empty. Her fingers are still curled, as if trying to hold on to something.

There were bruises.

There was a dent in the wall.

And Crystal smiled like she had something to prove.

A breeze catches through the screen, lifting the edge of a paper towel and sending it tumbling. I track its path as if anything could hold my attention longer than the static in my chest.

And then—a knock.

I glance up, my heart already recognizing the rhythm before my eyes catch up. Wes leans against the doorframe, backlit and casual, but something deliberate sits in the tilt of his shoulders. His smile is small, barely there, but it cuts through the fog in my head like a knife through gauze. His eyes catch mine like he's been looking for them all day. For a moment, the cabin feels less airless, like he's brought the outside with him. The sight hits me low in the chest, a quiet thud, like the ground shifting under my feet. I didn't realize how badly I needed to be found until now.

"Hey," he says, voice low but warm. "Noah could use a hand at the nature pavilion. Can you spare Emilia?"

Harper waves a dismissive hand without looking up. "Go on. We'll manage."

I'm already moving before she finishes the sentence, paintbrush forgotten, heart stuttering as I follow Wes out the door.

Because I know.

Noah didn't send for me.

✧Wes✧

The second she clears the door, I shift my hand to her back—gentle, not pushing, just there. A quiet promise. I can feel how tightly she's holding herself together, like her bones are trying to outrun whatever her mind won't let her say out loud.

We don't talk right away.

We just walk.

There's a stillness to her steps—not peaceful, but deliberate, as if the wrong sound will draw something out of the trees.

The air is heavier here, draped in the scent of wet soil and sun-warmed cedar. Ferns crowd the path edges, their fronds brushing my legs when the trail narrows, and somewhere deeper in the woods, water moves—not enough to see, but enough to hear if you listen.

The trail winds through the trees; pine needles crunch underfoot, the air thick with that humid, green scent that only comes after weeks of heat. Birds chirp somewhere overhead. The world keeps spinning, pretending not to notice a girl died yesterday and no one wants to call it what it was.

When we're far enough from camp that the silence feels like a blanket instead of a cage, I finally say it.

"You looked like you needed air."

That's all. No pressure. No demand for explanation. Just space.

We veer off the path toward the hollow just beyond the ridge where sunlight breaks through like it remembers us. I settle with my back against our tree, legs stretched out, and she drops her head into my lap. After a breath, she lies back, her eyes finding mine—wide, quiet, brimming with questions she won't speak.

I thread my fingers through her hair, not because it will fix anything but because she needs to feel how much she matters. "I'm here with you, babe."

✧Emilia✧

I don't know how to say it.

The words feel ugly. Ungrateful. Wrong.

But I say them anyway.

"I don't feel what I'm supposed to feel."

I pick at a splinter in the tree's roots, letting the silence thicken until it presses against my teeth. My mouth tastes like I've bitten into a penny.

Wes doesn't flinch; he just keeps twirling a strand of my hair around his finger like we're talking about the weather.

"I keep waiting to feel something," I whisper. "Sadness, guilt... anything that would make me feel like a decent person. But it's just not there. Or," I pause, the words scraping on the way out, "it's there, but not the way it's supposed to be. I remember feeling the same way when Zach died. Everyone thought I was heartbroken, but I was just... free. And now with Chloe..." I shake my head. "It's worse. I'm relieved, Wes. And I hate that I am."

The words hang there, ugly, and raw, and I want to scrape them back into my mouth before they can rot the air between us.

Wes looks down at me, brow furrowed, steady, and warm. "That doesn't make you a monster," he says.

My throat tightens. "You're sure?"

"I'm sure." His hand finds my cheek, thumb brushing along the bone. "She hurt you. Intentionally. You don't owe her grief."

"But everyone else—"

"Everyone else didn't live inside your skin."

I blink hard, trying not to let the heat behind my eyes fall.

He's quiet for a moment, then softer still: "And even if it wasn't an accident... I'm not sure everyone would call it wrong."

The forest stills around us; the breeze pauses mid-breath. My heartbeat thunders so loud it feels like the moss beneath me should be trembling.

I stare up at him, breath stuck. I don't know how to name it, but I know what he means.

I sit up, and before I can overthink it, I'm in his lap, arms locked around his neck. He holds me like he always does—like I'm something worth protecting.

We kiss. Slow. Steady. Like we're remembering how to exist without apology.

I pull back enough to rest my forehead against his. "It's a shame we have to go back."

He smiles, tired and real. "Yeah."

"It's only in these stolen pockets of time that I feel like I can actually breathe."

"Then we'll keep stealing them."

His lips brush mine again—soft, sure—and for a few seconds the weight of the world disappears.

Dinner hums with brittle cheer—smiles stretched too thin over a crack no one wants to look at. Even the light feels performative—gold slanting through the windows as if it's trying too hard. Every laugh comes a half beat too loud; every scrape of a tray

sounds like a door shutting on a conversation no one will have.

Camp is wrapped in gold; dusk flares off the mess hall windows, trees casting shadows like long fingers across the dirt. Inside, voices rise in forced bursts as the scrape of metal trays and shuffle of chairs fill the gaps where no one dares say her name.

I sit close to Wes, pressed into his side like it's the only thing that makes sense. He runs his thumb across the back of my hand under the table, casual and constant—a tether.

At our table, the world pretends everything is fine.

Sophie and Lila sketch talent-show ideas on a napkin. Jesse and Valentina trade song lines and argue over chords. Someone jokes about glitter and glue; laughter follows like muscle memory.

But beneath all of it, the wrongness coils—a thread pulled too tight under the surface.

No one talks about Chloe.

Or the van.

Or the way Crystal keeps floating through every room like she's glitched into a different reality.

And then—she's here.

Crystal glides toward our table, all teeth and honeyed efficiency. "Emilia," she says, voice bright and brittle. "Can I borrow you for something?"

I sit up, pulse snapping. "Sure."

"Aubree too; we need the karaoke machine from the old hall."

Aubree groans dramatically. "Why me? Send Mason out there."

Crystal's smile tightens. "You'll manage."

Aubree throws the full wattage of flirt at Wes. "Sure you don't wanna come help me instead? Could be fun." She bites her lip and gives him a come-hither look.

He doesn't rise to the bait. "I'm good right here," he says.

She pouts. I don't speak.

I already know we're going.

And I already know how it'll go—the words, the tension, the silence between them that cuts sharper than anything she'll say.

The woods swallow us quickly.

Camp sounds slide away behind us, replaced by gravel crunch and cicadas. The air smells of damp leaves, moss, and something older—an underlying rot of wood and time. The path to the old camp hall is barely visible now, overgrown and choked with thistle; the kind of place you forget exists until someone drags you toward it.

Blackberry brambles snag at my jeans, thorns catching like they don't want to let go. The canopy thickens; the air cools and the light dims until it feels later than it is.

A thin ribbon of mist threads low between the trunks, and the shadows take on that deep, green-black shade that makes it hard to tell where one tree ends and the next begins.

Aubree keeps pace beside me, ponytail swinging, voice slicing through the quiet. "You know he flirts back when you're not around, right?"

I don't answer.

She smiles, all teeth. "Wes. He's sweet, yeah. But that doesn't mean he doesn't want better."

Still I say nothing.

She moves closer. "He could have anyone. Someone lighter. Someone fun."

Her words slide under my skin like barbs—sharp, deliberate, planting something toxic.

But I don't show it.

I keep walking.

The old camp hall looms into view like a forgotten memory—roof sagging, shutters askew, a skeleton of its former self. The kind of place that used to hold laughter and now holds echoes.

Aubree sighs. "Seriously? For a karaoke machine?"

But I'm not listening to her anymore.

I'm listening to the quiet.

To the weight of the air.

To the sense that something is waiting inside.

Not a machine. Not a ghost. Something deeper—something waiting.

17

Smells Like Secrets

✧The Hunter✧

The sky bruises violet as the last of the daylight bleeds into the trees. I linger at the edge of the trail above the old path, shadows spilling long from the pine and hemlock that shield me. From here, hidden beneath their hush, I watch two figures just ahead—Emilia and Aubree. Unaware. Unbothered. Their voices carry on the still air like smoke.

I don't need to see Emilia's face to read the truth in her spine. Shoulders drawn high, body wound like wire ready to snap. The tension is alive in her, almost luminous.

Aubree's voice slices through it—sharp, saccharine, threaded with cruelty dressed up as charm. Poison in a perfume bottle. She's taunting her. Twisting something that still bleeds.

I can tell who it's about by the way Emilia flinches, the way Aubree sharpens her voice like a blade. I recognize the shape of the wound before I hear it spoken.

My head tilts. Curious.

There's a kind of person who kicks what's already broken. Who sees a crack and jams their fingers into it—not out of panic, not for self-preservation. Just for fun. A certain sickness in that. I study her the way a biologist might study a diseased animal. Not with malice. With interest. Awe, even.

It stirs in me like the hush before a storm, a reverence that tastes almost holy. To witness cruelty in its purest form is to be reminded why I was made for this.

People like her, creatures of rot and spectacle, don't belong in the natural order.

What I do isn't rage. It's not revenge. It's restoration. Balance. Silence where there was noise. Stillness where there was chaos.

There's a rhythm to it—a method. A ritual. Not for gods or ghosts. Just for the world to breathe a little easier again.

They push through the warped double doors of the abandoned camp hall. Their flashlights flicker like dying stars, swallowed up by the dark inside. Most see rot. Mildew. A crumbling shell of something that once mattered.

But I see beauty.

Decay is the most honest form of art. Moss in the cracks, vines threading through shattered windows like veins crawling back to a long-dead body. The scent of mold and old wood rises like incense in a forgotten chapel. To most, this is death.

To me, it's rebirth.

The door groans closed behind them.

I listen to the hush that follows, the gap they leave behind. My hands itch to fill it.

And I move. Slow. Silent. The woods exhale around me. No need to rush.

I already know how this ends.

And in my mind, it's beautiful.

✧Emilia✧

The old camp hall stretches in front of us like the fossilized ribcage of some giant, long-dead animal. Skeletal beams arch above, groaning with every shift of the wind. The air inside is thick and sour—mildew, wet wood, and something else beneath it. Sharp. Acrid. Like the ghost of a cleaner left to rot.

I wrinkle my nose and sidestep a tilting stack of gear crates, brushing my fingers along the cool metal edge to steady myself.

This place doesn't look like storage. It looks like a cemetery.

The silence presses closer here, padded with mildew and shadow. It feels less like a building holding old things and more like the building itself is the dead thing, its ribs split open to show the rot inside.

Busted paint cans. Mold-ridden felt hats. Plastic bins sunk halfway into the floor like the building itself gave up trying to hold them. Abandoned junk from a camp trying to pretend it's still fully functioning. Still innocent.

Aubree snorts behind me, too loud in the quiet. "This is a graveyard. Why the hell would Crystal think karaoke was a good idea?"

"I don't get this shit either," I mutter, flicking cobwebs off an old duffel bag. My voice cuts sharper than I mean it to, but I don't bother softening it. "Probably thinks music will distract everyone long enough to forget one of your friends just died."

It lands. I hope it does. I want it to.

Because I'm sick of watching everyone pretend. Pretend Chloe's death wasn't suspicious. Pretend this camp is still some idyllic, golden-summer bullshit.

Aubree mutters something I don't catch—thin, defensive. She turns toward another teetering stack of boxes. "If I find a raccoon in here, I'm quitting."

The image flashes in my mind—Aubree shrieking as a raccoon lunges at her fake lashes. It makes me smirk. A real one. Fleeting, but there.

I move deeper into the hall, stepping lightly. The decay is thicker back here, the air colder. My flashlight narrows into a pale ribbon slicing through shadow. It feels like the building is watching.

Every shift of my light feels answered, like shadow sliding just out of sight. My skin prickles. Not with cold. With attention.

Behind me, something creaks—not loud, but deep, like old wood remembering how to breathe. I freeze. Just the building settling, I tell myself. Just that.

To the left, a narrow archway sags like a tired sigh. Between two cabinets, tucked just out of reach. It might've been an office once. Or a practice room. Now it looks like a mouth ready to collapse in on itself.

I step through.

It's barely a room. Shelves buckle under the weight of forgotten instruments—guitars curled in on themselves, snapped strings like dead vines. A tambourine with a crack through the center. A ukulele with half its body missing. Music stands rusted at the joints.

I sweep my beam slowly. It's like looking through bones.

If the karaoke machine Crystal insisted still exists is anywhere, it'll be here.

I crouch, knees popping in protest, and lean beneath a collapsed table in the corner. It smells like dust, varnish, and something older. Something hidden.

Part of me hopes I don't find it.

Another part—quiet, sunken—hopes I do.

Just to have something to do.

Something that isn't thinking.

Something simple. Harmless.

Anything to stop the looping reel of Chloe's laugh, Chloe's absence, the space she left behind that everyone's too scared to name. Even a stupid karaoke machine feels like a rope to grab before I sink.

I should've known better.

✧The Hunter✧

I'm already inside.

The hall is a hushed cathedral of rot. Every breath tastes like mildew and old fear. Beneath it, I catch the bite of cedar and wet pine drifting in through the cracks — the forest's reminder that rot always feeds something living.

I move like water through shadow—silent, constant—drawn by the ghost-swirl of flashlight beams and a blurred figure ducking out of sight.

Not her. Not now.

Still... her presence stirs something. Tightens the thread. Sharpens the blade.

Her scent lingers faintly in the air—sweat, fear, shampoo masking it. Beneath it, the copper of possibility. I could follow it blind.

Let her stay hidden. I have something else to do first.

A voice slices through the stillness. Sharp. Mocking. Something about raccoons.

I still. Tilt my head.

Her. The intended one.

Aubree.

Noise in human form. She floods the world with it, choking out the silence like weeds in a grave. Pretty, yes. But hollow. Vicious. She plays at charm the way some people play with knives—grinning as they draw blood. She never sees the rot in herself.

But I do. And tonight, I respond to it.

My fingers flex around the handle of the knife—long, matte black, balanced just right. Ritual

settles over me as I adjust the bandanna over my face. Not for disguise. For focus. For breath.

Every step is a promise.

She's muttering to herself, wrestling with something heavy. The karaoke machine.

Her back is to me. Then she half-turns, arms full, smirking like she's about to say something clever.

And sees me.

Her eyes widen—shock first, then something else. Not disbelief. Not confusion.

Something behind her eyes clicks. A memory. A face. Her lips part like she might laugh it off, like this is some twisted joke she's in on.

There's calculation in it, too — the split-second gleam of someone who thinks charm might still save her.

She takes a single step back. Then another. Before her eyes land on the knife, voice catching, unsure: "What the fuc—"

Everything in her halts. The kind of fear that only comes when it's already too late.

I move.

The knife punches through the fabric of her shirt and sinks deep, low into the soft meat just above her hip. The air leaves her in a strangled wheeze, shock stealing her voice, her strength—everything. Her eyes go huge. Her mouth works around a scream that won't come. Her legs buckle inward like a puppet with snapped strings.

The hilt thuds home like a knock and I wrench the blade sideways.

Something tears. Wet. Sickening. A spray of warmth hits my wrist. Her scream rips free at last—high and broken, jagged with real pain. The karaoke machine crashes to the floor, the sound a violent punctuation. Cords tangle around her legs as she stumbles backward, blood streaking across the linoleum in wild, messy arcs.

She runs and I let her.

Three stumbling steps but then I'm on her.

We collide. My arm closes around her throat like a vise.

She kicks, thrashes, heel slamming into my shin. Her nails catch my arm, drawing lines of heat. The knife drives in again—higher, harder, angled up beneath her ribs. I feel it hit something solid, then give.

She gurgles. Warmth floods over my knuckles. Blood pulses in thick bursts against my chest. She shudders, her eyes bulging, her mouth twisting into something almost like a question. Her knees collapse. I ease her down. Not out of mercy—just control.

The world seems to wait with me, every groan of the rafters holding back, every shadow leaning close. There's intimacy in the pause, a quiet that feels almost tender.

I lower her slow, like something fragile.

She spasms. Twitches. Tries to speak.

I lean in. "No one ever actually wanted you," I breathe. "Especially not anyone who can see what's behind the mask."

Her eyes flutter. Then roll back.

She shudders once.

Then she's gone.

Her fingers twitch. One hand curls around nothing—an instinctive grasp for help that's not there. Her head slumps sideways, cheek pressed to the sticky floor.

I hold her a breath longer. Just to be sure.

Then I let go.

She crumples beside a crate, limbs folding like broken wings.

One shoe stays half-on, twitching against the concrete. Then still. Even the silence holds its breath.

Blood pools beneath her—dark and glossy, soaking into the floorboards. The hall accepts her, slow and silent.

The knife drips.

My breath fogs the air behind the fabric.

A minute passes. Maybe more. Time slips its leash. I stare down at what I've made, and for a moment,

everything is still. No footsteps. No voices. Just the tick of blood dripping, the hush of rot settling.

And then—I hear it. A shift. A breath. Soft. Sharp. Still in the room, I don't turn. I inhale and smile.

She watched. Not by choice. By gravity.

Just beyond the broken archway, a sliver of movement.

Her. Frozen. Barely breathing. I can see the tremble in her fingers, the rise of her chest. A rabbit in a snare. Beautiful in her fear.

I wonder how long she's been there. How much she saw.

Long enough, I hope. Long enough to understand what comes next isn't accident or madness. It is purpose, and she's already part of it.

Claimed in Blood

✧Emilia✧

I stand cloaked in shadows at the farthest corner of the abandoned camp hall, breath shallow, heart hammering like a warning in my ribs. The musty scent of old wood hangs in the air—familiar, almost nostalgic—but it's been tainted. Laced with something sharper. Fresher. Something that doesn't belong in a place meant for laughter. For music.

Blood.

The scent clings to the damp wood, thick and metallic, cutting through the mildew that usually owns these walls. It drips into the silence like rain off pine boughs, heavier, wrong.

It doesn't belong here. None of this does.

The distant laughter from the campfire has long since faded, replaced by the low thud of footsteps... and the brutal, unmistakable sounds of violence. A scuffle. A body hitting the floor. The ring of metal slicing through air.

I should be pressing myself behind the gear crates, should be hiding, escaping, but my feet betray me. I move closer. Toward the sound I just heard.

Why the hell am I moving toward it?

Is it concern? A death wish? Or something darker, rising like instinct?

My legs know something my mind refuses to name. Each step feels stolen, like the floor itself should splinter and send me crashing down, but it doesn't. It carries me forward—as though the shadows want me closer.

My chest heaves as silence settles again, thick, and ominous. That's when I see it, aglint of silver in the dim light.

But it's not the gore that freezes me. It's the way the light dances along the curve of the handle. I should turn away. Call for help. Find Wes. Do something. Anything. But my body won't obey the script of righteousness.

My chest tightens. My skin prickles—first with fear, then with something else. Something older.

It coils low in my stomach like smoke rising from ancient embers—warm and terrible and holy.

Not panic. Recognition as my eyes lock onto the knife. Not just any knife. That knife. The same handle I watched turn slowly in the firelight. The same blade that carved the symbol into the bark beneath the stars, promise written in pain and permanence.

My breath catches. The memory floods in, hot and electric.

That knife was never just a tool. It was part of him. An extension of his devotion—steel, sharp, silencing.

Heat unfurls beneath my skin like a secret coming alive. Because in this moment, I understand. It's not curiosity, not madness. It's devotion. A love so feral and consuming it would gut the world for me.

My breath stays caught somewhere between fear and certainty.

I step out from the shadows, feet silent against the warped wood. Moonlight spills through the dirty windows, casting silvery streaks across the floor.

He's standing at the center of it all. A body sprawled behind him. Crimson streaks the floor.

The tattered bandanna hides everything—except for his eyes.

Those eyes. Unmistakable, impossible to forget. He sees me but doesn't budge. Neither do I, not right away.

When I finally move it's slow, steady, my gaze never leaving his.

I reach him, my arm lifts. Fingers brush the edge of the bandanna. My hand shakes, just barely. But he doesn't flinch. Doesn't speak.

The cloth resists for a moment, snagging on the stubble along his jaw before it falls away.

And there he is.

My breath stutters. The world tilts, just for a second. But I don't look away. He's blood-splattered. Breathing hard. Still holding the blade. All I see is him though.

Maybe I should ask. Maybe I should demand an explanation. But there's no space left for questions.

Just him.

Just now.

I grab his face and kiss him—hard, hungry, like he's the last breath in a drowning world. It's not soft. It's not sweet. It's the collapse of everything false. The moment when the lie of innocence dies, and something older, truer takes its place. It's a collision of want and fury and desperate understanding. And he kisses me back with that same wild heat.

One bloodied hand cups my jaw. He caresses my cheek. My neck. The smear burns hotter than the kiss because it isn't just blood. It's proof. A brand the world will never see but I will never wash away.

Staining me with him. Not with tenderness, with possession.

And I let him because this isn't fear. This is belonging. This is home.

His mouth finds mine again—rougher now, a silent declaration. I meet him with equal fire, my fingers tangling in his hair as I pull him closer.

He lifts me backing into the wall, our bodies pressed so tight I can't tell where I end and he begins.

His hands roam—blood-slick, reverent. Everywhere he touches ignites. Not fire—but friction. Heat and ache and wanting.

Gripping me like he's terrified I'll vanish.

He reaches for one of the dusty mattresses leaning against the wall and throws it to the floor with a heavy thud, never breaking the kiss. It hits the ground crooked. Unceremonious. My back hits it seconds later, the springs groaning under the weight of us.

We shed layers like we're molting our old selves—frantic, clumsy, necessary. Clothes stick, heavy with sweat and blood, peeling away in awkward jerks. Fabric rasps against skin, each sound louder in the hollow room, like confession.

His skin is streaked in crimson—some dry and flaking, some slick and new. It smears where we touch so now I wear it too.

I feel the echo of our mark—carved into bark, carved into memory. Now carved in flesh, in heat, in breath.

We are one.

When he enters me, there is no hesitation. It's worship. A communion of flesh and breath and sin.

We move together like something inevitable. As if gravity always meant to pull us here.

The air trembles with our rhythm—each breath sharp, each motion deeper than the last. I lose the edges of myself.

All that's left is him. His blood becomes mine. My cries become his breath. Every thrust writes a vow across my skin that no language could hold.

He buries his face against my throat, whispering things too sacred for the air—things meant only for me.

My nails rake down his back, leaving fresh wounds in their wake. Crimson crescents, sealing our bond.

We fall together. Shatter together. Remade in the same breath. A single heartbeat stretched between two worlds.

The rafters groan above us, settling as if the building itself has borne witness and can finally exhale. Outside, the forest stays hushed, complicit.

We lie tangled on the mattress, blood drying between us like a second skin.

One breath. Then another. Our chests rise in unison—bare, stained, steady.

I don't know what this says about my mental state. I only know that something inside me has gone quiet—for the first time in years.

And in the silence...

There's peace.

Nothing left to hide.

Only truth.

Only us.

19

And Then The Past Spoke

☽ Sometime after midnight ☾

✧Wes✧

The mattress beneath me is cold now. The kind of cold that seeps into your bones when the night's fully sunk its teeth in. Blood has dried in slow, rust-red patches across my arm. Her leg. It clings like a second skin—silent, unrepentant.

Outside, the Oregon dark hums low and steady. Wind slides through warped cabin boards and rattles loose shingles, carrying the resin-sweet bite of pine. Crickets saw into the stillness, thin and relentless. The occasional crack of a branch under something we'll never see. But in here, it's just us.

Emilia shifts beside me. Not away. Closer. Her skin is warm, still flushed. Her breath steady but taut—drawn tight like a wire strung between knowing and asking.

But I already know what she's thinking. I always have.

I turn my head. The moon's silver touch filters through broken windowpanes, catching in her eyes—the kind of eyes that burn when they look straight through you.

"You wanna know when it started," I say, voice low. Even. "When I stopped just watching and started doing something about it."

She doesn't answer. Just gives the smallest nod, sure and solemn, like she already knows she won't be able to unhear what comes next.

I stare up at the ceiling, and for a second, I don't see warped wood or shadows—I see a memory carved into bone.

"I always hated how he talked to you. The way he looked at you like you were something he could break just because he could. I saw it in how you flinched, how you made yourself smaller—like if you were quiet enough, maybe he'd forget you existed."

My hand slides over hers. I don't squeeze—just hold.

"But that night... that night was different." The words hitch, barely. I force them out. "You'd just gotten home from the hospital. I was in my room. I saw your light flick on, and I looked out the window. And there you were. Sitting on the roof."

My gaze shifts, meets hers. I watch it hit—recognition blooming like wildfire behind her eyes.

"Your arm was in a cast. Lip split. One eye already swollen and purple beneath the stitches. You looked like you couldn't even keep it open anymore. And you were just sitting there. In the dark. Like you were deciding whether to go back inside... or disappear for good."

"My chest locked that night. Because I saw it—the edge you were balanced on. Not a thoughtless kind of edge, not just hurt. It was the kind where the sky looks too wide, where the air feels too thin, where a body starts thinking maybe the quiet would be easier than the weight. And I knew if you tipped, if you slipped even a breath too far, there'd be no pulling you back."

My jaw clenches.

"And then I heard him. Inside. Laughing. Your mom blaming you. Him telling her to stick to the story—you fell down the stairs."

The anger burns cold now. Steady. Controlled.

"That was it, Em. That was the last fucking straw."

Emilia doesn't move. Her eyes are wide and wet—but she's not looking away.

"He left like always. Headed to the bar. Took that same shortcut through the woods.

And I knew… I knew he'd be coming back the same way, drunk and full of himself. So I waited."

"I waited by that old pine tree at the bend, the one with the roots like claws. I had my hunting knife with me. The one my dad gave me. You remember it?" I ask, my voice barely above a whisper. "He gave it to teach me how to survive. But that night, I used it to make sure you did."

"When your father finally showed up, he was stumbling, bottle half-empty, already soaked in the stink of beer. He didn't even see me at first. Just kept walking."

"Then he squinted. Realized it was me. And he laughed—like it was some joke."

'Wesley fucking Mercer,' he slurred. 'Shouldn't you be at home missin' the woman that bled out bringin' your sorry ass into this world?'"

"He stepped closer. All swagger and slurs. Told me to go home before he knocked some sense into me too. Said I could get a taste of what you got."

I didn't move. Just said, 'Does it feel good? Hurting someone defenseless. Does it make you feel big?'

I remember watching his face twist. That flicker in his eyes when he realized—I wasn't scared of him.

"He lunged. Tried to grab me. But he slipped. Foot caught on a root. Went down hard."

"The bottle shattered, spraying shards of glass around us. He went for one, hand closing around the broken neck. The glass caught me clean across the arm—" I gesture vaguely toward my arm, "—right here. The sting barely registered. All I could think was how small that wound was compared to every one he'd carved into you."

"I didn't even flinch."

"I looked right at him while my blood hit the dirt. And I thought, If he thinks that'll stop me, he doesn't know a goddamn thing about love."

"I drove the knife into him. Once. Twice. Again. I don't even remember the number. Just the sound. Steel against flesh. His breath stuttering. The woods going silent. And when it was over..."

I turn back to her fully now, eyes steady.

"I wasn't sorry. I made him answer to someone who actually gave a damn."

I lift our joined hands to my chest.

"He deserved it. For what he did to you."

A beat of silence folds between us. Thick. Final.

"That night, I swore I'd never let anyone hurt you like that again. And I haven't."

I swore it once under my breath, knife still warm in my hand. I'm saying it again now—with her watching. With nothing left to hide.

✧Emilia✧

The air inside the cabin feels thick, like breathing smoke. My heart thrashes behind my ribs—wild, unmoored. Wes's hand is warm on mine, blood drying along his forearm. Our fingers stay twined. His confession doesn't crash—it rolls in slow, like thunder trailing lightning. Heavy. Inescapable.

I should be horrified. Should feel sick or scared or shattered.

But I don't.

Instead, heat blooms low beneath my ribs, a raw ache spreading like fire in dry grass. Something feral claws its way up from the hollow places I

thought I'd buried for good. It should terrify me—that this is what his confession awakens. But it doesn't. It feels... right. Like the part of me that always ached finally recognizes the hand that's been holding me up all along.

Because I remember that night all too well.

The ache. The numbness. The cold shingles beneath me and the endless sky above, stars blurred through one good eye. The sting of broken ribs, the taste of blood. The quiet question echoing in my head: What if I just don't go back inside?

And then... he was gone. Disappeared.

I never asked questions. I just let it be.

But now I understand why in my gut—for the first time after he vanished—I felt safe.

Wes's voice cuts into the quiet, softer now. "I killed Aubree the way I did... when I did... cause I needed you to see. To understand. Not just what I've done. But why."

I blink, stunned.

"Because I've seen how it's been eating at you," he says, his eyes locking onto mine like he's trying to anchor me in the truth. "The deaths. The mystery.

The guilt. But I'm not some stranger lurking in the woods. I'm the one who sees you. Always have."

The blood he's shed, on my skin. His truth in my hands.

And still, I feel nothing but safe.

I look at him. Really look.

The blood. The scars. The firestorm behind his eyes.

And I don't flinch.

Because this man—this broken, brutal boy who bled for me—is the reason I'm still standing.

I surge forward, mouth crashing against his with a soundless cry. A collision. A claim.

It's not a kiss—it's a reckoning.

Wes groans low in his throat, arms locking around me like armor. One bloodied hand cups my face, fingers splayed along my jaw. The other anchors at my waist, hauling me into him like he's starving and I'm the only thing that's ever fed him right.

But I'm not pulling away.

I press harder. Deeper. My lips part for him, and he takes—tongue against tongue, breath against breath—like he's trying to consume the silence that's lived between us for years. The taste of blood and sweat and salt tears into me, earthy and wild. His truth lingers there—iron and oath—and I drink it like something holy.

His hands roam, rough and reverent. Not graceful. Not delicate. Worship carved from ruin. He touches me like he's memorizing the lines of a prayer etched in flesh, and he's terrified he'll forget the words.

My fingers tangle in his hair and I tug—hard—dragging a growl from his throat that vibrates against my skin. He's already pushing me down, mouth breaking from mine only long enough to ghost down my throat, open-mouthed kisses that burn and claim. His stubble scrapes tender skin, his breath coming in sharp bursts, warm and ragged.

I arch beneath him—not in invitation, but in surrender.

Let this be the moment that replaces every one he shattered.

There's no space for hesitation. No place for shame. Just the ache of it, the need of it, the way our bodies seem to understand what we haven't spoken out loud: This isn't about forgetting the pain. This is about surviving it together.

He slides against me, his hips meeting mine in a rhythm that starts slow, reverent, like he's afraid I'll disappear. But I wrap my legs around him, pull him closer, deeper, and the restraint cracks open.

We burn like wildfire on dry earth.

Frenzied. Consuming.

His forehead presses to mine. His hand slides up my thigh, curling possessively around it as he moves inside me, filling every hollow space I never realized was empty until now.

We breathe in time. My name leaves his lips like a vow. His name tears out of me like salvation.

This isn't sweet.

It's sacred.

He rocks into me like he's praying, like every thrust is an apology for the years we lost. Like every inch of me is something he swore to protect and now refuses to let go.

And I let him.

I let him ruin me.

I let him make me whole—brick by bloodstained brick, with hands that never once let go.

No hesitation.

No fear.

Only this.

Us.

✧Wes✧

The silence that follows isn't empty. It's whole. Like a song played to the end, every note struck and heard.

She's tucked against me, cheek pressed to my chest, her breath rising with mine. The blood between us has dried like ink sealing a pact. Her fingers trace slow circles over the scar on my forearm—the one from years ago, the first time I stood between her and the world.

She doesn't recoil from it, doesn't look away.

I watch her in the low light. Not the way I used to—from across rooms, down hallways, where her pain was always just out of reach. No, I watch her here, wrapped in the aftermath of all the truths I

finally spilled. And I see something I never thought I'd earn:

Peace. In her. Because of me.

No more ghosts in her eyes. No more doubt in her hands.

She's still fire. Still fury and grit and unhealed scars—but she's with me. Trusts me.

And I swear—I'll spend the rest of my life keeping her safe in the ways no one ever did.

Not just from the monsters in the woods.

From the ones that left their fingerprints on her bones.

From herself, on the nights she forgets she's more than what they made her feel.

I press a kiss to her temple, eyes closing as the forest exhales around us—wind combing through fir boughs, water trickling somewhere unseen. The woods out here have always been merciless, but tonight they don't feel like a threat. They feel like witnesses. Like they've taken our secret into their soil and promised to keep it.

For once, I don't brace for what the future holds.

Because whatever it is—we'll face it together.

The truth between us—iron and flame. Sacred. Unflinching. Forged in everything we couldn't say until now.

Outside, the woods breathe like a sleeping beast.

Inside, so do we. Finally. Wholly. As one.

✦ 20 ✦

Before Breakfast

☽ Camp Day 38 ~ August 3rd ~ 5 Days to Go ☾

✧Wes✧

The water runs hot. Borderline scalding. It hits the scratches she left down my back like a promise—sharp and deliberate—and I lean into it. Let it burn. Let it remind me I'm alive.

Steam coils up around us like smoke, thick and heavy, curling against the cracked tile walls of the ADA shower stall. It's tucked behind the infirmary, rarely used—the kind of place no one thinks to look. Especially not just before dawn, when the camp still sleeps and the world feels suspended between dark and light.

She hasn't said a word. Neither have I.

But we're not quiet because we don't know what to say.

We're quiet because there's nothing left to question.

She's standing under the spray, bare shoulders rising and falling, eyes closed like she's letting the heat rinse last night from her bones. Her skin glows in the dim light—pale and marked and real.

I move closer, slow, and sure, letting the water pour over both of us. I reach for the bar of soap, lather it between my hands until it froths, then touch her waist.

She doesn't flinch. Doesn't feel the need to ask.

Just leans back into me.

I start with her shoulders, gentle as I work the suds across her skin. My hands glide over the curve of her arms, down to her wrists, around the places where she's still tense. I wash her like she's something sacred—something ancient and bruised and still beautiful. Like maybe if I'm careful enough, gentle enough, she'll start to believe she's safe. Like maybe this is the only prayer I'll ever need.

The water pounds steady against tile, echoing like rain in a chapel. In this stall—hidden, steaming, suspended—I feel the world shrink down to skin and heat and silence. No voices. No orders. No camp. Just us, carved out from the noise, like we've stolen a sliver of time no one else will ever touch.

She turns slightly when I shift, giving me access to her back. I trace each ridge of her spine with the pads of my fingers—the places I kissed last night, the ones I held while the world turned red. The soap slicks over her skin, and I watch it slide away, taking nothing I want to keep.

"You still okay with all this?" I murmur, voice low, brushing hair from the nape of her neck.

She looks up through her lashes and locks onto my eyes, then nods.

That's all I need.

I trail one hand around her ribs, let it rest just below her heart as I rinse the soap from her slowly. She sighs. Not out of discomfort. Out of relief.

I press a kiss to her shoulder, let my lips linger there for a moment longer than I need to.

We don't rush.

We enjoy this moment while we have it.

When we finally step out of the shower, the room's heavy with warmth and something quieter. Something softer.

She wraps a towel around her chest, water still dripping from the ends of her hair. I do the same, rubbing at mine until it sticks up in damp curls.

She stands at the sink, eyes lifting to the cracked mirror. I meet her gaze in it.

And what passes between us—it's not regret.

It coils invisible, binding us in ways no hand or chain could. A tether, yes—but also devotion. A vow. Something ancient in its quietness, as though the mirror itself bore witness to a promise spoken without words.

"So," she says, teasing, "are we supposed to just walk across camp in towels and hope no one notices?"

A grin tugs at the corner of my mouth as I tilt my head toward the bench by the wall. "I brought clothes."

Her brow lifts. "You packed a bag?"

"Last night. Before I came to find you," I tell her, voice dropping. "I didn't know exactly how it would go, but... I hoped."

She turns to face me fully, towel still clutched around her, eyes shining in the soft light.

"I hoped you'd see it. Everything. And still stay."

She steps closer. "I see you," she whispers, brushing her fingers over the scar on my forearm—left there the night I made sure he'd never touch her again. "Completely and forever."

That's all she says.

That's all she needs to.

We dress in silence, side by side like we've always done this. Like we always will.

She pulls on a dark green tank top I love on her, and those black cargo pants with the little mushrooms stitched at the seams. Her movements are casual, but I can't stop looking. Can't stop seeing her.

The scent of wet pine and soap clings to the air as we step outside. The sun's just beginning to break over the treetops, casting gold across the grass in a slow, blooming wash.

I bend and pick a sprig of white wildflowers near the path—delicate things clinging to the earth despite everything. She watches me, puzzled, until I tuck them into her hair. My fingers brush her temple. She doesn't pull away.

Then I kiss her.

Not with hunger this time.

With admiration.

With the kind of certainty that doesn't need to speak to be understood.

My hand lingers at her waist. Steady. Anchoring.

"I gotta help Noah with something at the pavilion this morning," I murmur against her lips.

She nods. "I'll find you later."

We kiss once more.

Not goodbye.

Never goodbye.

And then I walk away, already waiting for the moment she finds me again.

✧Emilia✧

The sun hangs high by the time I cross camp, though the breeze still carries the chill of morning in its folds. The woods whisper softly—branches creaking, birds rustling the hush with their wings.

Everything looks so normal.

It's absurd.

A jay scolds from somewhere overhead, sharp, and ordinary. Colorful pendant banners ripple in the breeze. Kids' sneakers—mud-caked, abandoned—sit neatly by a cabin step. Beyond them, the firs sway slow, their shadows long and cool across the dirt paths. For a moment the world looks

untouched, it feels almost wholesome—like a postcard no one will ever send.

I step over a root curling like a question from the dirt and try not to think about how last night shifted something permanent beneath my skin.

Death and desire.

Rage and reverence.

Wes's mouth on mine, his hands gripping my hips like a man unraveling. The feel of blood drying on my skin and his voice in my ear, low and broken with need.

He took a life for me.

Ravished me after.

And I let him.

Not just let. I met him there. Matched him.

Now there's no part of me untouched by what we did—by who we became beneath the trees and inside that stall with the water pouring down like absolution.

I spot Sophie and Lila near the arts table, cross-legged, surrounded by tangled beads and a puddle of spilled paint. The colors drip over the edge like a melted rainbow.

"Morning, sleepyhead," Sophie calls, grinning. Her hands are sticky with glue and glitter. "You look... recharged."

I arch a brow. "I slept fine, thank you."

Lila squints at me, stringing a bead onto cord. "No offense, but you've got a whole witchy forest nymph thing going on. Like you danced naked under the moon."

Sophie gasps, one hand to her heart. "With Wes, obviously! I bet you two were making out under the stars. Summer camp romance—I live for it."

I roll my eyes, lips twitching. "You two are ridiculous."

But they're not wrong.

And their teasing doesn't sting. It almost... feeds me.

They have no idea what happened—what really happened—but they can feel it. The shift.

The way last night's darkness bled into passion. The way Wes's hands on my body, his mouth against my skin, felt like worship. Like survival. Like belonging.

The way death and desire braided together so tightly I don't know where one ends and the other begins.

And through it all—Wes.

Steady. Brutal. Mine.

He's shown me again and again that I don't have to be afraid anymore. Not of the past. Not of what I am. Not even of what I want.

And standing here, with the sunlight catching on my hair and Sophie giggling about a crush she can't even imagine the depth of...

I feel powerful.

Not because I'm pretending.

But because for the first time, I don't have to.

"Admit it," Sophie says, tilting her head. "There's something different about you. Major energy shift."

Lila nods. "Like you finally stopped running."

I don't respond.

Because I did stop running.

But not because I found peace.

Because I finally chose him fully.

Instead, I reach out and squeeze Sophie's shoulder gently. "See you at breakfast."

✧

The lake sparkles through the trees as I approach. My schedule says I'm supposed to be here. The air feels thick with the heat of the day trying to settle in.

Crystal's already there, pacing. Clipboard in one hand, pen tapping a rhythm against it like a nervous heartbeat.

She doesn't even glance at me before launching into her usual prattle.

"Community service lake cleanup," she says briskly. "End-of-summer morale boost. You're helping me organize it."

My stomach knots.

"I noticed you didn't return with the karaoke machine last night," she adds with a pointed look. "Don't tell me you forgot."

I shrug. "Aubree ditched me before we got there. I wasn't going alone."

Crystal clicks her tongue. "Fine. Doesn't matter. You're organizing this cleanup now. Think of it as a growth opportunity."

We start to walk the perimeter of the lake, her voice filling the air with logistics and delegation. I half-listen. The water licks at the shore, and the dock casts long, slatted shadows like skeletal fingers.

It should've just been another morning.

But then I see it.

Tanner.

His body is half-submerged in the reeds, pale and bloated, bobbing softly with the ripples. One arm is twisted upward, frozen in a silent plea. The smell hits next—sweet rot undercut with stagnant algae, the kind of scent that belongs to something already claimed by the earth. The reeds bow as if the lake itself is pulling him deeper, trying to make him part of its silence.

I stop walking.

Crystal doesn't.

"Oh god," she mutters, and her voice isn't horrified—it's calculating.

The water around him is clouded, green-brown with stirred silt. Dragonflies skim the surface, undisturbed, their wings catching the light as if nothing has shifted.

My stomach turns. Not violently. Just enough to make the world tilt. The buzz in my ears drowns Crystal out before she even speaks.

"Okay. This is manageable. He must've taken out a canoe. Probably late. Probably tired. It's tragic, but we can frame it right."

She turns to me, "Emilia" —my name slamming me back into the moment—"no campers have been down here, right?"

Her eyes are managerial, not mournful. "I'll have Mattie pull him out before breakfast. Quietly. This doesn't leave our lips. Understand?"

But I'm not looking at her.

I'm staring at Tanner's face. At the bruises along his ribs. The gash at his temple. The unnatural angles of his limbs.

He did this.

After Chloe.

And I know it. Deep in my bones.

But what rises inside me isn't fear.

It's heat, pride, hunger. He did this for me.

Crystal's still talking. "We can't let this ruin the summer. We keep it calm. We stay in control."

Her voice fades into static—white noise on the edge of consciousness.

The water laps gently around Tanner's corpse. The reeds sway like nothing has changed like the lake itself understands silence.

And I smile—not in joy, not in mourning but in certainty.

✧ Emilia ✧

The kitchen smells like warm spice and lemon-slicked metal, the air thick with the hum of knives and quiet intention. Morning sunlight slants through the mess hall windows, glinting off trays of cut fruit and cooling muffins, but I move through it half-absent, my mind still tangled in shadows.

I slice melon with slow, steady rhythm—inhale, exhale, cut—trying not to replay what I saw in the woods. What Wes did. What he became for me. Not just the kill. The way he looked at me afterward, blood on his hands and worship in his eyes.

He'd meant every word, hadn't he? Every late-night promise. Every quiet I'd burn the world for you.

I used to think words like that were just air—empty promises meant to soothe, nothing more. But blood stains truer than ink. And Wes... Wes never spoke to soothe. He spoke to mark. To claim. And last night, with the knife, with his hands, he carved every vow into something the world could no longer ignore.

My chest tightens with something that isn't fear. It's awe. Gratitude. Something sharper. Something deeper.

Miss Dee doesn't miss a thing. She never does.

"Your body might be in the kitchen, girl," she says without looking up from her tray of cornbread, "but your spirit's out there floating somewhere with that boy of yours."

I startle slightly, my hands stilling on the knife. "Sorry. Just tired."

"Mmmhm." Dee glances over her glasses, the corner of her mouth twitching like she knows better. "You look lighter today. A little more sure of yourself. Like a girl who finally stopped asking for permission."

I say nothing, but my hands resume their motion—slicing, stacking, rinsing. The melon's juice runs cool across my skin.

When the last wedge is cut and placed neatly on the tray, I rinse my hands, the cold-water biting.

I breathe in.

"I'm gonna get some air," I murmur.

Miss Dee hums, like she was waiting for it.

"Don't go too far," she calls. "We still got cinnamon rolls to plate."

I smile faintly, but my chest is tight again as I slip out the back door into the thick morning air.

The morning sun hangs low behind the trees as I step onto the back porch and make my way around the mess hall's side path, the pine-needled trail muffling my steps. The air is still damp from yesterday's storm, cicadas humming in the hush between buildings.

I cut behind the staff cabins, intending to find Lila and Sophie before breakfast, but slow as voices rise around the corner.

The screen door creaks, but the voices carry before I even reach the porch.

Crystal's voice, sharp and brittle, slices through the humid air. "God, Lila, must you always embarrass me in front of the other staff? You looked like some kind of poorly dressed gremlin during flag duty."

Lila's voice cracks. "I was just wearing a hoodie. It was cold."

"You think people don't notice? You think they don't whisper behind my back about how I can't even control my own daughter?"

Silence. Then Lila's breath hitches. "I'm not something to control."

Crystal's tone drops, venomous now. "No, you're a reflection. My reflection. And I will not have you ruining what I've worked for just because you've decided to mope around and play best friend to the broken girls."

Lila's reply is soft, but steady. "Maybe I like the broken girls. At least they're real."

"Oh please," Crystal scoffs. "You don't like them, you want to be them. It's easier than being someone with potential, isn't it?"

My stomach twists. That voice. That poison. I know it well.

Then Lila, firm this time: "You don't get to talk to me like this anymore."

A beat of silence.

"I'm not staying with you after camp. I'm going to Dad's. And you can spin whatever story you want to the neighbors. I don't care anymore."

Crystal's laugh is hollow. "Oh honey. You'll come crawling back the moment he forgets you exist."

"Then I'll finally have something in common with you."

The silence that follows is jagged, sharp as glass. For a heartbeat, even the cicadas pause, the camp holding its breath as if it, too, waits for Crystal's reply. But none comes—only the brittle mask of control slipping in the twitch of her jaw, the tremor in her hand still clutching the clipboard like a shield.

The door slams. I duck back into the trees, my heart thudding, not just from what I heard, but from the look on Crystal's face in that final second.

For the first time, the director didn't look polished.

She looked small.

As I slip back toward the trail, my pulse still ragged, I realize something.

Lila wasn't just surviving Crystal.

She was breaking free.

And maybe, just maybe, I wasn't the only one rewriting what it meant to be a girl who lived through the darkness.

✦ 21 ✦

Let Her See

✧Emilia✧

The dining hall hums with a tension no one dares name. Not out loud. Not yet.

The usual morning chaos is dulled—like someone draped a thick sheet over the camp and dared us to pretend it's normal. There's noise, sure. Forks scraping plates. Juice being poured. Murmured conversation. But underneath it, there's an undercurrent. Hollow. Waiting.

The fourth empty seat at our table has become something more than a gap.

It's a warning. A wound.

Aubree's absence stretches long and uncomfortable across the room, the minutes piling up like stones. The air itself feels thinner, stretched taut like the silence before a scream. Even the light through the windows looks faded, washed in the pale gray of a sky heavy with rain that never breaks. Oregon mornings are rarely this still—no birdcall, no rustle through the firs. Just the hush of waiting.

Campers keep sneaking glances at the door, like they expect her to come in wild-eyed and laughing, brushing glitter off her shorts, and blaming a late night or a dead alarm clock. But the hands on the wall tick forward. And she still hasn't shown up.

"You don't think something happened to her, right?" Brianna whispers to Mason, voice just sharp enough to carry across the table. "She never came back to the cabin."

"I think I saw Crystal send her off for something after dinner," Harper murmurs, cautious. "And Tanner's still missing, too..."

She trails off, and I know the silence that follows. It's the kind that makes your chest tight.

"That's four," Valentina says under her breath. "Zach. Chloe. Tanner. Now Aubree."

The words settle like a curse.

Brianna scoffs, stabbing her yogurt with aggressive swirls. "Maybe she finally cracked. I've considered disappearing too, after hanging out with you freaks every day."

No one laughs.

A few heads turn toward her, frowns tugging at the corners of mouths, but nobody pushes back. Not yet.

I keep my hands still. My face blank. My breath even. The stillness around me is deliberate. A performance I've perfected. I don't flinch when people like Brianna try to poke the bear.

But across the table, Wes is watching me. And the way he watches—like he's memorizing something only he can see—it grounds me more than I expect. His gaze flickers like a struck match. Last night still hums in the space between us. The heat. The hunger. The violence. The vow.

I'm different now and he sees it.

And I think part of him has been waiting for it all along.

By the coffee urn, Dee speaks just loud enough to land like a dropped stone:

"Funny how it's always the same kind of folks that end up missing. Maybe karma's got better aim than we thought."

She doesn't look at us when she says it. Not exactly. But her words hang in the air like smoke, and for a moment, the table goes still. It clings to us, acrid and heavy, like woodsmoke after a fire.

No one breathes too deeply. No one wants to be the one to break it.

And then Crystal enters.

She walks in with that same clipboard clutched to her chest like armor, a tight smile stitched across her face. Her eyes flick around the room, scanning like she's measuring the temperature of the room and doesn't like what she feels.

"Aubree wasn't feeling well last night," she says, loud enough to command the room. "She was taken for medical care early this morning."

The lie lands smoothly, practiced. Too easy. It curdles in my stomach, thick and sour. I've heard enough adults lie to know the taste of it by now—syrup poured over rot, meant to sweeten what can't be swallowed.

"But don't worry," she continues, in that too-bright voice. "Today's schedule is unaffected. We've got a big week ahead, and we're not letting a stomach bug derail our momentum."

Chairs shift. Forks pause mid-air. Uneasy glances are exchanged.

She powers on, voice clipped, assigning roles like she's handing out party favors. "Noah is still leading the North Ridge foraging hike. Harper,

Jesse, Valentina, you guys are on stage duty; set it up, decorations, sound, lights. I want the talent show to feel like a grand finale, not a funeral."

Not a funeral. The words taste sour.

"Brianna, Mason—you're on lake duty with Trudy," she adds, and something sharp passes through her expression. "Tanner still seems to be... off trail, so I need you two to stay alert."

Her eyes don't quite meet anyone's. I don't think they ever have.

Across from me, Wes lifts his mug and takes a slow sip. His eyes never leave mine. Everything we haven't said sits heavy between us.

We both know Aubree didn't get medical care this morning. We both know Crystal doesn't know where she is. And worse—that Crystal doesn't even care.

That's when the final thread snaps inside me.

This isn't a storm she's failing to weather. She is the storm. The rot. The cause. And I'm done watching it spread.

Crystal turns on her heel, her shoes clicking out of the hall. Her clipboard held like a shield, again.

But it won't save her. Not this time.

✧Wes✧

She rises like a shadow peeling off the wall. Silent. Steady.

Her fingers find mine without hesitation, like we're made of the same blood now. There's a rhythm to us. A pulse. We move as one—no signal needed. No words.

We follow Crystal down the path that leads to her office. She's ahead of us but not out of reach. Not anymore.

Her voice drifts back, venom disguised as exhaustion. "Keep the kids happy. The parents fooled. The counselors in line..."

She kicks a root. Swats at a fly.

"No one says thank you. No one sees how hard I work. One little accident and suddenly I'm the villain."

She mutters to herself like the woods owe her something. As if she built this place with her bare hands.

But the forest listens better than she does.

It's listening now.

The firs lean closer in the breeze, branches creaking like old bones. Pine needles shift underfoot, the scent sharp and resinous, as though the whole forest is bracing for the weight of what's next.

I don't look at her. I'm watching Emilia. Her steps don't falter. Her grip doesn't slip.

She's not just following me anymore.

She's beside me, *with* me.

She's become what I always knew she could be—fierce, aligned, unflinching. Not an echo of my violence but a reflection of my devotion.

Crystal reaches her door and disappears inside.

I don't prolong this, I lead us around the building.

The office window lifts without a sound. I slide through first. Emilia follows.

Crystal turns, startled. "What the—why did you—"

I don't answer, no need to.

Three strides. One hand. Her head slams against the desk.

The thud echoes too loud in the cramped office, louder than it should, as if the wood itself winced. Dust shakes loose from the shelves, her clipboard topples. Blood spatters across her appointment calendar. The air tastes of copper and paper, sharp enough to sting the back of my throat.

She screams; I pause to listen. But there's no alarm. No voices. No footsteps. Only birdsong and wind.

I slam her again. Harder.

And again.

Her face splits at the brow. Her lip tears. The desk groans beneath her, tired of holding this lie together.

She claws at my arms, kicking wildly. I don't flinch. I don't stop until she's limp.

I look to Emilia. She's trembling but not with fear.

Her eyes blaze.

God, she's beautiful like this. Changed. Lit from within by something savage and sacred. A wildfire in bloom.

I draw the knife. Our knife.

It gleams, red-tinged already. As if it remembers what it's for.

"Em," I say, voice reverent.

She nods once. Her smile curves like something dangerous and true. She understands now. Everything. What I did. What I'd do again.

Not just vengeance.

Love.

With one swift motion, I open Crystal's throat. The room floods with silence and blood.

Emilia steps forward, calm as dusk. She brushes Crystal's hair from her face and tucks a camp flyer beneath her ruined hand like a benediction.

One final illusion, folded neatly into the truth.

We walk out hand in hand.

We leave the clipboard behind.

We don't need it anymore.

✧Emilia✧

The woods don't recoil they open.

My boots press soft into the earth, the blood on my hands drying in delicate filigree. I half expect the

trees to whisper judgment. To reach for me like they used to in my nightmares.

But they don't.

They part for us like they were waiting.

The breeze filters down in quiet ribbons, brushing across my cheeks like a blessing. Sunlight dapples through the leaves, painting gold across the path ahead.

I keep waiting for the weight to hit. For shame. For guilt. Something....

But there's nothing.

There is no ache in my chest. No ringing in my ears. Only clarity. A quiet I've never known. I thought this might break me, but it's the most whole I've ever felt. I shed the girl who trembled.

It feels less like stepping forward and more like shedding skin—peeling off something weak and brittle to stand bare beneath the pines. I became someone else entirely.

Beside me, Wes walks like a sentinel, eyes on the path, alert and still somehow calm. Ready to protect me. To defend me.

But I don't need defending anymore.

I'm no longer afraid of the dark. I *am* the dark.

And wherever we go next, we go together. Not with apologies but with fire.

22

Soft Earth, Quiet Fire

✧Emilia✧

By midmorning, camp moves like nothing's changed. Not on the surface. The dining hall has emptied, schedules resumed, and Crystal's absence—though unspoken—is obvious in how smoothly everything unfolds without her. There's no tension humming beneath announcements. No micromanaged chaos. No teeth hidden behind a clipboard smile.

Wes and I fall in with Noah and a small group of older campers as they gather at the trailhead for the North Ridge foraging hike, part of the day's pre-planned itinerary. No one questions Crystal's absence. They just... follow the schedule. As if letting things run smoothly is enough to forget.

But the woods don't forget. The air carries a damp sharpness, pine and loam and the faint sweetness of blackberries ripening in the heat. The earth holds a cool breath beneath the surface, and I feel it rise around my ankles with each step. It grounds me, but it also reminds me—this soil remembers what's been spilled into it.

The forest welcomes us with an early August hush. Sunlight filters down in uneven patches through the canopy, gilding moss and leaves with flickers of gold. Birds call to one another like a private conversation we're lucky enough to overhear.

Noah moves quietly at the front, steady and deliberate, pointing out the wild plants with a kind of reverence that slows everyone's pace. Wood sorrel with its lemony tang. Jewelweed nestled beside poison ivy like a secret antidote. Ramps still clinging to cool soil. Ripe blackberries glistening on thorny brambles.

He speaks with the kind of awe that makes you want to listen. Like the forest is a cathedral, and every plant is a prayer. For a moment, I forget what's buried beneath it all—blood, lies, and shadows that haven't yet finished settling.

I let my fingers brush the edge of a birch trunk. Feel the paper bark peel under my touch. Something in me is quieter here. Not healed. Not whole. But grounded, like Noah's voice has tied me back to the earth and told me I don't have to run anymore.

Later, we pause for lunch beneath a small birch grove. Clearwing butterflies drift through shafts of light like ghosts caught mid-dance. Campers settle into a loose circle on the forest floor, passing around sandwiches and crumpled chip bags like communion. Warm water, sticky fingers, sun on our backs.

Without Crystal's biting supervision or the inner circle's venom curling around every comment, the group breathes differently. Softer. Less guarded. There's laughter—real laughter—and for once, it doesn't sound like a mask. I laugh too. Easily. Like my lungs finally remembered how.

The sound feels foreign, almost fragile, like testing a new muscle. For a heartbeat I wait for guilt to rush in, to choke it off, but it doesn't come. The forest doesn't punish me for feeling light. It lets me. Maybe even urges me to.

Wes bumps his knee into mine. Just lightly. But the warmth lingers longer than it should. His presence has always been magnetic, but now it hums deeper, steadier, like a shared current we both recognize.

The fire pit comes to life at dusk.

The sky deepens from violet to indigo, the stars hesitant at first, then bold. The wood snaps and hisses beneath the flames, casting long shadows and soft light across the circle.

Smoke clings to our hair and clothes, that sweet-bitter scent of cedar and ash. Every spark that leaps feels like a reminder—fire consumes, but it also binds. It's warmth and destruction both, and we sit balanced between them.

Someone passes a bag of marshmallows, already half-melted. Laughter spills out across the clearing—genuine and full, like the forest itself is leaning in to listen.

Wes and I sit together on a low log, knees brushing, shoulders aligned. It's the kind of closeness no one questions. The kind that doesn't ask permission.

Sophie curls beside me, legs tucked under a shared blanket. Lila's on her other side; brow furrowed in concentration as she toasts a marshmallow to golden perfection.

She leans in, voice low with a smirk. "My mom's been M.I.A. all day. Could be a good thing… or a really, really bad thing."

I almost laugh, but it catches in my throat.

Lila doesn't know.

Not really.

She's still playing the same game we all used to—reading between Crystal's lines, bracing for the next petty explosion. She doesn't see yet that the storm is over. And that something deeper has moved in to take its place.

Jesse strums her guitar, the notes soft and smoky. Her voice drifts into a quiet cover of an old song, then one of her own. Her lyrics are simple but full—like a balm for the raw places we don't speak of.

The circle has shrunk. Five is down to two. But the space doesn't ache the way I thought it would. It feels clearer now. More honest.

No claws, no masks, no fake tears, or performative cruelty. Only flame and silence and the people who've stayed. The circle doesn't feel like a battlefield anymore, it feels like home.

✧Wes✧

The fire's down to embers when we slip away.

Most of the campers have already wandered off, tired or sticky or content. Their laughter lingers like smoke on the breeze.

Emilia and I walk the shoreline, slow, quiet, her hand in mine like it's always belonged there.

The lake is still. A mirror of stars and treetops, black glass catching constellations in a hush so absolute it feels sacred. The forest behind us breathes slow—crickets, frogs, the low pulse of wind.

The Cascade air has that particular bite to it—cooler once the sun drops, touched with damp earth and the resin of pine sap. It smells like endings. Like beginnings too. I breathe it in, and it tastes clean, sharper than anything I've earned.

It's the first time we've been alone since this morning, just us and the dark and the truth that's still unfolding between us.

I don't know why I speak first, maybe because I need to hear her say it, maybe because she deserves to say it out loud.

"How are you?" I ask, quietly. "Really?"

She doesn't answer right away. Just squeezes my hand, then exhales.

"I thought it might trigger me," she finally says. "Seeing it happen. Watching you... kill her."

Her voice is steady. Almost soft.

"But it didn't," she adds. "Not because I'm numb. Because it felt... right."

She stops walking and turns to me. Moonlight cuts across her face, catches the glint in her eyes like fire in the dark.

"I wasn't afraid of the death," she says. "I was afraid of myself. Of how easy it was to feel good about it. Like something clicked into place. Like it was always there. Waiting."

She looks away then, like maybe the words are too much.

"I thought that made me broken. Unlovable."

I shake my head. "You're not broken."

"I know," she says. "Because you looked at me like I wasn't."

She pauses, then asks it. The question she's already answered in her heart. But she wants to hear me say it.

"Tanner... It was you, wasn't it?"

I don't hesitate. "Yes."

No shame, no regret. Just truth.

And I see it on her face—the shift from question to understanding, from knowing to accepting.

"I saw him," I explain. "That morning, after Chloe. Just a flicker in the trees. I didn't know how much he saw, or if he heard anything. But I couldn't take the chance."

My voice is low now, grounded in the clarity I've never doubted.

"It wasn't about getting caught. It was about you. If I got dragged away, if they took me from you—who would protect you then?"

The words hang there, heavier than the night itself. I expect her to recoil, to remind me of what I've admitted, but instead her silence feels like acceptance. The frogs keep calling from the reeds, steady as a heartbeat, as if the world refuses to judge us.

The wind moves her hair. She doesn't speak.

She doesn't need to.

Because I see it in her eyes. She finally understands.

Not just what I did, but why.

She steps closer, presses her forehead to my chest. And when she speaks again, it's barely a breath.

"Thank you."

It guts me.

That someone like her—fierce and fragile, sharp, and sacred—would thank me for this. For blood and silence and devotion sharp enough to cut.

We walk until we reach a hammock strung between two pine trees, half-hidden where the woods kiss the water's edge.

I pull her in close, my arms wrapping around her like a promise I'd kill to keep.

Her head rests on my chest. My fingers trace the length of her spine.

We lie there like that, listening to the lake lap against the rocks. To the forest hum and the wind comb through the trees.

Her breath evens against my chest, syncing to mine until the two are indistinguishable. Above us, the branches sway, black lace against the stars. It feels less like sleep and more like surrender, not to weakness but to trust. The dark no longer threatens. It cradles.

And for the first time in a long, long time—we sleep.

Without fear, without masks, without pretending. Only truth. Only each other.

✦ 23 ✦

Two Days of Sunlight

☽ Camp Day 39 ~ August 4th ~ 4 Days to Go ☾

✧ Emilia ✧

I wake slowly, breath low, cheek pressed to the warm, steady rhythm of Wes's chest.

Pine-filtered sunlight spills across his skin in soft gold ribbons. The forest hums gently around us—leaves rustling high above, distant birdcalls echoing between branches. His arms are wrapped around me, one hand resting just above my hip. Our legs tangled. Our skin bare and warm.

And for the first time, I don't flinch from the intimacy of it.

I don't retreat from the softness or the certainty of what this might become.

The hush between us feels sacred. I watch the way his chest rises with each breath, the way sleep still lingers in the curve of his mouth. When he stirs and smiles like I'm the best part of waking up, something inside me settles.

This is real.

This is safe.

This is ours.

The forest seems to breathe with us, branches swaying overhead, sun spilling slowly through the canopy. A jay calls, sharp and sudden, before silence folds back in. For once, I don't brace for what's next. I let myself belong to this moment, as if the world itself has paused to witness it.

A sudden crunch of footsteps breaks through the quiet. I lift my head just as Sophie and Lila appear at the edge of the woods, their arms crossed and grins wide, as if they've stumbled onto a secret worth keeping.

"There you are!" Sophie calls, half scandalized, half delighted. "We've been looking for you all morning."

Lila squints at us through the slanting light, pretending to shield her eyes. "You guys slept out here? That's either adorable or deeply irresponsible."

They both burst into exaggerated kissy noises, dubbing it a "peak camp romance moment."

I should feel exposed. Embarrassed. But I don't.

Instead, I smile. Not sheepish, not defensive. Just... seen.

"It's just nice," Sophie says after a beat, her voice softer now. "To see you like this. Blooming instead of shrinking."

And I let that land.

Because she's right.

✧ Wes ✧

The day moves on like it always does.

The mess hall buzzes with clinking trays and groggy chatter. Outside, sunlight filters through the warped windows, catching motes of dust in golden streams. The smell of powdered eggs and cheap coffee hangs heavy in the air.

I drop our trays at the return just as Mattie's voice rises over the din. "She's just catching up on paperwork and end-of-camp stuff," he says, breezily. Too loud. A statement built for eavesdropping.

Across the hall, Dee raises an eyebrow but doesn't challenge it. Just offers him one of her infamous deadpan stares. Then glances at me, and the air shifts.

Something unsaid passes between us. I know she knows something—maybe not everything, but enough. And she's not going to say a word.

When I look across the room, Emilia's already watching; she caught it too.

Nobody says anything. Because not saying things is the safest language here. And yet... the camp runs smoother now. Like some invisible tension has snapped.

Without Crystal shouting orders or stirring up chaos, things just... work. Counselors fall into step. Campers settle more easily. The schedule holds like scaffolding, no one realized had already been built by steadier hands.

Jesse, quiet and capable, starts filling in the gaps. Not barking commands—just being there. Checking the docks. Walking kids to activities. Giving reminders like she's offering kindness, not control. She doesn't need a title to lead. She trusts people to rise, and they do.

✧ Emilia ✧

After dinner, Wes and I wander down to the docks. The lake is a mirror of dusky pink and deepening blue, glassy and still.

We don't talk about Crystal.

We don't talk about the camp, or the missing, or what we've buried in silence.

Instead, we trade pieces of ourselves in fragments: my old treehouse with the rope ladder that always tangled. His obsession with frogs when he was nine. Old songs we half-remember and hum to place.

His fingers play with a piece of my hair, twirling it absently. My head rests on his shoulder, the dock creaking beneath us. The air smells like damp wood and distant firepit smoke. The kind of quiet that isn't empty—but earned.

The lake holds the last of the sun like molten glass. Gnats hover in gold-lit swirls. Somewhere across the water, a loon calls—a long, mournful note that ripples through the stillness and into my bones. It sounds like a warning. Or maybe a promise.

It feels like a breath between storms, a heartbeat of stillness before the noise returns. We both know it won't last but for now... It's enough.

☽ Camp Day 40 ~ August 5th ~ 3 Days to Go ☾

✧ Emilia ✧

The morning begins with bunk ladders creaking and the hiss of hot water through ancient pipes. Steam curls into the hallway, fogging mirrors and soaking the air in heat.

I stretch beneath my thin blanket. My muscles ache, but it's a good kind. Deep. Spent. My chest feels... light.

On the other side of the room, Brianna is cross-legged on her bed, loudly dissecting Jesse's not-so-secret crush on me, voice pitched just high enough to be overheard.

Mason—already in here for some reason—of course, adds a gross comment. I ignore it.

They're the same. Loud. Smug. Pretending the world hasn't shifted around them. But I can see it now—the way they cling to each other, the way they burn brighter trying to hold their ground. There's a fracture in their foundation. A crack in the armor.

And for the first time, I admit it:

It feels good to see it splinter.

Outside, the day is bright and crisp. I find Sophie perched at a mess hall picnic table, her journal open, pen poised. She hums softly, distant, like she's writing her way through something only she understands.

I pause.

There's something eerie about the peace today. Like the air itself is holding its breath, already anticipating what's coming.

The quiet before thunder.

Clouds drift high and thin, veiling the sun in a pale shimmer. The kind of sky Oregon wears before a storm, light turning strange and metallic, shadows stretching sharper than they should. My skin prickles like the day itself is warning me.

The day ends in lavender light.

Fireflies rise from the brush like floating embers. Laughter carries from the campfire circle. Somewhere behind the trees, a volleyball thuds into grass, followed by cheers.

I watch Emilia.

She moves like someone finally unburdened. The way she brushes past Brianna's barbs without reaction. The way she stands straighter. The way her eyes find mine like she's no longer afraid to be seen.

She loves me completely now—not secretly, not tentatively. But openly. Fully.

The part of her that always did, now freed.

Sophie and Lila dance barefoot across the lawn, giggling, twirling like it's the only thing that matters. Around the fire, Valentina leans into Noah's shoulder, laughing too hard at a joke I didn't hear. Jesse's guitar hums soft and low. Two campers are curled beside her, heads on her knees. Harper is braiding someone's hair. Nurse Trudy, for once, isn't holed up in the infirmary, she's sipping tea beside Dee, both of them chuckling at something we'll never know. They are a rare, welcomed sight.

No one suspects what's already happened.

Or what's still coming.

But something's shifting. If you pay attention, you can feel it.

Like a weight lifting.

Like the edge of something bigger.

For a moment, it feels like a real summer camp again.

Just two days of sunlight.

✦ 24 ✦

Ritual Heat

☽ Camp Day 41 ~ August 6th ~ 2 Days to Go ☾

✧ Emilia ✧

The late afternoon sun presses down like a weight, thick and smothering, as Wes and I lean against the screen porch railing of the mess hall. The air is heavy, stifling, as if the whole camp is holding its breath, waiting for something that can't be named.

The resin-sweet tang of sunbaked pine drifts in from the tree line, heavy and cloying in the heat. Even the flies move more slowly, circling lazy arcs as if the air itself has thickened. My skin prickles beneath the weight of it, every nerve tuned to the coming shift.

The usual sounds of camp life—the clatter of dishes, half-hearted laughter—feel brittle and forced, like a flimsy mask stretched too thin.

From the field below, we catch Mattie's voice, low but clear. He's assigning Mason to inventory duty at the old gear shed.

Wes and I exchange a look that needs no words. This is it. The moment has come.

Mattie's eyes flick toward us for a heartbeat—a subtle glance loaded with meaning. Is it acknowledgment? A warning? Or something darker, a secret understanding? We don't dwell on it.

When Mason slips quietly into the trees, disappearing beneath the thick canopy, we fall into a tense silence.

My hand finds Wes's.

No words are necessary. Everything is decided.

✧ Wes ✧

Emilia leads me down the overgrown back path toward the gear shed, the air cooling beneath the trees, a sudden relief from the relentless heat—but inside me, the fire burns hotter.

The forest floor smells damp and loamy, rich with August decay: fallen pine needles, moss clinging to rocks, and the faint, sharp tang of crushed ferns underfoot. Sunlight filters in fractured shafts through the dense canopy, catching dust motes and cobwebs alike, painting the world in a trembling gold. The air feels alive here, thick with expectation and the quiet insistence of something older than the camp itself.

The shed stands neglected, its wood swollen and cracked. It doesn't feel abandoned; it feels consecrated, as if the forest itself chose this place for what we're about to do. This forgotten place now feels like sacred ground. Our cathedral of reckoning.

Inside, Mason is bent over a pile of dusty gear, oblivious to our approach. The scrape of his fingers against the metal and canvas fills the air.

I draw the knife slowly from my belt, the blade catching the fading light, flashing cold and unforgiving.

I don't just draw it, I show it. Let the light catch and dance along the edge as I turn the blade in my fingers, letting it gleam like a magician's final trick. I can feel her watching. Not flinching. Not afraid. Her gaze steadies me—no, sharpens me. I want her to see it all. I want her to remember this, every flicker of light off steel, every breath I take before the blade sinks into him. This is for her. Not just vengeance. Not just justice. A performance. A consecration.

Mason senses the shift before he turns.

His eyes widen as the silver edge slices through the stale air.

I speak low, deliberate, each word a verdict:

"For standing by. For laughing. For everything you refused to see."

He raises his hands instinctively, but it's too late.

I move like a shadow—precise, controlled.

The first cut opens him like paper—clean, decisive, a red seam splitting his arm. He yelps, staggering back, hand clutching the wound as blood sprays across the nearby tarp. The metallic tang hits my tongue, thick and coppery, as if the air itself has turned to rust. His cry rattles the shed walls, echoing too loud for such a small place, and for a heartbeat, the sound feels less human—more like an animal caught in a trap. I don't pause. The second slash catches his side, lower, messier—skin parting over muscle, blood pouring warm and fast. He tries to stumble away, but I catch his shoulder and shove. He falls hard, elbow cracking against the concrete floor, a scream torn from his throat.

Emilia stands in the corner, silent and burning with fierce intensity, the heat of her gaze setting the room aflame.

Every movement I make is for her. Each strike a sentence spoken in blood.

I carve away his defiance, piece by piece. Each slash echoes like a hammer on stone in the quiet of the shed. The scent of warm blood mingles with the musk of sunbaked pine still clinging to my skin, the smell tangling with sweat and the faint rust of old tools. Mason's protests are sharp, desperate—animalistic. And yet, I feel my pulse steady, tethered to Emilia's unwavering gaze. Every movement is a word, every strike a sentence in a language written for only us. The moment stretches, taut, like a drawn bowstring—ready to snap, or to release something sacred.

The blade sinks into his stomach with a dull, wet crunch—thick resistance, like dragging steel through soaked rope. He lets out a guttural choke, and I twist, grinding the edge inside him, feeling tissue tear around it like it's trying to hold on. It's not clean. It's not quick. But it's raw, real, and Emilia sees it. Every inch of it.

Mason's eyes fill with shock and betrayal as his strength bleeds out onto the floorboards.

Glancing toward her, I make eye contact before pinching the blade between my thumb and first two fingers and sliding them down it, dragging the blood off the tip in a slow arc, casting droplets like a crimson vow into the stale air.

A communion of vengeance and devotion.

I hear the sound of his blood hitting the floor—soft, rhythmic, almost like rain. Behind me, Emilia doesn't speak. But I can feel her approval in my bones.

His body falls limp. The silence that follows is thick, settling over us like dust.

Without warning, Emilia crosses the room in a heartbeat. Her lips crash onto mine—a collision raw and desperate. The taste of blood and sweat and fire fills me.

We collapse together, tangled among rusted tools and spilled blood. Her kiss is feral, urgent—an animal unleashed. It's as if the violence hasn't ended but transformed, heat rolling from one ritual into the next.

I groan low, answering her hunger as her hips grind fiercely against me. Our bodies speak a new language—wild, violent, sacred. This is no gentle reprieve. This is a reckoning.

✧ Emilia ✧

Wes flips us with fluid, breath-stealing strength, pinning me beneath him as my back hits the blood-slick floor of the shed. It's cold. Damp. Grimy. But none of that matters.

All I feel is him—his weight, his heat, the tremble of violence still simmering in his muscles. And the burn in me, that primal hunger he's awakened and now refuses to tame.

He kisses me like he needs it to survive, dragging his mouth down my neck, across my collarbone, teeth scraping just enough to sting. I whimper, arching into him as his hand slides between us, rough and blood-warm, pushing up my shirt before yanking open the button of my shorts.

The fabric catches briefly at my hips, and then he bites my inner thigh—hard enough to bruise, to brand. My breath shatters on impact. It's not gentle. It's reverent in its own savage way, a mark of devotion inked in teeth. Then he rips my soaked panties away like they offend him, baring me fully.

I should feel exposed—embarrassed, maybe. The light that filters through the cracks in the wood slats paints me raw and open. But the way he looks at me now—like I'm not just something he wants, but something he worships—makes me feel untouchable. Powerful. Transformed.

I've never been looked at like this before. Not with lust alone—but with hunger, awe, obsession. I'm not just his altar. I'm the offering, too.

"Damn, you're already soaked for me, baby," he murmurs in awe. "Dripping, and we've barely even started."

He lowers himself between my legs, settling there like it's his rightful place, his blood-slick hands gripping my thighs so tight I swear he could leave fingerprints in my bones. But he's not holding me down. He's holding me closer. Closer still. Like he can't bear the space between us.

His tongue finds me slowly, dragging through my folds before circling my clit with aching precision. I gasp, body jerking as sensation blooms and burns. One hand stays locked around my thigh; the other slips between us, and then his finger presses inside me—curling, working that tender spot with ruthless patience while he keeps sucking.

Lapping. Devouring.

"Fuck," he groans against me. "You taste so goddamn good Em."

I cry out as he adds a second finger, stretching me, pumping rhythmically while his tongue flicks and presses, relentlessly. It's not just sex—it's worship, and he's unrepentant in his reverence. I twist beneath him, clutching at his hair, grinding into his face like I need him to crawl inside me just to get close enough.

"Cum for me," he murmurs, voice hoarse with need. "Let me feel it."

And I do as I'm told.

The orgasm tears through me like a quake—violent, holy, unstoppable. I shudder as the pleasure crests and crashes, my thighs trembling against his jaw.

But he doesn't stop.

He keeps going, licking me through it, cleaning me up with his tongue like he's starving. Like it's not enough to taste me once—he needs it again. I convulse around his fingers, another wave ripping free from the first, until I'm sobbing with the pleasure, breathless and undone.

Only then does he pull back, eyes blown wide with hunger and devotion. My chest heaves. My limbs feel unmade. And still, he moves with that same reverent intensity—unbuckling his belt, sliding his jeans and boxer briefs off, positioning himself above me like a prayer made flesh.

I close my eyes, overwhelmed by the sensation, but he doesn't let me look away.

His fingers curl under my chin, lifting it until my gaze locks with his.

"I want you to see what you do to me," he growls, grinding his length against my slick entrance. "Look at me, Emilia. Look at what you make me."

Then he pushes into me in one deep thrust.

I scream. Not from pain—but from the staggering, stretching fullness of it. Of him.

He doesn't move right away. Just holds there, buried to the hilt, hands bruising my hips.

"You take me so fucking good," he whispers, voice rough and trembling. "So tight, so wet, made for me."

Then he moves—thrusts building into a savage rhythm, not rushed but relentless.

Each one feels like a vow, his body telling mine what he hasn't yet said aloud: I am yours. You are mine. Forever.

He praises me with every breath—how perfect I feel, how proud he is, how good I am for him—and it shreds me. Breaks something open in my chest that will never close again.

"That's it, Em," he groans. "Give it to me."

When I cum again, it's loud and shaking, my whole body locking up as I pulse around him. He follows a heartbeat later, groaning my name, spilling deep inside me, body shaking from the force of it.

We collapse together, tangled and soaked in sweat and blood and something even more primal—love, twisted and raw, deeper than devotion.

And when the silence returns, I whisper it against his ear, low and sure.

"We have one more thing to take care of."

His eyes open slowly, a smile, cruel and knowing, curves his mouth. "Brianna."

✧ Wes ✧

Time stutters around us. Nothing moves. Nothing dares.

The blood beneath us begins to dry. Mason's body already feels like a dream—distant, unimportant. The only thing that exists is her. Emilia.

I look at her—truly look—and feel that same stunned reverence flood my chest.

She's glowing in the twilight seeping through the cracks. Her skin streaked with crimson. Her thighs marked with my grip. Her lips still parted, eyes wild, chest rising with every uneven breath. And

yet, she's never looked more serene. More untouchable. More... mine.

I kneel beside her and start to strip her the rest of the way. Not like before—not desperate, not hungry. But slow. Careful. Devotional. Like each ruined thread is a layer of the old world peeling away.

I pull my shirt off, and when I reach for her hand, our fingers slot together as naturally as breath.

Naked and born anew, we step outside the shed. Not as killers.

As something more.

The forest greets us like a cathedral after confession—quiet, golden, and waiting. The blood on our skin dries under the dying sun. But inside, we are brand new.

✧ Emilia ✧

The woods greet us like they've been waiting.

Evening begins to settle in, draping gold light over everything—branches, bark, the backs of our hands. The air is thick with heat and hush, a breath held long and low. Even the light feels reverent, like the forest knows what we've done and approves.

We walk in silence, our bodies sticky with sweat and blood, the rawness between us still pulsing just beneath the skin. The path bends and narrows as we pass the old, abandoned camp hall.

The lake is close—but far enough from camp that no one will stumble upon us. This part of the woods belongs to no one but us.

When the clearing breaks open and the lake stretches out before us, still as glass, I release Wes's hand and move forward without hesitation.

The water is a shock to my skin, biting and cold and bracing in the best way. My breath seizes as I wade deeper, blood unspooling from my thighs and wrists in delicate red ribbons, swirling like silk beneath the surface.

The water bites with a mountain-fed chill, the kind that seeps into bone and shocks breath from the lungs. The lake smells faintly of peat and forest detritus, rich and ancient. Small ripples edge out from my legs, sending tremors across the mirrored surface. A breeze brushes through the pine line, carrying the faint rustle of osprey wings overhead and the whisper of distant streams tumbling over stones. Every sense is heightened—the shock of cold, the weight of the sky, Wes's presence behind me—melding into a moment that feels bigger than us, timeless and untouchable.

I sink until my toes barely graze the lakebed, arms out, eyes skyward.

Let it all wash away.

Let me keep only what matters.

For a long breath, I float, weightless, letting the water rock me gently, steadying me. Then I let my legs sink, lowering until my toes brush the sandy bottom, and I rise slowly to stand. The lake laps around my waist, cool and biting, a sharp contrast to the lingering heat on my skin. Droplets run down my shoulders, over my ribs, and I let the sensation ground me.

That's when I feel him moving through the water, deliberate and steady. The current shifts subtly as he nears, brushing against my back, the quiet rhythm of his breathing blending with mine—it draws me into the moment fully.

His hands find my hips from behind, firm and grounding, steadying me as we sway together in the gentle waves. I lean back into him instinctively, feeling the press of his chest along my spine. He doesn't speak. He doesn't need to. Every movement carries intention, reverence, a quiet promise in the weight of his presence.

We linger like that for a heartbeat stretched into eternity, water rocking around us, the sky above turning violet and indigo in the fading light. He shifts slightly, tilting me just enough so my back curves naturally against his chest, letting my arms float free without losing contact with him.

I close my eyes for a fraction, letting the silence, the water, and him wash through me. The moment is charged, sacred, still. It holds us in a quiet gravity that feels larger than ourselves. My fingers press lightly against his arms, and I can feel the pulse beneath his skin, steady, strong, tethering me as surely as the lake supports us.

We remain there together, his arms around me, my body partially floating. The chill of the water blends with the warmth of our bodies. And in that charged silence, I know there is nothing to rush, nothing to force—only this. Only us. Only the hush of the forest and the open sky above, bearing witness to our transformation.

Then his fingers find my hair.

He lifts the soaked strands from my neck, gathering them in both hands, running them through the cool lake water with aching care. He combs through the tangles with his fingers, washing away the blood and salt and memory like he's rinsing off an obsolete version of myself.

Each strand slips slick through his fingers, and with every pass it feels like a vow: to strip away what was broken, to leave only what has been remade. My scalp tingles under his careful touch, a tenderness so sharp it cuts deeper than any blade.

It isn't sexual. It isn't possessive.

It's holy.

He baptizes me in silence, and I let him.

There's a weight in his silence, one I understand. Neither of us needs to name what we've become. The lake can't forgive us. But it can witness us. And that's enough.

When he finishes, I turn to face him again. His hands rise to cup my face, palms wet and shaking slightly with everything he's holding. His forehead rests against mine, our breath mingling, shallow and warm between the cool evening air and colder water.

His voice is low, steady.

"I'd do it again," he murmurs. "A hundred times."

There's no fear in his voice. No apology.

Only truth. Only promise.

And I feel it too.

There's no turning back.

We're not just in this.

We are this.

And in the hush between heartbeat and twilight, something begins to rise—not guilt, not fear, but purpose. Dark. Holy. Inevitable.

25

Devotion & Decay

☽ Camp Day 42 ~ August 7th ~ 1 Day to Go ☾

✧ Emilia ✧

Lake water still clings to my skin as I step onto the muddy bank, barefoot and dripping, the cool breeze whispering over damp limbs. The blood has washed away, but the weight of what we've done presses deeper now, settling like sediment into my bones. Beside me, Wes shakes out his hair and reaches for my hand, offering that boyish, crooked smile he used to give so easily.

We're naked. Cleansed. Baptized in violence and devotion.

The lake behind us is already knitting itself closed, ripples fading into glassy stillness beneath the pine-crowded ridge. Mist clings low over the tree line, carrying that wet-cedar scent Oregon mornings always hold, cool and heavy as breath. It feels like the forest has swallowed our secret whole, tucking it away in its moss and marrow.

"We can't exactly stroll through camp like this," I say, glancing down at our bare skin with a smirk.

Wes gives a soft laugh. "Tempting, though."

"There's a box of old uniforms in the abandoned hall," I add, remembering the storage room I'd stumbled into while looking for the karaoke machine. "We'll grab something."

I pause. My voice dropping lower. "I'm not putting those blood-soaked clothes back on. But I'm not leaving them behind, either."

He nods. "We'll wash them later. Come on."

The abandoned camp hall is still, steeped in silence and decay. The air smells like mildew and dust and something sweeter—faintly rotten. Aubree's body remains in the corner, half-cloaked in shadow. The scent of her has begun to rise.

The air is dense with mildew, sour-sweet rot, and the faint mineral tang of water that has seeped into the warped floorboards. Moonlight pushes through cracks in the roof, catching dust like pale smoke. Every surface bears the mark of time—moss at the windowsills, vines creeping along the outer wall—but here, with her, it feels less like decay and more like consecration.

Neither of us flinches.

This place has become sacred, a reliquary for our purpose.

I cross to the dusty storage closet and yank it open. A faded cardboard box sits inside, surprisingly intact. I pull it free and pop the lid. Inside are vintage counselor uniforms—shorts and T-shirts in sun-bleached colors, the old Camp Silver Hollow logo stitched at the chest in thread barely clinging to fabric.

I toss a navy shirt and olive shorts to Wes. "Not your usual look, but it works."

He catches the clothes one-handed and steps into the shorts first. They hang low on his hips, slightly too big, the waistband dipping just enough to pull my gaze without shame.

He heads towards the hall's back entrance, then pauses. "We should stage them."

My brows lift.

"For Brianna," he says, a grin pulling at his mouth—but it doesn't hide the malice glinting in his eyes. "If she finds them like this, together… it'll gut her. She's been feeding on fear for years. She deserves to taste her own medicine."

A slow, cold smile spreads across my face. "Poetic justice."

He holds up the shirt, then tosses it back to me. "I'll put this on after. Don't want to ruin my nice new shirt with Mason's blood."

That makes me laugh, soft and sharp.

I change quickly, the fabric clinging to my damp skin like a second self. It feels good to be covered again—but different. Like new skin for a new creature.

Wes nods toward the shed. "Let's get Mason."

Together, we return.

The body is curled behind the crates, jaw slack, and arms limp like a marionette with its strings cut. Wes rolls out the tarp in silence, hands deft and practiced, then arranges Mason's limbs with clinical precision. He wraps him tightly, then hoists the bundle over his shoulder with ease.

For a flash, I see Mason not as he is now, but how he'd laughed in the mess hall, voice sharp, and mocking. The contrast almost undoes me—not with doubt, but with clarity. This is the shape of justice. The transformation from arrogance to silence, from swagger to stillness, made beautiful by Wes's hands.

I watch his muscles flex, how effortlessly he carries the weight of the man who once made snide jokes around the firepit.

"You're stronger than you look," I murmur, my voice edged with admiration.

Wes shoots me a sly smile. "You're just now noticing that?"

A few drops of blood trickle down his back, winding across his skin like dark vines. I watch them snake over the muscles of his shoulders and feel something deep in my chest bloom and tighten.

Back in the hall, he unrolls the tarp with quiet care. Wes lifts Mason's corpse beside Aubree's and arranges their bodies with deliberate precision. Not just death—art. Message. Retribution.

"They're almost poetic," I murmur, stepping back.

We don't linger; we have work to do.

Hand in hand, we step out into the pale hush of moonlight. The night feels reverent, like it's bearing witness.

At the edge of camp, Wes leans in, voice warm at my ear. "Last night you'll have to share that cabin with anyone."

I smile. "Finally."

✧

The kitchen buzzes with low morning clatter—knives hitting cutting boards, the hiss of bacon grease, the thunk of a biscuit cutter against dough. I stand beside Wes at the counter, hands dusted in flour, mixing with methodical calm.

Miss Dee hovers by the stove, spatula in hand, eyes flicking over us.

"You two clean up nice," she states dryly.

I glance up. She isn't smiling, but there is something in her gaze, a glint of recognition. Understanding.

"Shame about all those disappearances," she adds, like she's just talking to the frying pan. "But you know... sometimes the trash takes itself out. Or gets helped along."

Wes stays silent, and I nod once, slow, and certain.

Dee flips the bacon with a snap. "Told you before—karma finds a way. And sometimes," she adds, looking at us now, "you get lucky enough to watch it work."

No judgment. Just quiet approval.

✧

Wes sits beside me at the staff table, our thighs brushing beneath the bench. I'm wearing the deep purple shirt he'd picked out for me weeks ago at Bargain Cove—the one I'd claimed didn't suit me.

But now?

Now it feels like armor. Like it had been waiting for this version of me all along.

Across the room, Brianna sits alone.

Her hair is curled, glossy, and styled exactly right. Lip gloss gleaming, winged eyeliner precise. But her shoulders are too tight. Her smile too brittle. The cracks show in the places she can't control.

Valentina and Jesse linger nearby, then slide into the seats beside her—not out of loyalty, but discomfort. Sympathy. The kind that's just close enough to pity.

"He never showed," Brianna mutters, stabbing her eggs. "Mason. We were supposed to meet up after curfew."

Jesse shifts. "Someone said he was out by the gear shed late yesterday."

"Yeah," Valentina concedes. "Doing inventory or something?"

Brianna doesn't look up. But Wes and I catch the flicker in her eyes. Not fear. Not confusion. Possession, cracking.

Wes's hand brushes mine under the table. I meet his gaze. No words. Just understanding, this is it.

"I'll take these up," he says quietly, reaching for his tray, then mine, then Sophie's.

Sophie raises an eyebrow. "You don't have to..."

Wes smiles. "What kind of gentleman would I be if I didn't?"

I watch him walk away—broad shoulders, calm steps, the faint twitch of anticipation in his jaw.

Sophie leans in. "That's new. The domestic thing."

I smirk. "He's full of surprises."

She studies me for a moment, then lowers her voice. "I don't know what's going on with you two. And I'm not asking. But I've never seen you like this before."

"Like what?"

"Steady. Confident. Like someone lit a fire under your ribs, and you're not afraid to let it burn."

I don't reply. Just give a small smile.

She squeezes my hand. "Just... be careful. And if you need me, I'm here. No questions asked."

"I know."

Then Wes returns, wiping his hands with a napkin and flashing us both that crooked, golden-boy grin.

"All right, ladies," he announces. "Ready to face the day? Sophie, I believe the arts and crafts hall is calling your name."

✧

The sun has climbed higher, burning the dew from the grass in soft curls of steam. I stand casually near the path that leads to the gear shed, listening.

I hear Brianna before I see her—her steps heavy, posture sharp.

She stops in front of me, arms crossed. "You seen Mason?"

I tilt my head. "Actually... I saw him last night. With Aubree."

Her expression falters. "Aubree? She hasn't been around in days."

I shrug. "Guess she showed up after lights out. I saw them slip into the old camp hall together. Looked... cozy."

She stares at me, blank for a moment. Then her features twist, bitter and venomous.

"Mason wouldn't. I'm not some sad, pathetic nothing like you. Men don't leave me."

I don't say a word. Don't have to.

Brianna steps closer, her voice a low sneer. "That sunshine boy of yours? He won't last. Guys like that don't stay with girls like you. It's just a matter of time before he sees what's under the surface and runs."

Still, I stay quiet. Let her talk. Let her break herself open.

Her perfume—potent, artificial berry—cuts against the damp pine air, jarring in its insistence. That scent, that presence, has filled cabins and hallways like a shadow they couldn't shake. Now, watching the strain in her jaw, the way her hands clench too tightly around nothing, I realize she is the brittle one. The forest would outlast her. The silence would outlast her. *We* already had.

She turns to go, muttering, "Would be just like Aubree to show back up only to steal a man."

Then she stalks off, heading straight for the hall.

I wait a beat, then smile at the thought of the hall greeting her.

✦ 26 ✦

She Bloomed in Blood

✧ Emilia ✧

The door creaks open ahead of me, low and strained like the groan of something old and unwilling. It sounds almost... reluctant. Like, even the building can sense what's about to happen and wants no part in it.

I don't follow her right away.

I wait in the shadows just beyond the threshold, my back to the peeling wood, the breath caught in my lungs stretching long and still. I let the silence hold me. Let the moment hum.

Let her step into it.

Let her see.

Let it take hold.

Inside, the long room is suspended in airless hush. Dust drifts like pollen through slanted beams of fading gold. The air is thick—rank with mildew and the first real curl of decomp—but beneath the stink, there's something deeper. A kind of reverence.

Mason and Aubree are slumped just where we left them, their limbs arranged in careful mockery of peace. A tableau built of consequence, composed of silence and rot. Their presence weighs on the space like relics at a shrine.

Her heels scuff against the warped floorboards. Slower than usual. Uncertain.

The sound rasps through the room like sandpaper. I picture the forest outside—quiet, watchful—and for a flicker, it feels like even the trees are leaning closer, waiting for the moment she understands.

They falter after a few steps. I hear it in the rhythm. That hesitation. The first sliver of doubt.

The silence catches her by the throat.

"Oh, my god."

The words fall out broken, small, human.

She steps in further, cautiously now. Like the room itself is warning her back.

I watch from the dark as her eyes catch on their bodies. Her brow knits, lips parting soundlessly. Her arms twitch at her sides.

"No." She whispers. "No, no, no—"

She blinks hard, like she can blink this away.

"Mason?" she says, her voice cracked. "Aubree?"

But they don't answer.

No one does.

Then Wes moves.

He emerges from the shadows like he was part of them all along, fluid, and quiet, a storm held in a man's skin. One arm catches her across the chest, yanking her back against him in a brutal snap. Her spine slams straight. Her scream barely escapes.

His other hand flashes forward, the blade already angled at her throat.

She freezes.

Dead still.

She lets out a breathless, high-pitched gasp—but no movement. Her body goes rigid with the recognition of how fast things just changed.

"What—what the fuck—" she stammers, breath shallow and sharp. "What are you doing? I didn't—please don't—"

"There it is," Wes murmurs in her ear, voice low and slow. "Fear."

Her voice cracks harder. "Wait—wait, please. Wes, whatever this is—whatever you think—"

He presses the blade closer, flush to her skin, just enough to let her feel the edge. "Shhh," he whispers, like a lullaby. "We saved this moment just for you."

The blade kisses her neck—just a scratch, a red line that opens like a warning. She jerks slightly, a sob punching up into her throat.

Then Wes shifts the blade. Turns the hilt toward me. No command, no explanation. He doesn't have to; I'm already moving.

My hand closes around it like it's always been mine.

Because it is.

She sees it happen, and her eyes go wide—not just in shock, but in real recognition.

"No—" she gasps. "What the actual fuck? Are you serious right now?! This is insane—Emilia, you—you're pathetic," she spits suddenly, desperation sharpening into venom. "You think this makes you strong? You'll always be nothing. He'll see it, and then he'll leave."

She thrashes suddenly, jerking hard, but Wes is already repositioning—snatching both wrists behind her back and locking them with his forearm. He braces her against his chest like dead weight. A single, brutal shift that makes her cry out.

"Let go of me! You're insane—this is fucking insane—"

Her voice breaks into raw sobs, high and frantic, the kind that scrape the throat bloody. For a heartbeat, I almost see the girl she used to be—the one who always thought she was untouchable, untouching. But that version of her is gone. The only thing left is this: her body pinned, her words stripped of power, her fear blooming like a wound.

Wes doesn't move. Doesn't flinch. He holds her firm, knowing exactly what I'm about to do.

The room narrows to a tunnel—her, me, the knife—and Wes as witness, nothing else. My hands don't shake. My breath doesn't falter. All the years of silence, of shrinking myself, of swallowing the pain whole, every one of them sharpens to this point.

I step in, slow and certain, and for the first time—her panic stops being denial.

It becomes belief.

“Oh god,” she cries. “Emilia, no. Please don’t—please don’t do this—”

But I already am.

The first stab lands just below her breastbone, angled slightly up. It’s not graceful. It’s not elegant. The blade drives in with thick, shuddering resistance—like trying to cut through wet rope. It jars all the way up my arm, vibrating through bone and tendon, until it buries deep, and the warmth floods up to my wrist.

The sound she makes is wet and startled—half scream, half gasp—as the blood hits my skin in a sharp spray. My lips. My cheek. It drips hot down my neck.

And I don’t flinch.

There’s no panic.

Just a feeling I can only call right.

Wes tightens his hold, anchoring her from behind. His forearm locks beneath her arms, her wrists twisted behind her spine. Her legs buckle instantly. But he braces her—like a display. Like a monument.

I yank the blade free with a grunt, my chest heaving.

"You always wanted me to fall apart," my voice shaking not from fear, but from release.

The next stab plunges into her lower abdomen. I feel her jolt—her whole body twitching like a puppet cut loose. Blood spills fast, slicking over my fingers as I withdraw the blade.

"You just never thought you'd be the one bleeding for it."

I stab again. Higher, just beneath her ribs. Then again. Lower, toward the hip. I aim. I breathe. I strike. There's a rhythm to it. A silence between the beats. Each thrust lands with purpose.

I keep going, driving the blade into her thigh, deep and decisive. Then again, in her belly. And still—Wes holds her.

✧ Wes ✧

She doesn't hesitate anymore. She doesn't tremble. Each thrust of the knife is measured. Sure. A rhythm of becoming.

She's not unraveling—she's becoming. Blooming in blood, in purpose, in fury.

I watch the way her body moves—shoulders tense, jaw set, eyes gleaming with purpose. Blood runs down her forearms, flicking in arcs across her collarbones. Her curls are wild, stuck to her face in damp tangles.

She's not fragile. She's fury incarnate. And I've never loved anything more in my life.

Her purple shirt clings to her in soaked patches, dark with blood, clinging like a second skin. She looks like something reborn in fire and violence. Something holy.

Brianna's gasps have become quiet, rattling things. Her body sags in my grip, but I won't let her fall—not yet.

Not until Emilia's done.

I shift my grip, lifting her just enough to bare her chest fully. Her head lolls back against my shoulder.

I hold her upright, not out of mercy, but out of reverence. Because this isn't just vengeance, it's transfiguration. Something darker. Something divine.

And I want her to have all of it.

✧ Emilia ✧

The knife slips from my fingers, at last.

It clatters to the floor, landing with a sound that echoes far too loud in the quiet that follows.

My chest heaves. My hands shake. But I've never felt more steady in my life.

I close the last bit of space between us and take his face in my hands—sticky with blood, trembling with everything we've become.

I kiss him. Hard.

Over Brianna's shoulder, our mouths crash in a collision of breath and ruin. He releases one hand and fists my hair. My fingers knot the neckline of his shirt. The kiss tastes like blood and something deeper. Something permanent.

Brianna's body sags one last time and then slips from his arms. She crumples to the floor with a thick, wet sound.

But we don't stop. I press against him, greedy for it now—not frantic, but certain. His mouth finds mine again with slower hunger, more sure now, more final.

This isn't aftermath. It's absolution. Consecration. The blood rite of becoming.

His lips tell me what my heart already knows.

You're mine, I'm yours. This is real.

We hold each other in the hush that follows, blood cooling between our skin, breath mingling in the stale air.

No more masks, no more running, no more shame. We are the dark now. Unstoppable and completely unapologetic.

And at long, brutal last—Free.

Outside, the forest waits—silent, endless, patient. But inside this room, something new has taken root. Not mercy. Not forgiveness. Something hungrier. Something that will not die.

✦ 27 ✦

What Remains

✧ Wes ✧

The abandoned camp hall smells like copper and pine and something heavier—like reverence that's just started to rot.

Sunlight cuts through the grimy windows in fractured beams, splashing across the blood on the walls, the floor, our skin. It catches Emilia's profile in strange, haunting light—streaks of gold and crimson painting her cheekbones, her collarbone, the cling of her shirt where it's still soaked through. She's too still, but it's not fear—it's the kind of stillness that comes after fire.

My jaw is stiff with dried blood. I can feel it tightening every time I move, flaking down like war paint.

Her eyes meet mine for a beat. Wide, alive. Not wild—just raw.

We don't speak.

We just stand there, suspended in the hush that follows something holy. Or hellish. The difference feels paper-thin.

Then she exhales—sharp and dry, almost a laugh. "Well," she mutters, tugging at her ruined tank top, "clearly we can't just walk back into camp like this, unless we wanna be burned at the stake."

I tilt my head. A smile curls, slow and crooked.

"Lake bath?" she deadpans.

I bow—flourish and all. "After you, my lady."

And just like that, she laughs. Real this time. Short and bright and breathless, like it's catching her by surprise.

We don't need much. Just each other. We move together, vanishing into the trees like ghosts—trailing blood and something heavier in our wake.

✧ Emilia ✧

The lake is cold, a shock to the system.

I wade in fast and let it hit me. Let it bite at my skin and steal the heat from my chest. I dunk under, hold my breath. When I come up, I scrub at my arms and hair, the water turning pink around me in slow-dissolving spirals. Like smoke.

For a moment, I just float there, hair spreading out around me, the sky wide and endless above the tree line. My lungs ache from holding, but it feels like the first real breath I've taken in years. The water presses close and cold, leeching everything out—the blood, the fear, the jagged edges of who I was before this. I almost feel weightless. Almost new.

Wes slips in beside me without a word. The silence holds us—easy, unbothered. For one suspended moment, there's no death. No blood. No fear.

Just water, and him. And the wild, impossible relief of still being whole.

I float in place, the lake lapping just under my chin, and watch Wes tread water a few feet away—his curls wet, face soft. There's no sharpness in him right now. Just warmth. Just him.

He catches me staring and grins, cocky but soft around the edges.

"What?" he crooned. "You're looking at me like I hung the stars."

I roll my eyes, but the smile won't stay down. "You're ridiculous."

He shrugs, "and you love me."

"Unfortunately." But my voice lacks bite.

There's no armor left between us. Not after the blood, the truth, the way he still looks at me like I'm something holy and whole.

"Mmhm. Liar." He swims closer, voice dipping low. "You're finally letting yourself. That's different."

I blink at him. Something stutters in my chest.

"...What makes you say that?"

He stops just in front of me, water dripping from his lashes. "Because you're not waiting for the part where I leave anymore."

My throat tightens.

"You used to kiss me like you were bracing for impact," he adds. "Now it's like... you're home."

I feel it then, low, and deep and warm—something breaking loose inside me.

"I used to think if anyone really saw me—all of me—they'd run."

He lifts a hand. Brushes a wet curl from my cheek. "I'd never run," he whispers, "you've been mine since before you knew."

I laugh—quiet and startled. "God, you're cheesy."

He grins. "Hopelessly."

I lean in, pressing my forehead to his chest.

And for once, I let it be simple.

"I love you," I murmur.

"I know," he says, smiling. "I love you more."

By the time we step out and dry off in the wild summer air, I feel stripped down to bone—but in a good way. Like everything unnecessary has been burned off.

I dig through the dusty old box we left stashed in the camp hall's back closet. Most of the stuff is moth-eaten junk, but I find a faded blue shirt that's soft with age, oversized, and stretched at the collar. It smells faintly like cedar and mildew and something I can't name, but it'll do.

Wes throws on a green plaid button-down that shouldn't work on anyone. It looks like it time-traveled here from a 1983 gas station.

But somehow on him? It works too well.

He notices me staring and just lifts one brow. Smirking back, I don't bother pretending I wasn't.

But the moment sobers quickly.

I rake my fingers through my damp curls. "We should probably go get Crystal's body out of her office," I say. The words are quiet, but they land with weight.

He nods, rubbing a hand over the back of his neck. "Bring her here. Leave her with the others."

There's a beat of silence.

"No one's coming back to this place," he adds. "Not this summer. Maybe not ever."

My throat tightens. I nod. "Yeah. Let's just... get it done."

✧

We move through the trees like shadows. Avoid the main paths. Step quiet.

When we reach Crystal's office, I push open the door—and freeze.

It's clean.

Not just cleaned—sterile. Staged. Sanitized. There's no blood, no body, no broken lamp.

The couch is straightened. The floor is gleaming. Brochures aligned. Her sweater—gone. Her nameplate—gone. The Polaroids—gone. Every trace of her has just been erased.

Even the air smells... ordinary.

Not copper. Not ozone. Not the singed chemical tang of a shattered bulb. Nothing but stale coffee and the camp's natural lavender cleaner.

Like a ghost wore perfume and vanished.

A chill creeps over my arms, prickling goosebumps. The room doesn't just look empty—it feels hollowed out, like someone scooped the soul right out of it. The air always carries dampness, the faint musk of earth and rain, but here it's sterile, bleached of everything real. It's like standing in a stage set, not a place that ever lived or bled.

I step forward like I'm walking into someone else's memory. "What the hell..."

Wes's voice is tight. "She was right here."

He crosses into the room, eyes darting, like he's trying to summon back the mess, the blood. "The lamp was—" He stops short. Frowns.

Someone scrubbed this place like they were erasing a crime scene from reality, not hiding it, unmaking it.

"Someone cleaned it up," I whisper. "More than cleaned. Like she never existed."

He meets my gaze. His jaw ticks. We both know what this feels like.

It feels like we're not the only ones rewriting the truth.

I scan the room one more time. "We didn't imagine it... right?"

Then—clank. A low metallic sound slices the air. We both turn to the window.

Mattie. Shovel in hand. Standing outside the maintenance shed like he's been there all along.

✧ Wes ✧

We approach slow. Careful. I shift in front of her, out of habit, just in case.

Mattie looks up when we get close. His face is unreadable as always, but there's something ancient in his eyes. Like he's already seen the worst this place can offer.

"I was thinkin' it might be you two," he says, calm as anything. "Already took care of Ms. Crystal."

Emilia stiffens. "What do you mean... 'took care of'?"

Mattie shrugs, hoisting the rope onto his shoulder. "Same thing she'd always have me do with the others. Been cleaning up this place since before either of you was born."

My fingers brush Emilia's. I can feel her pulse jump. Mine stays steady.

"Sure would be a big help if you told me where the rest are," he adds, voice like gravel. "Haven't found 'em yet."

"How did you know?" she asks softly.

He doesn't flinch. "I always know. Camp's got a way of whisperin' bones don't stay quiet forever."

Then he meets our eyes full-on. No shame, just waiting.

I answer. "Old camp hall. Past the trails."

He blinks slowly. "Didn't think anyone remembered that place was still standin'."

There's a pause. His expression doesn't change, but something in the air softens.

"They'll be gone without a trace by morning," he says. "Like it never happened."

The way he says it makes the forest seem thicker and older. Like he's not just a man with a shovel but something the woods themselves made to keep their secrets buried. For the first time since all of this began, I wonder if we've stepped into a story that isn't entirely ours.

We don't ask what else he's erased. We don't ask who came before. Some questions belong to the dark.

I give a nod. That's all.

He tips his hat like nothing about this conversation was unusual. And simply turns back to work.

✧ Emilia ✧

We walk away, and the forest feels... watchful.

Still. But not in a way that makes me shiver. In a way that feels like bearing witness.

I glance at Wes. He's still got that faint little smirk—like this doesn't rattle him at all. Like this was always going to be part of the story.

The closer we get to camp, the louder the normal world becomes.

The smell of grilled hot dogs drifts across the lawn. Someone strums a guitar too loudly, a messy chord spilling out into the open air. Someone yelling across the lawn. This should all feel safe, ordinary. Instead, I feel split in two—one foot in their world, the other still in the shadows where the truth rots.

We pause at the edge of the clearing.

Blood cleaned off. Fresh unstained clothes. Faces set. The world didn't change. But we are not the same.

I glance back one last time, Mattie's still there. Still moving. Still cleaning. Still very much real.

We step into the sun like nothing happened.

Sophie spots us. "Hey!" she calls. "We were just about to grab food. You guys disappeared on us."

Wes gives her a grin. I try to match it.

Lila eyes his shirt and snorts. "What in the upstate thrift store hell is that?"

I break, laughing hard and sudden.

Wes twirls. "Exclusive one-of-a-kind camp couture."

"Looks like something my dad used to wear to power-wash the driveway in," Lila shoots back.

Sophie watches me more quietly. Her eyes flick to my hair, my shirt, the subtle change in my posture.

She doesn't say anything, just gives me a look that says: I know enough. I'm not asking.

And it means more than I can say.

✧

The lunch line crawls forward. Someone's humming. Someone's shouting about missing ketchup.

Sophie glances at us. "So, talent show. You two performing?"

"Nope," I say instantly, grabbing a tray.

"Rude."

Lila eyes Wes. "You?"

He shrugs, all false innocence. "Tell me what to do, and I'll do it."

Sophie gasps. "Dangerous offer."

By the time we sit, we've brainstormed a dozen terrible acts: Wes lip-syncing Britney, Wes reciting

Shakespeare in a bear onesie, Wes doing weird bird calls. We laugh more than we should.

Then Lila says it—quiet, offhand. "I haven't seen my mom in days."

My heart hiccups.

Sophie tries to smooth it over. "She's probably just..."

"No." Lila's voice hardens. "I told her I'm done pretending we're fine. I'm moving in with my dad." She looks toward the mess hall doors. "Maybe that's what broke her."

I look at Wes, he doesn't say anything. Just reaches under the table and laces our fingers together, squeezes, and holds on.

✧

Later, we head to the girls' junior counselor cabins—and stop dead.

It's empty. Not messy, not abandoned; wiped completely clean.

Beds made. Photos gone. Journals gone. Even the pink soap Aubree left in the bathroom is gone.

"This is exactly like Crystal's office," Wes says behind me.

I nod once. I can't seem to speak.

✧ Wes ✧

I move to her fast. Take her face in my hands. Kiss her forehead. "Come on," I whisper. "Let's get ready."

I can tell her shower was hot, steam curling out of the bathroom like something exorcised as she exits, her skin damp and glowing, curls pinned back—I forget what words are.

"You're beautiful," is the only thing I can conjure followed by a grin as I catch my breath.

"But—since I'm attempting to behave—I have something for you." I pull the dress from behind my bag. Soft black cotton. Simple. Quietly perfect.

"I bought it the day we stopped at that store," I admit. "I saw it and just... knew it was yours."

She stares at it. At me. "Wes..."

"Wear it for me?"

I watch in awe as she shimmies the dress on, taking the new confident and comfortable in her own skin, Emilia all in—bare shoulders, soft cotton skimming her hips, curls falling loose around her face.

My breath catches. "Holy shit," I murmur. "You're gorgeous."

✧ Emilia ✧

Wes stands there like something carved out of shadow and intent. His black button-down clings across his chest, sleeves rolled to his elbows, the fabric stretched just enough to hint at the quiet strength beneath. His jeans hang low on his hips, broken in and effortless. The knife—our knife—rests hidden against his back, but I feel it like gravity.

His curls are still damp, falling over his brow in messy waves. His eyes hold me in place—blue and burning, reverent in a way that makes my throat tighten.

He looks like danger dressed in devotion. Like a promise no god ever dared make me.

"You're not so bad yourself," I murmur, voice catching on something tender.

We move toward each other like we're remembering something ancient. No fear, no shame. A chaste breath before the curtain lifts, and for now, we're just two people who lived through the storm. Two people who didn't flinch. Two people who found each other in the blood and didn't let go.

Outside, the sky deepens to lavender and dusk. Across the lawn, the talent show lights blink to life—soft, golden, surreal.

Whatever's next, we'll meet it together.

28

Beneath the Lights

✧ Emilia ✧

The talent show unfolds beneath a canopy of fairy lights, strung from tree to tree like a stitched constellation, casting the lawn in a soft golden haze. The makeshift stage creaks with charm, a few crooked boards and faded paint giving it the perfect amount of camp nostalgia. There's a gentleness in the air tonight—like the forest is holding its breath with us.

The laughter, the nervous chatter, the burst of applause—it all feels brighter under this sky.

Even the shadows feel softer tonight. The trees aren't looming, they're listening. The breeze carries the smell of grass and citronella candles, like the woods are in on the magic.

Valentina zips around like she's powered by static electricity and sheer will, clipboard in hand, barking last-minute instructions and encouragements in equal measure. She's a flurry of theater-kid urgency and unshakable optimism.

Then Jesse appears, moving slower, steadier, her calm a contrast to Val's spark. She and Valentina reach Wes and me with matching expressions of low-key panic.

"With Crystal gone, no one's here to do the intros," Jesse says, pressing her thumb to her temple. "She was supposed to emcee."

"I mean, I could do it," she adds with a dry laugh. "Wouldn't be the weirdest thing I've taken over since she ghosted. But considering I'm singing tonight, that might come off a little... self-congratulatory."

Valentina adds quickly, "We all know Wes has been dying to perform that cursed Shakespeare number Lila and Sophie wrote, but we could really use ya."

Wes gasps like he's been personally betrayed. "You mean to tell me I don't get to dramatically monologue in a bedsheet toga tonight?"

Jesse snorts. "Not unless you want to traumatize the first-years. Seriously though. Will you do it? Just read the intros, keep things moving?"

He places a hand over his heart and bows with flourish. "Your emcee for the evening, at your service."

The show begins, and I find a spot among the other counselors and younger kids. I sit on the ground with my knees hugged to my chest, the grass still warm from the day. The first acts are what you'd expect—off-key singing, an out-of-sync ukulele duet, a magic trick that ends with someone shouting, "You weren't supposed to actually eat the card, dude!"

And somehow, it's perfect.

Then Lila and Sophie take the stage, sitting back-to-back on mismatched stools, each with an easel in front of them. They shout for audience suggestions— "A dinosaur in a tutu!" "A haunted smoothie!" "Valentina's stress levels!"—then race to sketch them. The results are chaotic and barely decipherable, but somehow still brilliant. Their banter is effortless. Their friendship is more of an art than anything they draw.

Next, Jesse steps onto the stage, guitar in hand, and the tone shifts. Her voice is low and sure, threading through a melody I've heard her hum all summer. The lyrics ache in that quiet, brave way—about staying when it's hard, about being seen, about choosing love when it would be easier to run.

The sound threads through me like pine smoke—thin, clinging, impossible to wash out. Her voice doesn't just fill the air; it settles into the cracks of me I thought I'd boarded shut. Oregon nights always hum with crickets and wind, but right now it feels like the whole forest is holding still, listening with me.

When the last note fades, no one claps right away; we all just breathe.

I feel it in my ribs—the ache of it. That kind of song doesn't end. It lingers. It settles. It reminds you of every version of yourself you thought you had to bury.

Then come the theater kids, led by Valentina in a hat made entirely of glitter and papier-mâché drama masks. They launch into a musical number with more energy than precision, waving cardboard props and hitting every exaggerated jazz hand like their lives depend on it.

Between each act, Wes appears with a stage whisper and a smirk, twisting Crystal's careful transitions into something absurd—deadpan jokes, dramatic pauses, even a bit where he pretends to forget his lines and blames it on "emotional whiplash from the haunted smoothie painting."

And I… watch him.

The way he walks. The way he holds space. How he turns performance into care makes the crowd feel like they matter.

It's not just charm; it's grace in disguise. A kind of quiet reverence for the moment, like every laugh he earns is sacred. He makes it look effortless.

He looks back at me during one of the transitions and winks. My chest instantly loosens.

Jesse and Valentina step forward, arms around each other, glowing. The show ends the way they say it always has.

"If you haven't performed yet," Valentina calls, "you're not off the hook. It's time for the camp song. Come up here and sing it with us."

A few brave souls wander forward. From the stage, Sophie locks eyes with me.

"Come on," she yells. "Camp rite of passage!"

"Hard pass," I mouth automatically.

But then he catches my eye. Wes has moved and is now standing behind Sophie and Lila. He's not beckoning, not teasing, simply watching. Steady. Still.

There's no push in his gaze—just patience. Just belief. And somehow, that undoes me more than pleading ever could.

The way he looks at me isn't performance. It isn't pressure. It's the kind of gaze that makes the air heavy with possibility, like the lights strung overhead aren't just for show but a map leading me toward him. My chest aches—not from fear, but from wanting to stop hiding.

Like every wall I've built is suddenly see-through. And I'm tired of pretending I don't want to be known.

Something shifts, I sigh, roll my eyes, and head towards the stage.

The lights glow. The first chords ring out. And I step into the music beside them.

✧ Wes ✧

After the applause fades, the crowd begins to scatter—some trailing toward the fire pit, others melting into the trees. There's a soft hum in the air, like static left behind after lightning.

Lila turns to Sophie, still buzzed from the performance. "I'm actually kind of excited to live with my dad," she rejoices, like she's just now realizing it's true.

Sophie bumps her with a grin. "We're staying up all night. No sleep 'til the rides home tomorrow."

They disappear into the dark, laughing, and plotting mischief, still tethered to the night's glow.

I stay back with Emilia. She's close—shoulder brushing mine, curls still a bit damp from the night air—and every time she exhales, it's like I can feel her letting go of something old. The weight she's carried since we were kids. Each breath feels like it's rewriting her shape—less armor, more softness. And I'm lucky enough to witness it.

I don't move, I allow myself to memorize this—her skin warm against mine, the sound of crickets and laughter drifting on the breeze. Like the universe finally exhaled.

Before I can say anything, Jesse appears out of the shadows, eyes bright. "Thank you," she says, breathless. "For stepping in. I *might* be addicted to performing, but I wouldn't have been able to do it if you hadn't helped."

Then she turns to Emilia, grinning. "And honestly? I'll allow it." Glancing back towards me, "He's officially earned the right to keep your heart."

She hugs me quick and hard, then winks at Emilia and vanishes toward Noah and Harper, who are huddled around Valentina, who's giving exaggerated bows.

I turn back to her, brushing a curl behind her ear. My fingers linger, tracing the edge of her cheekbone.

"You ready for your reward?" I ask, voice low. "I know where Dee hides the good snacks."

✧ Emilia ✧

The mess hall is mostly dark when we slip inside, moonlight spilling in through the high windows like silver mist. The quiet hum of the old freezer, the creak of the floorboards—it's the kind of silence that only exists in places that have held too many secrets for too long.

Wes leads me to a locked cabinet, fumbles with a key, and pulls out a tray of brownies wrapped in a towel. From the fridge, he snags a can of whipped cream with a grin like a kid on Christmas.

"You," he says, shaking the can with theatrical flair, "have earned this."

I hop onto the counter, feet swinging. "Wow. Dream date."

He sprays a cloud of whipped cream directly into my mouth, then his.

"Romantic, right?" he says, voice muffled. "Nothing says 'forever' like sugar foam."

I swipe whipped cream from my lip and move to smear it across his cheek. "You're ridiculous."

But he catches my wrist and draws my finger slowly to his mouth, eyes locked on mine as he licks it clean.

"Only for you," he murmurs.

The kiss that follows is slow and sweet, full of laughter and soft breath, the taste of sugar and something warmer.

His hand drifts to my hip. My fingers knot in the collar of his shirt. The kiss deepens—lazy, heat curling low and slow, like the first promise of a fire.

"Oh, hell no."

We both freeze.

Ms. Dee stands in the doorway, arms folded, her expression hovering somewhere between judgment and amusement.

"You two are not about to desecrate my kitchen with whipped cream and hormones."

Wes opens his mouth but closes it just as fast.

Dee steps forward, her tone firm but kind. "You've both got good heads on your shoulders. You know where the line is. And when it's time to cross it. You've got a sense of justice most people never find."

Then her voice drops just slightly. Her gaze sharpens, not accusatory; just... aware.

"Camp Silver Hollow has a way of waking things up in people."

There's a pause; it hums with something old like a story that doesn't get told out loud.

The kind of truth that lives in roots and riverbeds. It makes the hair rise on my arms—not in fear, but recognition. Like she's seen what we are, what we're becoming, and she's already made peace with it.

Then she turns away and mutters, "Next year, I'm hiding the good snacks better."

We walk the quiet path beneath the stars, hand in hand, the night still warm and full around us. Fireflies glow in the dark like floating embers. The air smells of damp cedar and cooling earth, the kind of scent that only comes after a long summer day finally exhales. Every sound carries farther at night, the far-off laugh by the firepit, the whisper of wind shifting in the branches. It feels like the whole camp is watching, waiting, but for once not intruding. The silence between us isn't empty. It's steady. Whole.

We've walked this path a hundred times this summer, but tonight it feels different—like it remembers. Every secret. Every scream. Every kiss. The forest doesn't forget.

At our tree, I stop, my fingers trace the symbol Wes carved there. It's worn smoother now, weathered, like us. But it's still here, still ours.

"You always said you'd be there for me," I whisper. "I didn't know what that meant—not really, not to the full extent. But now I do, you've shown me."

Wes steps closer, thumb brushing my jaw.

"You never had to earn it," he says. "You just had to believe I meant it."

I kiss him, not to prove anything. Not to claim, or ask, or answer; just to feel the promise of him.

His heartbeat steadies mine. The scent of pine and summer sweat and him wraps around me like a memory.

His arms fold around me, one at my waist, one braced behind me against the tree.

There's no rush, only this, only us.

When we finally break the kiss, he rests his forehead against mine, breath warm.

"Forever," I whisper.

He answers without hesitation. "I'm not going anywhere."

And for the first time in years, I believe him.

We stand there wrapped in stars and pine, the bark warm against my spine, his breath still catching on mine.

His hand slips from the tree to cup my jaw, thumb brushing the hollow beneath my cheekbone. He studies me like I'm made of starlight and breath, like touching me might unmake him.

"I love you," he murmurs. No fanfare. No question. Just truth.

"I know." I nod, threading my fingers through his hair. "I didn't realize I could love someone as much as I love you."

I kiss him—slow, deep, sure. Not desperate. Just... here.

His arm tightens around my waist, pulling me flush against him, and I feel it—the heat between us, steady and rising, like a tide that won't crash but will carry us wherever it wants to go.

He kisses me again, and again, until we're both a little breathless, a little undone. My hands find the buttons on his shirt, undoing them one by one, slower than I ever have. Like this time, I want to remember what it feels like to peel him open.

His shirt slips off and pools at our feet. His skin is warm beneath my palms, familiar now but no less holy. I reach for his belt, and he watches me, eyes dark but soft.

"You sure?" he asks, voice low.

I answer by lifting the hem of my dress and tugging it up and over my head, baring everything in the hush of the woods. The air kisses my skin. His gaze drags down and back up, reverent. Not possessive. Not hungry.

Just in love.

He steps closer, hands settling on my waist, and leans in to press a kiss just below my collarbone.

Then another, lower. Then again, like he's tasting the places that never get touched.

I reach for the button of his jeans and ease them down, his boxer briefs with them. He does the same, his thumbs curling under the band of my panties, dragging them slowly down my legs. They catch around my knees, and he drops with them, his mouth brushing the inside of my thigh as he looks up at me like a prayer.

He stays there, on his knees, hands smoothing up the backs of my thighs as he leans in and kisses the soft skin again. Then again, then higher. The kind of kisses that aren't about seduction—they're about devotion. About knowing me.

"You have no idea what you do to me," he murmurs between kisses. "How lucky I feel just to be here. Like this. With you."

I brace my hand on the tree as he parts my legs just enough and runs his tongue along the seam of me in one slow, deliberate stroke.

My breath stutters. My hand curls tighter against the bark.

He does it again—teasing, gentle, a single swirl of his tongue, then a kiss, then another, a quiet moan escapes my lips, and his grip tightens around my hips as I tip slightly forward, trying not to fall apart on my feet.

"That's it," he whispers against me. "Let me hear you. Let me feel how much you want this."

"Wes," I whisper, voice broken at the edges.

He looks up again, mouth shiny, eyes soft and wrecked. "I could stay here forever," he says, voice thick. "You taste like home." He presses a final kiss to the inside of my thigh. "But I need to be inside you."

He takes my hand, guiding me gently down to the soft moss at the base of the tree, like we're lying down inside the earth itself. It smells like pine and damp soil and summer.

He kisses me as he settles between my legs, our bodies bare and unguarded in the dark. His touch is careful but certain, like he knows this isn't just sex—it's something older, something predestined.

When he slides inside, it's deliberate, slow, full. My lungs stutter—not from surprise, but from the way I feel the pull at my heart.

I wrap my legs around him, arms looped around his neck, and for a moment we breathe—forehead to forehead, chest to chest.

"Okay?" he whispers.

"Always," I say, and I mean it with every inch of me.

We move together as if the forest made us for this. Like the stars above are holding their breath. The moss cradles me, damp and alive beneath my back, and I can't shake the sense that the forest is memorizing us. Every rustle of pine, every shimmer of starlight feels like a witness. It doesn't feel wrong. It feels like we were meant to be here—that the earth itself is rooting for us.

I feel him everywhere—his hands, his breath, his love—woven so deeply into me, I couldn't untangle him even if I tried.

His hips roll slowly against mine, a steady rhythm that builds with each breath. His hand cups my cheek. He keeps looking at me. Really looking—like if he blinks, he might miss something sacred.

And maybe he would.

Because this feels like a prayer answered. Like the version of me I tried to smother is finally free and wild again, blooming beneath him.

The pleasure builds low and warm, like sunlight through water, curling inside me with every gentle thrust.

He lowers his head, pressing a kiss to the curve where my shoulder meets my neck. It lingers there, his lips soft against sweat-damp skin, and I feel the shiver ripple down my spine.

"Emilia," he breathes against my throat—like a vow, like a plea. He says my name again, quieter this time, and it unravels something deep in my chest.

His hand slides up along my ribs, slow and grounding, until his fingers cradle my jaw. He tips my face toward him and kisses the edge of my mouth, then the corner of my smile, then finally my lips—deep and patient, like he's trying to memorize how I taste when I trust him.

I kiss him back through a sigh, my hips rising to meet his as he sinks deeper. The rhythm stays steady. Sure. Every movement unhurried and thick with meaning.

"That's it, Em," he whispers, his breath catching. "Let me feel all of you."

When he pulls back to look at me, his gaze is glassy—wrecked and worshipful.

"You feel so fucking good," he murmurs, voice breaking. "I could spend forever right here. Just loving you."

He leans down and presses another kiss, this time to the space just beneath my collarbone, my heart stammers under his touch. And still, he moves inside me, not rushing, not claiming—just giving himself over to every inch of me.

I slide my hand into his hair, fingers curling, and he moans low at the touch, hips faltering just slightly before he finds the rhythm again.

"Fuck" he rasps breathlessly, "you're so perfect like this." The swell of it rises—pleasure and ache and love tangled together until I don't know where one ends and the other begins.

"Look at me," he whispers. "I want to see your face when you cum."

It's not just my body coming undone; it's every version of me that thought she had to be small. Every part of me that learned silence as a form of survival. And he sees it. All of it.

I arch against him, thighs trembling, and the sound that escapes me is small but real, a breathless cry that's more thank you than anything else.

His hand tightens around mine in the moss.

"That's my girl," he murmurs, forehead pressed to mine. "Give it to me, Em. I've got you. I've always got you."

And I fall apart. Quietly. Entirely. Wes and the forest the only witnesses to this soft collapse.

My body pulses around him, and he falters—his breath catching, hips stuttering—then with one final thrust he breaks too, groaning low and desperate against my neck. His whole-body shudders with it—arms caging me, face pressed to my skin like he's trying to disappear into me completely.

He stays there for a long moment, still trembling, still inside me.

Then finally, slowly, he lifts his head and looks at me like I'm the only thing left in the world.

He kisses me again—soft, slow, tender, like he's sealing something in place.

The world is quiet, but I'm not. Not anymore.

29

The Quiet That Follows

☽ Camp Day 43 ~ August 8th ~ The Last Day ☾

✧ Wes ✧

The final breakfast bell rings, and the dining hall buzzes with that chaotic energy unique to endings—campers laughing a little too loudly, dragging out rituals they suddenly realize they'll miss. Sunlight spills through the tall windows, catching in the dust that hangs like glitter midair.

I sit beside Emilia at our usual table, our trays mostly untouched. Around us, the circle has shrunk—just Jesse, Harper, Noah, and Valentina. The table feels softer this morning. Quieter. Like something sacred is dissolving beneath the surface.

We talk about the summer in that coded way survivors do. The words say, remember the bonfires and talent shows, but underneath they whisper, *we made it.*

Jesse leans forward, brushing a loose strand of hair behind her ear. "I'm really glad you two stuck it out," she says, looking between Emilia and me. "You didn't have to. But you did. And it changed things."

Harper nods, chewing on the end of her spoon before grinning. "No offense to them, but once the inner circle started ghosting, this place got way more peaceful."

I laugh, but I feel Emilia go still beside me. I glance at her. Her smile flickers but doesn't hold. She's quiet this morning in a way that makes my chest ache.

Before I can ask, the dining hall doors burst open. Sophie and Lila tumble in like a matched set of small tornadoes. Still high on fairy lights and adrenaline, they chatter nonstop, replaying the talent show, promising weekly letters, already mourning people they haven't even left yet.

Lila bounces on her toes. "The buses just pulled in!" she announces. "Some parents are here already."

Jesse stands like she's flipping an internal switch, sliding into Crystal's abandoned role with practiced ease. "Alright, everyone—grab your things, say your final goodbyes, head to the horseshoe drive. Let's not make anyone wait."

The room ripples into motion. The noise doesn't sound like breakfast anymore. It sounds like unraveling. Forks scraping plates, chairs legs dragging, sneakers pounding—every sound is too sharp, like the walls themselves know they won't hold us much longer. For a second, I simply sit there, trying to memorize it all. Because tomorrow, the silence will feel like a ghost. And just like that, the end officially begins.

✧ Emilia ✧

Outside, the camp is alive with motion—duffel bags flying, arms thrown around shoulders, tears spilled freely into each other's necks. I watch it all unfold like a memory already fading. Like I'm hovering just outside myself, watching someone else live it.

The air smells of pine needles and exhaust, laughter cutting jagged through it like broken glass. I tell myself this is normal—that last days always hurt—but my chest is tight in a way that feels different. Like the ground itself knows I'm not ready to leave.

The goodbyes hurt everyone more than I expected. Kids clutch each other like if they let go, summer will vanish. They promise to write. To call. To visit. They say it like a vow. Like if they believe it hard enough, it'll make it true.

I help a group of first-years find their luggage. I scan Jesse's clipboard one last time, ticking names off the manifest.

That's when I see him: a tall man, standing beside Sophie and Lila near the gravel path. His hand rests gently on Lila's shoulder, his eyes creased in a smile that mirrors hers. Kind, steady. There's a quiet in him that looks familiar; it must be her dad.

Sophie points my way, and when his eyes meet mine, he gives a nod, soft and warm. I nod back, returning the smile.

Slowly but surely, the buses fill, the air shifts, and the camp falls quieter.

I'm back at Wes's side again by the time the three of them—Lila, Sophie, and her dad—approach.

"We just found out we only live, like, 45 minutes apart!" Sophie says, practically vibrating with excitement. "That means we can hang out all the time!"

Lila clutches her arm. "Every weekend. Sleepovers. Coffee dates. We're basically family now."

Her dad smiles, extending his hand. "Brian Vaughn. I've heard a lot about both of you. Thank you for looking after my girl."

Wes shakes his hand. I offer mine too. His grip is warm. Grateful.

"We're just two towns over," he says. "If you're ever up for a visit, Sophie's welcome anytime. We'd love to have her."

I nod, adding, "Maybe she can come to our place, too." The words feel strange in my mouth.

Because our house... the one with Vince's anger echoing in the walls and my mom's silence pressed into the wallpaper like mold—how do you invite someone into that?

But I smile anyway. Pretend it's easy. Maybe pretending is how it starts.

The girls hug again. Hard. Reluctant. Brian thanks us softly, especially for being so kind to Lila after Crystal vanished. Then he places a protective hand on her shoulder, and they walk away.

Sophie watches until their car disappears down the long stretch of gravel road, lined with Douglas Firs, that crowd so close they swallow the sky. Her eyes don't move. Not until they're completely gone.

✧ Wes ✧

The camp is mostly empty now, just the bones of it left behind. Everything echoes more sharply. Even the pine-scented air feels thinner without the sound of kids running through it.

Somewhere, a screen door bangs shut, and the sound carries forever. The cabins already look abandoned, shadows gathering in their eaves. The place that roared for six weeks has gone hollow in a single morning.

I stand by the car, one hand braced on the roof, watching Emilia rearrange something in the trunk. There's a tenderness in the way she moves—like she's holding the moment gently in her palms, knowing it's about to vanish.

She catches me staring and lifts a brow. I tilt my head and smile, the *come on, let's get this show on the road* kind of smile.

Very mom-and-dad energy, as Lila would say.

I turn and call toward the cabins. "Let's go! If we leave now, we might beat the other counselors to the first gas station."

Sophie comes flying up the path, sandals slapping against gravel, hair bouncing. "I almost forgot my sculpture!" she pants, holding up a misshapen piece of ceramic wrapped in newspaper with a triumphant grin.

She tosses her duffel in the trunk like it owes her money.

"Careful," Emilia says, helping her fold the seat forward. "Don't crush whatever that is."

Sophie beams and slides into the back. Emilia clicks the seat into place and moves to get in herself.

But before she can, Dee crosses the drive toward us, a small woven basket tucked in the crook of her arm.

"I packed a few things," she says, holding it out. "Snacks. I know how you kids get on the road."

Emilia accepts it with both hands, her smile quiet but real. "You didn't have to..."

"I wanted to."

Then she steps in and hugs her. Not a quick side-hug. Not a pat. It's full-body, intentional, and steady.

"You two are good people," she says into her ear. "Not just for getting through this summer, but for the way you moved through it."

Emilia holds on. I see it in her shoulders—that moment of stillness, of letting it land.

When Dee pulls back, she turns to me with a nod. "You drive safe now."

I'm already in the driver's seat when I catch movement out of the corner of my eye.

Mattie stands at the edge of the tree line, arms folded, half-shadowed. Watching.

I raise my hand. Not big. Just enough.

He doesn't wave but nods.

It's something.

✧ Emilia ✧

The highway unfolds like a ribbon of silence.

The forest gives way to long stretches of farmland, the kind that ripple gold in the wind. Sophie chatters for a while, still half-high on adrenaline, reliving every moment of the summer in breathless bursts.

But slowly, her voice fades. Her head tips to the side. She's asleep before we pass the third exit.

The basket from Dee rests in my lap. I run my fingers along the woven edge, then glance out the window. Everything looks different now.

Wes's hand slides over to my knee. His thumb brushes once, gently.

"What're you thinking about?"

I pause. The previous form of me would have lied. Would've said, *Nothing. I'm fine.* But I'm not her anymore.

"Camp changed me," I say. The words feel big, but right. "Something in me started to heal. But now I have to go back. To my mom. To Vince. That house." I shake my head. "None of it changed. But I did. And I don't know how to survive it the same way I used to."

He's quiet for a beat. I glance over, expecting hesitation. There's none.

"You don't have to survive it the same way," he says. "We've got each other fully now. We can build something new. Even if the rest of it stays messy."

I let his words sink in. They don't fix anything, but they offer a way through.

Eventually, Sophie stirs behind us, stretching and rubbing her eyes. "I can't wait to tell everyone at school," she says through a yawn. "Well... maybe not everything." I catch her eye in the rearview mirror, and we both smile.

We stop at a gas station somewhere near the county line. Stretch. Grab drinks. Watch Sophie talk the cashier's ear off about camp. The parking lot smells of diesel and hot asphalt, the kind of place where time feels stuck. Across the road, hayfields roll toward the hills, their edges ringed in blackberry thickets. I lean against the car, sipping my drink, and the sunlight feels sharper than it did at camp—as if the real world wants to remind me it's less forgiving, that it's already trying to resume. I can feel it in my bones.

✧

The trees begin to thin. Familiar signs rise along the roadside—gas stations we never stop at, the diner with the rusted roof, the turnoff that means we're almost home.

And that's when it hits me hard. We're not just leaving camp. We're going back.

But something inside me won't fit into the house I left behind. Camp didn't fix me. But it showed me something—who I am when the weight isn't crushing me. That girl is still in here, I'm still her.

Even if the world asks me to shrink again, I won't, not this time.

This time, I'm not just surviving; I'm choosing.

✦ 30 ✦

Homecoming Heat

✧ Emilia ✧

Sophie launches out of the car the second Wes pulls into the driveway. She doesn't even look back, doesn't grab her bag—just shouts something about going to Janelle's and disappears down the sidewalk in a blur of tangled hair and leftover camp adrenaline.

Her absence leaves a sudden silence in the car, like her energy had been the thing holding everything light. I sit there, frozen, the keys still jangling faintly in the ignition. The stillness presses in on me, louder than Sophie's chatter ever was. Through the windshield, the house looms—sun-faded siding the color of old bones, blackberry vines creeping along the chain-link fence like they've been trying to strangle it for years. Somewhere down the block, a dog barks and a lawnmower drones, perfectly ordinary sounds that only make the dread in my chest feel sharper. I don't move. My fingers curl tight in my lap; maybe if I grip hard enough, I can keep the past from crawling under my skin.

The house stares back at me. Quiet. Still. But I can feel it buzzing under the surface—an old, familiar hum of dread wrapped in peeling siding and sun-faded curtains.

Wes doesn't rush me. He unbuckles, gets out, then circles to my side and opens the door without a word. His presence alone steadies something shaky in my chest.

I stand slowly, the driveway warm beneath my sandals, the late-summer air clinging humid against my skin. Wes's hand slides to the small of my back.

"You here with me?" he asks, voice low.

"I dunno," I admit.

He nods like he expected that. "We don't have to be afraid of this place anymore."

But I am. Even now. Even with him beside me. Because this place remembers who I was. Because the ghosts in that house wear faces, I know too well.

I swear I can smell it already—cheap liquor soaked into carpet, grease clinging to the kitchen walls, the stale weight of words that were always meant to wound. The air itself feels thick, like it's waiting for me to break the silence I left behind.

I glance up at the front door. It hasn't changed. Still chipped paint, still rusted around the knob. But something in me has. And maybe that will be enough.

Wes leans down, his forehead briefly brushing mine. "Whatever happens in there," he says, "we walk through it together."

And I believe him.

✧ Wes ✧

She carries more weight in her shoulders with every step toward the house. I see how it sits heavy in her joints, how it tries to curl her back in on itself. I want to lift it off her, to break whatever pieces are still clinging from the life she's finally ready to burn down.

I grab the bags. Hers first, then Sophie's. I open the door, and the moment it swings inward, the air shifts. The hinges groan like they resent being used, and the air that spills out is stale, heavy with cigarettes and mildew. It smells like time stopped the day we left, like nothing here has shifted.

"Look who finally decided to show back up," Vince's voice barks from the living room, sharp and slurred like it's been aging in cheap whiskey. He doesn't even look up, sprawled across the couch like he owns the place. A bottle clinks against the floor as he shifts.

His legs are splayed like a warning. Like he's claimed every inch of this room by sheer force of arrogance. The TV flickers quietly behind him—reruns, probably, or nothing at all. Just background noise for a man who's always been louder than life ever deserved to let him be.

Marla's curled in her usual corner chair, clutching a threadbare throw pillow with stuffing poking at the seams as if it might save her from what she knows is always to come. It looks more like a child's security blanket than comfort for a grown woman. Her hair hangs limp, unwashed, eyes bloodshot and glassy. She doesn't even look up when Emilia steps inside, and that absence of recognition burns worse than any insult. Doesn't even try to pretend she's sober. "Let's just all calm down," she mutters, words slurred, limp, and useless.

At her words, Vince starts to rise.

"She's not about to walk back in here like she runs shit," he snaps, staggering upright and turning fully toward Emilia, wiping his mouth with the back of his hand. "I don't care how many kumbaya songs you sang or who fucked out in the woods"—glancing toward me.

He's moving toward her now. Not fast—he's off balance—but his intent is loud. Heavy. Threatening.

And that's when Emilia looks at me, her eyes are steely. There's a flicker in them, a flash of something sharp, ancient, a silent signal that needs no words. She glances toward the heavy flashlight by the door.

I nod. The understanding hits like thunder inside me. It's time.

I close the distance in two strides, intercepting Vince before he reaches her. My hand clamps around his wrist, twisting. I slam him into the wall so hard the plaster cracks. He wheezes as his ribs buckle inward with a choked scream.

He thrashes, but I've got leverage and fury on my side. I drive my knee into his gut, winding him, then yank him off the wall merely to slam him back again, harder.

"Don't fucking move," I snarl, teeth clenched.

But he's still trying, still mouthing off.

Until Emilia steps beside me. Flashlight in hand.

Her grip shifts once. Then again. Like she's adjusting for weight or memory. Like she's thinking of every time she wished for something heavy enough to stop whoever her mom was prioritizing over her.

She doesn't hesitate.

The first swing clips his cheekbone, jolting his head sideways with a fleshy crack, skin splitting open like fruit under a tire. He roars in pain, but before he can recover, the second hit lands hard at the curve of his temple. The dull thud is sickening—like metal on wet wood. Bone gives a little under the force, fracturing inward, his balance buckling.

Then the third blow comes down brutal and clean. She swings from her core, flashlight gripped like a hammer, and it smashes straight into the bridge of his nose with a crunch so sharp it silences the room. His septum caves, blood erupts, dark and fast, splattering across my shirt in a wide, arterial arc.

He drops to one knee, groaning—stunned, disoriented. I let him fall the rest of the way, then kick his leg out from under him for good measure. His skull meets the floor with a wet, final thud that makes the air seem thinner somehow.

Marla screams.

"Stop it! Stop it!" she shrieks, lurching to her feet, but goes down hard. She hits the floor with a slap, sliding on Vince's blood, her jeans soaking it up.

For a second, she lolls there, soaked, stunned, her hands twitching like she doesn't know what to reach for. Maybe the bottle. Maybe the past. Maybe me. But she's too slow, too broken, too late.

The blood beneath her spreads fast. She sees it now, really sees it—what he was. What she let happen. And for once, the silence she's always used to shield herself cracks open into something raw and real.

"I'm your mother," she sobs, trying to back away on shaking arms. "I raised you—I cared for you—"

✧ Emilia ✧

"No, you didn't."

My voice comes out low and trembling—but it builds with every word, fueled by everything I've carried for years.

"You watched Dad beat the shit out of me. You sat on your ass and let it happen. Lied, for him. And after he was gone, the only thing you cared about was their attention." Gesturing towards Vince's body, "For years, putting the wants of men over the needs of your own daughters. What kind of mother does that?"

My throat tightens, voice angrier but more self-assured now.

"I raised Sophie. I kept food in the house. I cleaned your puke, paid your bills, and hid every bruise. You didn't raise me. You just made sure I survived long enough to resent you for it."

She sobs harder, clawing at the floor like it might open up and save her.

Wes steps beside me. Still. Silent. I reach behind him and curl my fingers around the knife still sheathed at his lower back. The same knife he used to end so many of my nightmares.

It feels right that I end this one with it too.

"Emilia," Marla gasps, "Please—baby—"

I step forward, her eyes widen as I kneel. The blade catches the light. I don't wait, I drive it into her chest. One quick, clean, brutal thrust.

Her body jerks under the force, ribs resisting for a breath before giving way. The sound isn't loud. It's wet. Final.

She gasps, blood bubbling on her lips, eyes wide with shock. I twist the blade.

Her hands flutter weakly at my wrists.

The house seems to hold its breath. The AC unit hum turns too loud, a grotesque lullaby underscoring the wet sound of Marla's final gasps. I feel the pulse of her heart against the hilt—strong for a beat, then wavering. Then nothing, and she goes still.

Once again, I find myself drenched in blood. It coats my wrists, my fingers, splattered up my arms.

My hands tremble, but not with regret. The blood drips down my wrists, hot and sticky, falling to the linoleum in tiny red constellations. I stare at them like they might rearrange themselves into something holy. For once, I don't feel like a ghost in this house. For once, it's the house that feels haunted by me.

I don't feel light.

But I do feel free.

Rage doesn't leave your body all at once. It lives in your knuckles and your breath. But for the first time, mine has somewhere to go that isn't just inward.

I look at Wes. When he looks at me, I crash into him like gravity snapped.

I grab his shirt and shove him hard into the kitchen. The hum of the refrigerator vibrates through his spine. One hand against the door, the other bracing the counter beside him. I plant my palms flat against his chest, holding him there like a challenge—caged and still—just how I want him.

Our mouths collide, messy and frantic. I yank at his belt with shaking fingers, the leather catching on the button of his jeans.

"I need you," I whisper, the words trembling against the charged air between us.

My knees hit the tile, cool and gritty against my skin.

My hands tremble—not from fear, but from something messier. Need. Grief. Devotion. A prayer disguised as desire.

I want to undo him. Strip him down to his bones the way he sees through mine. I want to worship him like he's the only clean thing left in this house.

Like if I give him every part of me, maybe I'll remember I was never dirty to begin with.

Every nerve in me feels raw, strung too tight, like the violence cracked something open that only he can fill. The kitchen still reeks of iron and rot, but the warmth of his skin cuts through it, grounding me. My pulse hammers so fast I can taste it at the back of my throat. I want to devour him the way this house tried to devour me—completely, without mercy, until there's nothing left but us.

I press hot kisses to the waistband of his jeans. Then lower. Tongue teasing, fingers fumbling. I unzip him, tug his boxers down, take him in my mouth like he's the only thing keeping me upright.

Blood streaks drying across my body. My skin's tacky with sweat and adrenaline. But I don't care.

He's hot against my tongue, the taste of skin and salt grounding me in this body, this moment. I suck slowly, letting the weight of him fill my mouth, my throat burning a little with effort.

His groan is sharp and broken. One hand grips the counter, the other fists in my hair—tight enough to hold me there, like he's anchoring us together.

He bucks forward instinctively, and I brace my hands against his thighs, pushing him back just enough to take control again. I want this slow. Intentional. I want to make him fall apart on my tongue like I'm the only safe place left in the wreckage.

"Fuck, babe—"

I take him deeper, slow, and filthy, tongue working over every sensitive inch. His hips jerk. He lets out a strangled breath, knuckles white where they grip the counter. Every moan he gives me is a thread stitching something torn back together—like if I love him hard enough, I can unmake every hand that ever hurt me.

There's something frantic in both of us now—like we're trying to fuck the violence out of our bloodstreams. Like if we don't touch enough, we'll become unmade.

He growls, low and animalistic, and hauls me up by the hair—not rough to hurt, but like he needs to feel every inch of me in his grip, to anchor himself in something that's still alive.

His mouth crashes into mine, filthy and hungry, slamming me back against the refrigerator. He yanks my shorts down and rips my underwear off.

His hands roam, rough and claiming. Then he grabs under my thighs and lifts me, carrying me the few feet to the counter like I weigh nothing.

My ass hits the counter, and his fingers slip between my thighs—testing, teasing— "You're always so goddamn wet for me, Em," he gasps, lining himself up and driving into me with one hard, perfect thrust.

I cry out, finally feeling whole.

The room disappears. The blood. The ghosts. The house. There's only Wes. His body. His hands on my hips. His mouth on my throat.

Every thrust is a reclamation.

I claw at his back, not just for pleasure but for proof—I'm still here. In this body. In this house. And he's in me, not to take but to anchor.

The cabinet digs into my spine, hard and grounding. Every sound he makes becomes mine. Every breath he steals from me, I give back twice over.

"I want to live inside your chest," I pant, clinging to his shoulders. "Nest behind your ribs. Sleep wrapped around your fucking heart."

"You've already climbed in," he growls, "and you're never allowed leave."

My legs lock tighter around his waist. Every snap of his hips is a promise. Every kiss, a vow.

I cum with a cry, shaking in his arms. He follows, groaning into my shoulder as his grip on me turns bruising and devout all at once.

For a moment, I can't tell where I end, and he begins. My body shakes, still wound tight from everything I unleashed, but in his arms, it feels like the shaking has somewhere to go. Like every scream I swallowed over the years, finally tore its way free through pleasure instead of pain. His sweat mingles with mine, the scent of him sharp and human, drowning out the ghosts that used to own this space.

✧

A broken home remade in the heat of ruin. The ghosts are still here, but they're quieter now—watching, maybe, but no longer steering my hands.

The kitchen smells of blood and sweat and sex.

I'm still perched on the counter, legs draped around him, his head buried against my throat. My skin's flushed, sticky, glowing with effort and aftermath.

It should feel wrong, but it doesn't. It feels like taking myself back; proof that this place doesn't own me anymore.

Wes finally pulls back, just enough to meet my eyes. His thumb drags across my jaw. I think we're both still fully catching up to what just happened.

But I know this:

We're not going back. We're moving forward. And this house—this life—it's ours now.

Even if we have to burn it down again tomorrow.

We'll do it together.

Outside, the cicadas scream, their chorus rising like a warning and a promise. The house stands silent behind us, blood still wet on the floorboards, the air thick with ghosts.

But for the first time, I don't feel like I belong to it. It belongs to me.

✦ 31 ✦

Blood, Sweat & Silence

✧ Wes ✧

For a while, all I can hear is her breath. The kind of breath that isn't trying to hide anything anymore—shaky, alive, real. Her body still wrapped around mine; her fingers still tangled in the back of my shirt like she's holding on just in case the past tries to take her again.

I press a gentle kiss to her collarbone and ease back, only far enough to let my hands find my jeans on the floor near the fridge. They're half inside out, sticking to the tile from sweat and blood and everything we didn't try to stop. I tug them up with a grunt.

Emilia chuckles quietly beside me, soft and hoarse. "Thanks for not fully ripping them this time."

I glance over my shoulder. She's crouched, retrieving her underwear from under the cabinet where they slid mid-frenzy, dangling them from one finger like evidence.

"They looked too pretty to ruin," I murmur, watching her slip them back on, then adjust her shirt back down into place with a kind of ease that shouldn't be possible in a kitchen still painted in blood.

But that's the thing about Emilia. She doesn't shy away from aftermath. She meets it where it's bleeding and builds a life on top of it anyway.

I turn toward the living room. The air is heavy again but not like before. Not dread. Just… finality.

"Come on," I say, voice low. "We've got some cleaning up to do before Soph gets home."

Vince is in the dead center of the room, one leg kicked awkwardly outward from where he tried crawling and failed. His blood pools beneath his head, a halo that's already half-dried at the edges. Marla's a few feet away, twisted like a fallen mannequin. Her jeans are soaked in red, knees slick where she slipped, chest gaped open from the knife.

Emilia doesn't look away.

She grabs the bucket and bleach from under the sink. I grab the plastic tarp and tape from the garage—because yeah, I've thought about this before. Maybe not this exact scene, but close enough.

The smell is already turning. The air thickens with it—copper and iron laced with something sour, already veering toward rot. It mingles with the faint tang of bleach from the open bottle; a clash of sterility and death that makes the room feel less like a living space and more like a morgue with curtains drawn.

We wrap Vince first. Blood seeped into the floorboards beneath him, dark and tacky. When I shift him, there's a wet sound that clings to the air, meat pulled free from the wood. His jaw clicks once when I roll him, and Emilia doesn't even blink.

There's blood smeared along the wall where I slammed him—cracked like a spiderweb behind it. The plaster flakes with every movement, little bits drifting down like dust stirred from an attic.

"I'll patch that later," I say, almost to myself.

Emilia nods. "Add it to the list."

The flashlight lies half-lost under the coffee table, its metal casing coated with now tacky blood. I nudge it out with my boot and wipe it clean, placing it back by the door.

She's kneeling in a puddle of it now, scrubbing where Marla's blood slicked across the wood. It stains her palms, but her movements are steady. Controlled.

Her breath catches once, just once, like the effort costs more than she'll admit. I can see the tendons in her wrists strain with each stroke, but her jaw stays locked. She's not just cleaning—she's daring the house to remember her this way, not as the girl who hid here, but the woman who gutted her ghosts.

It's like she's trying to scrub out years, not just blood—like if she cleans deep enough, she can peel the house's memory from the floorboards. And maybe she can. Maybe we both can.

We work in silence for a while, only breaking it with the occasional request— "More bleach," "Help me with the bag," "Don't forget under the couch."

"This feels..." she starts, then trails off.

"Necessary?" I offer.

She exhales. "Yeah. That."

The rhythm of our hands becomes almost ritual. Scrub. Bleach. Rinse. Repeat. It's not just mess we're cleaning—it's grief, layered like dust on every surface. Every stroke of the rag feels like a small act of rebellion. Like we're sanding down the ghosts and daring them not to return.

Eventually, she looks up, sweat glistening along her hairline. "What are we doing with them?"

"I've got a plan," I tell her. "Somewhere no one will find them."

She studies me for a long second. Not shocked. Not scared. Just... assessing. Then she nods. "Okay." That's it. That's all she needs.

We finish the living room first. Mopped, scrubbed, renewed. Every inch of blood erased like it was never there. But we'll always know. The floorboards will know.

I move the tarp-wrapped bodies to the garage to deal with tonight, after Sophie's asleep. When I return, Emilia's leaning against the wall, arms limp at her sides, a faint red smear across her jaw like war paint. She looks at me and says, "Shower?" Without hesitation I take her hand.

✧ Emilia ✧

The bathroom is still warm from the day, but the moment Wes twists the knobs, and the water starts pounding against the tile, steam begins to rise. It swirls up slowly, curling along the mirror as the air thickens between us.

There's no ceremony to it. No hesitation. I peel off my shirt—stiff with blood and sweat—and let it fall into the pile already forming near the sink. The rest follows. The cotton clings as I strip it away, sticky with everything we've survived.

Wes is already stepping into the tub, jeans gone, boxers peeled away, water running hot and steady over his shoulders. When he turns and offers his hand, I don't just take it, I fold into him.

The curtain swings closed behind me, sealing us inside a space that feels quieter than the rest of the house—like the walls are holding their breath.

The hiss of the shower is the only sound, steady, and endless, drowning out the creaks of the old house. Steam curls into every corner, blurring edges, softening the tile into something that almost feels like sanctuary. For the first time in hours, maybe days, the world shrinks to nothing but this heat and his hands.

The spray hits my chest first—hot enough to sting, then soothe. I tilt my head back and close my eyes as the water races down my body, dragging flecks of blood and grit in its wake. It turns pink at my feet. I watch it disappear down the drain without flinching. What's left clings to the tile grout and my cuticles, too stubborn to leave all at once.

Wes's hands are on my hips, steadying me like I might break if he lets go.

Neither of us speaks.

He shifts behind me, runs a hand down my spine, gentle as rain. Then I feel the soap—his hands lathering slow, starting at my shoulders, and working lower. Each touch deliberate. Dedicated.

He kneels, his fingers tracing the backs of my calves, scrubbing at the dried blood there before rising to my thighs. His lips press once, just above my knee. Not lust. Not pity. Just love, bruised and quiet.

When he stands again, I meet his eyes. Then take the soap from his hands.

I lather his chest, slow and reverent. Trail suds along his ribs, across his shoulders, over the curve of his biceps. I scrub under his fingernails, then reach up and run my fingers through his hair, working shampoo into his scalp until he sighs, leaning into it like he's letting go.

Neither of us has ever said we're okay. But right now, in this small porcelain space, we are.

Okay doesn't mean whole. It doesn't mean healed. It just means we're still moving, still choosing each other in the wreckage. And for me—that's enough.

I tip my head under the stream, rinsing, eyes closed. When I blink through the curtain of steam and drops, Wes is watching me. His expression is soft. Open. Like he knows we're still standing in the ruins, but we're already rebuilding.

He reaches up and brushes a strand of wet hair from my cheek and kisses me. Just once. Just enough.

Then he reaches past me and shuts off the water.

✧

I towel off slowly, wrapping the fabric around my body like armor. My skin is pink from the heat. My hair drips down my back.

Wes stays in the bathroom, toweling his hair dry. I leave him there and walk barefoot down the hallway, cool wood planks pressing into the soles of my feet.

The house feels… different. Not fully safe, not yet. But quieter.

The weight it used to hold is still here, but it's shifted. Like something's finally given way. Like the foundation cracked just enough to let the light in.

I pause in the doorway of our bedroom that Sophie and I have always shared. The posters on the wall are faded and peeling, the old mattress in the

corner of the room; messy, and only half-made. The burned-out lamp on the dresser is still there. So is Sophie's stuffed rabbit, wedged between two pillows.

It's still the same room, but I'm not the same girl who left it. I sit on the edge of my bed and let the silence settle around me. Let it belong to me.

This is where I grew up and where I bled and where I dreamed of getting out.

Now I picture something else—Sophie asleep in a big bed in her own room, safe. Wes's boots by the door. Me in the kitchen, windows open, the air filled with something other than fear.

It's not a plan, not even a promise. Just a possibility; a version of this life that might not be perfect but might finally be ours.

Through the half-open window, I hear the night insects humming in the blackberry thickets outside, their chorus rising with the damp breeze that carries the sharp resin of fir needles. The house exhales with it, old wood groaning, as if it knows change has finally come.

I pull on clothes, breathe, and I let it settle in—this fragile hope blooming beneath all the blood.

This house isn't haunted anymore. Not if I don't let it be. Not if I become the thing it's afraid of. Maybe I already am.

The girl who returned isn't the one who left. She doesn't cower in corners or swallow screams. She bleeds and rebuilds. She sharpens her teeth and calls it healing.

The walls can keep their scars. The floorboards can keep their whispers. I'm not erasing the past—I'm folding it into my skin, into my breath, into every step I take across this house. If it remembers me, it will remember the version that refused to die here.

She walks the same creaking floorboards, but now they echo different. Less like a warning. More like applause.

✦ 32 ✦

Where the Roots Take Hold

✧ Emilia ✧

Sophie opens the front door like she's bracing for the usual bomb to go off. Her fingers twitch at her sides like she's ready to bolt if the moment cracks. I can almost see the calculations in her head—where to duck, what to say, whether to trust the quiet.

Her footsteps are slow. Cautious. Her eyes flick from the coat rack to the floor, expecting to find broken glass or a bottle just barely holding onto the edge of the counter. She pauses like she's listening for the slurred drawl of Vince's voice from the couch, or the sharp crash of Marla knocking something over in a drunken stupor.

But there's only silence; serene sacred silence.

It's the kind of silence that feels too wide for a house like this, as if the walls themselves don't know what to do without the usual chaos to absorb. The air tastes lighter, detergent, and dust instead of smoke and sour beer, the faint buzz of the fridge replacing what used to be shouting.

The TV hums low in the background, I'm curled up on the couch, legs folded beneath me, a blanket draped over my knees. Wes sits beside me, arm thrown around me over the back of the cushions like it's the most natural thing ever. Like we belong there, and maybe we finally do.

Sophie lingers in the doorway like she's waiting for something to lunge at her.

Her gaze sweeps the room once, then again slower. Her brow furrows. She takes one step forward, hesitant, like she's afraid to breathe too loud in case it breaks whatever spell this is.

Her eyes skim over the couch, over the floor. No ashtrays overflowing. No passed-out figures. No Vince, sprawled in boxers with a beer balanced on his stomach. No Marla with a half-lit cigarette and a slurred insult ready to go.

Just me and Wes, curled up on the couch with a blanket between us, the warm glow of the lamp softening the corners of the room, a random re-run humming low in the background.

It's not the silence that unnerves her. It's the softness. The way the cushions hold their shape. The scent of detergent instead of vodka. The fact that no one's yelling, or slamming cabinets, or crying in the bathroom with the door half-shut.

She doesn't speak. Doesn't move past the threshold. Just stands there, gripping the strap of her backpack like she's waiting for someone to tell her this is all a trick.

"Hey you," I say, gentle. "Come sit?" I pat the spot next to me.

She doesn't move. Just stares at us like we're strangers who broke into her house and replaced her life with something too quiet to trust. Her eyes glint with suspicion, the kind that comes from years of learning that quiet never lasts. She shifts her weight like she's already rehearsing the next escape route, waiting for the moment the calm will curdle into something sharp.

Finally, her voice cuts through the stillness, wary and thin.

"...Where's Mom?"

Wes shifts beside me, casual in the way people get when they're trying too hard not to seem rehearsed. He scratches the back of his neck "she, umm, took off."

Sophie blinks, not quite processing.

I add, "With Vince. Something about Florida and motorcycles and some buddy of his with a shop down there."

A long beat of silence like she's waiting for the punchline. But there isn't one. She frowns. "She really just... took off?"

Wes nods. "Didn't even bother to finish her bottle."

Her lips part, confused. I can see her trying to plug this version of events into everything she knows and coming up short.

"Guess she decided to stop pretending that we matter," she says, soft.

Sophie's eyes flick between us again. Two calm bodies. No shouting, no danger, just warmth and something that might pass for safety if she knew what that felt like.

And for a second, she looks like she might cry. Not because she's sad. But because peace—real, lingering peace—feels more foreign than anything else we could've said.

Her voice is quieter when she says, "It's weird. Seeing you two like this."

Wes raises a brow. "Watching TV?"

"No. Just... here. On the couch, ya know?" She shrugs. "It's just different. No one's drunk. No one's yelling. And dead serious, cleaner than I've ever seen it"

She doesn't elaborate on what we all know: most of her life, this space reeked of vodka and stale cigarettes, claimed by Marla's shrieking or Vince's foul laughter echoing through the walls. Usually, Sophie would just attempt to slink past the chaos unnoticed, unheard. But not tonight.

Tonight, there's simply... peace.

"Ya hungry?" Wes asks, shifting to look at us both. "I bet there's at least a few packs of ramen somewhere in that haunted-ass pantry."

"In this economy?" I deadpan. "Good luck."

Sophie grins, the smallest crack in her armor. "Maybe we can pretend we're on Chopped. Make something edible out of whatever's left in the freezer and Mom's old SlimFast packets."

"In that case, we're definitely fucked," I mutter, already standing.

We migrate to the kitchen, the three of us moving like something close to normal. Sophie pulls out a sketchpad, takes her spot at the table, and starts doodling like that was her regular evening routine. Like she hasn't spent years tiptoeing around landmines.

I watch her hand move, fluid and unafraid, like maybe this house doesn't feel like a trap anymore.

Like maybe she can create something here again that isn't about surviving.

It hits me then—how deeply we've all been starving for this level of ordinary. Something as simple as Sophie dragging a pencil across paper feels radical, like proof that the house can still hold creation instead of destruction.

Wes and I dig through cabinets. It's a scavenger hunt of sad condiments, off-brand cereal, and expired canned soup. But we manage. A pot of water bubbles on the stove for Mac n cheese. I pull out a rock-hard, half-eaten pack of freezer-burned Dino Nuggets from the back of the freezer. Sophie makes gagging noises, but she'll eat anything we set in front of her.

By the time we all sit down, the table is cluttered with a patchwork of paper towels, chipped plates, and mismatched forks. But we're together, and it's quiet. Still. Soft.

"I don't remember the last time we did this," I say, my voice low. "A real dinner. Even something this simple."

Sophie shrugs. "Maybe before Dad died, but I don't remember it."

That lands like hard, but not in a way that breaks anything, just the truth, spoken plainly.

We eat in silence for a minute. The clink of forks against cheap plates fills the room like music. Sophie hums under her breath, barely audible, Jesse's tune from camp. Wes refills her glass of water without a word.

I look around the table. At my sister, chewing thoughtfully, flipping pages in her sketchbook between bites. At Wes, calm and steady beside me. At the warm light over the stove, the clean counters, the open window letting in a breeze that smells like late summer.

It's not perfect, but it is ours. And for the first time in years, the tight coil behind my ribs begins to ease. Not completely—but just enough to let something else in. Something softer, it feels like the beginning of something better—raw, imperfect, but undeniably ours.

✧ Wes ✧

The night is deep and still. No street sounds or passing chatter. Save for the hum of crickets and the faint rustle of branches.

The kind of night that used to stretch into nightmares. Now for the first time it stretches into something else—quiet resolve.

Emilia stands watch near the edge of the driveway as I open the garage and pull the tarp-covered bodies toward the trunk of my car. They're heavier now. Not physically, but symbolically. This isn't just cleanup. This is closing the door for good.

I load Vince first, then Marla. Each body hitting the lining of my trunk with a dull, final thud. Emilia doesn't shrink; I can feel her watching me with those steady eyes.

I climb into the driver's seat. My hand finds her thigh automatically, I tell myself it's for grounding her but maybe it's grounding me too; because this part, the after, still demands something from both of us.

"Okay..." she says, voice small but firm. "Now what?" The engine hums to life. "Now," I murmur, "we take them where your father's been all these years."

We drive with the windows cracked. No music. Just the quiet stretch of pavement beneath us.

The farther south we go, leaving the last glow of town behind, the road darkens, swallowed by the

Lupine Forest. Out here, the pines and firs crowd close, their trunks silvered by moonlight, their shadows thick enough to feel like watching eyes.

I know these woods from childhood warnings—don't wander too far, don't get caught after dusk. Now we drive straight into them with a trunk full of ghosts.

She doesn't ask, but I feel the question sitting between us—warm and quiet, like something already forgiven. Like she's giving me space to tell it in my own time.

"You're wondering about it," I say, voice barely louder than the wind "that night, 9 years ago." She doesn't answer, I graze my thumb back and forth on her thigh.

"Used my dad's car, drove til I couldn't see lights anymore," I tell her. It lands gently, not a bomb—just the answer she already suspected. A puzzle piece she never needed to force.

"I knew the woods would hide it. You remember all the stories whispered about those trees—how they'd swallow you whole if you weren't careful? Everyone always said stay on the path, don't wander too deep... I figured; it was perfect, nobody goes there. Nobody notices. Everything stays hidden, just like it should."

Her fingers squeeze mine, but she still doesn't speak. I let the silence stretch, letting the memory sink in without spelling it out any further. The road narrows, then disappears into gravel. I park near the edge of a dark trail, headlights cutting through trees that remember everything.

We hike quietly, flashlights off. Just the waning moon above and the sound of our own breathing. Twigs snap underfoot like the forest is whispering warnings we don't need anymore.

"This is it," I whisper, pointing to an old pine whose roots jut up through the soil like claws trying to drag the earth open. "He's there." I gesture a little off to the side. "We'll put them close, but not with him."

She nods. I pass her the shovel, the handle solid and heavy. She sinks her fingers around it, takes a steadying breath, and drives the blade into the dirt with a swift, sure motion—each thrust a quiet act of finality, like marking the forest itself as witness.

✧ Emilia ✧

The dirt is stubborn. Dry in places, then suddenly too soft, like the ground can't decide if it wants to let go. But I keep going, each thrust of the shovel into the ground is a release. A ritual. The air smells like wet leaves and metal. My palms are already blistering.

I glance toward the gnarled oak. He's down there. The man who broke so much of me, and now I'm here to bury the rest.

"Good fucking riddance," I mutter.

The silence is thick, but not empty, just full of history. The forest presses close, damp air heavy with moss and loam, the canopy blotting out all but scraps of moonlight. Every breath feels like it's borrowed from something older, something that's been waiting for us to finally return what never belonged above ground.

When I finally speak again its words I didn't know I'd been carrying. "You did it. All those years ago. Before I ever knew. You ended it."

Wes stays quiet, he doesn't try to explain. I think about all the years I spent wondering if anyone saw me, if anyone cared enough to try. And now, watching Wes move through this darkness for me, I wonder how I ever doubted I was worth saving.

"I didn't think I mattered back then," I continue, breath catching. "But you stepped in. You gave me space to breathe when I didn't know I was suffocating."

He looks at me, eyes shadowed but sure. "You did." His jaw working like he's chewing on the right words before he speaks again.

"I saw you," he says quietly. "Even back then. I always saw you." Before turning and heading back to the car.

I watch from the edge of the clearing as Wes lifts my mom's body from the trunk. He doesn't grunt or curse or hesitate. Just wraps his arms around her like she weighs nothing and carries her to the grave we dug—to the place where this ends.

The moonlight brushes over his shoulders as he lowers her in, catching on the ridges of muscle beneath his shirt, the raw strength in every movement. But it isn't just his body that steals my breath, it's the care in how he does it. The way he honors even the worst of them, for my sake.

When he straightens, I don't look away. Not from his arms, his hands, or the weight he carries. Not from the man burying ghosts just to give me a life without them. Not from the man who's never asked me to explain the scars—only made sure I'll never have new ones.

Then he goes back for Vince, less deferential, his jaw now set in a hard line all pretense of respect evaporated.

He hefts the second body out, chest flexing as he adjusts the dead weight across his arms. The moonlight catching his biceps, the low dip of sweat-darkened fabric clinging to his spine.

I should be thinking about the bodies. About the fact that we're committing crimes in the woods under cover of darkness, where the weight of the stories we grew up hearing about these woods make the night feel charged in a way that's impossible to ignore.

But all I can think about is him. His strength. His silence. The way he's always carried the worst of my past like it was his to hold—and somehow still makes me feel like something precious in the middle of all this rot.

He doesn't notice me watching. Doesn't know that between every shovelful of dirt, I'm falling in love deeper and deeper.

Not for what he says but for what he's always been willing to be for me.

We fill the grave together. The soil darkens and flattens as the woods hold their breath.

Wes steps close and brushes a smear of dirt from my cheek, his touch featherlight. I lean into it, eyes burning, but steady.

"Thank you," I whisper. "For knowing what I needed... before I even knew it myself." The wind rustles the leaves above us, but the clearing remains still.

The dirt stains our palms, gets beneath our fingernails, proof that we put them down ourselves. That we didn't look away.

We leave the dead behind. The ground holds them quiet, the trees standing sentinel, rooted deep in secrets they'll never tell.

We walk back into the darkness together—not afraid, not looking back—toward something that finally feels like peace. Not perfection but freedom.

Behind us, the Lupine Forest keeps its secrets. The roots take hold. The ground settles heavy and final. And for the first time, the past belongs to the dirt instead of us.

33

As Time Turns

✧ Wes ✧

Time doesn't just pass. It shifts, settles, and reshapes as summer gives way to fall, akin to a breath exhaled. I can tell Emilia keeps expecting something to snap. A bottle. A voice. Maybe herself... But the quiet holds. And slowly, she starts to trust it.

The house changes with us, slowly, like something thawing. Gone are the cigarette butts and sour beer cans. Gone is the mildew soaked into the baseboards. We strip the place bare and start again. Not to forget what happened here—but to make room for what's still to come.

The walls hold the damp weight of years, soaked through with the same gray drizzle that stains the town outside. When the rain comes, it threads in through the old window frames, carrying the scent of wet pavement and moss from the sidewalks. The floors creak like they remember boots heavy with sawdust, even though the mill's been shut down for decades. Little by little, the house exhales that history, and something cleaner begins to settle in its place.

The kitchen's the first to wake up. Emilia stocks the fridge with real food. There are clean dishes in the cabinets, and a spice rack on the counter. A coffee pot that warms the air most mornings; it smells like cinnamon and ground beans instead of the rot that once was, like something lived in. Like a real home.

Sophie takes over what used to be her and Emilia's shared bedroom, claiming it fully. She picks out the paint herself, something soft with flecks of sparkle that catch the afternoon light. It covers her by accident and splatters the ceiling on purpose. She blasts music and sings loudly while she works, and for the first time, I don't see her brace for impact when the floor creaks.

Paint fumes cling to the air, sharp and sweet, mixing with the faint scent of rain drifting through her open window. Dust motes float in golden light, stirred by her dancing. Each laugh shakes the tension from the walls, as though the house itself is soaking in her joy.

Emilia leans against the doorframe, watching her. I stand behind Emilia, watching them both. They don't see me, I don't want them to. This is their moment—this healing—and I'd never get in the way of it. But I'm here, anchoring the edges, holding steady.

This is our family now, and no one will take it from us.

My dad still lives next door, same house, same quiet. He spends most of his time at Mercer's Hunting and Fishing, the little shop on Main where the town still has a bit of life left in it. The smell of gun oil and river mud never quite leaves the old, warped wood floors. Locals stop in as much to swap fish stories as to shop. His place. His rhythm. Doesn't come by much, but he waves when he sees me. Leaves gear on our porch sometimes—hooks, oil, fire starters, a camping blade he thinks I might like. He doesn't say it, but I think he's proud of me. We don't need to talk about the past. Some things are just understood. And for us, that's enough.

☽ October 31, 2014 ☾

By the time Halloween rolls around, the porch is a crooked little shrine to spooky season. Paper ghosts hang from the eaves. Pumpkins crowd the steps. Sophie's out trick-or-treating with her friends in a costume made of glitter, netting, and Emilia's old scarves. Her laughter echoes down the street, loud and unafraid—like it never learned to be scared in the first place.

I finish hanging the swing just before dusk—reclaimed wood, knotted rope, sanded smooth and strong. It hangs from a thick branch that arches over the yard, catching the last of the leaves as they fall. I built it solid, built it for them.

I watch her move through our space like she's finally started believing it's hers. Not all at once, never all at once. But there's a softness to her now—a stillness.

She laughs more, sleeps deeper, even walks with her head up instead of bracing for the world to land another blow.

And sometimes, when I catch her smiling at nothing—just the sun or the way Sophie dances barefoot in the kitchen—I think about that girl in the front row of our senior year history class.

☽ Ashgrove High School — Senior Year ☾

She sat three rows ahead of me, always on the edge of her seat like she might bolt if someone spoke too loudly. Her hair was shorter then, and she wore that same frayed hoodie as armor. I used to count the threads unraveling from her left sleeve.

She didn't talk much. But once, she muttered a comment under her breath that made the teacher choke on his coffee. I laughed, so did she. Not at me, just… to herself; that laugh wrecked me.

Every day, I wanted to speak to her; to say, I see the way you flinch when people get too close. I know what kind of house makes you afraid of loud voices. I wanted to tell her that the gray drizzle outside the window didn't dull her; it framed her. That in a place where most kids cursed the rain and the fog, she carried something brighter, something the weather couldn't smother. I wanted to say her silence was louder than most voices I'd ever heard.

But I never said a word.

She had no idea how many times I pulled back from saying her name. How many times I watched her walk home purely to make sure no one followed. How many times I told myself it was better this way.

But now she's here in *our* house. In *my* arms. And every version of me who once stood in silence is finally home.

Emilia curls in close beside me, our bodies swaying slowly in the twilight; the fire pit's lit, the cider's warm. We don't need words; our silence is comfortable.

I reach for the knife I keep sheathed at my back, the one that used to be mine alone. The one I carried through fire and blood, now it belongs to something softer. I angle the blade into the wood at the back of the swing, careful, deliberate.

Stroke by stroke, I carve the symbol we etched into each other this summer. Etched into skin, locked in memory, a silent vow—the moment I finish, I look up, and our eyes lock instantly.

It used to be a mark of survival, a tether to the moment everything cracked open. Now, it's something steadier; a root sunk deep.

She wore a smile of quiet amusement over our shared secret. The swing creaks beneath us as we sway, the logs crackle, the sky deepens.

Sophie barrels through the gate, cheeks flushed, hair wild, arms full of candy. She's missing half her costume and still glowing from the high of the night. "Is that cider?" she asks, not waiting for an answer before snatching a mug.

She drops into a chair, curls her feet under herself, and launches into stories—how she won the unofficial candy trade, how some mom gave out full-size bars, how she definitely should've won best costume but got robbed. Her voice dips and lifts like a song, and we let her play.

Eventually, her words slow, and her eyes grow heavy. She stumbles toward the house, tripping on her own scarf, giggling at nothing.

And then it's just us—me, and Emilia, the swing, the fire, the hush of leaves drifting through the dark. She shifts closer, her leg presses against mine. I turn toward her, and she's already reaching.

✧ Emilia ✧

The kiss starts slow—warm, content, kissed by firelight and cider—but it deepens quickly. His hand slips beneath my sweater, palm dragging heat along my spine. I rise onto my knees and shift into his lap, straddling him on the swing.

Wes groans softly against my mouth. "We've had enough outdoor sex this year to last us a lifetime."

I laugh, breathless. "Fair."

Without breaking the kiss, he lifts me in one smooth motion, carrying me inside without another word.

The door clicks shut behind us. Shadows stretch long across the floor. The scent of apple pie lingers faintly in the air—one of my candles burning low on the dresser. The bed is turned down. The sheets are clean. The room feels like home; a quiet, lived-in kind of peace.

He doesn't rush. He undresses me slowly, like unwrapping something he's waited all day to touch. My sweater peels off. Then his shirt. Fingers skim down my spine, tugging gently at my waistband until I'm bare to him and aching.

I fall back onto the mattress with a sigh and a shiver. He follows, trailing open-mouthed kisses from my neck to my navel, kneeling between my thighs like he's exactly where he belongs.

His eyes meet mine—dark, starved, ravenous—as he lowers his mouth.

The first flick of his tongue makes me gasp, hips twitching. He holds them down with firm hands, licking slow and deep, each stroke more devastating than the last. His tongue circles my clit—slow and devastatingly precise—until the air leaves my lungs in broken moans. My fingers knot in his hair. My mind is blank, my lungs are empty, and I am entirely consumed by this feeling.

"Mmmh, that's it," he groans against me, the sound rumbling through every nerve. "You taste like fucking heaven."

My body jolts when he slides a finger inside—slick, deep. I cry out, head thrown back.

"Oh—fuuu—"

"So tight," he growls, curling his fingers at the perfect angle. "Clenching around me like you need it..."

A second finger follows and I whimper, thighs shaking, hips instinctively rolling against him. His mouth never stops moving—tongue flicking, sucking, fucking owning me with every relentless stroke.

"Please," I pant, barely able to form the word.

"You wanna cum?" he murmurs, voice filthy and full of love. "Cum for me, Em. Give it to me."

He growls into my clit, lips locking around it, sucking hard as his fingers stroke that raw, trembling place inside me—and I break.

It hits hard. Blinding. My moan rips out of me, long and wrecked. My entire body arches and locks, pulsing tight around his fingers as he groans like the taste of me is the only thing he needs to survive.

Even as the pleasure crests and begins to fall, he doesn't stop—tongue still lapping, fingers still coaxing, kissing me through it like he's worshiping every spasm.

By the time he crawls up my body, my chest is heaving, skin flushed and soaked in afterglow. He kisses me deeply—open and messy—and I moan softly into his mouth, tasting myself on his lips.

His kiss doesn't feel like victory; it feels like coming home, like being wanted whole.

He turns me gently onto my side, one arm loops around my waist, the other hooks under my thigh, lifting it over his own. The thick weight of his cock nudges at my entrance, and I let out a breathless sound, half-ache, half hunger.

"Wesss—" I gasp as he pushes in, slow and thick and overwhelming. I arch instinctively, legs trembling.

He groans deep in my ear, "feel that?" As he sinks into me, "All mine." I whimper in response, pushing back further until his hips are flush to mine.

Each thrust is deep and angled, his hand splayed over my belly to keep me tight against him, rocking me into every stroke. His breath shudders against my neck as I moan with each slow, perfect slide.

"Fuck," he pants, "gripping me so tight, you feel so fucking good."

A broken gasp escapes me—louder this time—"right there," I pant, pressing back, chasing more, as he hits that spot relentlessly every breath a plea, "don't stop."

"Never," he growls, kissing along my shoulder. "I've got you. Take it." His fingers slide between my legs again, circling my clit with breathtaking accuracy. My thighs tremble. My sounds turn desperate—sharp little cries that punch the air with every thrust, every stroke, every command.

"Arch for me," he groans. I obey, curving into him, and the angle nearly undoes me. My hand claws for the sheets as a sob catches in my throat.

"I want to feel you come undone around me," he whispers. "Cum for me again."

I shatter on cue. My cry breaks the quiet, my core locking, legs spasming, heart pulsing as I orgasm with a guttural, helpless moan. It's overwhelming—pure heat and surrender, and still, he holds me through it, his pace faltering only as he chases his own edge.

Even as the waves fade, he doesn't stop, his fingers still circling that raw, swollen place between my thighs. I'm wrecked. Shaking. Still quivering from the first, too sensitive and too desperate not to chase more. Every thrust drags a sound from me I can't hold back. Each one building, coaxing, claiming; he slams into me harder, rougher, groaning brokenly against my skin.

He drives in one last time—deep, final—and stills with a raw, possessive groan as he spills inside me. I feel it everywhere, the heat of it. The feel of him thick and pulsing, buried so deep it aches up my spine, it's enough to send me over the edge again.

My breath catches. My body clenches hard around him, another helpless cry ripping from my throat as a second orgasm crashes through me—smaller, sharper, but no less wrecking.

He curses against my skin, shuddering through his release, like the feeling of me clenching down around him is too much, and still he holds on.

We lie there in the silence that follows—his arm still tight around me, my skin hypersensitive, every inch of me humming with the echo of him.

He presses a kiss to the top of my spine, my neck, my shoulder, his breath warm, his love wordless. Then pulls me in tighter, like even skin-on-skin isn't close enough. Our breath evens out in sync, the sheets warm with our shared heat.

I let the quiet take me. Wrapped in him. In us. We fall asleep tangled in each other. Limbs knotted, sheets rumpled, and the same as every night since we returned from camp, I no longer feel like I'm burning; I feel like I'm home.

☽ December 12, 2015 ☾

✧ Emilia ✧

Sophie's sixteenth birthday is loud, chaotic, and an absolute masterpiece; we throw her a big party, a real one, the kind you see in movies.

Streamers dangle from trees. Glittery gold balloons float above the table, pizza boxes stack high. Lila brings decadent cupcakes piled with buttercream, Wes cues up a playlist of girl-power anthems and indie tracks from their campfire nights, and I thread twinkle lights through the trees until it looks like a fairytale backyard.

They dance barefoot, singing at the top of their lungs, as they twirl with paint on their hands and glitter in their hair. The grass is damp underfoot, but no one cares. The air is cool, carrying that mix of woodsmoke and sea salt that always clings to Ashgrove in the fall. Their laughter rises above it, wild and unbroken, the kind that makes neighbors peek out their windows and smile.

Sophie cries when she opens our gift—a leather-bound art journal and real charcoal pencils. She hugs Wes hard; she hugs me longer.

I catch her mid-laugh, frosting on her cheek, and something in my chest pulls tight. She's nothing like the girl I once carried through fire. But she survived her own way, and now... she shines.

It's not just a birthday. It's a declaration of survival, of joy reclaimed, of a girl finally given the kind of love that sticks.

☽ April 17, 2017 ☾

✧ Emilia ✧

Spring comes like forgiveness, slow and sure. The house doesn't creak anymore, it's settled; the air smells like lemon and rosemary, not stale beer, and old cigarettes. The windows stay open, soft breezes replacing silence.

Sophie leaves for school with a journal tucked under her arm, ready to tackle the last couple semesters of her senior year. Her hair's longer, her laugh is louder, she's becoming someone whole.

Lila visits almost every weekend now that she got a car for her 17th birthday. They cover the picnic table in paint and dreams. They talk about the art school they're applying to after graduation. About futures, about volunteering at camp someday—just to see it again.

Wes and I never stop working, still clocking hours at the theater; still sneaking popcorn and kiss behind the storage racks, and laughing when the reels jam. We build this life one day at a time.

Sophie's sculpture—the one she made at camp and ran back for—sits in the living room. Spiraling wood and clay. You can see the press of her fingers if you look close enough. A quiet echo of who she was, a reminder of how far we've come.

The garden is blooming after two years of love being poured into it. Wes worked it with bare hands and quiet patience. Now it bursts with green: basil and peppers, tomatoes climbing trellises. Each row neat, each corner tended, he calls it his peace project.

When the sun burns through the clouds, the soil steams faintly, rich, and alive. The scent of rosemary drifts up with each breeze. A crow perches on the fence post, cawing like it knows the garden is claimed. Sometimes I think Wes isn't just growing food—he's coaxing the earth itself into forgiving him.

While I sit sideways on the swing Wes built, back resting against the wide armrest, swaying gently. One arm stretched out, fingers drifting over the carved symbol—the one he left there for me, for us. Our mark. A promise kept.

Looking across the yard—Sophie sits at the table, scribbling in her journal, toes in the soil. Wes kneels near the edge of the garden, sleeves rolled up, dirt smeared across his forearms—and I can't help but marvel that this is actually my life. Our life.

The air is soft, sweet with spring, and for once, I'm no longer always waiting for the other shoe to drop. There's no running. No pretending.

I didn't outrun the dark. I planted it. Watered it. Let it bloom. And somehow, it became my shelter.

✦ Epilogue ✦

Ashgrove, Oregon

☽ June 9, 2025 ☾

The porch swing creaks in a slow, familiar rhythm, fireflies blinking across the lawn like tiny sparks of memory. Emilia sits curled into Wes's side, her legs tucked beneath her, a glass of lemonade sweating on the armrest beside her. The air is thick with summer, cut grass, lavender from the garden, and something sweeter still: anticipation.

Out on the street, the asphalt still holds the day's heat, radiating faintly even as night settles in. Houses sag in quiet rows, paint peeling, porches leaning, the whole suburb a reminder of better years when the logging mill kept everything alive. The mill's long gone now, but the town breathes in its own way—rain-slick, moss-softened, and stubborn enough to keep going. Their house is no different.

Inside, a small duffel bag waits by the front door, already packed. Her bathing suit. A flashlight. A locket Emilia let her borrow, tucked secretly into the front zipper pocket.

“I still can’t believe she’s old enough to go,” Emilia murmurs.

Wes hums, resting his chin on top of her head. “She’s ready. You’re the one who’s not.”

“I know.” Emilia smiles against his shirt. “But still.”

A cicada hums somewhere in the distance, the low, steady drone threading through the night. Once, that sound had carried terror, echoing through a cabin with thin walls and thinner safety. Now it folds into the evening like background music, softened by the scent of cut grass and the safety of Wes’s arm around her. The fear feels impossibly far away—like something that happened to another version of herself.

She reaches down and tugs gently at the hem of her old camp T-shirt, faded navy, the Silver Hollow logo nearly worn away from a decade of memories she never let herself throw out. She’d dug it out that morning, half nostalgic, half superstitious; the moment had felt big enough to warrant it.

"I just got off the phone with Jesse," she adds. "She said everything's all set. Cabin assignments, schedule, all of it."

Wes grins. "Let me guess, the one closest to the lake?"

"Of course," Emilia says. "Best view for stargazing. And Jesse's already planning to sneak her extra marshmallows on s'mores night."

He chuckles. "I'm so glad Jesse stayed."

"Me too. After that summer... I think we all could've walked away. But she didn't. She stayed. She rebuilt something broken. Made it into something real."

Under Jesse's leadership, Camp Silver Hollow had quietly become the kind of place they'd all once wished it could be. Safe. Magical. Honest. She'd kept the people who genuinely cared, Noah, Valentina, and even Dee, who eventually softened enough to stay on as kitchen manager. A few years ago, Sophie had started volunteering. Now, at twenty-five, she was signed on again, this time as a senior staff counselor, ready to lead the arts and crafts hall.

"She'll be there too," Emilia adds softly. "Ivy will have Sophie watching out for her."

Wes leans over and presses a kiss to her temple. "That helps."

A breeze stirs, brushing through the wind chimes and lifting the edge of the porch curtain. From inside, small footsteps patter across the floor and up the stairs, ending in the soft slam of a bedroom door, probably one last check on the flashlight.

Emilia laughs under her breath. "Do you ever think about that night in the old hall?" Her voice cracks the quiet like a pebble tossed in still water, rippling out into the dark.

Wes's breath catches slightly, but he nods. "All the time."

"When you looked at me, really looked, and didn't hide anything. You let me see the worst of it, and I didn't want to run."

His hand finds hers, and he squeezes it gently. "You didn't just stay. You saw me. That was the night everything changed."

A silence settles, thick with memory. Not just fear or fury, but the spark beneath it. The clarity. The rush.

"I felt more alive in that moment than I ever had," Emilia admits quietly. "Like something wild in me finally had permission to breathe."

Wes's thumb brushes over her knuckles. "I know. Me too. It was never just about survival, was it?"

She shakes her head slowly. "It was a reckoning. And it brought me so much closer to you."

"It was the beginning," Emilia whispers, barely louder than the hush of the wind.

The porch swing rocks beneath them, old and steady, its wood etched with initials carved long ago. Wes runs his thumb over the groove absentmindedly, still carrying the same knife sheathed on his belt.

"You know," Emilia says after a pause, "sometimes I think about that summer like it was a story I read once. Too twisted to be real. Too heavy."

"But it was real," Wes says. "All of it."

She nods, her gaze drifting toward the stars, bright and endless above the trees.

"I never thought we'd end up here. With her. With this life."

Wes brushes a curl behind her ear. "You earned every second of it."

There's a beat before Emilia adds, "You did too. Taking over Mercer's, you didn't just keep it going—you brought it back to life."

Wes shrugs, modest as always. "When my dad was ready to shut it down in 2017. Someone had to step in."

"And you did more than that," she says. "You built something solid. Steady. You gave us the kind of life I never even dared to dream about having. Enough for me to stay home with her after she was born. You gave us this."

Even after all these years, he still looks a little surprised when she says things like that.

"I just don't wanna turn into him," he admits. "So work obsessed and shop focused, I miss

everything else." He glances instinctively toward the faint glow of porch light next door—his dad's house, still standing, still quiet. The siding sags, the gutters choke with moss, the place as weathered as the man inside. They don't talk much, but it works for them.

"Never," Emilia says, her voice firm. "You show up. Every day." A pause. As her thoughts drift off back to camp. "She's going to be okay there, right?" she asks again, softer now, like the question has lived in her for weeks. "Even with everything that happened back then."

Wes threads his fingers through hers, his grip warm and steady. "She'll be better than okay. That place gave us everything."

"Even if it almost took it all away first."

He leans in until his forehead rests gently against hers. "But we're still here."

A beat of silence.

"Mom?" Ivy calls from the hallway. "Can I bring the bug net and the binoculars? Oh, and my journal, the leather one?"

They both smile. “Of course,” Emilia calls back. “But only if you promise not to catch your counselors.”

Another giggle. Then the sound of retreating footsteps. Emilia exhales, content “she’s going to love it.”

She hopes—no, she believes that Ivy’s story will be bright, her battles few. But some quiet part of her knows that if the world ever tries to dim her, their daughter will burn anyway. She’s her mother’s daughter, but she’s his, too. That spark, that fire, they passed it on, whether they meant to or not.

Wes tightens his arms around her, eyes on the fireflies winking across the yard like tiny ghosts of summer's past.

“She’s going to make her own story,” he says. “We already made ours.”

The swing creaks again, slow, and steady, carrying them forward into the hush of summer.

✦ Copyright ✦

www.ingramcontent.com/pod-product-compliance
Lightning Source LLC
La Vergne TN
LVHW090544110826
845146LV00001B/16

* 9 7 9 8 9 9 6 0 4 7 8 0 2 *